SLOWLY, LEO REACHED out and picked up the pawn. "If you must cheat, why don't you do it properly," he said. "You insult my intelligence to imagine that I wouldn't notice. Do you think I'm blind?"

Cordelia shook her head. "It's not really possible to cheat at chess, but I do so hate to lose. I can't seem to help it."

"Well, I have news for you. You are going to learn to help it." He replaced her rooks in their previous positions. "We are going to play this game to the bitter end and you are going to lose it."

Cordelia stared furiously at the pieces. She couldn't bring herself to make the only move she had. She would be acknowledging she'd lost, once she gave up her queen. "Oh, very well," she said crossly. She shot out her hand, half rising on her stool. Her knees caught the edge of the table, toppling it, and the entire game disintegrated, half the pieces tumbling to the carpet.

"Why, of all the graceless, brattish, mean-spirited things to do!" Leo, furious, leaped up. He grabbed her shoulders, half shaking, half hauling her toward him.

"But I didn't do it on purpose!" Cordelia exclaimed. Then matters became very confused. He was shaking her, she was yelling, his mouth was on hers. His hands were hard on her arms and her body was pressed against his. An overpowering tidal wave of desire raced through her blood. Everything she had felt before was but a faint shadow of this wild abandoned hunger. . . .

The Diamond Slipper

JANE FEATHER

BANTAM BOOKS

NEW YORK   TORONTO   LONDON   SYDNEY   AUCKLAND

The Diamond Slipper

A Bantam Book / February 1997

All rights reserved.
Copyright © 1997 by Jane Feather.
Cover art copyright © 1997 by Alan Ayers.
Insert art copyright © 1997 by Pino Dangelico.

ISBN: 0-553-57523-6

Published simultaneously in the United States and Canada

Bantam Books are published by Bantam Books, a division of
Bantam Doubleday Dell Publishing Group, Inc. Its trademark,
consisting of the words "Bantam Books" and the portrayal of
a rooster, is Registered in U.S. Patent and Trademark Office
and in other countries. Marca Registrada. Bantam Books,
1540 Broadway, New York, New York 10036.

PRINTED IN THE UNITED STATES OF AMERICA

OPM   10 9 8 7 6 5 4 3 2 1

The Diamond Slipper

❀

Prologue

Paris, 1765

"NO ... PLEASE, NO MORE." The words emerged as barely a breath through the woman's dry, cracked lips. Feebly she tried to push aside the silver chalice held to her mouth.

"You must take it, my dear. It will make you well." The man held her head in the crook of his elbow. Her eyes were closed and she was too weak to resist as he tipped the contents of the chalice down her throat. At the familiar bittersweet taste, the woman groaned faintly. Her head fell back against his arm, and gently he lowered her head to the pillow. He hung over her, staring down at her beautiful white face, the skin so translucent he could almost see through to the bones of her skull. Then her eyes opened. For a moment they were as clear and brilliant as they had ever been.

For a long moment, her dying gaze held his. Then her eyelids dropped, her lips parted on a struggling sob of a breath.

The man stepped back into the shadows of the bed-curtains. He took up a glass of wine from the bedside table and sipped, his cold brown gaze never leaving the woman's face. It wouldn't be long now.

A whimpering snuffle came from beyond the bed-curtains. He moved them aside and stepped into the warm, firelit chamber. A nurse sat beside the fire, rocking a double cradle with her foot.

"Should I bring the babes to her, Your Highness?"

The man went over to the cradle. He looked down into two matching pairs of bright blue eyes, two sets of rosy cheeks, four dimpled fists clutched on top of the pale pink blankets.

Were they his? He would never know. And it didn't matter now. "Yes," he said. "They will bring the princess comfort, but don't let them tire her."

"No, of course not, sir." The nurse bent to scoop up the two snuffling bundles. She smiled and kissed them. "There, my pretties, your mama is waiting to see you." She carried her burden to the bed.

The prince sipped his wine and stared into the fire. The nurse returned the infants to their cradle in a very few minutes. "Her highness is so weak. I don't believe she'll last the night," she said sadly.

The prince didn't reply. He returned to his deathwatch in the shadows of the bedcurtains, listening to the rattle of his wife's labored breathing. He was still there when the sound stopped.

He approached the bedside, leaned over, pressed his lips to hers, felt their cold deadness, the total absence of spirit in her body. He straightened slowly and lifted the woman's fragile right wrist. He unclasped the charm bracelet she wore, holding it up to the dim light of the lamp burning at the bedside. The dainty charms glittered and glowed, shockingly frivolous in this dark chamber of death. He slipped the bracelet into his pocket and called for the nurse.

Chapter One

THE PROCESSION OF gilded coaches, plumed, gaily caparisoned horses, and officers resplendent in the blue and gold uniforms of Versailles wound through the great gold gates of the palace, coming to a halt in the center of the massive square.

"Look at those two carriages!" a fair-headed girl hanging perilously far out of an upstairs window exclaimed to her companion leaning out beside her. "They are both to carry me into France. Which do you prefer, Cordelia? The crimson one or the blue one?"

"I can't see it makes much difference," Lady Cordelia Brandenburg responded. "Of all the ridiculous things. There's the Marquis de Durfort riding into the city as if he'd traveled all the way from France, when instead he only left Vienna an hour ago."

"But it's protocol," the archduchess Maria Antonia said in shocked reproof. "It's how it has to be done. The French ambassador must enter Vienna as if he's come all the way from Versailles. He must formally ask my mother for my hand in marriage on behalf of the dauphin of France. Then I will be married by proxy before I go into France."

"Anyone would think you hadn't been promised to the dauphin for the last three years," Cordelia stated. "What a stir it would cause if the empress refused the ambassador's request." She chuckled mischievously, but her companion didn't see the joke.

"Don't be absurd, Cordelia. I shan't allow you to be so impertinent when I am queen of France." She wrinkled her pert nose.

"Considering your bridegroom is only sixteen, I imagine

you'll have to wait awhile before becoming queen," Cordelia retorted, not in the least affected by her royal friend's scolding.

"Oh, pshaw! You're such a wet blanket! When I'm dauphine, I shall be the most popular and important lady at Versailles." Toinette twirled in a crimson swirl of silk as her hoop swung out around her. With an exuberant gesture, she began to dance around the room, her dainty slippered feet faultlessly executing the steps of a minuet.

Cordelia cast a glance over her shoulder and then turned back to the considerably more interesting scene in the court below. Toinette was a gifted dancer and never lost an opportunity to show off.

"Now, I wonder who that is," Cordelia mused, her voice suddenly sharp with interest.

"Who? Where?" Toinette came back to the window, pushing Cordelia to one side, her fair head a startling contrast to her companion's raven black curls.

"There. Dismounting from the white stallion. A Lippizaner, I think."

"Yes, it must be. Look at those lines." Both girls were passionate horsewomen, and for a moment the horse interested them more than its rider.

The man drew off his riding gloves and looked around the court. He was tall, slim, dressed in dark riding clothes, a short, scarlet-lined riding cape swinging from his shoulders. As if aware of the observers, he looked up at the creamy ocher facade of the palace. He stepped back and looked up again, shading his eyes with his hand.

"Come in," the archduchess said. "He's seen us."

"So what?" Lady Cordelia responded. "We're only looking. Don't you think he's handsome?"

"I don't know," Toinette said with a touch of petulance. "Come away. It's shockingly bad etiquette to stare like that. What would Mama say?"

Cordelia had little difficulty imagining what the empress Maria Theresa would say if she found her daughter and her daughter's friend staring out of the window like a pair of oglers at the opera. However, something kept her at the window, even as Toinette tugged at her arm.

The man continued to look up at her. Mischievously, Cordelia waved and blew him a kiss. For a moment he looked thoroughly taken aback, then he laughed and touched his fingers to his lips.

"Cordelia!" The archduchess was scandalized. "I'm not going to stay in here if you're going to behave like that. You don't even know who he is."

"Oh, some equerry, I expect," Cordeila said airily. "I doubt we'll come across him in all the palaver." She plucked half a dozen yellow roses from a bowl on the deep windowsill. Leaning as far out as she could, she tossed them down. They fell in a cloud around the horseman, one of them landing on his shoulder, caught in the folds of his cloak. He extricated it and carefully inserted it in the buttonhole of his coat. Then he doffed his plumed hat and bowed with a magnificent flourish, before moving out of sight as he entered the palace below the window.

Cordelia laughed and drew back from the window. "That was amusing," she said. "It is fun when people enter the spirit of the game." A contemplative little frown drew her thin arched eyebrows together. "An ordinary equerry wouldn't be riding a Lippizaner, would he?"

"No, of course not." The archduchess was still annoyed. "You've probably been flirting with a senior official from Versailles. He must assume you're a kitchen maid or something."

Cordelia shrugged. "I don't suppose he's important. Anyway, I'm sure he won't recognize me close to."

"Of course he will," Toinette scoffed. "No one else has such black hair."

"Oh well, I'll just powder it," Cordelia declared, selecting a grape from a bunch in a crystal bowl and popping it into her mouth. A silver clock on the mantel chimed prettily.

"Goodness, is that the time?" she exclaimed. "I must fly, or I'll be late."

"Late for what?"

Cordelia looked for a moment unnaturally solemn. "I'll tell you before you go to France, Toinette." And she had whisked herself out of the room in a cloud of primrose yellow muslin.

The archduchess pouted crossly. Cordelia didn't seem to mind that their friendship was about to come to an end. Versailles had decreed that when Maria Antonia married the dauphin and came to France, she must leave behind everything that was tied to the Austrian court. She was allowed to take none of her ladies, none of her possessions, not even her clothes.

Disconsolately, she plucked grapes from the bunch, wondering what secret Cordelia was holding these days. She was as ebullient and mischievous as ever, but she was always disappearing mysteriously for hours at a time, and sometimes she had the air of someone dealing with a weighty problem. Which was not in the least in character.

Cordelia, well aware of her friend's disgruntled puzzlement, sped down the corridor toward the east wing of the palace. She couldn't risk confiding in anyone: Not only was the secret too dangerous, but it was not hers to tell. Christian's livelihood was at stake. He was dependent upon the goodwill of his master, Poligny, the empress's court musician, and to lose it would mean losing the empress's patronage. And he would certainly lose that goodwill once he accused Poligny publicly of stealing his pupil's compositions. The accusation must be made from an unassailable position.

Cordelia turned down a little-used corridor and entered a long gallery through a massive wooden door. She was in the west wing of the palace. The gallery was lined with heavy tapestried screens. She ducked behind the third one.

"Where have you been? Why can you never be on time,

Cordelia?" Christian's great brown eyes were filled with anxiety, his mouth taut with concern, his countenance pale.

"I'm sorry. I was watching the arrival of the French wedding party in the courtyard," she said. "Don't be cross, Christian. I've had a brilliant idea."

"You don't know how dreadful it is to hide here, trembling at every mouse," he whispered fiercely, a tight frown wrinkling his broad brow. "What idea?"

"Supposing we produce an anonymous broadsheet, saying that Poligny's latest opera was actually written by his star pupil, Christian Percossi?"

"But how could we prove it? Who's going to believe an anonymous accusation?"

"You publish your original score in the broadsheet. Sign the statement 'A friend of the truth,' or something like that. Include a sample of Poligny's compositions to show the difference in the two hands. It'll be enough to start people talking."

"But he'll have me thrown out of the palace before anything can happen," Christian said glumly.

"You're such a pessimist!" Cordelia exclaimed, her voice inadvertently rising from the undertone they'd both been using. "Sometimes I wonder why I bother with you, Christian."

His smile was a little sheepish. "Because we're friends?"

Cordelia groaned in mock frustration. She and Christian Percossi had been friends for five years. It was a secret friendship, because within the rigid hierarchy of the empress Maria Theresa's court a close friendship was unthinkable between a humble pupil of the court musician and the Lady Cordelia Brandenburg, goddaughter of the empress and bosom companion of her daughter, Maria Antonia, known to her intimates by the diminutive Marie Antoinette.

"Listen," she said, urgently taking his long, slender, musician's hands within her own. "The empress is known for her fairness. She may be as starched as a ruff, but she won't permit Poligny to cast you off without a fair hearing. We just have to ensure that she sees the broad-sheet and the evidence before Poligny can move against you. And we have to make certain that Poligny is taken by surprise. He mustn't have time to create a defense by at-tacking you."

Still holding his hands tightly, she stood on tiptoe to kiss him lightly. "Don't lose heart, Christian. We *will* prevail."

Christian hugged her. Once, they'd thought they felt more for each other than simple friendship, but their naive experimentations had quickly convinced them both that they were not destined to be lovers. But he still enjoyed the feel of her lithe suppleness beneath her court dress, the scent of her skin and hair.

Cordelia drew her head back, smiling up into the musi-cian's hungry brown eyes, enjoying the angular beauty of his face. Her hands moved through his crisp fair curls. "I do love you, Christian. Even more than I love Toinette, I think." She frowned, puzzled at this novel thought. She'd never before attempted to grade her feelings for her two best friends. Then she shook her head in characteristic dismissal of such an irrelevant issue. She wouldn't fail either of them if they needed her. "Try to get the evidence together and we'll talk later. But now I must go."

Christian let his hands fall away from her and looked helplessly into her face. "I wish we didn't have to hide in corners, snatching moments to talk. It was much easier when we were children."

"But we aren't now," Cordelia stated. "And now I'm much more carefully watched. Besides, once you spring your surprise on Poligny, no one must suspect my involve-ment. Then I can work on the empress in your favor . . . or at least," she amended, "on Toinette while she's still here." She gave his hands another quick squeeze, trying to infuse him with some of her own optimistic determination. Chris-tian was so sensitive, so easily cast down. It was because of his undeniable genius, of course, but it could be somewhat irritating.

"I'm going now. Wait for five minutes before you leave." On tiptoe she kissed him again and then was gone from behind the screen, leaving Christian with the faint fragrance of orangeflower water that she used on her hair and the lingering impression of her quicksilver personality like the diffusion of a fading rainbow.

Cordelia slipped backward into the long gallery. She smoothed down her skirts, turned to stroll casually toward the door at the far end of the gallery, and came to face to face with the man who rode the Lippizaner.

He turned from his contemplation of a particularly bloody hunting scene on a tapestry on the far wall. He still wore his scarlet-lined riding cape, startling against the impeccable white of his ruffled shirt.

"Well, well," he said. "If it isn't the flower girl. Where did you spring from?"

Cordelia was for once in her life at a loss under the quizzical scrutiny of a pair of merry golden eyes, aglint with flecks of hazel and green. Her heart was suddenly beating very fast. She told herself it was fear that her clandestine exchange with Christian had been overheard, but for some reason she didn't seem to find that worrying. Something else was causing this tumultuous confusion, the moistening of her palms.

"Cat got your tongue?" he inquired, lifting a slender dark eyebrow.

"Behind the screen . . . I was behind the screen." Cordelia finally managed to speak. "I . . . I was adjusting my dress . . . a hook came loose." She gathered the shreds of her composure around her again, and her eyes threw him a defiant challenge, daring him to question the lie.

"I see." Leo Beaumont regarded her with amused curiosity. Whatever had been going on behind the screen had had little to do with dress repairing. Hooks and eyes didn't cause such a delicious flush or such a transparently guilty conscience. He glanced pointedly toward the screen, and his eyes filled with laughter as he thought he understood. A secret assignation. "I *see*," he repeated, amusement bubbling in his voice. "I'm hurt. I thought your kisses were exclusively for me."

Cordelia swallowed and inadvertently touched her lips with her tongue. What was happening to her? Why wasn't she telling him to mind his business? She told herself that she had to stay in order to prevent him from looking behind the screen and identifying Christian. "Who are you?" she demanded with a rudeness that she hoped would distract him.

"Viscount Kierston at your service." He bowed solemnly, seemingly unperturbed by her lack of finesse.

An English viscount. No mere equerry, then. Cordelia nibbled her lip. His eyes continued most unnervingly to hold her own blue-gray gaze. Close to, he fulfilled the promise of her distant window observation. She found herself taking inventory. Tall, slender, with a broad forehead and pronounced widow's peak, his hair, almost as black as her own, confined in a bag wig at his nape. There was something disturbingly sensual about his mouth, a long upper lip above a deeply cleft chin.

Lucifer! What was she thinking? Her mind flew to Christian, cowering behind the screen, but his image seemed to blur under the English viscount's steady gaze and her own rapt bemusement.

"You now have the advantage of me," he prompted gently, noting the elegance of her gown, the silver pendant at her throat, the pearl-sewn ribbon in her hair. "I take it you're not a flower girl or a parlor maid, despite your fondness for kisses."

Cordelia flushed and said awkwardly, "I trust you'll keep that little incident between ourselves, my lord."

His mouth quirked. "But I found your greeting on my arrival quite delightful."

"It was unwise of me to throw the flowers, sir," she said stiffly. "I am sometimes unwise, but it was only a game, and I intended no discourtesy, or . . . or . . ."

"Excessive familiarity," Leo supplied helpfully. "I assure you I didn't take it in the least ill, and to prove it to you, allow me to make good a distant promise." Taking Cordelia's chin between finger and thumb, he kissed her before she fully grasped what he meant. His lips were cool and pliant, yet firm.

Instead of withdrawing in shock and outrage, Cordelia found herself responding, opening her lips for the strong muscular probe of his tongue, greedily inhaling the scent of his skin. His hands moved over her back, cupping her buttocks, lifting her toward him. She pressed herself into his body, her breath swift and uneven as hot waves of hungry passion broke over her. She nipped his bottom lip, her hands raking through his hair, her body totally at the mercy of this desperate craving.

Leo drew back. He stared down at her, his own passion fading slowly from his eyes. "Dear God," he said softly. "Dear God in heaven. What are you?"

Cordelia felt the color draining from her face as the wild, uncontrolled passion receded and she understood what she'd done. Understood what, but not why. Her body was still on fire, her legs shaking. With an inarticulate mumble, she turned and fled the gallery, holding up her skirts with one hand, her hoop swinging, her jeweled heels tapping on the marble floor.

Leo shook his head in bewilderment. What had started as a little playful dalliance with an appealingly mischievous young woman had taken an astounding turn. He wasn't used to losing himself in the kisses of an ingenue, but whoever she was, she weaved a powerful magic with that unbridled passion. Reflectively, he touched his bitten lip. Then with another little shake of his head, he turned to leave the gallery.

He glanced sideways at the screen from where the girl had emerged. Presumably, it concealed some young man who had fallen victim to that tidal wave of desire. He tapped his fingers lightly against the wooden frame. "It's quite safe for you to come out now."

He left the hidden lover to make his escape and strolled toward the guest apartments, a deep frown drawing his sculpted eyebrows together.

Christian emerged when the booted footsteps had receded. He looked up and down the gallery. There was no sign of Cordelia. What had been going on? He'd heard them talking, but they had been too far along the gallery for him to make out the words. But then there'd been a long silence, a silence enlivened only by the shuffle of feet on the marble, the rustle of rich material. Then he'd heard Cordelia's racing steps out of the gallery. What had happened out here? Who was the man? And what had he been doing with Cordelia?

Frowning fiercely, the young musician made his way to his own humble chamber over the kitchens.

A flunky was waiting for Leo in the salon of the guest apartments. "Lord Kierston, Her Imperial Highness requests your presence," he said with some haste. "She is in audience with Duke Brandenburg. If you would follow me."

Leo followed the flunky through the corridors of the palace. He was familiar with the intricacies of the place after a visit six years earlier, when he'd had a private audience with the Austrian empress on behalf of his own family, who claimed kinship to the Hapsburgs through a distant cousin. Like most English noble families, the Beaumonts had relatives and connections across the continent, and there was always a home and a welcome to be had at any royal court.

But for the last three years, Leo had spent most of his time at the court of Versailles, cultivating the friendship of his sister's widower, Prince Michael von Sachsen, because only thus could he keep a watchful eye on Elvira's children.

"Ah, Viscount Kierston, how delightful that you could be part of this historic occasion." The empress greeted him cordially. Maria Theresa was now a widow of fifty-three and after sixteen children, her former beauty was just a shadow. She gave him her hand to kiss, then waved him to a chair. "We are very informal this afternoon," she said with a smile. "We are discussing the arrangements for Cordelia Brandenburg's marriage to Prince Michael von Sachsen."

Leo bowed to Duke Brandenburg the prospective bride's uncle, with the bland expression of an experienced diplomat. "My brother-in-law wishes me to stand proxy at the marriage of your niece, Duke. I trust that meets with your approval."

"Oh, most certainly." Duke Franz Brandenburg smiled with his fleshy lips, revealing yellow teeth, pointed like fangs. "I've examined the marriage contracts, and all appears to be in order." He rubbed his hands together in a gesture of satisfaction. Cordelia's price was high, but Prince Michael von Sachsen, the Prussian ambassador to the court of Versailles, had not even bargained.

Leo contented himself with a short nod. Michael had decided very suddenly to take another wife, some young virgin who would bear him a male heir. Twin daughters could be sold in the matrimonial market when the time was right, but they could not inherit, and could not perpetuate the name of von Sachsen. Cordelia Brandenburg, the empress's goddaughter, was a most eligible bride for a von Sachsen prince. At sixteen, she would be well tutored in the social requirements, but otherwise unsophisticated, inexperienced, and, of course, a virgin.

Leo's only interest in his brother-in-law's prospective bride was as a stepmother to his twin nieces. They were at the age now when they needed the softening influence of a mother. Their father was a distant autocrat, leaving their daily care in the hands of an elderly indigent relative whom Leo despised. Louise de Nevry was too narrow-minded to supervise the education and welfare of Elvira's spirited children.

He became suddenly aware that his hands were clenched into fists, his jaw so tight, pain shot up the side of his head. He forced himself to relax. Whenever he thought of his twin sister's sudden death, an almost unbearable tension and unfocused rage would fill him. It had been so unnecessary. So abrupt. Her marriage had changed her certainly, dampened her wonderful exuberance, and her ready laughter was heard less often. But when he'd left her and gone to Rome that February of 1765, she'd been as full of life, as beautiful as ever. He could still see her deep blue eyes, their mother's eyes, smiling as she bade him farewell. There had been a shadow in the depths of her eyes that he had put down to melancholy at their parting. They had always hated to be too distant from each other.

A week later she was dead. And now when he conjured up her image, all he saw was that shadow in her eyes, and now he remembered that it had been there for many months, and that sometimes her laughter had sounded strained, and that once he had surprised an expression on her face that he had never seen before. Almost of terror. But Elvira had laughed when he'd probed, and he'd thought nothing of it until after her death. Now he could think of little else.

"Lord Kierston?"

He returned to his surroundings with a jolt. The empress was talking to him. "I understand you have assurances from the French king that if Cordelia is wed to Prince Michael, she will be permitted to accompany my daughter to Versailles," the empress asked.

The assurances were actually from Madame du Barry, the king's mistress, but, as they all knew, the du Barry's word was as good as the king's. "Yes indeed, Your Majesty. His Majesty understands that it will be hard for the archduchess to leave everything and everyone she knows behind her on her marriage to the dauphin."

"My daughter will embrace France as her country," Maria Theresa stated. "She knows her duty. She knows that she was born to obey." She nodded decisively. "And Cordelia, of course, will be delighted to accompany Marie Antoinette—and to accept such an advantageous marriage. You have discussed this with her, Duke?" She turned to Franz with an inquiring smile.

The duke shrugged. "I saw no need to do so, madame. Cordelia also knows that she was born to obey. Now is time enough to tell her of her good fortune."

Good fortune? Leo's face was expressionless. Michael was a desiccated Prussian prince of rigid temperament; a sixteen-year-old might well be a trifle skeptical of such good fortune. Michael had not been as rigid when he'd married Elvira, but her death had darkened him in some way.

"So, my niece will wed Prince Michael by proxy and will accompany the dauphine to Versailles. You, Viscount, will be her escort, I understand."

"Yes, Duke. It will be my honor and privilege." Leo inclined his head in acknowledgment, thinking wearily of how tedious it was going to be accompanying some simpering debutante on such a long and arduous journey.

"Cordelia should be informed immediately. Send for Lady Cordelia." The empress gestured to her secretary, who bowed and left the room with swift step. "I would have this matter settled before the festivities of the wedding truly begin. We will be done with all business so we may enjoy ourselves on this joyous occasion with a free heart." Maria Theresa smiled benignly.

Cordelia stared down at the Latin text in front of her. The words made no sense; the grammatical structure was impenetrable. As she stumbled over the translation, she could sense the puzzled impatience of Abbé Vermond, the archbishop of Toulouse, who tutored both Cordelia and Marie Antoinette. Cordelia never stumbled. She took great pleasure in the intricacies of the Latin language, as she did in philosophy, history, and mathematics. Unlike Toinette, whose attention span was almost nonexistent, Cordelia was in general a bright, quick pupil. But not today.

She was alternately hot and cold, alternately filled with confused embarrassment and bemused anger when she thought of the exchange with the Englishman. And then when her body remembered the imprint of his through the light muslin of her gown, when her lips remembered the cool pliancy of his mouth, when her tongue remembered the taste of his mouth, she was awash with pulsing longing that she knew she should consider shameful, and yet she could find within herself not one iota of guilt or shame. It was pure exciting pleasure.

She glanced sideways at Toinette's fair head bent over her books. The archduchess was doodling in the margin of the text, idle scribbles of birds and flowers. She yawned, delicately covering her mouth with her fair white hand, her boredom palpable in the warm room filled with spring sunshine.

Had Toinette ever felt these strange stirrings, this heady flush of an unknown promise? Cordelia was certain she hadn't. Toinette would have confided such mysterious longings to her friend.

There was a knock at the door. Toinette sat up, blinking the daze from her eyes. Cordelia looked over with only mild curiosity at the flunky who stood in the doorway. "Lady Cordelia is summoned immediately to the empress."

"What could my mother want with you?" Toinette asked, frowning. "Why would she see you without me?"

"I can't imagine." Cordelia wiped her quill carefully and laid it on the blotter beside the inkstand. Such a summons was unprecedented, but one didn't keep the empress waiting. "If you would excuse me, *mon père*." She curtsied to the archbishop and went to the door. The flunky bowed her out and escorted her to the empress's audience chamber, although she knew the way perfectly well.

She entered the audience chamber, her eyes swiftly taking in those present. A quiver of shock and surprise went through her at the sight of the English viscount standing behind the empress's chair. Dropping her eyes, she made a deep obeisance to the empress and thus missed the expression in the viscount's eyes. Her uncle, his gouty leg propped on a footstool, his hand resting on the silver knob of his cane, gave her a curt nod.

Leo turned aside, struggling to regain his composure. This was Cordelia Brandenburg! No simpering debutante but a mischievous, challenging, and sensual young woman. Just as Elvira had been before her marriage.

"Cordelia, my dear, your uncle has arranged a most advantageous match for you," the empress said without preamble. "Prince Michael von Sachsen is the Prussian ambassador to the court of Versailles. As his wife, you will take your place in that court, and you will be able to remain as friend and companion for Marie Antoinette."

Cordelia's mind whirled. She couldn't immediately take it in. She was to be married as well as Toinette? They would be going to France together? It was too good to be true—that she might be free of her uncle's tyrannical rule and the confines of the Austrian court. And live instead in that glittering palace of Versailles, in the fairy-tale world of the French court.

"Viscount Kierston, the prince's brother-in-law, will stand proxy for your wedding, which will take place the day after the archduchess's proxy marriage to the dauphin." Her uncle was speaking now in his flat assertive tones.

Leo turned slowly back to the room. Cordelia stared at him. "You . . . you are to be my husband." She didn't know what she was saying, the words spoke themselves.

"Proxy, child . . . proxy," the empress corrected sharply. "Prince Michael von Sachsen is to be your husband."

"Yes . . . yes, of course." But Cordelia barely heard the empress. She looked at the viscount and a warm river of excitement gushed through her veins. She couldn't put words to its cause; it seemed to spring from some bubbling source existing both in her mind and in her loins. It was as strange and terrifying a sensation as it was wonderful.

She smiled at Leo and the look in her eyes was so nakedly sensual that Leo was afraid that the others in the room would see it and wouldn't fail to read it correctly. He stepped forward, drawing something from his pocket.

"I have a betrothal gift from Prince Michael, Lady Cordelia. He kept his voice toneless and he avoided meeting her eye as he placed a small package in her hand. "You will also find a miniature of the prince." He stepped back, out of her line of sight.

Cordelia opened the flat velvet box and unwrapped the tissue. She withdrew a gold, pearl-studded charm bracelet and held it up to the light of the window. The jeweled charms swung together in the slight breeze.

"Very pretty," approved the empress.

Leo frowned. He hadn't thought to wonder about the prince's betrothal present. It had seemed unimportant. But the bracelet had been Elvira's, a gift from her husband on the birth of the twins. His mouth thinned. Michael kept a tight hold on his pursestrings, but to give a new wife a gift from a dead one seemed insensitive to say the least.

"Oh, look, there's another charm!" Cordelia was momentarily distracted from her emotional turmoil. She picked up a tiny diamond-encrusted slipper. "See how delicate it is." It lay in the palm of her hand, the diamonds glittering in the light. "He must mean it to be my own special charm."

"We will send the bracelet and the charm to the jewelers, Cordelia, and they will attach the slipper," Maria Theresa said briskly, returning to business. "Leave it on the table there. Now take a look at the miniature of Prince Michael."

Cordelia reluctantly laid down the bracelet and unwrapped the small circular package that had accompanied the box. The portrait of her future husband looked up at her from a lacquered frame. It was hard to get any sense of the person behind the flat image. She saw pale eyes under beetling brows, a thin straight mouth, a jutting jaw. His hair was concealed beneath a curled and powdered wig. He looked humorless, even severe, but since she was accustomed to dealing with both characteristics in her uncle, she was untroubled by it. He had no obvious physical defects that she could see, except for his age. He was definitely not in the first flush of youth. But if that was all to object to in her future husband, then she was luckier than many of her peers who were sold, regardless of inclination, to whoever suited their family's needs.

Her gaze darted toward Viscount Kierston. Was he married? That strange fizz of excitement was in her blood again. Her eyes widened and she almost took a step toward him. But he moved away and there was such a sharp warning in his own eyes that she recollected herself abruptly.

"How recent is the portrait?" she asked dutifully.

"It was taken last month," the viscount replied.

"I see. And does the prince have a miniature of me?"

"Yes, of course," her uncle said with a touch of impatience. "He received it months ago. One wouldn't expect Prince Michael to offer for you sight unseen."

"No, of course not," Cordelia murmured. "But I, of course, must accept him as my husband." It was almost sotto voce, but Leo heard it. His lips twitched despite his unease at the unnerving intensity of her gaze.

"The viscount will be your escort on the journey to Versailles," the duke stated, thumping his cane on the floor. He hadn't heard what she'd said, but he knew his niece and guessed it was something impertinent.

"I will be most grateful for His Lordship's escort." Cordelia curtsied demurely to the viscount. "I am obedient to the wishes of my empress and my uncle in all things." Her eyes flicked upward to meet the viscount's, and again he was taken aback by the light of passion blazing in the blue-gray depths. What was she? An innocent on the verge of sensual awakening? Or a woman who had held the secrets of that territory in her blood since birth?

The fine hairs on the nape of his neck prickled with the chilling certainty that he was going to find out.

Chapter Two

CHRISTIAN LURKED IN the corridor outside the empress's audience chamber. He knew that Cordelia was with the empress and her uncle. The whole palace was abuzz with rumors. Gossip traveled on the tongues of servants faster than a panther on the heels of prey, and Lady Cordelia's name was on every tongue. Nothing specific had been said, but it was generally agreed that the arrival of the French delegation concerned Lady Cordelia's future as well as the archduchess's.

Christian nibbled a loose cuticle as he hovered in a window embrasure. He knew they wouldn't be able to speak openly in the public corridor, but he was too apprehensive and curious to wait patiently for Cordelia to seek him out. Something peculiar had happened earlier between her and the man in the gallery. He wanted to know what, and whether it had any bearing on whatever was happening now.

The door to the audience chamber opened, and a tall man in dark riding clothes emerged. He stood for a minute in the corridor, and his expression, which had been calmly neutral a second earlier, suddenly came alive. Christian didn't know who he was, but the glint in the hazel eyes was so inviting he almost stepped out of the window embrasure toward him. A puzzled frown drew the stranger's eyebrows together, and the light in his eyes was suddenly speculative. Then his taut mouth relaxed, turning up at the corners in an attractive smile. Still smiling to himself, he strolled down the corridor, passing Christian without so much as a glance, his short scarlet-lined riding cape swinging with his long stride.

Christian wondered what it was about the stranger that was so charismatic. He seemed to possess a curiously magnetic quality. Then he shrugged off the question and resumed his vigil. The empress was keeping Cordelia for an inordinately long time. Duke Franz Brandenburg emerged next, leaning heavily on his cane, his habitual scowl marring his jowly countenance. He stomped down the passage, ignoring the musician. A servant hurried past, half running, and still Cordelia didn't appear.

Christian turned to gaze down through the window into the court below. It was packed with wagons, carriages, and horses as the palace set about preparing to entertain those who had come to take the archduchess to her future life.

The light pattering of slippered footsteps brought him round to face the corridor again. Marie Antoinette was dancing down the corridor toward her mother's door. Toinette rarely walked anywhere.

Christian frowned as the archduchess was admitted to the audience chamber. Was there some trouble that both girls should be summoned to the empress? Had he and Cordelia been seen somewhere, exchanging urgent whispers in a corner of the gardens? In a fever of anxiety, he began to pace the corridor, unaware of the curious glances he drew from hurrying servants.

In the empress's private chamber adjoining the audience room, Marie Antoinette was embracing her friend with tears of joy. "I can't believe it, Cordelia. You're to come with me. I won't be alone."

"His Majesty has been very considerate, child." Her mother smiled benignly at the entwined fingers of her daughter and her friend. The friendship pleased her, largely because Cordelia, a year older and a great deal wiser than the archduchess, often had a sobering influence. Although it had to be admitted that Cordelia's vivacity sometimes led them both astray, Maria Theresa was confident that marriage and its heavy social burdens at the court of Versailles, not to mention motherhood, would squash any undesirable liveliness in both of them.

"Is this his portrait? Oh, let me see." Toinette picked up the miniature and examined it critically. "He's very old."

"What nonsense!" rebuked the empress. "The prince is in the prime of his life. A man of great wealth and influence at the court."

"How is it that the viscount is Prince Michael's brother-in-law, Madame? Is he married to the prince's sister?" Cordelia told herself it was a perfectly reasonable question and that she was only peripherally interested in the answer.

"Prince Michael was married to the viscount's sister," the empress told her. "Unfortunately, she died some years ago, leaving twin daughters, I believe."

But he could be married to someone else. Why could she not get Viscount Kierston out of her head? What possible difference could it make to her, whether he was married or not? Cordelia took herself to task, but her self-reproof seemed to lack conviction.

"Oh, then you're to be a mama immediately!" Toinette exclaimed, doing a little pirouette. "Shall you like it, Cordelia?"

Another thing no one had thought to tell her, Cordelia reflected, startled by this information. How could she tell whether she would be able to mother two unknown little girls? She wasn't ready to be a mother to anyone, she was only just beginning to try her own wings. "I hope so," she said, knowing it to be the only answer acceptable to the empress.

"You must pin the miniature to your dress," Toinette said. "Like mine." She gestured to the portrait of the dauphin that she now wore. Deftly, she fastened the prince's miniature to Cordelia's muslin bodice. She stood back, examining her handiwork, then gave a little nod of satisfaction. "Now you're properly betrothed, just as I am."

"Well, run along now. You must dress for the ball

tonight," Maria Theresa instructed with another fond smile. "You will both look so beautiful . . . two exquisite brides." She patted the fair head and the dark, then kissed them both. "Leave me now. I have some papers to read before dinner."

Toinette linked arms with Cordelia and danced her out of the imperial presence. "It's so exciting," she burbled. "I'm so happy. I was so afraid, although I didn't dare admit it, but now I'm not at all frightened about going. We shall take Versailles by storm, and everyone will fall at the feet of the two beautiful brides from Vienna." Laughing, she released Cordelia's arm and twirled away down the corridor. Cordelia's head was too full of her own turmoil to be able to enter the spirit of Toinette's exuberance, and she followed more slowly.

"Cordelia!" Christian grabbed her arm as she passed the embrasure. He jerked her into the small space. "What's going on? What's happening? Who was that man you were with in the gallery?"

Cordelia glanced over her shoulder. A majordomo had appeared around the corner of the corridor and was making his self-important way toward the empress's door. "I'm to be married," she whispered. "And the man was Viscount Kierston; he's to be my proxy husband. But we can't talk here. Come to the orangery—the usual place—at midnight. I'll be able to slip away from the ball then. I've had an absolutely brilliant idea that'll solve all your problems."

She put a finger on his lips when it looked as if he was about to protest, then darted another glance at the approaching majordomo before swiftly jumping on her toes and kissing his cheek. Then she slipped away, walking sedately down the corridor. Christian heard her polite greeting to the official as he waited for the man to pass before leaving the embrasure himself.

Cordelia was always full of brilliant ideas, but how could her getting married and presumably leaving Vienna solve any of *his* problems? It would simply mean that he would lose his best friend.

The gala reception that began the week of festivities to celebrate the archduchess's marriage to the dauphin of France was held in the Great Gallery. The high windows were opened to the expanse of torchlit gardens beneath, where colored fountains played, their delicate cascades reflected in the gold-framed crystal mirrors of the gallery.

Cordelia kept her eye on the clock even when she was whirled down the line of dance by hot young men in powdered wigs, their rouge running under the exertions of the dance and the heat of four thousand candles. Normally, she enjoyed dancing, but tonight she was distracted. Christian had given a recital earlier, his exquisite music transporting his audience. Poligny had nodded benignly throughout and had blatantly claimed the credit both for the composition and for his pupil's performance for himself. The empress had given Poligny a heavy purse at the end, enjoying the impression her musicians had had on her visitors. The patronage of geniuses was a royal obligation, but it was very satisfying to have it acknowledged. She would expect Poligny to share the purse with Christian, but Cordelia knew as well as Christian that he'd be lucky if he saw so much as a guinea.

Christian now circled around the gallery, dancing when he was obliged to do so, accepting compliments when necessary, making himself agreeable as a man who lived on patronage must do. He kept his angry chagrin at Poligny's treatment well hidden from the crowd.

The entire palace now knew that Lady Cordelia Brandenburg was to be married to a Prussian prince, ambassador at the court of Versailles, and the archduchess Marie Antoinette wouldn't have to make her journey into her new life alone. But Christian was desolate. Paris was a whole world away. Since the moment when he'd come upon an angrily weeping little girl in the orangery five years earlier, Cordelia had been his best friend. He'd comforted her on that occasion and on many another since, just as she had supported him, bolstering his confidence, always believing in him however many times Poligny cut him down, mocked him, made use of him. Only when he was with Cordelia did Christian believe truly in his own genius.

Cordelia avoided Christian as she always did in public, but she didn't seem able to be so discreet when it came to Viscount Kierston. Her eyes constantly searched the room for him. He was never on the dance floor, preferring to stand to one side in conversation with some high-ranking French or Austrian courtier. She noticed that he didn't seem to look much at the women, who for their part couldn't take their eyes off him—so distinguished in a pale gray silk suit, black striped waistcoat, and ruffled cravat, his unpowdered black hair confined at his nape with a gray velvet ribbon.

Was he married? Did he have a mistress? She couldn't stop thinking about him . . . couldn't stop looking at him. His image tormented her, the questions hurled themselves at her brain. She felt as if she were in the grip of brain fever, hot and cold alternately, and unable to concentrate on anything. Her partners found her distracted and almost brusque and rarely asked her for a second dance.

Cordelia didn't realize that the viscount was observing her as closely as she was observing him. Leo was thinking that she bore no physical resemblance to Elvira, who had been fair and statuesque, unlike this spritely dark beauty with the creamy skin and deep-set eyes that were sometimes blue as turquoise and sometimes gray as charcoal. But he was convinced that the two women shared something else. Passion and a sensual appetite that would drive a man wild. He had watched Elvira before her marriage work her magic with her rich laugh of pleasure and a careless toss of her blonde mane. Prince Michael had not been the first in her bed, but that was only to be expected when a woman as lively and sophisticated as Elvira waited into her twenties before accepting a husband. She had insisted that Michael had never questioned her about her past. He was a man of the world; he wouldn't have expected a woman of the world to be a virgin. But sometimes Leo wondered how true that was. Michael cultivated a smooth diplomatic courtesy and Leo had never seen it crack, but it was hard to believe there weren't some other currents beneath the surface.

Leo sipped champagne and watched the prince's destined second bride go through the motions of the minuet, gracefully but without enthusiasm. Her partner was looking bored. Lady Cordelia turned on the floor and once again her eyes met the viscount's. A flush started on her cheeks, her lips parted, her eyes glowed.

He swung away from her. Holy Mother, what was she doing? First some poor soul behind the tapestry screen and now she'd turned her enchantment upon him, God help him!

The palace clocks chimed midnight and the guests strolled through the gallery to the supper rooms, where burned champagne, green goose, quail in aspic, larks' tongues, salmon mousse, oyster barquettes, and crab patties awaited them.

Leo remained in the gallery, staring moodily out into the gardens, where the light from the windows spilled onto the lawns and the gravel paths. He sipped from his refilled glass. Behind him the musicians continued to play softly, the sounds of laughter and the chink of glass and china drifted from the supper rooms.

A figure appeared below him, on the curved stone staircase leading to the garden. She passed beneath the line of flaming torches edging the stone-flagged terrace, and her black hair shone with blue fires. Her gown of ivory gauze swayed gracefully around her as she stepped onto a gravel path running between the parterres and walked swiftly toward the orangery.

Now where in the devil's name was she going, sneaking away in the middle of the night? Leo put his glass down on the windowsill and strode from the gallery, down the great staircase to the doors opening onto the stone stairs. If this was another tryst, he was obliged in his role as Michael's proxy to put a stop to it. She was betrothed and could no longer run around like a schoolgirl pursuing her own butterflies.

He caught a glimpse of ivory disappearing into the darkness of the orangery and quickened his step.

Inside the sweetly fragrant glasshouse, Cordelia moved unerringly down the third alley, her feet clicking on the stone floor. Braziers were lit even on such a mild night, coddling the rare orchids, the exotic fruit trees, the lush grape vines in the arbor.

"Christian? Are you here?" Her voice sounded unnaturally loud in the silence as she came to the end of the aisle and looked around in the semidarkness.

"Here." Christian stepped from behind a palm tree. His face was pale in the gloom. "Is it true? You're to go to France, to marry some Prussian prince?"

"Yes," she said softly, "but listen. Why don't you accompany me? You can find a new patron at Versailles and be your own master, not a pupil any longer. If I can persuade the empress to release you, as a sort of wedding present, then you'll be free of Poligny."

"But even if the empress does release me, I have no money. How can I make the journey?"

"Why do you always look for difficulties?" Cordelia said impatiently, punching his arm with her small fist. "We'll manage something."

Christian still looked doubtful, but turned the subject to Cordelia's concerns. "Is this him?" He poked the miniature pinned to her dress with a fingertip, as if it were something disgusting or harmful.

"Yes. I have to wear it." She tipped it up and peered down at it. "Do you think I shall like him?"

Christian examined the miniature more closely. "He looks hard. But perhaps that's just the portrait," he added hastily, anxious to reassure her. "People always look too composed in portraits."

"Mmm." It was Cordelia's turn to look doubtful. "I wonder if he'll like *me*."

"Of course he will. How could anyone *not* like you?" He hugged her tightly to him. "I'm going to miss you so."

"No, you're not," she mumbled against his chest. "Because you're coming too."

"Are you both insane?"

Christian jumped back with a startled cry, his hands falling from her body. He stared over Cordelia's head into the pale glimmer of Viscount Kierston's face.

"Of all the stupid, reckless things to do. Lady Cordelia is betrothed; the palace is crawling with guards, officials, guests. And the two of you kiss and cuddle among the orange trees like a pair of village simpletons!"

Cordelia stared at him, forgetting the strange effect he had on her in her resentment at this furious and bewildering castigation. "We weren't doing anything of the kind, as it happens. Not that it's any of your business what I do," she stated, as Christian was still trying to recover his wits.

"You forget. I am to stand proxy for your husband," he said curtly. "That makes your business very much mine, my lady. And most particularly when it leads to this kind of self-indulgent idiocy. Have you given any thought to what would happen if you were discovered?" He stared at them, anger fading to exasperation. "What a pair of foolish children you are."

He turned to the still tongue-tied Christian and said more kindly, "Be off with you, now. Your business here is done. If you wish to do Cordelia a favor, you'll keep out of her way until she leaves here. It will be easier on both of you." A smile glimmered in the dimness and he patted

Christian's shoulder. "First love hurts, I know. But it does ease."

Christian looked blankly at the man who he assumed was Viscount Kierston, since he'd said he was Cordelia's proxy husband. But he seemed to have taken hold of the wrong end of the stick. Christian cleared his throat and said, "Of course I love Cordelia, sir, she's my best friend. But we're not *in* love, if that's what you're implying."

"No," Cordelia agreed tartly. "We were simply having a friendly conversation."

"A friendly conversation at dead of night, locked in each other's arms in a secluded orangery!" Leo scoffed. "What kind of a fool do you take me for?"

"One who's blind as a bat," Cordelia retorted. "Christian was just hugging me."

"I think I'd better go," Christian said, reading Leo's incredulity without difficulty. "We're not having an assignation, sir, but it's true that Cordelia shouldn't be here with me. It's not appropriate for the empress's goddaughter to make a friend of a mere musician." He spoke with a quiet dignity, bowed stiffly, and walked away.

Leo's exasperation faded. The lad's composure was convincing. Maybe he'd come to the wrong conclusion, but it didn't alter the fact that Michael's betrothed had no right to be doing whatever she had been doing, however innocent it might have been. He turned back to Cordelia, who now stood silent and still in the shadows. He crooked a finger at her. "Come here, my lady."

Cordelia stepped into the dim light. She returned his scrutiny. All her anger had dissipated and that strange thing was happening to her again. They were alone in this dark and fragrant place, and she could think of only one way to dispel the confusion raging in her brain, pouring through her veins with every heartbeat. "Would you kiss me, like you did this afternoon?"

"Would I *what*?"

"Please kiss me," she repeated patiently. "It's very important."

"My God, you are beyond belief!"

Cordelia didn't say anything, merely stepped up to him. He wanted to move back but he couldn't, it was as if she'd bound him with invisible threads. He could feel the heat of her body, smell the fragrance of her skin and hair. She looked silently up at him, her eyes wide and luminous.

"Please." She raised her hands to hold his face and then pulled his head down to hers.

Why couldn't he move? Why couldn't he stop this? But he couldn't. He couldn't resist the power of her passion or prevent the rush of his own. His hands encircled her throat, feeling the pulse beating wildly against his thumb. Her mouth opened beneath his, her tongue darting against his, tasting the flesh of his cheeks, the moist underside of his tongue, running over his lips. Her breasts rising above the low neckline cried out for his touch. His hands slid down the column of her throat, moved over the soft swell of flesh. A finger dipped into her neckline, and her nipple was hard and erect as he touched it. All the while her hungry mouth engulfed him, seeming to draw him up from his body's core, her demanding sweetness heady on his tongue.

With a supreme effort, he broke free of the web her body was spinning around him, a web whose gossamer strands were made up of her scent, her taste, the lithe feel of her beneath his hands.

"Holy Mother! *Enough!*" He pushed her from him and ran his hands over his face, his mouth, tracing her imprint on his flesh. "What kind of sorceress *are* you?"

Cordelia shook her head, saying with soft wonder, "No sorceress. But I love you."

"Don't be absurd." He struggled to regain his composure. "You're a spoilt and headstrong child."

"No." She shook her head again. "No, I'm not. I've never loved anyone like this before. Oh, once Christian and I thought that perhaps we loved each other in that way, but it didn't last a week. I never wanted him to kiss me the way I *needed* you to. I *know* what I feel."

There was such calm conviction in her voice, in her eyes, in her smile. She looked as smug and satisfied and as sure of herself as any cat with a saucer of cream.

Leo laughed, thinking desperately that maybe tolerant amusement would puncture her intimidating self-possession. "You know nothing, my dear girl. Nothing at all. You're at the mercy of a host of emotions you don't as yet understand. They belong in the marital chamber and you'll understand them soon enough. I blame myself. I should never have kissed you."

"I kissed you just then," she corrected simply. "Because I needed to."

He ran a hand through his hair, disturbing the thick black locks waving off his broad forehead. "Now, listen to me, Cordelia. It was all my fault. I should never have teased you the way I did in the gallery earlier. I didn't realize, God help me, that I was playing with fire. But you must now put all this nonsense about love behind you. You're going to be the wife of Prince Michael von Sachsen. That is your destiny. And you will only hurt yourself if you don't accept it."

Cordelia tucked a loosening ringlet behind her ear. "Are you married?"

"No." He answered the simple question without thought.

"Do you have a mistress?"

"Do I *what*?" The change of tack left him momentarily speechless, until he realized that it wasn't a change of tack at all.

"A mistress?" she repeated, tucking away another ringlet. "Do you have one at present?"

"Get out of here, Cordelia, before I really lose my temper."

"I wonder what that would be like," she said mischievously, then backed away as he stepped toward her. "Oh dear, I have made you cross. Well, you needn't answer me

now. I'll ask you again when you're more used to the idea."
She blew him a kiss, turned, and moved away into the darkness. He stood watching the glimmer of her ivory gown wafting as if disembodied until even that had vanished and he was left only with the lingering scent of her.

❀

Chapter Three

RAIN LASHED THE windowpane, and a chill draught set the flames in the hearth flickering. Prince Michael von Sachsen put down his pen and leaned toward the fire, holding out his hands to the warmth. April in Paris was not always a soft time of budding trees and nodding spring flowers; the wind and rain could be as raw as on any winter day.

He picked up his pen again and continued with his writing, covering the thick vellum page of the leatherbound book with a spidery sloping scrawl. At the end of the page, he laid down his pen. For twenty years he hadn't missed a daily entry: a scrupulously accurate accounting of his day, with every event, every significant thought punctiliously recorded.

He reread the entry before sanding the page and closing the book. He carried the journal over to an ironbound chest beneath the window. He took a key from his pocket and unlocked the chest's brass padlock. He kept the chest locked even when he was in the room. It contained too many dangerous secrets. He lifted the heavy lid and inserted the journal at the end of a row of identical volumes, each one with the year embossed on the spines that faced upward. His hand drifted over the spines. His index finger hooked the top of the volume for 1765, flipping it up. He opened it, standing with his back to the fire. The page fell open to February 6. There was only one line on the page: *At six o'clock this evening, Elvira paid for her faithlessness.*

The prince closed the book and replaced it in the chest. The lid dropped with a thud and he turned the key in the padlock, dropping the key back into his pocket. A green log hissed in the grate, accentuating the silence of the room, indeed of the entire house at this dead hour of the night. He picked up his neglected glass of cognac and sipped, staring down into the spitting fire, before turning restlessly back to the secretaire where he'd been writing his journal.

He opened a drawer and took out the miniature in its mother-of-pearl frame. A young, smiling face looked out at him. Raven black ringlets framed her countenance—fresh skin, large, deep-set blue-gray eyes, a turned-up nose that gave her a rather impish look.

Lady Cordelia Brandenburg. Aged sixteen, goddaughter of an empress, niece of a duke. Impeccable lineage and a very pleasing countenance ... but one that bore no resemblance to Elvira's. Cordelia was as dark as Elvira had been fair. His gaze lifted to the portrait above the mantel. Elvira, just after the birth of the twins. She reclined on a chaise longue, clad in a crimson velvet chamber robe. Her voluptuous bosom, even fuller after the birth, rose from a lace-edged bodice. A rich velvet fold caressed the curve of her hip. One hand rested negligently in her lap. Around her wrist glittered the charm bracelet that her husband had given her on the birth of the children. At first glance an observer would miss its curiosity, but the artist had caught the bracelet's intricate design, a ray of sunlight throwing it into sharp relief against the lush crimson lap. Elvira was smiling the smile Michael remembered so well, the one that drove him to madness. So defiant, so derisive. Even when she was terrified and he could feel her fear, she gave him that smile.

How many lovers had she had? With how many men had she betrayed him? Even now the question twisted in his soul like a fat maggot. Even now, when Elvira was no longer here to taunt him with her defiance.

He looked down again at the miniature on his palm. He had coveted Elvira in the early days, but he would never expose himself to such weakness again. He would take this woman because he needed an heir. And he needed a woman in his bed. He was not a man who enjoyed paying for his pleasures; it left a sour taste in his mouth. This fresh young woman would arouse his flagging energies, would bring him pleasure as well as the fruits of her loins. And she could occupy herself usefully with the twins. Leo was right that they needed more complex schooling than their governess could provide. The prince had little interest in them himself, but they needed to be educated in the duties of womanhood if they were to make satisfactory wives. He was already planning their betrothals. Four years old was not too soon to make the most advantageous connections for himself. They wouldn't marry for another nine or ten years, of course, but a wise man prepared early.

He hadn't mentioned these plans to their uncle as yet. But then, it wasn't really Leo's business, although he'd probably consider that it was. He was as devoted to the children as he had been to their mother. Her death had devastated him. He'd journeyed from Rome to Paris in less than a week when the news had reached him, and immediately after the funeral had left France for a twelvemonth. He would say nothing about what he'd done or where he'd been during that year of grief.

Michael took another sip of cognac. Leo's besotted attention to Elvira's children was a small price to pay for his continuing friendship. His brother-in-law was a very useful friend. He knew everyone at court, knew exactly which path of influence would be the quickest to achieve any particular goal, and he was a born diplomat. He was an amusing companion, a witty conversationalist, a superb card player, passionate huntsman, bruising rider.

And the perfect choice to take care of his friend's wedding details. Michael smiled to himself, remembering how delighted Leo had been at the prospect of the prince's remarriage. Not an ounce of resentment that his sister was to be replaced, just simple pleasure in the prospect of the twins having a mother, and an end to his friend's marital loneliness.

Yes, Leo Beaumont was a very splendid man . . . if a trifle gullible.

"Oh, Cordelia, I am so fatigued!" Toinette threw herself onto a chaise with a sigh. "I am so *bored* with listening to speeches, standing there like a dummy while they rattle on and on about protocol and precedent. And *why* do I have to play this silly game this afternoon?"

She leaped up again with an energy belying her complaint of fatigue. "Why do I have to announce in front of everyone that I renounce all claim to the throne of Austria? Isn't it obvious that I do? Besides, there's Joseph and Leopold and Ferdinand and Maximilian all in line before me."

Cordelia bit into a particularly juicy pear. "If you think this is tedious, Toinette, just wait until you get to France. The real wedding will be twice as pompous as all this palaver." She slurped at the juice before it could run down her chin.

"You're a great comfort," Toinette said gloomily, flopping down again. "It's all right for you, no one's taking any notice of your wedding."

"Yes, how very fortunate I am," Cordelia said dryly. "To be married in the shadow of the archduchess Maria Antonia and Louis-Auguste, dauphin of France."

"Oh!" Toinette sat up. "Are you unhappy that your wedding is to be so quiet? I didn't mean to hurt your feelings. It must be terrible to have no one taking any notice of you at such an important time."

Cordelia laughed. "No, it's not in the least terrible. I was only pointing out the other side of the coin. In fact, there's nothing I would like less than to be the center of attention." She tossed the core of her pear onto a silver salver and wiped her mouth with the back of her hand.

"Oh, you have the bracelet back from the jeweler." Toinette caught the flash of gold in a ray of sunlight.

"Yes, and it's most strange." Cordelia, frowning,

unclasped the bracelet from her wrist. "I didn't notice its design when I first looked at it, but it's a serpent with an apple in its mouth. Look." She held it out to the archduchess.

Toinette took it, holding it almost gingerly in the palm of her hand. "It's beautiful, but it's . . . it's . . . oh, what's the word?"

"Sinister?" Cordelia supplied. "Repellent?"

Toinette shivered, and touched the elongated serpent's head where a pearl apple nestled in its mouth. "It is a bit, isn't it? It's very old, I should think." She handed it back with another little shiver.

"Medieval, the jeweler said. He was most impressed with it . . . said he'd never seen anything like it except in an illustration in a thirteenth-century psalter. Don't you think it's strange if it's that old that it should only have these three charms on it? In fact, really only two if you don't count the slipper, which is mine."

"Perhaps the others got lost somewhere along the line."

"Mmm." Cordelia fingered the delicate filigree of a silver rose, its center a deep-red ruby. Beside it hung a tiny emerald swan, perfect in every detail. "I wonder who they belonged to. Where they came from," she mused.

"I expect it's very valuable."

"Yes," Cordelia agreed, clasping it once again around her wrist. "Part of me doesn't like wearing it and part of me does. It has a kind of ghoulish fascination, but I do love the slipper. Makes me think of Cinderella going to the ball."

She chuckled at her friend's incredulous expression. "Oh, I know I'm not a beggar maid rescued by a prince, but we *are* going to Versailles, which everyone says is a fairy-tale palace, and we're escaping from all this prim protocol, and my uncle will never again be able to bully me. We can dance our lives away if we want, and never again have to sweep the ashes in the kitchen. . . . Oh, lord, is that the time?" She started, exclaiming with a mortified cry, "Why am I *always* late?" as the chapel clock struck noon, the gong resounding through the courtyard beyond the window.

"Because you think it's fashionable," Toinette replied with a knowing chuckle. "What are you late for this time?"

"I was supposed to be in the chapel at quarter to twelve to rehearse my own proxy marriage with the chaplain. And I didn't mean to be late. It was the bracelet that delayed me." Cordelia grabbed another pear from the fruit bowl and headed for the door. "I don't suppose it'll matter. Father Felix never expects me to be on time."

"Your husband might," the archduchess commented, checking her reflection in a silver-backed hand mirror.

Cordelia grinned. "My proxy husband or the real one?"

"Prince Michael, of course. The viscount is just a puppet."

"Oh, I don't think that's the case," Cordelia said consideringly. "Leo Beaumont's no puppet. Anyway, I'm sure he's not expected to rehearse too." She blew Toinette a jaunty kiss as she left.

She had seen the viscount only from a distance since the encounter in the orangery two nights earlier. Strangely, she'd enjoyed the distance. She'd hugged the thought of him as a deep and joyful secret, treasuring his image, which had filled her nighttime dreams and her waking internal vision. But she'd been only half awake as she'd watched him from afar, dwelling on this extraordinary, all-encompassing, totally engulfing love that had felled her like a bolt of lightning, made her so hot with desire she could have been in the grip of a fever.

Now she was ready again for the man of flesh and blood. Her body sang at the thought of being close to him, of feeling his heat, inhaling his scent. Her ears longed to hear his voice, her eyes to feast upon his countenance. This afternoon, at the renunciation ceremony, he would be beside her, in Prince Michael's place.

She pushed open the door to the chapel and entered the dim, incense-fragrant interior. "I do beg your pardon for being late, Father." She became aware of Leo Beaumont's presence even before she saw him pacing restlessly before the altar. Her heart jumped into her throat. "I ask your pardon, sir. I didn't realize you were to be rehearsing too."

"I understand from Father Felix that you've never been taught that punctuality is the courtesy of kings," Leo said acidly.

"Oh, indeed, I know it's impolite." She came swiftly toward him, her eyes glowing in her radiant face. "But I was talking with Toinette. My bracelet has come back from the jeweler and we were admiring it and the time just went somewhere." She held out her hand to him, her fingers closing over his.

Deliberately, he pulled his fingers free and instead picked up her wrist, holding it to the light from the rose window above the altar. As always, the bracelet's curious design disturbed him. The serpent that tempted and ultimately destroyed Eve. Sometimes he had thought Elvira had been the embodiment of Eve and that Michael had picked his gift with pointed care. He noticed that the jade heart was now missing. It had been the charm Michael had given to Elvira. Presumably, he'd thought it more tactful to remove it before passing on the gift to Elvira's replacement.

He became suddenly conscious of Cordelia's pulse racing beneath his fingers as they circled her wrist. Her skin was hot. He looked into her face, and she smiled with such seductive radiance, her eyes so full of joyous excitement, that he dropped her wrist as if it were a burning brand. For an instant he closed his eyes against the blazing force of her invitation.

"Well, now you're here, let's be done with this business. I've other things to do with my time." He turned brusquely to the altar. "Father, if you're ready."

The chaplain came forward with an eager assent. "It won't take long, my lord. Just to make sure that you're both familiar with the ceremony and the blessing of the rings."

Cordelia stepped up beside Leo. Her skirts brushed his

thigh. She tilted her head to look up at him. "Don't be vexed, my lord. I'm truly sorry to have kept you waiting."

"It's not necessary to stand so close to me," he snapped in an undertone, taking a step sideways.

Cordelia looked hurt.

"I beg your pardon, my lord. Is something the matter?" The chaplain looked up from his prayer book, where he was searching for the relevant passages.

"No." Leo shook his head with a sigh. "Nothing in the world, Father." He stared straight ahead, trying to ignore the pulsing presence beside him. How on earth was he going to manage her on the long journey to Paris? Or did he mean, how on earth was he going to keep his hands off her?

The ceremony was short, and Father Felix was only too happy to race through it when he realized the viscount's impatience and Lady Cordelia's restless distraction. He closed the book with relief after ten minutes. "That's really all there is to it. The blessing of the rings will take five minutes, and, of course, there'll be an address to the congregation. You will make your confession before the service, Lady Cordelia, so that you will be in a state of grace when you make your vows."

"And His Lordship too?"

"As this is a marriage by procuration, my lady, Viscount Kierston does not have the same obligations."

"Quite apart from the fact that I don't practice your faith," Leo stated. "Now, if you'll both excuse me, I have some business to attend to."

Father Felix offered a blessing and disappeared into the sacristy.

"Oh, no, wait!" Cordelia gathered up her skirts and ran to catch up with the viscount as he strode out of the chapel. "Don't go yet." She slipped her hand into his arm, pulling him aside into a small side chapel. "What a relief it must be not to have to go to confession." She took a bite of the pear she'd been holding in her hand throughout the rehearsal. "I tend to be rather forgetful when it comes to remembering my sins."

Her chuckle was so infectious that Leo couldn't help a responding smile. "Selective memory has its uses." He couldn't drag his eyes away from her little white teeth biting into the succulent flesh of the pear.

"I was wondering if loving could be considered a sin," Cordelia mumbled through another mouthful of pear. "I don't know why it should have happened that I love you the way I do, but it's a fact, and I don't really believe that God would frown upon it."

"Oh, in the name of mercy, Cordelia!" Leo jerked his arm free. "You don't know what you're talking about." He glared down at her. "And you've got pear juice running all down your chin."

"But I do know what I'm talking about," Cordelia protested firmly, searching through her pockets. "Oh dear, I seem to have mislaid my handkerchief. They're such juicy pears, you see."

With a muttered exclamation, Leo pulled out his own handkerchief and scrubbed at her chin. "You have to stop this fanciful nonsense, Cordelia. Do you hear me?" He thrust his handkerchief back into his pocket.

"I hear you. But I don't consider it to be nonsense." She gave him a serene smile. "Tomorrow night, in the Hofburg chapel, you will be my husband."

"Proxy!" he cried, flinging up his hands in frustration. "Proxy husband!"

"Yes, well, that's just a detail." She looked around for somewhere to dispose of her pear core, then with a shrug shoved it into her pocket. "Don't you see, Leo? This is *meant* to be. I know it in my blood. There are some obstacles, I know, but nothing we can't overcome."

"Are you run quite mad?" He looked at her helplessly.

She shook her head. "No. Kiss me and you'll see what I mean."

"Oh no." He backed away from her, holding up his hands

as if to ward her off. She was Eve, and the serpent bracelet gleamed on her slender wrist as she reached for his hand.

"Kiss me," she repeated, her voice low and sweet, her eyes beckoning him with a siren's enchantment, her parted lips offering entrance to the lush secrets of her body. Her hand closed over his and she stepped up to him. Light from the stained-glass window played over her upturned face, and a bar of gold lay across her milk white throat. "Kiss me, Leo."

He caught her face between both his hands. The urge to bring his mouth to hers was overwhelming. His lips seemed to sing with the memory of the times he had kissed her, and she was looking up at him with all the expectant wonder of sensual awakening. He could feel his fingers deeply imprinting the soft skin of her cheeks. There was a demon here, in her or in himself, he didn't know, but somehow it must be exorcised. He looked down at her, his eyes seeming to pierce the shell of her body to the soul beneath.

Abruptly, his hands dropped from her face. He turned and strode from the chapel, and the door clanged shut behind him.

Cordelia bit her lip on her disappointment. She felt empty, as if she'd been promised something that had been incomprehensibly withdrawn. And yet she was certain that he *did* feel what she felt—that they were somehow bound to each other. It wasn't a certainty that she could imagine either ignoring or questioning.

❀

Chapter Four

LEO WAS BORED, but no one would guess it from his smiling attention, his easy conversation, his diplomatic appearance of pleasure in the evening. He disliked costume balls more than anything, and in Paris or London he would have appeared in his regular dress, maybe carrying a loo mask as token contribution to the festivities. But in Vienna he was a foreign guest, a member of a delegation, and it would be discourteous to spurn his hostess's entertainment. So now he was clad as a Roman senator in a purple-edged toga, but as if to emphasize his dislike of the entertainment, his loo mask dangled negligently from one finger.

He shifted from one foot to the other and watched the clock. At midnight everyone would be unmasked, and if he slipped away a little beforehand, he could return dressed as himself without drawing comment.

In the meantime he conversed with one half of his mind while his eyes covertly raked the throng for Cordelia. She'd been at the banquet, dressed in a gown of celestial blue quilted taffeta over a petticoat of palest blue. Her midnight black ringlets clustered on her white shoulders, caught up at the back in a pearl comb. Her wrist was circled with her betrothal bracelet, and he noticed how she played with it absently when her hands had nothing else to do.

He had tried not to look at her, but, failing in that, had concentrated on concealing his observation. She had cast him several speaking glances across the wide expanse of the banquet table, but he had refused to return them, pretending to see only the brilliant glitter of the chandeliers, the crystal sea of glass, the glinting planes of silver and gold salvers that stretched between them.

But he couldn't deny that she was entrancing. She bubbled with life, and her table companions were reflected in her light and laughter. She seemed to scintillate at the center of the people around her, and Leo again saw Elvira. No one could be in the same room with Elvira without becoming wittier, prettier, handsomer, livelier. Even Michael in the early days of their marriage had taken on some of her hues.

Amelia and Sylvie occasionally showed glimpses of their mother's spirit, but they were intimidated by their dour governess, who was under strict orders from her employer to stamp out any signs of unseemly liveliness in the girls and to train and educate them to know their duty.

Leo, suddenly aware of his clenched jaw, forced his thoughts back to the ballroom. He made some vague observation to his companion as they stood at the side of the ballroom, his eyes still searching the crowd of dancers for Cordelia. She would have changed into her costume after dinner, but he was sure he'd know her, no matter how elaborate her disguise. Nothing would conceal the essential Cordelia.

When his companion's attention was claimed by another guest, he took the opportunity to move away, strolling around the ballroom, avoiding the strategically placed firemen with their pumps—eight hundred of them stationed in the window embrasures to watch the thousands of candles. He'd been told that the empress had installed medicines, beds for emergencies, and physicians in the apartments surrounding the temporary wooden structure of the ballroom in the grounds of the Belvedere Palace. It struck him as typical of that monarch's obsession with detail.

A quadrille was being danced by four squares of couples. He paused to watch, his eye immediately falling upon a lissome figure scandalously clad in britches that molded her calves and thighs. A tunic covered her hips for the most part, but when she moved in the dance, the tunic moved with her, offering tantalizing glimpses of a small round bottom.

Her hair was pulled back from her brow and confined in a silk snood, her black silk loo mask covered eyes and nose, but Leo knew immediately that it was Cordelia. *What in Lucifer's name was she playing at?* He pursed his lips on a soundless whistle and glanced involuntarily toward the dais where the empress sat with her daughter, her sons, and the senior courtiers of both France and Austria. Did she have the faintest idea that her goddaughter was dressed in this scandalous fashion? Cordelia was safe from Duke Franz because his gout kept him from the ball, but she was still risking serious censure. And she was drawing every eye in her vicinity.

She was outrageous and utterly seductive. And after tomorrow evening's proxy marriage, she would be totally in his charge until he delivered her to Prince Michael. It would be his responsibility to see she didn't flout the conventions on the procession through France. There would be rigidly defined rules of etiquette for this ceremonial journey with its many stops as the French people were introduced to their new dauphine, and there would be no room for nonconformity, however appealing the rebel might be.

And she was *very* appealing. Even as he frowned with disapproval, he couldn't deny how much she stirred him.

The strains of music faded as the graceful dance ended. Cordelia smiled distractedly at her partner, then turned away, striding off the floor with the freedom of movement her costume allowed. It was clear to Leo that she was looking for someone as she circled the room, prowling with a long-legged feline grace that sent a shiver down his spine. Judging by the quiver of arrows on her back, she was playing Diana the Huntress. She didn't seem to be aware of the attention she was drawing. The stares, the whispers, scandalized, envious, and in many cases undeniably lascivious, followed her every step.

Michael would have a seizure if he could see her, Leo thought. But instead of being shocked, he wanted to laugh. Sheer madness. Encouraging her was the last thing he wanted to do. Dear God, whyever had he agreed to take on such a charge? But, of course, he'd been expecting a timid, obedient debutante. Instead of which . . .

Impatiently, he started to cross the room toward her, keeping her in his line of sight. She had paused beside the young musician, Christian Percossi, who was listening attentively to some bewhiskered general. Leo saw her brush her friend's arm in passing. Then a back obscured his view for a second, and when he had a clear view again, Diana the Huntress had vanished.

Frustrated, he stopped, looking around. Then he saw young Percossi making his way purposefully to the doors leading to the courtyard outside the ballroom.

Clearly another assignation. Leo's eyes rolled heavenward. He quickened his step, following the musician.

There was a nip in the night air; the stars were crystalline against their black velvet background. Leo shivered in his thin toga after the heated ballroom with its myriad candles and hot press of bodies. A red carpet covered by an awning ran from the ballroom to the main structure of the Belvedere Palace; flambeaux lit the pathway that disappeared into the glittering maw of the palace. There was no sign of his quarry, but Leo followed the path into the palace. The great entrance hall was unnaturally quiet. A lone footman hurrying across the vast marble expanse gave the viscount in his Roman costume a curious glance and seemed to hesitate, then a clock somewhere chimed the midnight hour and he continued hastily on his way.

Leo heard Cordelia's voice, low but both urgent and excited, coming from an antechamber to the left of the grand staircase. He entered the small room without ceremony and was relieved to find the two of them standing decently far apart beside the open window. For all their protestations of pure friendship, he hadn't been completely convinced. But this was clearly no lovers' tryst.

Cordelia sensed his presence and turned swiftly to the door. "Oh!" she said. "It's you."

"Yes, it's me." He advanced into the room. "What in the name of the good Christ are you doing in that costume?"

"I was just asking her the same thing, sir." Christian ran a distracted hand through his fair curls. He was dressed unimaginatively if decorously as a minstrel. "It's shocking, Cordelia. What if the empress discovers your identity? Or your uncle! Can you imagine what he would do to you?"

"Yes," Cordelia said cheerfully. "But he won't know, and neither will the empress. Only Toinette knows, and she would never betray me."

"Cordelia, you're impossible." Christian looked toward the viscount in unconscious appeal.

"Come over here, Cordelia." Leo took her hand and led her over to a wall mirror. "Now, take a look at yourself and tell me what you see."

Cordelia, head to one side, examined her reflection. It seemed a strange question; it was obvious what she saw. "Me, dressed as Diana the Huntress."

"No. You, dressed in the most provocative, seductive fashion."

"But it's a costume ball. It's part of the fun to be incognito and slightly shocking."

"You are not yet old enough, wise enough, or sophisticated enough to be enflaming men."

"Do I?" she interrupted. "Do I enflame you?"

Leo was speechless for a moment, and it was Christian who exclaimed, "Cordelia!"

"I didn't say it first," she said. "Do I enflame *you*, Christian?"

"No ... I mean, well, you *could* do." He ran his hand through his curls again. "It's just shocking, Cordelia. You're the empress's goddaughter and you're about to be married—"

"Precisely." Leo waded in, once more on track. He took hold of her shoulders, feeling the slender shape of them beneath his hands, and turned her once again to the mirror. "Look at yourself, Cordelia. You don't think of the effect you have on men. Every man in that ballroom was salivating when he looked at you, and you blithely swan through it all like some innocent fairy in a dream. I tell you straight, your husband will not appreciate such a performance."

He felt some of her ebullience leave the slim body under his hands. She sighed. "I don't see why you should both be so cross, when no one except ourselves and Toinette knows who I am. And it's past midnight, so I can disappear and no one will ever be any the wiser. Besides, I didn't notice anyone salivating over me."

"That, I suspect, is your only saving grace," Leo said aridly. "If you had calculated the effect you had, you would be quite insufferable."

Cordelia turned aside and stared fiercely out of the window. She was accustomed to being scolded for her high spirits, but not in this fashion, and certainly not by Christian. "Maybe it was a mistake," she conceded, her voice a little muffled. "So, can we stop talking about it now, please? I have something much more important to discuss."

"Something private?" Leo inquired with a raised eyebrow.

Cordelia turned back to face him, regarding him intently, her eyes glowing turquoise through the slits in her black silk mask. "I would like to take you into our confidence, my lord. I . . . I think perhaps you might be able to help us."

"Oh." The eyebrow almost disappeared into his scalp.

"Cordelia, I don't think—" Christian began hesitantly.

"Viscount Kierston will help us," Cordelia interrupted. "You will, won't you?" She laid a hand on his forearm, on the bare flesh exposed by the toga. Despite her preoccupation, her eyes darted upward, an almost startled expression in them as her fingers crossed over his warm skin. Leo pulled his arm from her.

"Go and change your clothes," he said, keeping his voice level only with an enormous effort. "I refuse to discuss anything with you in that outfit."

"But you'll both stay here and wait for me?" she asked urgently. "I won't be many minutes."

"Christian and I will further our acquaintance in your absence," he responded coolly.

"Very well." She whirled to the door. "Christian, you can explain the situation with Poligny while I'm gone. And then I'll tell you both of my plan when I come back."

The viscount shook his head as she vanished. "I find I need a glass of champagne to restore my equilibrium." He strode to the bellpull hanging beside the door and summoned a footman.

"Cordelia does sometimes have that effect," Christian ventured with a timid smile. "She's so full of energy and ideas, she often throws me off balance."

Leo's smile was a trifle rueful, but he didn't respond. He gave orders to the footman who'd appeared instantly, then said, "So, put me in the picture, Christian."

Cordelia flew upstairs to the small chamber she occupied when the court was in residence at the Belvedere Palace. It was nowhere near as elegant or spacious as her apartments in the Schonbrunn, although not as cramped as those in the ancient Hofburg Palace, but the court was accustomed to moving from one palace to another according to the empress's ceremonial obligations, and Cordelia was at home in any one of them.

She hauled on the bellpull and ran to the armoire, tugging the tunic over her head as she did so.

"My goodness gracious me! Whatever are you wearing, girl?" Mathilde appeared in the doorway within minutes of the summons. She'd been Cordelia's nurse and now performed the duties of abigail even as she continued to scold, caress, comfort, and doctor as if Cordelia was still her nurseling.

"Whatever would your uncle say? And the empress?" She closed the door swiftly at her back as if prying eyes might be in the corridor.

"Oh, don't you start, Mathilde." Cordelia emerged from

the tunic and tossed it to the floor. "Only Toinette knew who I was, and she thought it a famous joke. But I have to change now." She tugged at the waistband of her britches while examining the contents of the armoire. "I shall have the seamstress make me up a gown of sackcloth with a neck that goes up to my ears! That should satisfy the so prudish Viscount Kierston!" She grinned, her spirits quite restored as she kicked off the britches and shrugged out of the shirt.

"Now, what are you prattling about?" Mathilde picked up the discarded clothes as they flew about the room. "If someone had the sense to take you to task for such mischief, all well and good."

Cordelia didn't answer. She pulled out a gown of sprig muslin. "This should do. It's about as seductive as a haystack. Lace me, Mathilde." She gave the woman her back, grasping the bedpost as Mathilde hauled on the laces of her corset. "Good. Thank you." She put finger and thumb at her waist and nodded her satisfaction. "I suppose when I have babies, I shall grow the most enormous waist. Now, where are my stockings?"

Mathilde held them out wordlessly. She was accustomed to Cordelia's whirlwind.

"Fichu," Cordelia declared, stepping into her petticoat and gown. "I need a demure fichu that won't show a centimeter of bosom."

Mathilde shook her head in resignation and proffered a white cambric fichu. Cordelia fastened it at the neck of her gown. "Oh, my hair. I can't wear this snood, it'll give everything away." She pulled it loose, shaking her black curls free. "Be an angel and brush it for me quickly."

Mathilde did so, drawing the brush through the black tresses until they shone with blue lights.

"You're a darling, Mathilde, and I don't know what I would ever do without you." Cordelia threw her arms around the maid's neck and kissed her soundly. "Don't wait up for me. I can undress myself." She picked up her fan and danced out of the chamber, leaving a smiling Mathilde to tidy up after the cyclone.

The sounds of music still came from the ballroom as Cordelia jumped the last two of the sweep of marble stairs rising from the entrance hall. She didn't pause to catch her breath but hastened into the anteroom. She stopped in the doorway beneath a torch in a wall sconce and curtsied with formal deliberation.

"I trust you find nothing to object to in my costume, Lord Kierston." She raised her eyes, and the flaming torch was reflected in the dark irises.

"I would call it a vast improvement, madame," he replied with a cool bow.

"I have it in mind to instruct the seamstresses to fashion me one of those garments women wear in the sultan's harems," she said. "Something that covers every inch of my skin, with a veil over my head, so no one can see anything of me but my eyes. Would that suit you, sir? That way I could never be a temptation or—"

"Put a bridle on your tongue, Cordelia!" he interrupted, trying to hide a bubble of amusement, lowering his eyelids to conceal the glints of laughter he knew were alive in his eyes. Cordelia could cover herself in horsehair and she would still be a temptation, but he wasn't about to tell her that.

"Do I tempt you, my lord?" She glanced up at him with demure eyes, long black lashes fluttering in a perfect mockery of flirtation.

"Cordelia!" exclaimed Christian yet again. He'd never seen his friend behave in this manner. "Have you had too much champagne?"

She shook her head, her eyes still fixed upon the viscount. "Well, do I tempt you, my lord?"

"To many things," he replied dampeningly. "Few of them pleasant."

"I was only funning," she said, although she knew she hadn't been, but some devil inhabited her when she was in the viscount's company, and she couldn't seem to help herself. "I don't think you have a sense of humor, sir. If you had, you wouldn't wear that boring and unimaginative costume."

Leo glanced at his reflection in the mirror. "What's wrong with it?" He sounded chagrined.

"It's dull. I would have dressed you as a Roman legionnaire instead . . . in a short toga and leggings, and those sandals with the crossed laces that go up to the knee. Now, that wouldn't have been boring in the least. Oh, and a circlet of gilded laurel leaves around your head. *Very* appealing."

Leo was so occupied trying to sort out this image of himself so blithely presented that it took him a minute to realize that she'd thrown him off balance again. He glanced at Christian and saw to his further chagrin that the young man was grinning.

"Cordelia's very good at costumes, my lord," Christian volunteered. "She designs all the costumes for the plays the royal family put on in the theatre at Schonbrunn. I know what she was wearing tonight was shocking, but it *was* very clever."

Leo glanced again at his image in the mirror and caught himself reflecting that it *was* a very boring costume. A legionnaire's regalia would have been much more imaginative and exciting.

Dear God! What would he be thinking next? "She was as conspicuous as a flamingo in a dovecote," he stated repressively. "Now, could we get to the matter in hand? If Poligny is pirating Christian's work, then he must be exposed."

"Yes, but even if we do that, Christian's position here will be impossible, even with the empress's support. Poligny has so many friends, so much influence."

"That's what I told *you*," Christian pointed out, "and you accused me of being a pessimist."

"Well, I thought about it a bit more." Cordelia wandered over to the table and the bottle of champagne. "Is there a glass for me?"

"I'm afraid not." Leo sipped his own wine.

"Never mind. I can share Christian's." She suited action to words, taking Christian's glass from his unresisting fingers. "This is what I have in mind. Christian should expose Poligny in a broadsheet that will hit the streets the day we all leave Vienna."

Leo's gaze sharpened. The musician was leaving too?

"But won't that look as if I'm afraid to defend my position?" Christian took the glass back and sipped.

"It might, but not if your evidence is incontrovertible." She held out her hand for the glass, talking rapidly but succinctly. "It'll cause a stir at the very least, and the news will reach Paris, so that when you arrive there you should already be a celebrity and it shouldn't be difficult to find an influential patron. Everyone knows you're a genius. And if they don't, they'll discover it immediately, as soon as you begin to play. What do you think, sir?" She turned to Leo, who had been watching the interplay between the two with a degree of amusement. Their ease with each other was completely free of loverlike undercurrents; it reminded him of the way he and Elvira had been together.

Sorrow, as fresh as it had ever been, washed through him. He picked up the bottle and refilled his glass.

Cordelia, seeing the sudden shadow in the viscount's eyes, looked over at Christian. But Christian was frowning, absorbed in the business at hand.

"Do you think my husband might be prepared to sponsor Christian?" she asked, as the viscount took a sip of his wine and seemed to emerge from whatever black landscape he'd been inhabiting. "Just initially, I mean. Just to introduce him to the right people."

Leo stroked his chin and considered this. Embracing the cause of an impoverished young musician, even if he was a genius, didn't sound at all like Michael. "I wouldn't pin my hopes on it," he said eventually.

Christian looked crestfallen, but Cordelia said impulsively, "But supposing I asked for it as a wedding present? It wouldn't be a big thing."

Leo couldn't help laughing. "My dear girl, a bride doesn't march up to her husband at first meeting and demand a wedding present."

"I suppose not," she said glumly.

"Besides, I don't have the money for the journey," Christian pointed out.

"Oh, I have money, that's not a problem," she said with a return of enthusiasm. "I can lend you whatever you need."

"I don't wish to borrow money from you, Cordelia."

"Pshaw! False pride," she said dismissively. "You'll pay it back when you're rich and famous and known the world over. But you must have a sponsor in Paris. Perhaps the king . . ." She glanced interrogatively at Leo.

"It's not impossible. The king is a generous patron, but it's not easy to gain his notice."

Cordelia chewed her lip. She could think of the solution, but she wondered if it would be impertinent to suggest it. It would, of course, but nothing ventured, nothing gained. However, it would be unforgivable to put both men on the spot in front of each other.

"The champagne has made me very thirsty," she said. "I wish I had some lemonade."

"I'll fetch you a glass," Christian said instantly, as she'd known he would. He set the champagne glass on the table and hurried from the room.

Cordelia picked up the discarded glass and sipped, trying to think how to approach the delicate subject.

"I thought the champagne made you thirsty," Leo observed, leaning back against a pier table, folding his arms, regarding her with an ironical eye.

"I want to ask you something private," she said.

"Why do I have the sense of impending trouble?" He reached behind him for his own glass.

"Will you sponsor Christian?"

Leo closed his eyes briefly.

"Please. It wouldn't be that much trouble, would it?" She came up to him, touching his arm again. "He really is a genius. You'll see."

He opened his eyes and looked down at her. Immediately, he regretted it. She was gazing up at him, her cheeks flushed, her hair tousled around her heart-shaped face. His eyes became riveted to the deep dimple in her chin, the full sensual bow of her lips. She brushed her hair impatiently from her face, tucking it behind her ears, and his gaze fell upon the small shells lying flat against the sides of her head. Her earlobes were long, begging for the grazing caress of his teeth.

"Please," she said softly. "It would mean so much to me. Christian can't waste his genius here. It's not fair to the world!"

"How can I possibly be responsible for depriving the world of genius?" he said, his lips curving in an involuntary smile. "You could charm the birds out of the air, the fish out of the sea, Cordelia."

Her eyes glowed and he knew he'd blundered again. "Could I, my lord?" Her little white teeth clipped her bottom lip.

He caught her face in both hands, his fingers pushing into the tangled ringlets. His mouth on hers was hard, as if he wanted to punish both of them for this craziness that he couldn't help. His tongue forced her lips apart, probing, ravaging her mouth, almost as if he would thus penetrate her body to the obstinate, irresistible spirit that drove it. His hands were hard on her face as he fought through the mists of madness to control his surging arousal.

But unbelievably, she laughed against his mouth, her breath a moist and sweet whisper, and her tongue danced with his. Her body moved against him, her own hands moving unerringly to his buttocks, pressing his loins against her.

Leo started back, his hands falling to his sides. He stared at her, her flushed face, her smiling mouth, the dreamy arousal in her eyes.

"Get out of here."

Cordelia stood her ground. She ran her hands through her hair, pushing the disordered curls off her face. "Don't you think you could love me at all, Leo? Not even one little bit?"

With a savage execration, he pushed past her and strode from the room.

Cordelia snapped a thumbnail between her teeth. At least he hadn't said no. But perhaps simply following her instincts as she was accustomed to doing was a mistake. Perhaps honesty put him off because he was accustomed to playing the sophisticated games of flirtation before the glittering mirrors of Versailles. But she didn't know how to play those games. She didn't know how to be anything but herself.

Too keyed up to go to bed and in too much turmoil to manage to be coherent in company, she made her way to the formal baroque gardens of the palace, the night air cooling her cheeks. That explosion of passion had shaken her. There had been a moment when he had frightened her, when she had sensed in him a force that could sweep her away into some maelstrom in which she would lose all sense of her own identity.

She shivered, wondering with a deep liquid surge in her loins what it would be like to experience that unleashed force.

Chapter Five

FOR THE HUNDREDTH time that day, Cordelia took up the miniature of her husband-to-be and scrutinized it. It was as if each time she stared into that calm, expressionless countenance, she expected to find some clue to the man himself. She knew that her own miniature was a fair likeness of herself, but that somehow it didn't capture any sense of the person she was. Presumably Prince Michael was as frustrated by this as she was.

The clock chimed five. In one hour she would be married by proxy to the man whose face gazed out at her from the lacquered frame. And she knew herself to be woefully unprepared for marriage, for wifehood, for motherhood—either to mother the prince's two little girls or to bring forth her own child. The idea of going blind into the unknown made her skin prickle with anxiety.

Mathilde bustled in, her arms full of silver cloth. "Come, come, child. Time's hurrying along and you must be downstairs to meet your uncle at five minutes to six." She laid the gown on the bed, panting slightly, her cheeks flushed. The gown was so heavily stitched with silver thread and seed pearls that it weighed almost as much as Cordelia herself.

Cordelia put down the miniature and stood up. The gown she would wear for her second wedding was already packed in the leatherbound chests she would take to Paris. It was made of cloth of gold and was even heavier than this one.

She shook off her wrapper with an impatient gesture that masked her sudden apprehension, and stood still as Mathilde laced her and fastened the tapes of her panniers. They were so wide she would have to slide sideways through all but the widest double doors. She stepped into the first of her six petticoats.

Twenty minutes later she was finally hooked into the gown. Her hair had been powdered and dressed hours before, and when she examined herself in the cheval glass, she saw a woman who bore no relation to herself. A painted, powdered doll, with jeweled heels so high and clothes so stiff and heavy she could walk only with the smallest steps. She'd endured ceremonial dress on other occasions since she'd left the schoolroom, but familiarity didn't lessen its discomforts.

Duke Franz Brandenburg was leaning heavily on his cane, his watch in his hand, when his niece entered the small salon in the imperial apartments of the Hofburg Palace.

"You are late," he pronounced in his customary irascible manner. "I cannot abide unpunctuality."

Cordelia curtsied and offered no defense. It was four minutes to six, but a minute was as bad as an hour in her uncle's book.

"Come." He limped to the door. "It's the grossest incivility to keep Viscount Kierston waiting. He's being most generous in taking on such a charge, and there's no need to make it more irksome than it already is." Belatedly, he offered her his arm at the door. "He must be a very close friend and confidant of Prince Michael's to do him such service. Unless, of course, he's in his debt," he added waspishly. "That's probably it. No man in his right mind would voluntarily take on such a burden."

Cordelia kept her mouth shut as the cantankerous voice maundered on in his disparaging fashion. Not that she expected anything else from her uncle. His niece was a burden to him; therefore she must be to any other man.

Marie Antoinette would be married by proxy the following day in the Augustine church, which was large enough to accommodate the entire court. Cordelia's ceremony was to take place in the small Gothic chapel beside the riding school. The guest list had been kept small, but no concessions had been made in the formality of the ceremony.

The royal family were present, as were the senior members of the French delegation. The duke limped up the aisle, his cane thumping with every step, his niece on his arm. The bishop of St. Stephen's stood before the altar.

Where was the viscount? Cordelia's eyes darted around the dim chapel. The day was overcast and there was no evening sun to light the stained-glass windows. Shouldn't her husband, proxy or not, be waiting at the altar for her? No one seemed concerned about this, and her uncle, now mercifully silent, continued his measured progress toward the altar without faltering.

As they reached it, Viscount Kierston appeared from the shadow of a stone pillar, where he'd been standing in quiet conversation with another courtier. It was almost as if his appearance were an afterthought, it was so casual. Cordelia, mummified in her stiff wedding gown and lacquered, powdered hair, felt a surge of resentment that he should treat this . . . her . . . with such insouciance. It was a real marriage. As legally and religiously binding as any. The one that would follow in Paris would carry no extra weight or significance.

He stepped up beside her, according the duke a curt nod but ignoring Cordelia. His attitude might be careless, but his dress was as formal as hers. His midnight blue suit was richly embroidered with silver arabesques. His hair was concealed beneath a pigtail wig, the queue encased in dark blue silk and tied top and bottom with matching silk ribbons. Diamonds winked from the folds of his lace-edged cravat, sparkled on his long fingers, edged the silver buckles of his red-heeled shoes.

Cordelia decided he looked intimidating, severe in his elegance—but so very beautiful. Her earlier resentment vanished as quickly as it had arisen. She was conscious of every line of his lithe slender frame, of the sharply etched cheekbones, the sensuous mouth, the long, luxuriant black eyelashes, so startling against the white of his wig. Her pulse raced, her palms dampened in her silk gloves.

The bishop's voice droned on over her head, but the words meant nothing. Her uncle gave her away with a clear note of relief in his louder-than-usual voice, and she barely noticed. She heard only the moment when Leo Beaumont said firmly that he took this woman, Cordelia Brandenburg, to be his wedded wife. She closed her mind to the "in the name of Prince Michael von Sachsen," aware only of her rising excitement, the heady swirl of anticipation. Somewhere at the back of her brain lurked the knowledge that she was being a fool, that to play with this fantasy while she stood at the altar being married to another man was a recipe for disaster, but that didn't seem to dim the lustre of her fairy tale in the least.

What if she were really marrying Viscount Kierston? Fueled by this question, her own responses were so fervent they surprised even the bishop, who peered at her in the candlelight.

Leo's mouth tightened as he heard Cordelia make her wedding vows. He knew what she was thinking. She had declared that she loved him, and however much he might dismiss this as a youthful fantasy, the ring of sincerity in her voice, the power of it in her eyes, couldn't be so easily dismissed.

Any more than he could dismiss the power she held over him, against his will, against his deep-rooted convictions, against all rationality.

The bishop blessed the rings and they were returned to the little gold ring box, to be presented at the second wedding when the true bridegroom would do his part.

"Well, that went off fairly well," Duke Franz declared when they were outside again in the gloomy, high-walled medieval courtyard outside the chapel. "And I wish you joy of your charge, my lord." He took snuff, flourishing his handkerchief as if waving away the burdensome years of his guardianship.

Cordelia, receiving the congratulations of the empress, heard the sour comment, as did everyone else. It was so churlish it penetrated the shell she'd early constructed around herself. She turned to look at her uncle, a tear of hurt shining in her eyes.

Maria Theresa patted her shoulder, saying kindly, "You have always been very dear to us, Cordelia. I consider you as one of my own children, and I know that you and Marie Antoinette will continue to be close friends and companions."

Cordelia curtsied as low as she could in her voluminous gown without overbalancing and falling on her rear. "I am sensible of Your Majesty's every kindness to me over the years, and I cannot express my gratitude enough."

Maria Theresa smiled approvingly, turning to the viscount. "I trust you'll be able to instruct Princess von Sachsen in the nuances of life at Versailles during your journey, Lord Kierston. I know they have some different customs."

Leo bowed. "I will do my best, madame." He supposed it was a task that fell to his hand—one of the growing list of responsibilities that accompanied taking charge of Michael's wife. How he had ever agreed to this insane project he couldn't imagine. But then, if he'd imagined Cordelia, he certainly wouldn't have agreed. But how could any sane man imagine Cordelia?

How would Michael react to her? He expected some demure, totally inexperienced young girl of impeccable breeding, well versed in her role of total obedience to monarch, father, husband. And he was going to find himself wedded to Cordelia.

"Stand still, Amelia, while I tie your ribbon. You're such a fidget."

"Yes, madame." Sylvie's eyes met her twin sister's, and they both dissolved in giggles.

"For mercy's sake, child, what is the matter with you today?" Louise de Nevry, the children's governess, pulled Sylvie's hair back with an unnecessarily hard tug. She couldn't understand what got into them on days like this. From the moment they woke, they seemed to share some secret that sent them into fits of giggles at the slightest thing anyone said to them. And all the scolding in the world did no good. She tied the lavender hair ribbon in a cramped little knot and pushed the child away.

"Now, Sylvie, come here and let me do your hair."

"Yes, madame." Amelia stepped obediently forward, her rosebud mouth quivering with laughter. It was one of the girls' greatest entertainments, this switching of identity. If they awoke before Nurse came to them in the morning, they would exchange positions in the bed before she saw them, and Amelia would be Sylvie and Sylvie Amelia for the rest of the day. And no one would be any the wiser.

Madame de Nevry tied the braid with the green ribbon that identified Sylvie for her father, as the lilac identified Amelia, then she turned the child around and scrutinized her critically. "This levity is unseemly," she scolded as the girl struggled with her laughter. "Both unseemly and foolish. What could you possibly have to laugh about?"

She glanced around the schoolroom with its dark paneled walls, bare oak floor, sparse furniture. The uncurtained windows were kept firmly shuttered so that no noise or distraction from the world outside could reach the girls at their lessons. She could see no encouragement for laughter in their surroundings; it was all exactly as it should be.

"The prince will be waiting for you. Is that ink on your hands, Sylvie?"

Amelia held out her hands. Her nails were painted with a foul-tasting yellow paste to keep her from biting them. Not that Amelia bit her nails; that was Sylvie's habit. But Nurse hadn't even looked when she'd ritually anointed the supposedly bitten fingers that morning.

"What will your father think!" the governess grumbled.

"Go to the nursery and wash them at once." She looked up at the clock, worrying at her lip with her teeth; they mustn't be late for their weekly presentation to the prince.

Louise was a thin woman, with angular features and sparse gray hair that she kept hidden beneath a large wig on which perched a dormeuse cap. An embittered spinster, a distant relation of the von Sachsens, she was dependent on the charity of the prince, for which she was expected to educate his daughters. But since she had little education herself, serious study didn't feature too much in the schoolroom of the prince's Parisian palace on rue du Bac. Instead the girls were expected to sit still for long periods of time, holding their heads high, their shoulders erect, the posture maintained with the aid of backboards. They were taught to curtsy and walk with the tiny, quick gliding steps de rigueur at Versailles, so that they looked like two clockwork miniatures with their panniered skirts floating over the floor, seemingly unpropelled by anything as vulgar as legs and feet. Madame, an indifferent performer on the clavichord, nevertheless strove to impart the rudiments of the instrument to her charges, neither of whom appeared to show either interest or aptitude. It didn't occur to the governess that this lack might have something to do with her methods of teaching.

The child returned with her ink-stained fingers scrubbed red and raw by Nurse's pumice stone. She curtsied to her governess, holding out her hands for inspection.

"It's not like you to have dirty hands," Madame said. "Your sister is usually the one who gets more ink on her than on the page."

There was a snort of laughter from the other child. Madame stared suspiciously between her small charges. "Now stop that! I shall report this conduct to your father."

The girls exchanged quick looks and sobered swiftly. They saw their father once a week for ten minutes, but there was no question whose authority ruled the schoolroom. They knew that Madame de Nevry's knees knocked when in the presence of Prince Michael. They could tell because her face became even more pinched and pale, and she fussed and scolded even more than usual before the weekly presentation.

"Come, it's time to go down." The governess hustled the children out of the door in front of her. The schoolroom was under the eaves at the very top of the house, and they proceeded down three flights of back stairs, with worn carpet and faded flock wallpaper. Stairs used only by the servants.

In the small foyer at the bottom of the last staircase, Louise took one last look at her charges, straightening a green ribbon here, a crooked fichu there. "Now, you speak only when spoken to and you confine yourselves simply to answering His Highness's questions. Is that clear?"

The twins curtsied and murmured assent. They needed no reminding of the rules. Their father was a figure so distant and lofty in their lives, they couldn't imagine opening their mouths in his presence without a direct order.

The governess smoothed down her own skirts, adjusted her cap, and sailed through the door leading to the grand hall of the mansion. Her charges followed, all levity vanished as they concentrated on taking little gliding steps while keeping their heads still, their backs rigid. They entered the main part of the house only on these weekly occasions, but they were trying so hard not to make a mistake, they never saw anything of their surroundings, retaining only a confused mélange of gilt and soft pretty colors, rich carpets or the click of marble beneath their tiny feet.

A liveried, powdered footman bowed as they passed. The children ignored him because they had been taught that servants were not to be acknowledged unless one was giving an order. Another footman flung open the painted paneled doors, announcing in ringing tones, "Mesdames Amelia and Sylvie. Madame de Nevry."

The children entered before the governess, both keeping their eyes on the floor, aware of the great expanse of carpet stretching between them and the figure of their father at the far end of the salon. Everything seemed huge in this room. A console table on the wall beside the door was at the level of their heads. The sofas and chairs were made for giants. They would have to climb up the slippery legs in order to sit in them. But since they were never expected to sit down, the question was academic.

Prince Michael beckoned them over. He remained leaning against the mantel, something nestled in the palm of his hand. He was dressed for court. His pale eyes were sharp beneath his elaborately curled wig as he took in his daughters' appearance.

"Your report, madame."

The children held their breaths. Sometimes Madame would list a catalogue of minor offenses, things they had either forgotten or had never even been pointed out to them. They never knew why she did this, except that it seemed to happen when she had been complaining to Nurse about how her troubles were on her. Other times, she would report an uneventful week and the prince would dismiss them with a satisfied nod.

Madame curtsied. "Amelia continues to have difficulty mastering cursive, sir, and Sylvie is sometimes reluctant to practice her music."

Michael frowned. Was it Sylvie who wore the green ribbon or Amelia? He could never remember, although he'd decreed the identifiers himself. They both looked dutifully at the carpet, but he could see that they each held their dimpled hands tightly gripped in front of them. They seemed very small, and it astonished him how two separate individuals could be so utterly identical. Presumably, they had different characters—not that their individual personalities were particularly relevant to anything.

"Anything else?"

"A degree of unseemly levity, sir."

The children remained motionless.

How could such stiff, expressionless little dolls show unseemly levity? It struck Prince Michael as extraordinary.

However, he had other things on his mind and decided these peccadilloes weren't worth considering.

"I daresay their mother will correct these faults," he stated.

Louise looked as if she'd been struck by a lightning bolt. "I . . . I beg your pardon, sir? Their . . . their mother?"

Amelia and Sylvie forgot their fear and looked up, showing their father two pairs of wide blue eyes, two rosebud mouths, two small noses. Elvira's features. He could see nothing of himself in them, but their paternity didn't interest him. Had they been boys, it would have been very different. But girls were simply currency and he would spend them wisely. They were bidding fair to be as beautiful as Elvira, and if they fulfilled that potential, he should have little difficulty making advantageous marriages for them.

"B-b-but our . . . our m-mother's dead, sir." They spoke in stammering unison.

"Your first mother, yes," he said with a touch of impatience. "But you are to have a new mother. You may look at her likeness." He held out the miniature.

Amelia took it from him with a quick, darting movement as if she were afraid she was putting her fingers in a trap. The two girls stared at the face and said nothing.

Louise felt the earth slipping beneath her feet. A mistress in the house was bad news for a governess. She would have to make herself agreeable to the new princess, who could well threaten her hitherto undisputed authority over the girls.

"Pray allow me to congratulate you, Prince." She curtsied stiffly. "Is the marriage to be soon?"

"The wedding has already taken place by proxy in Vienna. Viscount Kierston is accompanying the princess here with the dauphine's party." He held out his hand for the miniature. Amelia handed it back with a curtsy, immediately lowering her eyes to the carpet again.

Louise struggled to keep the chagrin and vexation from her face. It didn't surprise her that her employer hadn't considered it necessary to impart this information before, but it surprised her that Viscount Kierston had kept silent about it. He was so interested in the girls, it seemed extraordinary that he wouldn't have hinted at something this important. She longed to see the portrait, but it seemed it was not to be. The prince dropped it into his coat pocket. "You are dismissed."

The little girls curtsied and backed out of the room. Amelia's hand crept into Sylvie's as they edged out of the door. Their governess, after another stiff curtsy, followed them. No one said anything until they were back in the schoolroom, then Amelia gave a joyful jump.

"She's so pretty."

"Yes, like a real princess," Sylvie agreed, doing a little dance. "And Monsieur Leo will be coming back too."

"Now stop that at once!" Madame was looking very pinched and cross. "I will not have you dancing and jumping like a pair of peasant hoydens."

The girls composed themselves, but their eyes still shone. For once they had the advantage of their governess. They knew that she hadn't seen the miniature of the new princess, and they knew how vexed she was.

"She had black hair, madame," Sylvie said kindly.

The governess wanted to ask the single burning question: How old was this new Princess von Sachsen? But she wouldn't demean herself by asking it of her charges. The majordomo would know everything. Monsieur Brion always knew everything before anyone else. It would be almost as demeaning to beg information from him, but it was necessary.

"It's time you were in bed," she announced.

The girls couldn't yet tell the time, but they knew it was far too early. The sun hadn't gone down and they hadn't had supper. They gazed at their governess in dismay.

"You have both been exceedingly ill behaved," Madame declared. "This unseemly laughter has to stop. You will have bread and milk for supper and go to bed immediately."

They knew protestation would only make matters worse. Just as they knew they were suffering for their governess's pique. At least in bed, tucked behind the drawn bedcurtains, they could whisper about this amazing new event and speculate in perfect safety about the pretty young girl who was going to come to live with them.

And Monsieur Leo would come with her. They hadn't seen him for weeks and weeks, and they missed the one ray of sunshine in their drab little lives.

Chapter Six

"ADIEU, MY DEAR daughter. Do so much good to the people of France that they will be able to say that I have sent them an angel." Maria Theresa embraced her weeping daughter for the last time. The whole Hapsburg family, the entire Austrian court, the highest echelons of the aristocracy, were all witnesses to this final meeting between mother and daughter in the great hall of the Hofburg Palace.

"Poor Toinette," Cordelia murmured, blinking back her own tears. "To have to make such a public farewell. She loves her mother so dearly. How will she manage without her?"

Viscount Kierston made no response. He too was moved by the poignancy of this farewell. The new dauphine of France knew that she would probably never see her mother again, and it seemed a brutal separation for a girl not yet fifteen. But the sentiments of private people had no place in the lofty reaches of international diplomacy. The archduchess's marriage to the dauphin would cement the vital alliance between Austria and France as nothing else could.

Still weeping, Toinette was escorted from the palace to the coach that would take her to her new country. She was accompanied by her brother, the emperor Joseph, who seemed nonplussed by his little sister's emotional state. Toinette had begged that Cordelia be allowed to accompany her in the coach as well, but the empress had refused. Her daughter must make her ceremonial departure from the land of her fathers in state. She must be seen to be strong, mature, ready to assume her royal duties.

As the coach moved sedately out of the courtyard, Toinette could be seen through the glass window, leaning back in a corner, her hand covering her eyes with her handkerchief, but as the carriage passed through the gates, she leaned out, gazing backward at her home, tears streaming down her face. Her brother's hand appeared on her shoulder, drawing her within.

"Her brother won't be much comfort," Cordelia observed. "He's so stiff and formal."

"You'll be able to be with her when we reach Melk," Leo said. "You had better make your own farewells now."

The empress took a fonder farewell of her godchild than Duke Franz did of his niece. Maria Theresa gave her a silver locket with her own portrait inside and embraced her warmly. The duke acknowledged her curtsy with a cold nod and the command that she obey her husband. Her marriage settlements were generous and she should be grateful to all those who had looked after her interests hitherto.

If she never saw her uncle again, she wouldn't shed a tear, Cordelia decided, moving to her own carriage, where Leo Beaumont waited to hand her in. The von Sachsen arms were emblazoned upon the panels.

"Your uncle has a harsh manner," Leo observed, with a frown. "I daresay he's uncomfortable with emotion."

Cordelia glanced up at him as he handed her inside. "There's no need to make excuses for my uncle, Viscount. I assure you there's no love lost on either side." Her face was tight, though, and her eyes were tinged with sadness. "My parents died of smallpox when I was a baby. If they had lived, perhaps this leaving would have been difficult. As it is, I can't wait." She seated herself on the crimson velvet squabs of the luxuriously appointed vehicle, her skirts billowing out on either side, filling the entire length of the bench. The tightness of her expression relaxed. "Is Versailles really as much of a fairy-tale palace as they say?"

"Only for the naive," he said dryly, putting a foot on the footstep.

"I don't consider myself to be naive," she protested.

He laughed, but not unkindly, as he stepped into the

coach. "My dear, you are an ingenue, you know nothing of the darker side of court life, but if it pleases you to imagine a glittering fantasy, then do so. You'll be disillusioned soon enough." He sat back on the opposite bench, careful not to tread on the flounced hem of her gown as he adjusted his sword to his hip.

"I might surprise you, my lord," Cordelia said, not at all pleased at his somewhat patronizing tone.

"I'm not sure that anything you do could surprise me," he observed amiably, determined neither to quarrel in the close confines of the carriage, nor to offer an opportunity for one of her impulsive flights of passion. And after this ceremonial departure from Vienna, he would be able to ride while his charge journeyed by coach in decorous solitude.

The carriage started forward. Cordelia leaned out of the window to watch the procession fall in behind her. There were coaches laden with baggage and servants. Mathilde was traveling with Cordelia's trunks at the rear of the procession. A troop of cavalry escorted the procession, banners snapping in the breeze, the sun shining on the embroidered ceremonial trappings, the silver of bridle and stirrup. At the very rear, spare horses were led by troopers, her own Lucette, a Lippizaner like the viscount's, among them.

"Is Christian traveling with your staff?"

"I believe so. But how he chooses to make the journey is up to him."

"I wish I could be a fly on the wall when the broadsheet hits the street tomorrow and Poligny finds himself exposed." She chuckled, fanning herself lightly.

Leo didn't offer a response. He had less confidence than Cordelia and Christian in the power of the truth to bring down someone as slippery and influential as Poligny, but the man would at least be embarrassed, especially by the defection of the pupil whose work brought the master his greatest credit.

"The empress was very gracious when Christian asked

her to release him," Cordelia continued, regardless of her companion's silence. "She even gave him a purse."

"Mm."

"How far is it to Melk?"

"Fifty kilometers."

The viscount was obviously not in a talkative mood. They were to stop for the night at the Benedictine monastery of Melk, and fifty kilometers of jolting on ill-made roads in such severely silent company was hardly appealing.

"Is something vexing you, my lord?" She offered what she hoped was an innocent and supplicating smile. "I'll try very hard not to be a tedious traveling companion."

"I'm very much afraid that if you try too hard, you'll achieve the opposite effect," he observed, leaning back, his arms folded, regarding her through half-closed eyes. She was wearing an enchanting velvet cap perched atop the piled mass of black ringlets. An Indian shawl was draped carelessly over her shoulders against drafts, and one perfectly rounded forearm rested on the sill of the carriage. Prince Michael's bracelet circled her wrist, the little diamond slipper clicking softly against the side of the door with the swaying of the carriage.

"That's unkind, but if you wish me to sit in silence, my lord, then I will." Cordelia folded her lips together, placed both hands in her lap, and stared fixedly at the carved wooden paneling above the viscount's head.

It was such an absurd picture that his lips twitched and the merry hazel glints appeared in his eyes. "What an annoying creature you are."

"Oh, that is unfair!" she protested. "I'm trying to be exactly what you wish in a traveling companion and you accuse me of being annoying."

"I don't recall describing my ideal traveling companion."

"Well, you implied a description. You want a stiff, starchy, ugly doll, who won't speak or smile or suggest anything in the least unusual in the way of entertainment."

"If that were my ideal, I assure you, my dear, that

you could never approach it," he said with a lazy grin. "If you remain on your seat and confine your remarks to the commonplace, I shall be well satisfied."

Cordelia made a face. "The commonplace is exceedingly boring, my lord. However, I have an idea how we may amuse ourselves." She fumbled in her reticule and produced a pair of dice with a little crow of triumph.

"See. I come prepared. We shall dice the time away. I do adore to gamble." She tossed the dice from hand to hand with an expert touch.

Leo raised his eyebrows. Gambling was the besetting sin of all courtiers in every court on the continent as well as at St. James's Palace in London. Fortunes were lost in an evening almost as fast as reputations. Prince Michael was no exception, although he preferred cards to dice, but whether he would look kindly on serious gambling by his wife was another matter. But perhaps her idea of gambling was of the schoolroom variety, for small coins or paper spills.

"Let's throw for high numbers," she said eagerly, rolling the dice between her hands. "What do you wager, sir?"

"Three ecus," he said, prepared to indulge her.

"Oh, pshaw! That's baby stuff. I wager four louis."

Clearly, Cordelia had progressed beyond paper spills. "I presume you can cover such a wager?"

Her eyes flashed indignantly. "You insult me, my lord."

He held up his hands pacifically. "No insult intended, I assure you, madame. I was unsure whether you had funds upon your person."

Cordelia returned to her reticule, withdrawing a heavy velvet purse. "I have five hundred louis in coin and notes," she stated. "My uncle's wedding gift. He would not have it said that he failed in his duty to his niece," she added with a sardonic smile. "It's my own money anyway, from my mother's estate, but Duke Franz always pretends that it's his own generosity that keeps me in funds." Her lip curled derisively. "I trust my husband is not ungenerous in such matters. I know for a fact that my mother's jointure is my own under the marriage settlements, so I hope he's not inclined to withhold it."

Leo frowned. He didn't think Michael would withhold his bride's estate, but neither did he believe he would hand it over to her without supervision. "It's not customary for a woman to have access to her own fortune. I'm sure your husband will make you a generous allowance."

"An allowance of my own money! It's so unjust."

Leo shrugged. "Maybe. But it's the way of the world and not to be changed by a slip of a girl."

"Don't be too sure, my lord." Cordelia thrust her irritation from her and tossed the dice again. "Come, let us throw. We don't have a flat surface, but we can toss them on the seat beside you. The disadvantage will be the same for both of us." She leaned over, the shawl slipping from her, revealing the deep cleft between her round breasts. The scent of her hair, so close to his face, filled his nostrils, the curve of her cheek entranced him.

The dice rolled on the velvet seat beside Leo, and he turned with relief to look.

"A four and a six." Cordelia sat back with a smile of triumph. "Let's see if you can do better, my lord."

Resigned, Leo tossed the dice. They came up three and a two.

"Ha! I win." She gathered up the dice and held out her hand for her winnings.

Leo drew out his own purse and handed her four louis, which she pocketed with such an air of gloating jubilation that he couldn't help laughing. "What a graceless winner you are. I trust you don't lose as badly."

"I rarely lose," she said smugly, tossing the dice in her hands again. "Shall we raise the stakes to five?"

It seemed a relatively harmless way to pass the time, and Cordelia's shameless exultation at every win was irresistible. And she won every throw.

Belatedly, it occurred to Leo that such a run of good luck was way beyond the average. She had gleefully pocketed twenty louis before the first suspicion entered his head. Casually, he turned sideways to watch closely as she tossed the dice. There was something about the way she flicked them that caught his attention. It was a little twist of her wrist that ordinarily would pass unnoticed, but he was beginning to find his continual losses somewhat tedious.

"Ha! I win again! You owe me another five louis, my lord." She held out her hand in her usual fashion.

"I wonder if I do," he said slowly, scooping up the dice from the seat beside him. They felt normal enough. He'd been throwing them for the last half hour without a qualm. He glanced up. Cordelia was looking transparently anxious and had withdrawn her open palm.

He tossed the dice in his palm, fixing her with a hard stare, watching the color rise in her creamy cheeks, waiting until her eyes dropped to her lap.

"These are weighted in some way, aren't they? *Aren't they?*" he repeated when she seemed disinclined to answer.

"How could you accuse me of such a thing?" Her color was high, her bottom lip clipped between her teeth.

"You cheating little fibster!" he declared, tossing the dice into her lap. "Show me how they work."

"I was going to give the money back to you." Her glowing eyes were enormous, fixed earnestly on his face.

"You'll forgive me if I doubt that," he said dryly. "Now, show me how they work."

"Oh, very well. But it's such a neat little trick. If you didn't know, you couldn't feel it. You couldn't, could you?"

"If I had been able to, I wouldn't be twenty louis the poorer," he said as aridly as before. "I'm waiting."

Cordelia leaned forward, almost into his lap, the dice cupped in her hand. "They're clipped at this corner. If you flick them onto the edge, they always fall either on the six or the four. It doesn't win every time, but most of the time."

She was far too close to him. Her scent, the deep cleft of her bosom, the midnight-black mass of curls were making his head spin, and when she looked up at him, a tentative smile in her eyes that were that moment as brilliant as sapphires, his breath caught in his throat.

"It was only a little fun, my lord." Her voice was both apologetic and defensive. "It wasn't as if we were playing seriously."

"I didn't notice we were playing for pretend louis. I tell you, Cordelia, that if I'd been playing with a man who used such tricks, I would take a horsewhip to him," he stated.

"Wouldn't you challenge him to a duel?" Cordelia asked in surprise, momentarily distracted from her own predicament.

"I wouldn't dishonor my sword with his blood," he said bluntly.

"Oh." She chewed her lip again, then rummaged through her reticule. "Here. Every one of them." She tipped the louis into his hand. "I suppose it was wicked, but I do so love to win. And I'd never do it at the tables."

She sounded so melancholy and aggrieved that amusement yet again shattered Leo's justified annoyance. It simply wasn't possible to be angry with her for more than a fleeting instant, even in the face of such outrageous behavior.

"I give you fair warning, that if anyone catches you cheating in the salons of Versailles, you will be ostracized, and not even the dauphine will be able to redeem you," he said with dire emphasis. "And if you bring such dishonor on your husband's name, he would be entitled to have you shut up in a nunnery."

"But I wouldn't!" Cordelia protested, horrified as much by the idea that he might consider her capable of such stupidity as by the contemplation of such retribution. "We only played with these tricks in the family. Toinette is just as bad as I am; sometimes it was the only way to beat the archdukes. And they were quite odious when they won and set all sorts of embarrassing forfeits."

"Well, I've a mind to set a forfeit of my own," he said thoughtfully, tapping his mouth with his fingertips as he examined her.

"What?" A little prickle of excitement ran over her skin. She leaned forward again. "How would you have me pay, sir?"

Leo realized his mistake immediately. Whenever he dropped his guard, he found himself blundering into the morass. Her lips were parted in unmistakable invitation, and the tip of her pink tongue ran slowly over them in a gesture so seductive that it took his breath away. Cordelia was not the least alarmed by talk of forfeits.

He sat back, saying indifferently, "I find this tedious." Closing his eyes, he rested his head against the seat back and to all intents and purposes went to sleep.

Cordelia frowned. She didn't believe for a minute that he was truly asleep. She rifled through the contents of her reticule with great sighs and rustles as if looking for something vital. Then she hummed a little tune, tapping her foot in accompaniment. Still the viscount remained apparently asleep.

She let down the window and leaned out to watch the passing scenery. "Goodness, you should see the crowds lining the wayside to watch us pass," she observed conversationally. "Oh, and there's a dancing bear on a chain. It looks very sad, poor creature. Oh, and look, they're chasing a pickpocket . . . and there's a gingerbread stall. It's just like a fair, with stalls and entertainers." She withdrew her head and regarded her still-somnolent companion. "It's a deal more entertaining outside than it is in here."

Leo gave up. He opened his eyes. "Has anyone ever suggested wringing your neck?"

"Not to my knowledge," she said with a twinkle. "But it's odious of you to pretend to be asleep. I wouldn't have disturbed you if you were truly fatigued, but you're not. And I have so many things I want to ask you."

"Serious things?" he asked suspiciously.

"Utterly. The empress told me you would use the journey to educate me in the particulars of life at Versailles. Toinette will have the comtesse de Noailles to tell her things, but I have only you."

"Very well." They had to do something to pass the time, and this seemed both safe and useful. "What do you wish to know?"

"Oh, a host of things, but before we begin, I have another wager ... no, not dice and not for money," she added, seeing his darkening expression. "Something much more important. Let us wager on the precise time of arrival at Melk. Whoever gets closest wins."

"And what are the stakes?" Why he was even considering it on past experience, Leo didn't know.

"If I win, I ride tomorrow instead of sitting in this stuffy carriage."

"And if I win?" One black eyebrow lifted.

"Your choice."

"Oh, now, that is tempting indeed." He stroked his chin, reflecting. Cordelia waited rather anxiously. She couldn't imagine what he'd choose.

"Very well. If I win, you will refrain from pestering or provoking me the entire day."

"Is that what you think I do?" Hurt clouded her eyes but he refused to see it.

"I want none of your blatant flirtation, none of your trickery. You will behave with perfect decorum in my presence, and you will speak only when spoken to. Agreed?"

Cordelia nibbled her lip. It seemed a poor wager but she didn't have much option. She'd just have to hope she won. She shrugged her agreement. "So, let's write our projections now and put them away until we arrive." She drew out a lead pencil and a small notebook from her reticule and handed them to him.

Leo didn't hesitate. He wrote swiftly, then tore out the page and tucked it into his coat pocket.

Cordelia took the pencil and paper. She frowned fiercely, chewing the end of the pencil, trying to calculate how far they had already journeyed. They would have to stop for refreshment and to change horses, and it would all be very ceremonious, so it would take time.

"Mathematics is not your strong suit?" Leo inquired with a solicitous smile.

"On the contrary," she retorted. "It's one of my best subjects." Stung, she gave up calculating and scribbled her projection. "There." She stuffed the paper back into her reticule and sat back. "Now we'll see."

"So, you have questions."

"When did your sister die?"

He hadn't expected that, but it seemed an understandable question. "Four years ago. The girls were nine months old." His expression was neutral, his eyes hooded.

"What did she die of?"

"What has that to do with the particulars of life at Versailles?" His voice was cold, his mouth suddenly tight.

"I'm sorry," she said swiftly. "Does it pain you to talk of her?"

She didn't know how much. But it wasn't so much pain as this deep tide of rage that threatened to burst its dams when he thought of the wastefulness of such a death, such a vibrant, precious life extinguished almost overnight. He forced himself to relax and answered her first question, ignoring the second. "She died of a fever . . . a very swift wasting sickness."

It was far too common a cause of death to surprise Cordelia. "You loved her very much?" she asked tentatively, her eyes grave now, her expression soft.

"My feelings for Elvira can have nothing to do with your new life, Cordelia," he said, trying not to snap. He could never bring himself to talk about his sister, not even to Michael, who always maintained an understanding silence on the subject.

"Elvira. That's a pretty name." Cordelia seemed not to have heard him. "Was she older than you?"

Clearly, she was not to be put off. "We were twins," he said shortly.

"Oh." Cordelia nodded. "Twins have a very special bond, don't they?"

"So it's said. Can we talk about Versailles now?"

"Your sister gave birth to twins. It must run in the family," Cordelia continued. "Perhaps you'll father twins when you marry. Have you ever wished to marry?"

"That is not a topic for this conversation," he declared frigidly. "If you wish us to continue, then you will confine yourself to pertinent questions."

"I didn't intend to be impertinent," she said, frowning. "I was just being interested and friendly."

Leo wondered if she was being disingenuous and then decided that he didn't wish to know. He offered no encouragement, and after a minute she said, "Tell me about my husband. What kind of man is he?"

This at least was an unimpeachable area of interest. "He's a man in his prime. A great huntsman, which makes him popular with the king. He enjoys court life and you'll find that you'll be invited to most of the sojourns at the other palaces, like Fontainebleu, St. Cloud, the Trianon, the Hotel de Ville. The court picks itself up and goes on these journeys four or five times a year. The king grows impatient if he stays in one place too long."

Cordelia was listening intently, but while this exposition on court travels was mildly interesting, it wasn't as pertinent as her husband. "But will I like him?" She leaned forward again, underscoring the seriousness of the question.

Leo shrugged carelessly and drew away from her maddening proximity. "How should I know, Cordelia. Many people do, but he has enemies. We all do."

"Is he kind?" Cordelia persevered, laying a hand on his knee. "Is he good to the children?"

He was a cold, indifferent parent, one reason why Leo was so anxious that they should have a concerned and caring stepmother. However, Leo kept this reflection to himself. "They are in the charge of a governess. I don't believe their father has much to do with them."

That, too, was not uncommon. She opened her mouth for another question when the blast of a trumpet rent the air. "Oh, we must be stopping somewhere. I own I shall be glad to stretch my legs."

Leo swung open the door when the carriage came to a halt in the center of a small village. He jumped down to the cobbled square and held out his hand to assist Cordelia in the delicate maneuver required to get herself and her wide skirts through the door. He dropped her hand the minute she was on solid ground.

Cordelia proceeded to tuck her hand in his arm. "You are my escort, proxy husband," she murmured. "You mustn't treat me as if I'm a pariah dog."

He looked sharply down at her. As he'd expected, she was smiling with that outrageous invitation in her eyes. "Behave yourself!" he commanded in a ferocious undertone.

Cordelia's smile broadened. "I haven't lost the wager yet, my lord."

He had no time to respond, as the village mayor came over to them, bowing low, offering the humble hospitality of his village. The dauphine and her brother were installed in chairs on a canopied dais in the center of the square, while village maidens brought them food and drink and the inhabitants of the countryside for miles around gazed in wonder at the august presence in their midst.

Cordelia and the viscount were escorted to the village inn, where hospitality for the dauphine's retinue was provided. There were so many people milling around in the small, low-beamed taproom that conversation was impossible and the heat rapidly became insupportable. Cordelia dabbed her forehead with her handkerchief. "Pray excuse my, my lord." She withdrew her hand from his arm and turned to leave the inn.

"Where are you going?"

"A matter requiring privacy, my lord." She gave him an impish smile and pushed her way to the door.

Leo drained his tankard of ale with a heartfelt sigh. Twenty-three days of her close company!

Cordelia found the single privy with a line of courtiers waiting to use it. Her nose wrinkled at the noisome little shed. It wasn't constructed for women with skirts five feet wide. She turned and made her way through the village into the fields beyond. A blackberry bush provided sufficient cover and the air was a deal fresher, despite the circle of cows solemnly regarding this extraordinary creature who'd appeared in their midst.

She'd just moved her skirts and petticoats out of the way when she heard the crackle of footsteps beyond the bush. Of all the inconvenient moments for some village laborer to come along! She was not particularly embarrassed. Most of the public privies in Schonbrunn had no doors on them, and the commodes behind the screens in the corridors were hardly private.

"Cordelia, what the devil are you doing out here?" The viscount sounded distinctly annoyed and very close. She could see his feet beneath the bush.

A local peasant was one thing, Viscount Kierston quite another. "I'm behind the bush," she said hastily. "Don't come any closer."

"What the hell . . . Oh!" Laughter filled his voice. "I do beg your pardon."

Cordelia shook down her skirts and emerged from her open-air closet. "it was hardly chivalrous to follow me, my lord."

"When I see my charge hastening into the countryside at a moment when the dauphine and the emperor are about to reenter their carriage, chivalry doesn't come into it," he retorted. "Why couldn't you use the village privy like everyone else?"

"Precisely because everyone else was using it," she declared, smoothing a wrinkle in her skirt. "Women are at a serious disadvantage, you should know, Lord Kierston."

He laughed again. "I see your point. Now come along.

The carriages behind ours can't leave until we do." He took her hand, hurrying her back across the field, forgetting in his amusement to keep his hands off her.

Cordelia, for her part, made no protest at this unceremonious escort.

They reached the palatial monastery of Melk at six in the evening. The dauphine and the emperor had already entered the imperial apartments by the time the von Sachsen carriage passed beneath the west gate of the monastery, which dominated a bend of the Danube below.

Cordelia looked at the dainty fob watch pinned to her gown. She opened her reticule and drew out her folded sheet. "What did you project, sir?"

Leo pulled out his paper. "Six-thirty," he said with a confident smile. Half an hour out on such an impeded journey was barely worth considering.

But Cordelia laughed, her eyes gleaming with pleasure. "Six twenty-seven. See." She held out her folded sheet. "I never estimate regular times because in the real world nothing ever happens so neatly. I win."

"Yes, you do. But there's no need to crow."

"But it was clever of me," she insisted.

Leo stepped out of the carriage. "Yes, you may ride," he said, giving her his hand. "And I shall enjoy a peaceful day alone in the carriage."

Her face fell so ludicrously that he felt perfectly repaid for her gloating.

"How could you possibly wish to travel in a stuffy carriage?"

"As I said, it will be peaceful and quiet. . . . Ah, here's the monk who will show you to your apartments." He handed her over to a smiling monk who introduced himself as Father Cornelius and declared himself responsible for the disposition of the monastery's honored guests.

"Your maid will be directed to your apartments as soon as she arrives, Princess." He gestured courteously toward the entrance to the building. "Her Highness the Dauphine has requested that you be lodged in the imperial apartments."

Cordelia hesitated. She turned back to Leo. "You will not ride with me tomorrow?"

"That was not part of the wager." He couldn't help enjoying this tiny moment of revenge.

But Cordelia was not long at a loss. "I'll ensure in future, my lord, that I phrase these matters correctly." She swept him a perfectly executed curtsy and glided away with Father Cornelius, leaving Leo wondering whether he'd won or lost that exchange.

Chapter Seven

"I AM so unhappy, Cordelia!" Toinette flung herself into her friend's arms when Cordelia entered the dauphine's boudoir ten minutes later. "How can I bear to go so far away?"

"Now, now, Toinette, this is most undignified," the emperor protested, at a loss as to how to deal with his little sister's tears. He was not an unaffectionate man, but he'd been schooled to control his own emotions at all costs and was both embarrassed and shocked by Toinette's unbridled grief.

"Hush, now." Cordelia stroked her back. "It won't be so bad when you get used to it. Think of how excited you were before at the thought of being queen of France. Think of lording it over the court at Versailles. Think of all the amusements . . . think of the freedom to do as you please."

Toinette hiccuped in her arms, but her violent sobs slowed. Finally, she straightened and sniffed vigorously. "I know you're right, but it's so *hard*. I'll never see Mama again. Or my brothers and sisters."

She dabbed at her nose with her handkerchief and said with a brave attempt at composure, "I will try to master myself. But I will dine in my apartments tonight . . . Cordelia shall bear me company."

"Good God, girl, you can't do that!" Joseph protested. "You are receiving the hospitality of Melk. It would be considered unforgivably discourteous to hide yourself away."

"But I am *ill*!" Toinette cried. "So fatigued. And I feel so unwell, brother."

"That is no excuse," he stated flatly.

"His majesty is right, Toinette." Cordelia took her friend's hand, chafing it. "The abbot would be slighted if you don't appear." Slipping her arm around Toinette's shoulders, she drew her toward the bedchamber next door. "Shall you wear the diamond collar tonight? The one the king sent you from France?" The two disappeared into the neighboring chamber, and soon Toinette's voice could be heard responding to Cordelia's cheerful chatter.

The emperor sighed with relief. Cordelia had always been able to calm Toinette in one of her emotional outbursts. "I will return to escort the dauphine to dinner," he declared to the ladies-in-waiting, and took himself off to the tranquility of his own apartments.

When Cordelia left Toinette an hour later, the dauphine was almost her usual cheerful self. Cordelia had made her laugh with a wicked mimicry of various members of the French entourage, and Cordelia was still grinning at her own performance as she made her way to her own chamber in the imperial suite.

Mathilde was waiting impatiently. "You have but a half hour before the viscount comes to escort you to dinner," she scolded. "He sent a messenger an hour ago, saying that you were to be ready by eight o'clock, and here it is already half past seven."

Cordelia's heart did an involuntary little skip at the thought that she would soon be in Leo's company again. "Her Highness needed me." She drew off her gloves, tossing them onto a chair. "Oh, I don't wish to wear that gown, Mathilde, it makes me look sallow." She gestured disdainfully to the gown of dull yellow taffeta lying ready on the bed.

"What nonsense. You've never looked sallow in your life," Mathilde declared. "The gown is well suited for dining in a monastery. It shows less of your bosom than some others."

"But I don't wish to show less of my bosom," Cordelia said, flinging open the door to the armoire. "It may be a monastery, Mathilde, but everyone will be wearing their finest raiment and I shall look a positive dowd in that."

Mathilde tutted. She was a very devout woman, and half-naked women gamboling around a monastery deeply offended her. But while her influence on Cordelia was both maternal and extensive, it didn't encompass choice of dress. Cordelia always had her own idea of what was right for her and for the occasion.

"Well, hurry up, then," Mathilde said, gathering up the despised dress. "I'll not be blamed by the viscount for your being late."

"Of course he wouldn't blame you." Cordelia selected a scarlet silk gown and pranced over to the cheval glass, holding it up against her. "He already knows that tardiness is my besetting sin." She tilted her head, examining her reflection. "I think I will wear this tonight."

"Scarlet in a monastery!" exclaimed Mathilde, scandalized, unhooking Cordelia's traveling dress.

"Oh, you are a prude." Cordelia swiveled to kiss her on both cheeks. "Besides, cardinals wear red, don't they? It's a very suitable color." She stepped out of the unhooked dress as it rustled to her feet. "Have I time to wash? I feel so dusty from the journey." She darted across to the washstand, dipped a washcloth in the ewer, and scrubbed her face vigorously, before sponging her bosom and raising her arms to wash beneath them.

"Maybe they do. But it's not decent to go about a monastery with your bosom uncovered." Mathilde, still grumbling, dampened a handkerchief with lavender water. "Such a harum-scarum creature you are. Sit down and let me do your hair." She pushed her down onto the dresser stool, giving her the lavender handkerchief.

Cordelia dabbed the lavender between her breasts, under her arms, behind her ears. "That's better. I swear I was reeking like a stable hand."

"Keep still, will you!" Mathilde pulled the brush through tangled ringlets before deftly twisting the gleaming mass into a chignon at the nape of Cordelia's neck. She loosened the side ringlets so that they framed her face, and fixed a pearl comb in the chignon. She examined her handiwork in the mirror, frowning. Then she nodded in silence and went to fetch the scarlet gown.

Her expression as she hooked Cordelia into the garment was so disapproving that Cordelia almost gave in. But she knew the scarlet suited her complexion as well as it suited her present mood. She was feeling dangerous, fizzing with anticipation, her blood flowing swift and hot in her veins. She told herself it was the sense of freedom, of release from the prison of rigidity that had been the Austrian court. It was the sense of her life opening up before her, of the golden glories of Versailles that awaited her.

The sharp rap at the door brought her swinging to face it as Mathilde hurried to open it, and she knew as her breath caught in anticipation that it was Leo Beaumont who did this to her. It was love—ungovernable, unbidden, incomprehensible, invincible.

Leo stood in the open doorway. He saw before him a radiant creature, all scarlet and black, with eyes as lustrous as sapphires, a warm red mouth slightly parted over even white teeth, the small, well-shaped head atop a long slender neck. The rich swell of her bosom rose invitingly above her décolletage. Her waist was so small he could span it with his hands. He had seen her so many times in the last days, but he felt now as if he were seeing her for the first time. She seemed surrounded by an aura of danger and temptation. The air around her was electric, charged with passion; he could almost hear it crackle. Anyone touched by that charge would surely burn, he thought with a chill of foreboding.

"I am ready on time, you see, my lord." Cordelia curtsied, seeking to mask the depth of her feelings in a light teasing tone. "Mathilde is very disapproving of my gown. She says scarlet is too bold a color to be worn in a house of God. But as I pointed out, cardinals wear red hats. Do you have an opinion on the subject, sir?" She rose slowly, with a coquettish tilt of her head.

"I doubt your gown will draw undue remark, since all

eyes will be turned upon the dauphine and the emperor," he said dampeningly. "If you're quite ready, let us go down." He stepped aside so that she could precede him into the corridor.

"How ungallant of you," Cordelia murmured as she glided past. "I could almost be hurt at such a snub."

"But of course you aren't," he commented dryly.

She looked sideways at him. "Not in the least, my lord, since the only eyes I'm interested in are yours. I couldn't care less if I'm invisible to everyone else."

Leo drew a sharp whistling breath through his teeth. "You will stop this nonsense, Cordelia. I warn you that I begin to lose patience."

"I won the wager," she said, giving him a serene smile, taking his arm. "Now, don't look daggers at me or people will wonder what's amiss between such a newly married couple."

He had no time to respond as he would have liked because they had reached the great hall of the monastery, where those guests of sufficient importance were already assembled to dine at the abbot's table.

Toinette was pale but composed as she sat between her brother and the abbot. Princess von Sachsen and her escort were seated immediately below the royal couple, and Leo was obliged to grit his teeth and dwell silently on ways to put an end to his charge's incorrigible flirtation. Throughout the interminable meal, Cordelia's sunny smile never wavered, her conversation was never less than entertaining, and it was clear to the exasperated Leo that she was dazzling everyone by the sheer force of her personality. Even the abbot succumbed and was patting her hand toward the end of the meal and laughing heartily at her sallies.

Cordelia was exerting herself for Toinette, who she knew would be unable to hold her own in the conversation. The dauphine's pallor and silence went unnoticed under her friend's scintillating chatter.

"Now we shall have music," the abbot announced

genially, as the second course was removed. "It aids the digestion, I find."

Cordelia craned her neck to look from the dais where the royal party dined down into the main body of the hall. She hadn't seen Christian when they'd first taken their seats, but now she found him sitting at one of the far tables. He looked up immediately as if he felt her gaze, and raised his glass in a salute. He looked a little lost, she thought. He'd been apprenticed to Poligny at the age of ten and had spent all the intervening years at Maria Theresa's court. Now, like herself and Toinette, he was venturing into an unknown future in a foreign land. But unlike the girls, he had no path mapped out for him.

She glanced sideways at Leo. If she didn't have a path mapped out for her, how much simpler this tangle of feelings would be to unravel.

A Gregorian chant rose from the rear of the hall, and the table fell into appreciative silence as the exquisite plainsong filled the vast space, rising to the high rafters. The music continued until the abbot invited his guests to attend chapel for benediction.

"I thought you didn't practice our religion," Cordelia observed, kneeling on the hard stone, her skirts billowing out around her. Her knees were accustomed to the discomfort, cushions being reserved at court only for the empress and the aged of the highest aristocracy.

"When in Rome," he responded calmly, kneeling at his pew.

"I love you," she whispered. She hadn't meant to say any such thing, but he was so close to her that she could smell the faint lingering perfume of dried lavender and rosemary that had been stored with his linen. The air around her was imbued with his presence, so powerful that for a moment she lost all sense of her surroundings.

Leo prayed for inspiration. How was he ever going to resist her? He was aware of the blue fire in her eyes as she gazed at him from behind a hand that shielded her face, hiding her unprayerful countenance from the rest of the congregation. He was aware of the curve of her white neck, the little ear peeking between glossy ringlets, the swift rise and fall of her breasts. He reminded himself that she was another man's wife, but that fact hardly seemed real in the present circumstances.

When the service was over, the weary travelers were free to seek their beds.

Toinette summoned Cordelia to accompany her. "I know you're tired, Cordelia, but will you sit with me until I'm in bed? I feel so miserable still."

It was a royal command couched as a friend's plea for comfort. Something else Cordelia had grown accustomed to over the years.

Leo made his way to his own apartment. His servant was waiting to undress him, but he sent him away to his bed after the man had poured him a generous cognac and removed his shoes and coat. A fire had been lit in the grate. The late April evenings were still cool, and the stone walls of the monastery retained a chill even in high summer.

Leo sat down beside the fire in his stockinged feet and shirtsleeves and drew a small table with an inlaid chessboard toward him. Frowning, he began to rearrange the pieces in a problem that had eluded him for a week. It would take his mind off his heated blood. He might not be able to untangle the confusion in his brain, but the pure, simple clarity of the chess pieces and the clean lines of a chess problem could be managed.

Cordelia sat with Toinette until the dauphine fell asleep, then, yawning deeply, she made her way to her own chamber. Mathilde was dozing by the fire and rose sleepily to her feet when Cordelia came in.

"Just unhook and unlace me, Mathilde, and I'll manage the rest myself," Cordelia said through another deep yawn. "You need your own bed." She rubbed her eyes, then began to unpin her hair while Mathilde unhooked her gown. "I'm going to ride on tomorrow's journey. Is my habit unpacked?"

"I'll see to it in the morning." Mathilde shook out the scarlet dress and hung it up in the armoire. "We'll be making an early start, I gather." She unlaced Cordelia's corset and untied the tapes of her panniers. Cordelia kicked off her shoes, rolled down her garters and stockings, and plumped onto the bed with a groan.

"Go to bed, Mathilde. I can manage now."

"Well, if you're sure." Mathilde didn't waste time in protest. "I'll wake you in plenty of time in the morning." She bent to kiss her nursling and bustled out to her own bed in the servants' quarters.

Cordelia fell back on the bed in her thin linen shift and gazed up at the embroidered tester overhead, almost too tired to get under the covers. The fire crackled merrily in the hearth, and her eyelids drooped. She came to with a jerk, her heart pounding. Sitting up, she looked around the candlelit chamber for what had startled her.

A mouse scurried across the floor, disappearing into a hole in the wainscot.

She got off the bed and went to the dresser to brush her hair, knowing that if she slept on it unbrushed it would be a hopeless tangle in the morning. The silence of the room was broken only by the hiss and spit of the fire and the gentle ticking of the clock on the mantel. Cordelia realized that she was restless, almost too tired to sleep. Her mind was racing, filled with questions and speculation about the life that awaited her. What kind of man was her husband? What of his children? Were they looking forward to her arrival? Or dreading it?

She couldn't stop the tumbling thoughts or control her growing apprehension. She told herself it was because it was late and she was tired. If she could sleep, she would be her usual cheerful self in the morning, ready and eager to face whatever the day might bring. But for some reason, all desire to sleep had left her.

She moved restlessly around the room. One wall was lined with bookshelves. At first glance they looked to contain no volumes that might soothe a troubled soul. All very academic titles, mostly Latin and Greek. Obviously, the monks expected their guests to be of a scholarly turn of mind. Her hand drifted along the spines and alighted on a volume of Catullus's poems. Lighter fare than Livy or Pliny.

Cordelia pulled the slender volume from the shelf. She leaned against the bookshelves, idly leafing through the pages. And the wall began to move at her back. As she leaned against it, it creaked and groaned and swung inward. It was the strangest sensation and it all happened so fast Cordelia had no time to react. The section of shelving turned inward, and Cordelia found herself on the other side in a strange chamber, staring backward at the hole in the wall.

Leo looked up from the chessboard at the creaking groan from the wall of bookshelves at his back. He turned and stared, his mouth dropping open. Cordelia, barefoot, in a thin linen shift, stood in his room, gazing up at the gaping shelves with astonishment.

"How ... how ... how did that happen?" She spun round, relatively unsurprised at seeing him. It would take a lot to beat the astonishment of the last minutes. "Oh, Leo. I didn't realize you were next door. Look!" She pointed back at the wall again. "It ... it just opened. I was leaning against it and abracadabra! I was only looking for something to read." She brandished the Catullus as if she needed proof of her statement.

Leo was recovering slowly from his own astonishment. His first reaction was that Cordelia had deliberately engineered this little trick, but her amazement was clearly genuine and he couldn't see how she could have known in advance about the mechanism. "Go back to your own chamber and I'll try to close it from this side."

"Oh, how tame!" She stepped farther into his room, fulfilling his every fear. "Why do you think it's here? Isn't it intriguing?" Her hair was cascading around her shoulders in a blue-black river, ringlets framing her face, her eyes gray now, glowing like charcoal braziers in the firelight. "What was it for, do you think?"

"Presumably, it suited someone to have secret access to the next door chamber," he answered, trying to sound cool and in control. "Now go back to bed."

"Do you think it was for assignations?" Her eyes gleamed wickedly, but he didn't think she was playing her usual flirtatious games; she seemed genuinely fascinated by the situation. "In a *monastery*. How shocking." She turned to look back at the hole in the bookshelves again. "But I suppose these are the guest apartments. But what was some monkish architect doing designing such a thing?" Laughter bubbled in her voice. "Maybe monks have their secrets too."

"I'm sure they do. Now, will you go back the way you came, please."

"I can't sleep. I'm all excited and apprehensive and wrought up," she said cheerfully. "And you're not sleepy if you're playing chess. Are you doing problems? I like doing them too. But since there are two of us awake, shall we have a game?" She bent over the chessboard and without further ado swept aside the pieces of his problem and began to set the board up for a game.

"Cordelia, I was doing that problem!" he protested. "How dare you sweep it away like that?"

"Oh, I do beg your pardon." She looked up at him through her hair. "I didn't mean to be discourteous, but I thought you agreed to play a game." Again, he was certain that she was behaving without artifice. This was the impetuous, high-spirited Cordelia who had thrown flowers at a stranger from an upstairs window.

"I did not agree to anything. You didn't give me a chance to voice an opinion," he snapped. "Put those pieces down and go to bed at once." He smacked the back of her hand as she placed the black king on its square.

"Ow." Cordelia looked injured, rubbing her hand. "There was no need to do that. And why should we both sit alone and sleepless, when we can do something pleasant that will take our minds off the things that are making it difficult to sleep?"

She sounded so rational, her expression radiating bewildered hurt, that Leo felt the now familiar bubble of inconvenient laughter forming in his chest. Laughter and the equally familiar surge of desire at the lines of her body beneath the thin shift. While he was struggling for composure, Cordelia took advantage of his momentary disadvantage. She hooked a stool with her toe and plunked herself down before the chessboard. Removing a black and a white pawn, she held them in clenched fists behind her back, juggling them, before stretching her hands out to him.

"Which hand do you chose, my lord?"

It seemed that short of bodily removing her, he was destined to play chess with her. Harmless enough, surely? Resigned, he tapped her closed right hand.

"You drew black!" she declared with a note of triumph that he recognized from the afternoon's dicing. "That means I have the first move." She turned the chess table so that the white pieces were in front of her and moved pawn to king four. Then she sat back, regarding him expectantly.

"Unusual move," he commented ironically, playing the countermove.

"I like to play safe openings," she confided, bringing out her queen's pawn. "Then when the board opens up, I can become unconventional."

"Good God! You mean there's one activity you actually choose to play by the book! You astound me, Cordelia!"

Cordelia merely grinned and brought out her queen's knight in response to his pawn challenge.

They played in silence and Leo was sufficiently absorbed in the game to be able to close his mind to her scantily clad presence across from him. She played a good game, but he had the edge, mainly because she took risks with a degree of abandon.

Cordelia frowned over the board, chewing her bottom lip. Her last gamble had been a mistake, and she could see serious danger in the next several moves if she couldn't place her queen out of harm's way. If only she could intercept with a pawn, but none of her pawns were in the proper position, unless . . .

"What was that noise?"

"What noise?" Leo looked up, startled at the sound of her voice breaking the long silence.

"Over there. In the corner. A sort of scrabbling." She gestured to the far corner of the room. Leo turned to look. When he looked back at the board, her pawn had been neatly diverted and now protected her queen.

Leo didn't notice immediately. "Probably a mouse," he said. "The woodwork's alive with them."

"I hope it's not a rat," she said with an exaggerated shiver, and conspicuously united her rooks. "Let's see if that will help."

It was Leo's turn to frown now. Something had changed on the board in front of him. It didn't look the way he remembered it, but he couldn't see . . . and then he did.

Slowly, he reached out and picked up the deviated pawn. He raised his eyes and looked across at her. Cordelia was flushing, so transparently guilty he wanted to laugh again.

"If you must cheat, why don't you do it properly," he said conversationally, returning the pawn to its original position. "You insult my intelligence to imagine that I wouldn't notice. Do you think I'm blind?"

Cordelia shook her head, her cheeks still pink. "It's not really possible to cheat at chess, but I do so hate to lose. I can't seem to help it."

"Well, I have news for you. You are going to learn to help it." He replaced her rooks in their previous position. "We are going to play this game to the bitter end and you are going to lose it. It's your move, and as I see it, you can't help but sacrifice your queen."

Cordelia stared furiously at the pieces. She couldn't bring herself to make the only move she had, the one that would mean surrendering her queen. Without it she would be helpless; besides, it was a symbolic piece. She would be acknowledging she'd lost once she gave it up. "Oh, very well," she said crossly. "I suppose you win. There's no need to play further."

Leo shook his head. He could read her thoughts as if they were written in black ink. Cordelia was the worst kind of loser. She couldn't bear to play to a loss. "There's every need. Now make your move."

Her hand moved to take the queen and then she withdrew it. "But there's no point."

"The point, my dear Cordelia, is that you are going to play this game to its conclusion. Right up to the moment when you topple your king and acknowledge defeat. Now *move*."

"Oh, very well." She shot out her hand, half rising on her stool, leaning over the board as if it took her whole body to move the small wooden carving. Her knees caught the edge of the table, toppling it, and the entire game disintegrated, pieces tumbling to the carpet. "Oh, what a nuisance!" Hastily, she steadied the rocking table.

"Why, of all the graceless, brattish, mean-spirited things to do!" Leo, furious, leaped up. Leaning over the destroyed board, he grabbed her shoulders, half shaking, half hauling her toward him.

"But I didn't do it on purpose!" Cordelia exclaimed. "Indeed I didn't. It was an accident."

"You expect me to believe that?" He jerked her hard toward him, almost lifting her over the board, unsure what he intended doing with her, but for the moment lost in disappointed anger that she could do something so malicious and childish. Cordelia's protestations of innocence grew ever more vociferous.

Then matters became very confused. He was shaking her, she was yelling, his mouth was on hers. Her yells ceased. His hands were hard on her arms, and her body was pressed against his. Her mouth, already open on her indignant cries, welcomed the plunging thrust of his tongue. Her hands moved down his body. With an instinctive certainty of what was right, she gripped his buttocks through the dark silk of his britches. The hard bulge of his erect flesh jutted against her loins, and she moved her body urgently against his as her tongue drove into his mouth on her own voyage of exploration, demanding, tasting, wanting. She was aware of nothing but the wanting—an overpowering tidal wave of desire that throbbed in her loins, raced through her blood, pounded in her pulses. Everything she had felt before was but a faint shadow of this wild, abandoned hunger.

Leo fought for clarity, but he could feel every line of her body under his hands. Her skin burned beneath her shift, heating his palms as he ran them over her, learning the shape of her, her curves and her indentations. He gripped the loose material at the back of the garment and pulled it tight so that her body was molded by the linen. He looked down at the pink glow of her breasts beneath the white, the hard crowns jutting against the material, the dark shadow at the apex of her thighs. And all hope of clarity was lost to him.

Her lips were parted, her breath swift as he examined her shape. She put her hands on her hips and lifted her head with a challenging triumph, her eyes scorching with their passion and hunger. With a rasping breath, he dragged the shift over her head and put his hands on her body. His caresses were rough and urgent, and she met each hard stroke with a swift indrawn breath of arousal, thrusting her body at him, wanting him to touch every inch of her, to brand her skin with his mark.

She fell back across the chess table under the pressure of his body. The sharp edges of the fallen pieces pressed into her bare back but she didn't notice, caught up in the red mist of this wild desire. Her hips lifted for the hands, now caressing her inner thighs, opening her petaled center, finding the exquisitely sensitive core of her passion. The waves built in her belly, built to an unbearable crescendo when she thought she would die. And then she did, toppling slowly from a scarlet height of ecstasy into a soft blackness that leached every ounce of strength from her body, and she could hear her own sobbing cries of abandoned delight.

Leo held her against him as the shuddering joy convulsed her, his hands under her back as she sprawled across the chess table. He held her until her eyes opened and she smiled, her face transfigured with a wondrous radiance.

"What did you do to me?"

"Sweet Jesus!" He slid his flat palms out from under her and straightened. His golden eyes were almost black as he stared down at her, spreadeagled in such wanton abandon across the table.

"For God's sake, get up!" His voice was harsh. He pulled her upright onto her feet. "Put your shift on." He pushed her toward the white crumpled garment on the floor. The deep imprints of the chess pieces were on her back as she bent to pick up the shift. "I don't believe myself," he muttered, aware of his own arousal now as a painful need.

Cordelia turned back to him, clutching the shift to her bosom. "I still don't understand what happened." Her eyes were bewildered beneath the still-misty radiance of fulfillment. "We didn't—"

"No, we didn't," he interrupted harshly. "But what I did was bad enough. For pity's sake, go to bed, Cordelia, and leave me alone."

For once her impulsive protest died on her lips. She turned back to the gaping bookshelves, still clutching her shift. He tried not to gaze at the long sweep of her back, the perfectly rounded bottom, the slender length of her thighs. He tried, but failed.

At the bookshelf she said over her shoulder. "I really

didn't intend to knock over the board. It was truly an accident."

"It doesn't matter," he said wearily.

"But it does. I don't want you to think that I'd do something that despicable." She had one hand on the shelf, her earnest gaze seeking his.

Leo gave a harsh crack of laughter. "My dear girl, in the list of the evening's despicable events, that one is hardly worth considering."

"That wasn't despicable," she said, her voice very low. "Nothing so wonderful could be wrong."

Leo closed his eyes. "You don't know what you're saying," he said. "Now, go to bed."

Cordelia slipped through the gap into her own chamber and pushed the shelf back in place. She needed Mathilde's wisdom, but it would have to wait until the morning. She fell into bed, as limp as a kitten, and was asleep in seconds.

Chapter Eight

DAWN STREAKED THE sky when Mathilde entered Cordelia's bedchamber accompanied by a maid carrying a ewer of steaming hot water. The girl set this on the dresser before turning to rekindle the fire against the early morning chill.

Cordelia slept on behind the bedcurtains as Mathilde laid out her riding habit and repacked the trunk with the clothes she'd worn the previous day.

"Bring the princess a pot of coffee, girl. She'll need something to warm her; there's a nip in the air."

The maid curtsied and left the chamber, where the fire now burned brightly. Mathilde drew back the bedcurtains.

"Wake up now, child. The bell for prime rang some ten minutes ago and breakfast is to be at seven in the great hall."

Cordelia rolled onto her back and opened her eyes. For a moment she wondered where she was. Then the wave of memory broke over her. She sat up, rubbed her eyes, and looked ruefully at Mathilde.

"I'm in love."

"Holy Mary, not with that young musician, I trust!" Mathilde exclaimed. "He's a nice enough lad, but not for the likes of you, m'dear."

"No, not Christian." Cordelia sat cross-legged on the bed. "The viscount."

"Holy Mother!" Mathilde crossed herself. "And since when has this happened?"

"Oh, since first I saw him. I believe he feels something for me too, but he won't say so."

"I should hope not. What honorable man would declare his feelings for another man's wife?" Mathilde pushed a loose gray lock back beneath her starched cap.

"Mathilde, I don't *wish* to be married to my husband," Cordelia said with low-voiced intensity.

"Well, there's nothing to be done about it, girl. It was the same with your mother. It's the same with most women of your class. They marry where advantage leads them, not their hearts."

"Men's advantage," said Cordelia bitterly, and Mathilde didn't contradict her. "My mother didn't love my father?"

Mathilde shook her head. "No, your mother loved outside her marriage, and she loved with all her heart. But she did nothing to be ashamed of." Mathilde raised a warning forefinger. "She was honest to her deathbed."

"But unhappy?"

Mathilde pursed her lips then she sighed and nodded. "Yes, child. Desperately so. But she knew where her duty lay, and so will you."

Cordelia began to massage her feet, frowning fiercely. "My mother stayed at the Austrian court. There's no freedom there. Perhaps if she'd been at Versailles—"

"No, don't you be thinking any such thing," interrupted Mathilde. "You'll be in trouble worse than a snake pit, thinking like that."

"I think I already am," Cordelia said slowly, pushing her thumbs hard into the sole of her foot, keeping her eyes on her task.

Mathilde sat down heavily on the end of the bed, her face grim. "What are you saying, child? Has the viscount had knowledge of you?"

"Yes and no." Cordelia looked up, flushing, biting her bottom lip. "What you told me happened on the marriage bed didn't happen, but he touched me in ... in very intimate ways and ... and something wonderful happened to me. But I don't understand quite what."

"Mercy me!" Mathilde threw up her hands. "Tell me what happened."

Cordelia did so, somewhat haltingly, her face burning even though Mathilde had cared for her since infancy and

knew all her most intimate secrets. "But if what we did was
not intercourse, Mathilde, what was it?" she finished.

Mathilde sighed. This situation was more troublesome
than if her nursling had lost her virginity in an explosion of
passion. Initiation was rarely pleasurable however passionate, and was unlikely to encourage repetition. But true
pleasuring once experienced was a different matter.

"There are some men who are willing and know how to
pleasure a woman, child. But for the most part, they're not
interested in more than their own satisfaction. You'd best
put what happened behind you and forget about it. Be
grateful for a gentle husband and as many babes as you can
conceive. It's the best a woman can hope for."

Cordelia dropped her foot, saying blunting, "I don't
believe that, Mathilde. And I don't think you believe it
either."

Mathilde bent over her to take her face between her
hands. "Listen to me, dearie, and listen well. You must take
what's given you in this world. I'll not watch you fade away
from wishing, as your mother did. You're strong, I've made
you so. You must look for what you *can* have, and forget
what you can't."

"My mother didn't care for my father?"

"She didn't see what there was to care for in him because
she was too busy pining for what she couldn't have."
Mathilde released her face and straightened, her expression
suddenly hard and determined. "I've not raised you to
hanker for the impossible. I've taught you to take what you
have and make the most of it. Now, get up and get dressed.
We don't have all morning."

Cordelia swung her legs off the bed and stood up, just as
the maid reappeared with the coffee. "Oh, lovely. Thank
you. I can't tell you how I long for coffee. Thank you for
taking the trouble." She smiled at the maid with such
warmth that the girl beamed and curtsied before filling a
cup and handing it to the naked princess.

"No trouble at all, Your Highness." Still beaming, she backed out of the chamber.

"I really wouldn't have thought it of the viscount," Mathilde muttered. "If I didn't know how you always get your way, I'd not understand it at all. He seems such an honorable man."

"But he *is* an honorable man." Cordelia came quickly to Leo's defense. She took a deep revivifying gulp of coffee. "And I really didn't try to make it happen, it just did. And he made it stop, even though it must have been difficult for him."

"Aye, that it must," Mathilde said grimly. The thought gave her some satisfaction as she laced her charge a little more tightly than usual.

Cordelia endured without a murmur of protest. When Mathilde was this upset, it was best to let her get it out of her system. Involuntarily, she glanced at the bookshelves. Could she make them open again? She didn't know exactly how it had happened last night. Was there a knob she'd accidentally pushed, or a switch? Or did one just lean against the books at a certain spot? Not that she'd ever find out. They'd be long gone from this place in an hour.

"There, you'll do." Mathilde twitched Cordelia's starched stock into place at her neck. "Hurry away now." She waved her hands at her, shooing her from the room. Cordelia couldn't decide whether her nurse was vexed as well as concerned.

Deeply thoughtful, she stepped into the corridor just as Leo, in riding dress, emerged from the next-door chamber. "Good morning." She felt strangely shy. She curtsied, her eyes lowered.

"Good morning." His expression was somber, his eyes lightless, his mouth taut. He gestured curtly that she should precede him down the staircase to the hall.

Cordelia, most unusually, was tongue-tied. Throughout the ceremonial breakfast, her eyes kept drifting to his hands and she would remember where they had been on her body and a surge of glorious memory would flood her with warmth. It was a relief to concentrate on the ceremonies as the dauphine took farewell of her brother Joseph, who would now return to Vienna, leaving his little sister to journey without family to Strasbourg, where she would be formally received into France.

Toinette was less emotional at taking leave of her brother than she had been of her mother, but it was still a solemn moment when the emperor escorted his sister to her carriage for the last time.

"I see you intend to ride today, my lord." Cordelia gestured toward Leo's riding dress, speaking to him for the first time since she'd greeted him on the stairs. It was supposed to be a neutral comment, but her voice sounded strangely intense to her ears in the monastery's busy, noisy courtyard.

"Yes," he said shortly. "We will ride behind the cavalry and to the side of the coaches." He surveyed the scene, frowning, looking for his groom with their horses.

"What made you change your mind?" Cordelia ventured. "You said yesterday that you would travel in the peace and quiet of the carriage if I was riding."

His brow darkened. "You're in my charge, Princess. Much as I might lament it, I'm responsible for you. If you're going to make anyone's life a misery, it had better be mine rather than some poor groom's."

He ordered his groom to help Cordelia to mount.

Cordelia cast Leo a covert sidelong look. His face was drawn, dark shadows beneath his eyes. He looked as if he hadn't slept a wink—a man haunted by conscience. She thought remorsefully of her own deep and dreamless sleep untroubled by guilt.

Leo mounted his own horse, waiting until Cordelia was settled in the saddle, the girths tightened, stirrups adjusted. Her Lippizaner mare was a beautiful animal, and he assumed that like the Hapsburgs with whom she'd grown up, she was an accomplished horsewoman, so he wouldn't need to worry about her safety on such a prime beast. But he also guessed from what he knew of her that Cordelia would chafe at the necessity of keeping her place in the procession.

"We will keep to a walk," he stated. "We cannot overtake the dauphine's carriage without offending protocol, so I'm afraid it will be dull riding."

"But we could leave the procession," Cordelia suggested. "Branch off across the fields and rejoin it later."

"That kind of suggestion is why I wouldn't entrust you to a groom," he said grimly.

Cordelia closed her lips tightly, gathered up the reins, and fell in beside him. The procession wound its way along the banks of the Danube as the sun grew stronger, burning off the early morning mists. Leo said not a word, and finally Cordelia could bear it no longer.

"Please talk to me, Leo. I feel as if I'm in disgrace, but I can't see why I should be."

He said gravely, "You don't seem to understand, Cordelia. What happened last night was unforgivable. I lost control."

"You feel you have betrayed your friend and my husband," she ventured.

Leo didn't answer. It wasn't as simple as that. He also felt he had betrayed Cordelia. She was in his trust and he'd betrayed that trust.

"I don't know anything about this man, my husband," Cordelia said into the silence. "It doesn't feel like a betrayal when I don't even know him, but I *do* know that I *love* you."

She looped the reins and then let them run through her fingers. The mare raised her head and high-stepped delicately. "I've been thinking," she said hesitantly while Leo was still trying to gather his forces in the face of her calm declaration. "While I accept that I'm married to Prince Michael, I don't see why I can't still be your mistress.

"It's perfectly acceptable in French society, I'm told," she rushed on as he exhaled sharply and seemed ready to break in. "If two people are in love but are forced to marry their family's choice, it's understood that society will turn a blind eye if they pursue a liaison discreetly. Even the king says so."

"And just who told you that?" he inquired, finding his voice at last.

"A cousin of Toinette's. He said that husbands say to their wives, "I allow you to do as you please, but I draw the line at princes of the blood and footmen." She glanced interrogatively at him. "Is that true?"

"What's true for some is not necessarily true for all," he pointed out dryly.

"But it *is* the court attitude, though. I mean, the king has had mistresses who were closer to him and more influential than the queen. Madame de Pompadour was the most important woman at the court for over twenty years. And isn't that true of Madame du Barry now? And I know all about the Parc aux Cerfs, where the king keeps his prostitutes," she added with the air of one delivering the coup de grace. "It's all true, isn't it?"

"Yes," he agreed, unable to refute any of what she'd said. Cordelia was rather better informed than he'd expected of one reared in the strict moral atmosphere of the Austrian court.

"Then there shouldn't be any difficulty. I could be your mistress and my husband's wife." She gazed at him from her great blue eyes, a picture of earnest sincerity.

"My dear girl, you seem to expect Versailles to be some magical place where the usual rules don't apply, and all you need do is wave your wand to make whatever you wish come true." He sounded as impatient as he felt. "Even supposing such a fairy story were the case, and I do assure you it isn't, does it occur to you that I may not wish for a mistress?"

"Oh." It hadn't occurred to Cordelia. "Do you already have one?"

"That is beside the point," he said frigidly, wondering with a degree of desperation why he couldn't seize hold of this ridiculous conversation and break it off.

"I don't think it is at all. If you do have one already, it would be difficult, because one wouldn't want to hurt anyone's feelings unduly."

"Cordelia, I have not the slightest interest in taking you as my mistress. Neither interest nor inclination," he stated baldly, staring fixedly at the clouds of dust created by the cavalry on the road ahead.

"Oh," she said again. She swallowed uncomfortably. "Don't you care for me, then?"

He refused to look at her. "I care more for other things," he said resolutely. "I took advantage of your innocence last night, Cordelia, for which I beg your pardon. I can only assume I dipped too deep in the cognac. It will never happen again."

"But I would like it to happen again," she said simply. "I don't mean to sound bold or . . . or wanton, although I suppose I am being. But Mathilde said that very few men know how to give pleasure as well as take it, and it seems that when one finds such a rarity then one should work to hold on to it."

"Who the hell is Mathilde?" It was all he could find to say in response to that curiously artless yet appallingly knowing speech.

"My nurse . . . or at least she was my wet nurse and she's looked after me since my mother died. She was my mother's maid and I think they were about the same age. Mathilde knows everything about anything and she's amazingly wise."

"You confided in her?" Leo pushed a finger inside his stock, loosening the starched linen. He seemed very hot suddenly.

"I needed to understand what happened. I wasn't sure you would tell me if I asked you."

"I will tell you precisely what happened." He spoke with a cold finality. "I allowed a situation to develop in which I lost control. Fortunately, I came to my senses in time to prevent the worst happening. You will now forget everything about last night. You will stop talking nonsense about love and liaisons. You will treat me from now on with a scrupulous distance as I will treat you. Do you hear me, Cordelia?"

She nodded. "I hear you."

"Then don't forget it." He nudged his horse's flanks and the animal broke into a trot, drawing ahead of Cordelia.

She knew not to catch up with him as he rode a few lengths ahead of her. A few days ago, she would have allowed her impulse free rein and cantered up beside him, but she was learning things these days that had no place in the schoolrooms of her past life. She would not be downcast, Cordelia told herself fiercely. She would cultivate patience, a vastly underrated virtue, she was sure.

The day's journey was as tedious as the previous day's despite the freedom of horseback. In fact, Cordelia decided it was more tedious, since she was obliged to ride in silence, her eyes fixed upon Viscount Kierston's straight back ahead of her. She'd hoped he would be a little more friendly when they stopped for refreshment, but Toinette demanded her friend's company at the al fresco luncheon on the banks of the river. Leo, having seen her safely ensconced at the dauphine's side beneath the trees, surrounded by the fawning burghers of the local township, went off on his own, and Cordelia looked for him in vain.

Leo strolled down the procession of carriages, horses, pack mules, and wagons. He was distracted, his mind in a ferment, and at first he didn't hear the woman's voice behind him. On the second "My lord, a word with you, I pray," he glanced over his shoulder.

A tall angular woman with sparse gray hair tucked up beneath a starched cap dropped a curtsy, but there was nothing subservient about her manner. She met his eye with a quiet dignity and an indefinable challenge.

"Mathilde, sir," she said when he looked puzzled.

"Oh, yes, of course." He ran a hand over his chin. Cordelia's nurse—the woman who knew what had happened the previous evening. He could detect no judgment in her frank gaze, however. He was not accustomed to concerning himself about the opinions of servants, but he thought with a flash of puzzling discomfort that he wouldn't wish to be on the wrong side of Mistress Mathilde.

"I wished to discuss Cordelia with you," she said.

There seemed no point pretending to misunderstand her. He gestured that she should accompany him along the bank to where it was quieter. "I understand Princess von Sachsen confided in you the unfortunate events of last night," he began stiffly.

"I know most things that go on with my babe, my lord."

"So I understand."

"You should know, my lord, that the girl's like her mother. When she loves, she loves hard. And when she loves, she loves for all time."

"I don't know what you're saying, woman!" Leo exclaimed softly. "She's married to Prince Michael."

"Aye, married to him, but she loves you, sir."

"Are you as mad as Cordelia?" Leo swished at a bramble bush with his riding switch. "Whatever she feels, the facts cannot be altered to suit her own desires."

Mathilde nodded wisely. "I told her that, my lord. But she's not always inclined to take notice of what doesn't suit her."

"And I suppose my feelings in the matter are also an irrelevancy," he declared, with a sharply indrawn breath.

"You'd not foster this foolishness, then?"

"No, of course I wouldn't. *I'm* not a headstrong, spoiled brat."

"Then you'd best manage yourself around her, my lord. Because I doubt the lady will keep away from you," she said bluntly.

Leo found that he didn't resent the woman's advice or her blunt manner. She spoke but the simple truth. He had much more experience, much more sophistication, a much stronger will than sixteen-year-old Cordelia. It was for him to manage them both. Fleetingly, it occurred to him that in her absence the goal seemed much easier to accomplish than in her presence. "I would not harm her, Mathilde."

She looked at him for a long moment, then said, "No . . . no, I believe you wouldn't, sir. But that's to the good, because anyone who does harm to my babe does harm to me." The seemingly benign peasant woman had somehow disappeared, in her place a strangely menacing presence with the blackest eyes that were full of an ancient knowledge and a great threat.

Witchcraft sprang to Leo's mind. This was no ordinary nurse defending her nursling. This was a woman who knew things that a man was better off not knowing. "Well, it's to be hoped you can prevent her from doing harm to herself," he said roughly, controlling the urge to leave her in unseemly haste. Then he nodded, turned, and strolled back to the picnic.

The dauphine returned to her carriage, lamenting bitterly to Cordelia that her position made it necessary for her to journey in the state carriage while Cordelia had the freedom of her horse.

"It's not much of a freedom, Toinette. We can't overtake your carriage, so we have to crawl along behind you." Cordelia leaned into the window of the carriage. "Poor Lucette doesn't understand why she has to be so docile."

"I'd still rather be you," the dauphine said with a disgruntled frown.

Cordelia laughed bracingly. "No, you wouldn't. You're going to be queen of France, remember?" She stepped back as the royal coachman cracked his whip and the afternoon's progress began.

"Come, Cordelia. We mustn't keep people waiting." Leo spoke behind her. He was holding Lucette; his groom had the reins of the viscount's own mount. "Let me put you in the saddle." He cupped his palm for her foot and tossed her up. The smile she gave him was so radiant, it took his breath away.

"Shall we ride companionably this afternoon?" she asked,

confiding artlessly, "I was so lonely this morning." She turned her horse beside him as they fell in behind the cavalry. "I do wish we didn't have to swallow their dust."

"We can ride to the side." He suited actions to words, Cordelia following him. The talk with Mathilde had cleared Leo's mind. Last night had been an aberration that by some miracle had been stopped in time. It was ridiculous to imagine that he couldn't control his own desires. He had always been a man of honor and resolution, and that had not changed. Cordelia was in his charge. She was a sweet if spoiled and willful child, and he was a grown man, twelve years her senior. He would cultivate an avuncular amiability in their dealings. There was no reason to force Cordelia to ride alone. She was such a gregarious creature it was as unkind as it was unfair to punish her for his own lack of control.

"Shall we have another wager on the time of our arrival this evening?" She glanced sideways at him with transparent pleasure in having company again.

"What stakes this time?" He sounded amused, indulgent, as one might humor an enthusiastic child.

Cordelia frowned. That tone was almost worse than vexation. She shrugged carelessly. "Oh, I don't know. It was just a way of passing time, but I don't think it's really that amusing."

Amiable avuncularity did not find favor, clearly. Leo let it drop, inquiring with neutral interest, "What kind of studies did you do in Schonbrunn?"

To his astonishment, he realized that he'd opened a floodgate. Cordelia began to talk eagerly and fluently about philosophy, mathematical principles, German and French literature. She was educated far beyond the norm for her sex, and he found himself wondering what Michael would make of this aspect of his bride. Elvira had told him once that Michael despised bluestockings and she'd learned to pursue her own intellectual interests out of his ken. Leo hadn't thought much about it then. Many men were suspicious of educated and eloquent women. He had assumed that Elvira had access to her husband's library, social entrance to the various salons that abounded in Paris, and didn't go short of intellectual stimulation. But Elvira had been older and both more sophisticated and devious than Cordelia. Would Cordelia learn quickly enough what it was wisest to keep from her husband?

When they stopped to cross a tributary of the Danube at Steyr, Leo left Cordelia in the charge of his groom and went to confer with the French delegation. Cordelia was fascinated by the operation involved in getting such a massive procession across the single-track wooden bridge. She trotted along the riverbank, the groom in attendance, watching as the great coaches lumbered and swayed perilously close the the edge of the creaking bridge.

"Cordelia?"

"Christian!" She turned with a cry of delight. Christian was astride a gangling chestnut gelding with an ungainly gait and looked far from at home. But he was not a natural equestrian. "How I was hoping you would come and find me. I'm not permitted to go off on my own down the procession. Protocol." She wrinkled her nose in laughing disgust. "Are you enjoying yourself? Are you comfortable? Is there anything I can do for you?"

"No, nothing." Christian looked up at the red ball of the sun sinking below the river to the west. "A messenger came hotfoot from Vienna this morning. He brought me a letter from Hugh. You remember Hugh, he played the violin in Poligny's concerts."

"Yes, yes." Cordelia nodded eagerly. "What did he say?"

"The cat is really among the pigeons," Christian said with a chuckle of satisfaction. "Everyone's read the broadsheet. Poligny is defending himself from the rooftops, but Hugh said people are talking and pointing the finger. The empress hasn't said anything as yet, but palace rumor has it that she's thinking of sending him away."

"Oh, how wonderful!" Cordelia clapped her hands. "The

story will reach Paris long before we do. You'll be a celebrity already."

Christian looked thoughtful. He plaited his mount's coarse mane with restless fingers. "I was thinking that perhaps I should go back to Vienna. If Poligny is really out, then there'll be . . ." He stopped, habitual modesty preventing him from continuing.

"There'll be a vacancy for court musician, and who better to fill it than Poligny's star pupil," Cordelia finished for him. She leaned over to take his hand. "Oh, love, I want whatever's best for you. But I shall miss you dreadfully. Particularly now that everything's become so confused."

"Confused?"

"It's this awkward business of being in love with the viscount," she said with an almost despairing sigh. "And after last night, I know he feels more than he'll admit to—"

"What about last night?" Christian interrupted.

Cordelia felt herself blushing. "Well, something happened. I . . . I accidentally blundered into his chamber and, well—"

"He didn't *ravish* you?" Christian's brown eyes were suddenly ablaze.

"Oh, no," she reassured hastily. "Nothing quite like that. But . . . things got rather out of hand." She looked at him helplessly, a rueful smile on her lips.

Christian leaned close to her, his eyes piercing in his pale angular face. "Did the viscount take your virginity, Cordelia? If he did, I'll kill him."

"Oh, no. You can't do that," Cordelia exclaimed. "And no, he didn't," she added, seeing that Christian was almost ready to fling himself from his horse. "I'm just so confused now."

Leo's voice reached them as he cantered toward them along the bank. "I give you a good evening, Christian. Cordelia, you need to cross the bridge now." He drew up next to the musician, nodded pleasantly, and added, "I trust you find your accommodations satisfactory, Christian."

Christian stared at the viscount, the fire still in his eyes. A tide of color spread over his pale features, then as swiftly faded. "Yes, thank you," he said stiffly.

"Christian was telling me of the reaction in Vienna to our broadsheet," Cordelia said excitedly. "It's everything he hoped it would be. In fact, he's wondering whether he should return to Vienna and try for Poligny's position."

"I'm not wondering that any longer," Christian announced as stiffly as before. "I'll be staying with you." He stared hard and meaningfully at the totally bewildered viscount before digging his heels into his mount's flank and cantering away, his usually graceful body jouncing around in the saddle like a sack of flour.

"Now, what's eating him?" Leo inquired, taking Cordelia's rein and urging her horse around toward the bridge.

Cordelia, who knew perfectly well, muttered something inaudible, jerking her reins free of his grasp. She had the conviction that Leo would not care for anyone knowing about last night. And he would not understand her need to confide—even in someone as close to her as Christian.

Chapter Nine

PRINCE MICHAEL WAS not completely satisfied with the suite of rooms allocated to him and his bride at the Chateau de Compiègne. However, since the apartments set aside for the dauphine would not be completed before her arrival the following day because the workmen hadn't been paid, he decided it would be tactless to complain if the furnishings in his own suite were a trifle shabby.

The prince had traveled with the king and the dauphin to meet Marie Antoinette at Compiègne. The dauphine was still a day's journey away, but Louis had decided to honor his new granddaughter by coming out to greet her. He was in great good humor and had been delighted when it occurred to him that Prince Michael might wish to ride out to meet his own bride. The prince had accepted with appropriate gratitude what amounted to a royal command couched as invitation, although he would have preferred to welcome the princess on his own ground. Rushing to meet her seemed to indicate a somewhat unseemly eagerness. The girl was only sixteen, after all, and must not be encouraged to expect too much attention from her husband.

However, he was here at Compiègne and, the following afternoon, would ride with the king and court some fourteen kilometers to the edge of the forest where he would meet his second wife.

He took out the miniature from his pocket, examining it with a frown. She did look very young, but now Michael saw a boldness to her eyes that he instinctively disliked. She held her head with an almost challenging stance, gazing out of the mother-of-pearl frame with an uncompromising air.

Michael's frown deepened. He snapped his fingers

irritably at his servant who was unpacking the prince's portmanteau. The man hastened to put a glass of wine into his master's outstretched hand.

Michael sipped, not taking his eyes off the miniature. When he'd first looked at it, he'd seen no resemblance to Elvira. But he'd been looking at the coloring, the shape of the face. Now he wasn't so sure. There was something uneasily familiar about the girl's expression. She was much younger than Elvira had been at her wedding; she came from the strict formality of the devout Austrian court. How could there be any resemblance to the flamboyant, sophisticated, flirtatious Englishwoman who had destroyed his peace?

His fingers tightened around the stem of his glass. It would not happen again. He would take this unformed, untutored, inexperienced little innocent and mold her to his own requirements. If she showed any signs of exhibiting Elvira's character traits, he would erase them without compunction. And they would be easier to deal with in this young girl than they had been in Elvira. He would have a submissive, faithful, duty-bound bride, who knew her obligations and learned swiftly how to please her husband.

"Sir . . . sir, your hand!" The voice of his servant broke into his rapt concentration.

Michael looked down at his hand. Somehow he had snapped the glass stem between his fingers, and a shard of glass pierced his skin. "God's blood!" he swore, tossing the glass into the empty grate. "Fetch me a bandage, man! Don't stand there like a booby."

"Tomorrow we will reach Compiègne, where the king and the dauphin will be waiting to greet Marie Antoinette." Leo's expression was a study in neutrality. The procession had reached Soissons, thirty-eight kilometers from Compiègne, and he stood with Cordelia outside her bedchamber in the riverside inn that accommodated the royal party for the night.

"I know." Absently, Cordelia twirled a ringlet around her finger before sucking it into her mouth. They were within a day's ride of journey's end, and her customary ebullience was fast ebbing.

Throughout the journey Leo had been pleasant and friendly, but his manner had been more avuncular than anything else, and he had somehow ensured that they were never alone together, except when they were riding. Any attempts to move the conversation onto the subject of their future relationship had met with stony silence and his rapid departure. Since his company was all-important to her well-being, Cordelia had quickly learned to behave as he dictated. She amused him with her light and frequently insightful chatter, discussed weighty subjects with due gravity, and tried very hard to control the need to declare her love at every second sentence. And while the prospect of meeting her husband remained in the future, she had managed very well. But now time was slipping away. Once she was given into her husband's charge and Leo relinquished his responsibility for her, she saw only a frighteningly unknown landscape.

"Has it occurred to you that your husband might also be there waiting for you?"

"Yes." She chewed the end of the ringlet. It had occurred to her more than once in the last hours. "But I rather assumed he'd be waiting in Paris."

"He might be. But I have a feeling he will be at Compiègne."

"I won't have to go to his bed until the formal wedding is solemnized," she said almost to herself, through her mouthful of hair.

But Leo heard her, and the mumbled words reminded him how much she belonged to another man. "That is a thoroughly disagreeable habit." Roughly, he flicked the sodden ringlet from her mouth.

"I only do it when I'm thinking disagreeable thoughts."

"I don't suppose it occurs to you not to speak such thoughts in public," he snapped.

Cordelia took a deep breath. This was her last chance. "Leo, I know you don't want me for a mistress . . . no . . . no, please listen to me," she begged, seeing him prepared to silence her. "Please let me speak, just this once."

"Not if you're going to say what I think you're going to say," he responded curtly. "I have told you I don't know how many times, that I will not listen to your nonsense—"

"No, this isn't nonsense," she interrupted eagerly. "I'm not properly married to the prince, only by proxy. It hasn't been consummated or anything, so it could be annulled, couldn't it?"

"*What?*" He stared at her in disbelief. This was a new angle, even for Cordelia.

"I could explain that I don't want to marry him. That it was all a big mistake. I could tell him that he wouldn't want to be married to someone who couldn't bear to have him for—"

"Have you completely lost your wits, girl? You are as firmly married to Michael as if you'd been married in St. Peter's by the pope himself. The settlements are drawn up, your dowry is in place. . . . Dear God, you have your head full of fairy stories." He ran a hand through his dark hair that tonight he wore uncovered and unpowdered.

"I don't believe it can't be done," she persisted stubbornly. "I don't believe I can't have you for husband instead."

"Now, just you listen to me." He took her shoulders, speaking through compressed lips. "Get this into your head. I would not marry you if you were the only woman on earth." He shook her to emphasize the savage statement and had the dubious satisfaction of seeing her eyes cloud with hurt, all eagerness, conviction, and determination blotted out. "You seem to think that all you have to do is wish for something and it will come true. But you forget, Cordelia, that there are other people involved in these fantasies of yours. People who have their own opinions and wishes. I do not wish to be part of your fanciful caprices. Do you understand? Is that plain enough for you?" He shook her again.

Cordelia was stunned by the power of his words, the savagery of his rejection. "I . . . I thought you liked me," she said, her voice catching, her eyes filling with tears.

Leo swore, a short sharp execration. "Whether I like you or not has nothing to do with it. I am sick to death of being woven into your whimsical notions of how to rearrange your destiny."

"Won't you even stand my friend?" she asked painfully. "May I not talk to you as I talk to Christian?"

"You tell Christian such things?"

"I tell Christian everything. We've always shared all our confidences."

Leo closed his eyes briefly. "And I suppose you told your friend about Melk?" He didn't need her confirmation. The young musician had been glaring at him as if he were Attila the Hun ever since they'd crossed the Steyr.

Cordelia didn't respond, but continued to gaze at him, her eyes darkest gray with pain.

"Dear God!" he muttered almost despairingly. He couldn't bear her to look at him in that way.

"Won't you stand my friend?" she repeated with sudden urgency, laying her hand on his arm. "I have need of friends, Leo."

She would need friends, both in her marriage and as she negotiated a path through the obstacles of life at Versailles. It was not something he could deny her even if he wished.

"I will stand your friend," he stated without inflection. Then he turned aside to open the door of her chamber. "Good night, Cordelia."

"Good night, my lord." She slipped past him, averting her face.

Mathilde's appraising gaze was shrewd. Her nursling was

very pale, her eyes shadowed. "We'll be meeting the prince soon, I daresay," she observed casually as she unhooked and unlaced.

"Probably tomorrow." Cordelia pulled pins from her hair. Her voice was tight with suppressed tears. "But I won't have to go to his bed until after the wedding is solemnized."

"Aye." Mathilde contented herself with the simple agreement. Something had made her nursling particularly fragile at the moment, and it didn't take much to guess what. The viscount had presumably dealt the death blow to Cordelia's hopes, and Mathilde was not going to undo that with offers of sympathy and comfort. Her task now was to prepare Cordelia for her wedding night. She had ensured that the girl was not in ignorance of the carnal side of marriage. Viscount Kierston had carried that education beyond the boundaries that Mathilde considered necessary, but there was no point crying over spilled milk. She would impart a few more words of wisdom on the wedding night itself, when Cordelia would be at her most receptive.

She tucked Cordelia into bed as if she were once more a child in the nursery, kissed her good night, snuffed the candles, and left the room quietly.

Alone, Cordelia pulled the covers up over her head, burrowing into the darkness. It was something she'd done as a child when something bad had happened and she'd instinctively blocked out the world as if by not seeing it she could erase the bad thing. But she was no longer a child, and the defenses of childhood didn't seem to work. Even in her burrow, the wretched thoughts focused, took on almost concrete form, crystallizing her despair.

She didn't want to be married to anyone but Leo. The thought of being touched by anyone but Leo filled her with disgust and dread. How was she to endure what had to be endured?

Resolutely, she pushed the covers away from her face and lay on her back. Feeling sorry for herself would achieve nothing. She must look at what she feared and face it.

Leo didn't like his brother-in-law. The recognition inter-rupted her train of thought. How did she know that? He'd never said anything, but there was a look in his eye when the prince had been mentioned—a dark, brooding look that was banished so swiftly that sometimes she thought she'd imagined it.

Did it perhaps have something to do with Leo's sister? Had he been a tyrant in their marriage?

Should she be afraid of more than the physical act of marriage? Should she be afraid of the man himself?

The thought was so startling, Cordelia sat upright. Surely Leo would have warned her if he knew anything bad about her husband. Surely he would never have encouraged the marriage, played the part in it that he had done. Leo was too honorable to do anything against his conscience, as she knew only too well.

Cordelia lay down again, huddling beneath the feather quilt against the night chill. There now seemed so much she needed to know.

She'd begun the journey as if in an enchanted dream. The wonders of love had bathed everything in a soft rosy light. Ahead of her lay the golden palace of Versailles and a new life of freedom and pleasure. But that dream was now shat-tered by the coming dawn. Her love could never come to fulfillment while she was married to an elderly stranger. She was no longer adrift on a sea of rich promise, she was cold and frightened, shivering on the shore of a shrouded lake as for the first time since Vienna the reality of her situation became clear.

She rolled onto her side, drawing up her knees, trying to relax. She needed to sleep. But sleep evaded her. She tossed and turned, her head filled with disconnected thoughts and formless fears. She wondered if Toinette was going through the same agonizing apprehension and wished that they could have spent this night together, as they had spent so many nights of their girlhood, curled up in the same bed, exchanging secrets and dreams.

She finally fell into a heavy sleep just before dawn and awoke unrested, leaden, and miserable when Mathilde drew back the bedcurtains.

"Put out my riding habit, Mathilde, please. I think the fresh air will be good for me. It might wake me up." She yawned as she sat on the edge of the bed, her body aching and tired.

Mathilde cast her a knowing glance. "Bad night?"

"I'm tired and out of sorts, Mathilde." Cordelia jumped up and buried her head in Mathilde's comforting bosom, her arms clasped tightly around her maid's waist. "I'm frightened and miserable."

Mathilde hugged her and stroked her hair. "There, there, dearie."

Cordelia clung to her as she had done so often in her childhood, and as always Mathilde's strength infused her. After a few minutes, she straightened and smiled a little waterily. "I'm better now."

Mathilde nodded and patted her cheek. "Things are never as bad as you expect them to be. I'll fetch some witch hazel for your eyes." She produced a cloth soaked in witch hazel, and Cordelia lay back on the bed, the soothing cloth pressed to her aching eyes, while Mathilde brushed out her riding habit of blue velvet edged with silver lace.

She was still feeling wan when she left her chamber, but at least knew that she didn't look as bad as she felt. Leo was standing in the inn's stableyard watching the ostler saddle their horses. He turned at her approach and gave her a nod of greeting. Her quick covert examination told her that he hadn't slept much better than she had. He looked pale and drawn. Perhaps this wasn't such a joyful day for him after all. But after what he'd said, how could she think that? She had to stop indulging in fantasy.

"There's no reason why I shouldn't ride today, is there, my lord?" She flicked her whip against her boots. She had determined to greet him normally, to speak to him as if that wretched scene had never taken place, as if he had never spoken those dreadful words. But her voice was tight and the tears were a hard nut in her throat, and she found she couldn't look him in the eye.

"You may ride this morning. But after lunch you should travel in the coach. Your husband will expect you to be journeying in state," he said neutrally.

"Because to do otherwise would not be consonant with my position?" If she didn't think about Leo, if she concentrated only on neutral topics, the knot of tears would dissolve and her voice would sound normal again.

"Possibly." Leo fought the urge to stroke her cheek, smooth the tautness from her lovely mouth, banish her blatant unhappiness by denying what he'd said. But that way lay madness. He must stick to his guns or all his cruelty would have been for nothing.

"Is the prince much concerned with prestige and status and all its trappings?" She looked around at the entourage preparing to leave Soissons.

"Versailles is much concerned."

Was he deliberately evading the question? "But is my husband?" she persisted.

"I believe he is," he responded, swinging into the saddle. "But as I said, Versailles is ruled by the trappings of protocol."

Cordelia gave her foot to the groom who was waiting to help her mount Lucette. "Is the prince more concerned than the average?" She gathered the reins together and turned her horse to walk beside his out of the yard.

Leo frowned. Elvira had once complained that Michael had very rigid attitudes. He hated deviations from what he considered due process. He had certain unvarying rituals. When Leo had pressed her for specifics, she'd laughed it off and changed the subject. But he remembered being faintly disturbed by the exchange. In fact, he'd been faintly disturbed by many of their conversations at that time. As much by what Elvira refused to say as by what she did say.

"Sir?" Cordelia prompted.

He shook his head free of shadows and spoke brusquely. "I don't know. Michael is a diplomat, a politician. He follows the rules of all the games. He's concerned with appearances, but then so is everyone at Versailles. You will learn for yourself."

Cordelia had no heart for further questioning, and they rode in tense silence throughout the morning, stopping for midday refreshment on the right bank of the River Aisne. The local townsfolk crowded around the tables set up picnic-style, gawping at the dauphine and her entourage. Marie Antoinette was charmed with the rustic setting and the informality of the occasion. She summoned Cordelia to sit at her table and chattered like a magpie.

Toinette was clearly not apprehensive and certainly didn't look as if she'd spent a sleepless night. Cordelia reflected that the woebegone homesick girl had vanished, transformed into this delighted and delightful princess who reveled in the attention and the homage with a child's conspicuous pleasure mingled with the haughtiness of one who knew it was her due.

"Come, let us walk among the people." Toinette rose to her feet in a billow of straw-colored silk. She tucked her hand in Cordelia's arm. "We shall stroll among them and greet them. They are my subjects now and I do so want them to love me."

The people certainly seemed very well disposed to their future queen and reluctant to let her go when it was time to return to the carriages.

Lucette had been unsaddled and returned to the rear of the procession, and the coach with the von Sachsen arms on its panels stood ready. Leo was already waiting at the footstep. As Cordelia made her way over to him, Christian appeared from the crowd, leading his horse.

Cordelia's face lit up. With Christian she could be certain of her welcome. Christian's loving friendship was no fantasy. She gathered up her skirts and ran toward him. "Christian, how are you?" She stood on tiptoe to kiss him, forgetting the public arena. "I have been thinking of where you will lodge in Paris."

"Cordelia, you should know better than to indulge in public displays of affection," Leo reproved sharply as he came over to them. "And you too, Christian. You know as well as anyone that the closeness of your friendship needs to be kept out of the public eye."

Christian flushed. "I know where the boundaries of friendship lie, my lord," he said pointedly.

"My lord, do you have any idea where Christian should go when we reach Paris?" Cordelia asked quickly.

"I don't need the viscount's help, Cordelia," Christian protested stiffly. "I'm perfectly capable of looking after myself."

"But it's a strange city and Lord Kierston is sponsoring you. Of course he'll help you, won't you?" She turned her great turquoise eyes toward him. "You won't renege on a promise, I trust, sir?"

It was almost a relief, he thought, to see her eyes filled now with an angry challenge, rather than the haunting shock of one whose trust has been abruptly abused. He ignored the challenge, saying calmly to Christian, "I'll give you the address of a respectable and inexpensive lodging house. You'll be quite comfortable there until you get settled."

Leo opened the carriage door. "Come, the procession is moving." He handed Cordelia in and climbed up after her.

Cordelia leaned out of the window. "We'll talk about it when we get to Compiègne, Christian." She watched him ride away toward the rear of the column and then leaned back against the squabs.

"You will help him, won't you?"

"If he'll accept it." Leo turned his head to look out of the window. He regretted his necessary cruelty of the night before, but he was feeling much more than that regret at the moment. He had not expected to feel as he did. Bereft and sad. He had done his duty by Cordelia and by Michael. He had resisted temptation, all but that once, even though it had been the hardest thing he'd ever done. Now he would be out of temptation. Cordelia from the moment of her introduction to her husband would belong body and soul to Michael. But the knowledge filled him with drear regret.

They reached the town of Berneuil on the outskirts of the forest of Compiègne at three o'clock. Two outriders from the king's party awaited them with the news that His Majesty had decided to escort his new granddaughter to Compiègne himself. He and the dauphin were but five minutes away.

"An unlooked-for honor," Leo observed. "The king doesn't usually put himself out to such an extent."

When Cordelia didn't respond, Leo stepped out of the carriage. "Come." He held up his hand.

Cordelia's hand merely brushed his she stepped down. Unconsciously, she lifted her chin as she looked around.

It was such an obvious attempt to gather courage that his heart went out to her.

"Take heart. Things are never as bad as you expect." He offered a bracing smile.

"I don't wish to be married to him," she said in a fierce undertone. "I love *you*, Leo."

"Enough!" he commanded sharply. "That kind of talk will do you nothing but harm."

Cordelia bit her lip hard. They reached the dauphine and her entourage, who were standing beside their carriages, awaiting the king. Toinette looked over her shoulder and caught Cordelia's eye. She pulled a face and for a moment it was as if their old mischievous relationship were restored, except that Cordelia couldn't summon the spirit to respond. Then the sound of hooves and iron wheels on the unpaved road filled the air, and the dauphine turned back hastily, straightening her shoulders.

The king's cavalcade entered the small town square with the triumphant sound of drums, trumpets, timbals, and hautbois. It was a massive company of guards, soldiers, cavaliers, and coaches.

The king stepped out of the first carriage, accompanied by a young man who looked stiffly and nervously around the assembled company.

"Is that the dauphin?" Cordelia whispered to Leo, her attention diverted from her own misery.

"Yes. He's very shy."

Cordelia wanted to comment on how unattractive the young man was, but she kept the remark to herself, watching as Toinette fell to her knees before the king, who raised her up, kissed her warmly, and drew forward his grandson. Louis-Auguste shyly kissed his bride to cheers and applause from the spectators.

Prince Michael von Sachsen made his way through the crowd toward his brother-in-law. For a few minutes, he had observed the young woman standing beside the viscount. She was dressed in the first style of elegance, as he would have expected. Her expression was very serious, sullen almost. He'd had enough levity in his married life to last through several marriages, he reflected, not displeased by the girl's somber countenance. With luck, she would discourage his daughters' tendency to flightiness as reported by Louise de Nevry. Not that he could imagine either of them producing so much as a smile, but presumably their governess knew them better than he did.

"Viscount Kierston." He greeted his brother-in-law formally.

Leo had been watching his approach. He bowed. "Prince von Sachsen. Allow me to introduce Princess von Sachsen."

Cordelia curtsied. Her husband took her hand and raised her up. He kissed her hand, then lightly brushed her cheek with his lips.

"Madame, I bid you welcome."

"Thank you, sir." Cordelia could think of nothing else to say. The prince looked very like his miniature. He was not unhandsome. His hair was hidden beneath a wig, but his eyebrows were gray. His figure was a little stout, but not objectionably so—unless one was accustomed to the lean, athletic muscularity of Leo Beaumont.

She forced herself to smile, to meet his pale eyes. Leo, beside her, was staring into the middle distance. The prince frowned suddenly and a shadow flickered across the flat surface of his eyes. It was as if he didn't like what he saw.

"We will lodge at Compiègne this evening," the prince stated in a flat, slightly nasal voice, without a tinge of warmth. "I have arranged for the marriage to be solemnized formally when we reach Paris tomorrow evening. It will be a quiet ceremony, but I trust, Leo, that you will honor us with your company." He turned and smiled at his brother-in-law. A thin flickering smile that reminded Cordelia unpleasantly of an asp's tongue. She glanced up at Leo. His expression was frozen but he bowed and murmured his honor at the invitation.

Cordelia was struck powerfully yet again by the knowledge of Leo's dislike of the prince. It wasn't in what he said, but it was in his eyes. And she could feel some surge of rage emanating from him. What was it? She looked between the two men. Prince Michael was offering his snuff box. Leo took a pinch with a word of thanks. Superficially, there was nothing untoward about the scene or their manner to each other, but beneath that surface Cordelia would swear ran deep currents of antagonism.

Why? It had to have something to do with Elvira. But what?

Leo struggled as always with the maelstrom of emotion his brother-in-law's presence always evoked. Michael was alive. Elvira was dead. Leo had not been at his sister's deathbed, he had known nothing of her illness until she was dead. But had Michael done everything possible to save her? The question tormented him as only the speed of her death had done. The speed, the suddenness. One day she stood in the sun, glowing and radiant and filled with life. The next she had been a wasted body in a coffin. And he hadn't been there to save her, or to suffer with her. And he would never know if everything that could be done had been done.

"Come, we should return to the carriage." The prince indicated the royal party, who were reentering their own vehicles. "I will travel with you. There's room, I believe?" He addressed this polite query to Leo.

Leo pushed aside the ghosts of grief and anger and brought himself back to the sunny afternoon. "I'll leave you to become acquainted with your wife, Michael. I'm happy to ride.

"I bid you farewell, Cordelia." He bowed and held out a hand to the silent, watchful Cordelia, who realized with a sick shock that he really was going to abandon her here.

She curtsied, giving him her hand. Her eyes wide and vulnerable, her voice unusually forlorn. "I am so accustomed to your company, sir, I don't know how I shall go on without it. Will we see you at Compiègne?"

"No. I believe I shall return directly to Paris. Now you have your husband's escort, you can have no need of mine, my lady." He stared steadily at her, willing her to lose her air of desolation. It would certainly draw Michael's attention.

"Then allow me to thank you for taking care of me, sir." She seemed to have recovered herself. Her smile was brittle, but it was still a smile.

"The pleasure was all mine." He raised her hand to his lips and kissed it.

The touch of his lips seared her skin through her gloves, and for a telltale second her love glowed in her eyes with such piercing intensity that he almost had to look away. Then she took her husband's arm and turned from him.

Leo watched them move off through the bustling crowds, then he spun on his heel and walked away. He felt empty. The thought of Cordelia with Michael was suddenly unendurable. The thought of his hands on that fresh skin, his touch arousing that wonderful candid sensuality, brought bitter bile to his throat. Elvira had never confided anything about Michael's lovemaking, and her brother had respected such delicacy, even though it was unusual reticence from his robustly candid sister. Now he was tormented with an obsessional curiosity that was as painful as it seemed voyeuristic.

"Lord Kierston."

He stopped and turned at the hail from Christian Percossi. His expression was not encouraging. He didn't need the young musician's accusatory comments at this point. But Christian looked as bereft and miserable as Leo felt.

"Will she be all right?" Christian was out of breath, his hair disheveled, a lost look in his soulful brown eyes.

"She's with her husband."

"Yes, but what kind of man *is* he?" Christian was wringing his long slender hands. "Does he know how special Cordelia is? Will he be able to appreciate her?"

Leo exhaled slowly. "I hope so," he said finally, turning away again, before he remembered that the young man was in some way dependent upon him. "When you reach Paris, go to the Belle Etoile on the rue Saint-Honoré. Mention my name. I'll find you there in a day or two."

"Do you go to Compiègne now?"

"No. I am going straight to Paris. Until later, Christian." He waved a dismissive hand at the young man and strode off, leaving Christian uneasily alone in the now rapidly emptying town square. After a minute he went off in search of his horse. He would follow the procession to Compiègne. Even if he couldn't speak with Cordelia, at least he'd be in the vicinity. It seemed inconsiderate of the viscount to desert her when she must need familiar faces around her.

Leo pushed through a door into a low-ceilinged tavern. "Wine, boy!"

The potboy scurried behind the bar counter and returned with a jug of red wine and a pewter cup. Leo gave him a morose nod and filled the cup. He drank deeply and settled back for a long afternoon in the company of Bacchus. Tomorrow was Cordelia's wedding and he planned to attend it with a shattering headache and his senses dulled with wine.

Prince Michael had handed Cordelia into the carriage and stepped inside after her. He took his seat, arranging the full skirts of his brocaded coat, adjusting his sword.

Fussy little movements, Cordelia thought. A man who concerned himself with detail, who needed things to be perfectly ordered. The antithesis of herself.

"I am honored you came to meet me, my lord," she ventured. The ice had to be broken somehow.

"Not at all," he said, finally satisfied with his dress and looking up at her. "In normal circumstances, of course, I would have awaited you in Paris. But since His Majesty was pleased to make this journey, it seemed appropriate that I should accompany him on my own errand."

Dry as dust, Cordelia thought. Surely he could have said something a little warmer, more encouraging. She glanced down at her hands in her lap. A ray of sun caught the serpent bracelet on her wrist. She touched it and tried again. "And I must thank you for this beautiful betrothal gift, sir. The diamond slipper is exquisite." She held up her wrist to show him. The little charm danced with the movement. "I was wondering about the other charms."

He shrugged. "I have no idea of their history. They were on there when I purchased it for my—" He stopped abruptly, thinking it was perhaps tactless to mention its original owner. The truth was that it was too good a gift to waste and he didn't believe in unnecessary expenditure.

Elvira had worn the bracelet well. When he'd bought it on the birth of the girls, it had been an extravagant and whimsical gesture that he now despised. He had thought that its intricate design seemed perfectly suited to the woman, and how well he had been proved right. The bracelet with its rendering of the serpent and the apple was made for Elvira—temptress, deceiver, liar, whore. She'd been a whore when he'd first taken her into his bed, and she'd been a whore on her deathbed.

The old red rage coursed through him, and he closed his eyes until he had it under control. It was over with. Elvira had paid the price. He had a new wife.

His eyes flicked open again, studying her. There was a boldness to this one too. He'd noticed it when she'd met his eye earlier. She should have lowered her gaze before her husband, but she'd returned his look with a challenging air that he didn't like one bit. However, she was young and innocent. The antithesis of Elvira. He would soon rid her of any undesirable bravado.

Cordelia wondered why he didn't finish his sentence, but she didn't prompt him. His face was closed and dark. What kind of man was this husband of hers? She would discover soon enough.

Chapter Ten

By the end of the evening at Compiègne, Michael was still undecided about his wife. She lacked the subservient modesty he had expected to find in one so young, brought up in the court of Maria Theresa. But her voice was soft, her tones sweet and melodious, and he could detect no sign of stridency or presumption in speech or bearing.

Also in her favor, she was perfectly at home at court. She had carried off her introduction to the king with impeccable grace, neither intimidated nor overbold, and His Majesty had clearly been pleased with her. A wife who was looked kindly upon by the king and was in the confidence of the dauphine would be a significant asset.

He decided to withhold judgment until he'd learned a little more of her. When the royal party finally took themselves off to bed, he went over to his bride, who was talking with or rather listening to an elderly duchess in full monologue.

"If you'll excuse me, madame, I must take my wife away."

Cordelia looked up at the slightly nasal voice at her shoulder, and for a second her relief at this rescue was clear in her eyes. But immediately she dropped her gaze as relief at one rescue merely heralded the moment she'd been dreading all evening. What would happen now?

Would her husband expect some physical intimacies? The thought of as much as a kiss made her shudder.

"Ah, yes, I wouldn't keep you from your wife, Prince." The duchess unfurled her fan, saying with a malicious smile, "It's well known how a young bride can enliven the energies of a man a little . . . past his prime, shall we say?"

Prince Michael merely bowed, not a flicker of emotion crossing his face. "I bid you good night, madame."

Cordelia curtsied to the duchess and stepped back to take her husband's arm. "What a witch!" she said.

"What did you say?" Michael couldn't believe his ears. He looked around to see if the outrageous comment could have been overheard.

"I said she was a witch," Cordelia repeated, seemingly unaware of her husband's shock. "What a nasty, malicious thing to say . . . to both of us."

"Are you accustomed to using such language in Vienna?" he demanded frigidly.

"Oh." Cordelia realized her mistake. She seemed to have started on the wrong foot. "I do beg your pardon, sir. I'm afraid I tend to be somewhat outspoken." She offered him a rueful smile.

"That is a tendency you will learn to control, my dear," he stated, clearly unmoved by the smile. "And you will learn too that the duchess's malice is minor compared with most at Versailles. If you pay heed to it, you will be a laughing-stock. I assure you I will not tolerate that in my wife."

This harshness was so unexpected, so severe, she couldn't keep the shock and dismay from her eyes as she continued to look up at him, the smile fading slowly from her face.

Michael watched her discomfiture with satisfaction, noting that her blue-gray eyes were actually quite lovely, made even more so by her distress. His loins stirred faintly.

In horror, Cordelia recognized the dawning of desire in her husband's eyes. It was an expression she had learned to distinguish in the last year, since her position at court had changed from child to debutante and she'd become the focus of attention for many a young courtier. But what she saw in her husband's suddenly desirous gaze gave her the shivers. There was a ruthlessness to this hunger.

"You understand me," he said.

Only too well. Cordelia nodded. "You make yourself very clear, my lord."

"Good. And so long as you hear me as clearly, then we shall get along very well. Come, I will escort you to our apartments." The prince took her hand and tucked it firmly beneath his arm. Cordelia wondered sickly if he was about to satisfy his sudden appetite.

"Will you be playing at cards tonight, my lord?" The noise from the card rooms flanking the salon indicated that the usual inveterate gamblers were settling in for the night.

"No, not tonight," he said curtly, parading her through the salon, nodding and smiling his asp's smile from side to side as he met familiar greetings. "Tomorrow will be a long day. The king has graciously suggested that we solemnize our marriage in the private chapel of the Hotel de Ville in Paris."

"I understood you to say it would be a very quiet ceremony." She would not let him detect the tremor in her voice as she fought to control her panic. She wasn't ready for her wedding night. Not tonight. She had prepared herself to endure it on the morrow, but she couldn't possibly face it unprepared.

"It will be. Just Viscount Kierston and a few close friends."

"And your daughters?"

"Good God, why should they be present?" He looked genuinely astonished at such a suggestion.

"I had thought it perhaps appropriate," Cordelia said. Obviously she'd made another error.

"Absolutely not," he stated with finality, opening the door to Cordelia's chamber. "They will be waiting at the house to pay their respects to you."

Cordelia pulled a wry face, averting her head as she stepped past him into the room. It didn't sound as if it would be a warm and encouraging moment of introduction. The prince moved inside after her, closing the door at his back. The wave of queasiness broke over her again. But surely he wouldn't do anything in front of Mathilde.

Mathilde rose from her chair, where she'd been mending

a torn flounce on one of Cordelia's gowns, and curtsied to her new master.

"You're the princess's maid, I understand."

"Yes, my lord. Mathilde. I've looked after my lady since she was a babe." Mathilde was the picture of anxious subservience as she curtsied again. There was no sign in this humble maid of the assertive woman whom Viscount Kierston knew. But both she and Cordelia knew that if Mathilde didn't find favor with Prince Michael, he could cast her out of his household without compunction.

"Mathilde was my wet nurse."

Michael frowned. "You need an abigail well versed in the fashions of the court. An elderly wet nurse is hardly an appropriate attendant for the wife of the Prussian ambassador."

Cordelia thought quickly. "It must be as you please, my lord," she said, trying to sound softly submissive. "You know better than I, of course. But Mathilde was in great favor with the empress Maria Theresa. She has often attended the dauphine and was in the empress's confidence."

Michael considered this. While they were a long way from Vienna, it was well known that Maria Theresa had ears and eyes in every court. It wouldn't do for an ambassador to offend the empress of Austria even in such a slight matter as the disposition of an elderly maidservant. "Well, we shall see how she works out. If necessary, I will employ a proper abigail for you, and your nurse can work under her as laundress and seamstress."

Cordelia glanced at Mathilde, whose expression was completely impassive as she remained in a deep curtsy. "I'm sure you will find Mathilde is as well versed in the duties of a lady's maid as any other, sir."

Michael looked annoyed at this persistence. "I will be the best judge of that. I doubt either of you know exactly what's required of such a position at Versailles. How could you, indeed?" He gestured to Mathilde. "Put your mistress to bed, woman, and send me word when she's prepared."

Cordelia's palms dampened.

"Be quick about it," he instructed, then turned on his heels and stalked from the room.

"I'm not prepared tonight, Mathilde." Cordelia paced the room with agitated step. "I don't think I could bear him to touch me tonight."

"You'll bear what comes your way, like women before you and those that'll come after," Mathilde stated calmly. "But I don't believe the prince will take you tonight. He's a man who goes by the book." She began to unhook Cordelia's gown.

"How do you know that?" Cordelia stepped out of her petticoat.

Mathilde shrugged, her fingers busy with Cordelia's laces. "There's much I know, dearie, that doesn't need the telling. But I'll say this. I don't care for that man. There's something underneath that we'd best watch out for."

"Like what?" Cordelia reached up to unpin her hair. Mathilde was adept at sensing what people tried to conceal about themselves, and her intuitive insight was always enlightening.

"I'm not sure as yet." Mathilde took the gown to the armoire. "I can feel a darkness . . . some secret he's holding. Time will tell."

Not too enlightening or at all reassuring, but Cordelia didn't press the issue.

Once Cordelia was in bed, Mathilde plumped the pillow behind her head and smoothed the coverlet. "I'll send for your husband, then." She straightened Cordelia's lace-edged nightcap and examined her critically. "Pretty as a picture," she said with a sudden fierce frown. "And a lamb for the slaughter if that man has his way," she added sotto voce as she left the room to fetch the prince. But he wouldn't have his way if Mathilde had anything to do with it.

Left alone, Cordelia's apprehension rose anew. She drew a loose ringlet into her mouth, sucking on the end, wondering whether Mathilde really knew Prince Michael's mind.

Michael came into the room, clad in a chamber robe of brown velvet. He had discarded his wig, and his gray hair was tied at the nape of his neck. It was rather sparse on top in contrast to his straggly eyebrows. Mathilde hovered by the door.

The prince approached the bed. He examined his bride and then, surprisingly, smiled. Again Cordelia was reminded of a flickering asp's tongue and was not reassured by the smile. She realized she was still sucking her hair and hastily pushed the sodden ringlet behind her ear.

"A very childish habit," he remarked, sitting on the edge of the bed. "But you are very young."

"I will grow up, my lord." Cordelia determined that she wouldn't let him see how he intimidated her. She met his gaze.

Michael didn't move for a minute, then ordered over his shoulder, "Leave us, woman."

The door closed softly behind Mathilde. Michael leaned over, took Cordelia's chin between thumb and forefinger, and brought his mouth to hers. Cordelia closed her eyes on a shudder of revulsion, then as the pressure of his mouth increased and his fingers tightened on her chin, she began to fight for breath. Her lips were pressed against her teeth. She could feel him trying to prise open her lips with his tongue and she kept them closed, resisting with every ounce of her will. And finally he drew back, his fingers falling from her face. She opened her eyes and read the naked arousal in his.

"You are a little innocent, aren't you?" he said with undisguised satisfaction. "You must learn to accommodate a man's needs rather more willingly, my dear."

He rose from the bed, his erection jutting against his robe. He stood looking down at her, his hands resting on his hips, and she could see the swelling beneath his robe.

She really was quite appealing, Michael thought. Apprehension and innocence became her remarkably well. Her attraction couldn't be more different from Elvira's sophisticated allure. And her youthful scent, the freshness of her skin, the blue-black lights in her luxuriant fall of hair were a refreshing change from the occasional harlots he'd enjoyed since Elvira's death.

"We will begin tomorrow," he said, swinging to the door. "I will see you in the morning. We make an early start for Paris."

"I understood that the royal party will be staying here for a few days." Cordelia was startled out of her numb shock.

"But we have no need to remain with them," the prince informed her. "You are not a member of the dauphine's household, my dear. You will not be required to attend upon her on a daily basis, and you have your own life to lead now." The door clicked shut behind him.

Cordelia scrubbed her mouth with the back of her hand, desperate to rid herself of the memory of his lips. Ever since she could remember, her life and Toinette's had been intertwined. From earliest childhood they had shared their secrets, their joys, and their troubles. On one level they had both known that the archduchess's destiny would be of great and public significance, whereas Cordelia would be permitted a more private future, albeit one not of her own choosing. And yet, until now, Cordelia realized that she hadn't fully understood how separate her life would be from Toinette's once their journey into the future was completed.

And only now did she fully realize how alone she was.

"Is it tonight that we will see our new mother, madame?" Sylvie put her thumbnail into her mouth and hastily spat it out. In her excitement she'd forgotten about the foul-tasting yellow paste.

"The wedding is to be solemnized at six o'clock," Madame de Nevry stated. "I have no idea what time your father and his wife will come to the house, but since I've received no instructions from the prince, I assume it will be after your bedtime. I daresay the princess will send for you in the morning." The governess picked up her Bible. "Now, finish your seam, Sylvie. Amelia, that hem is quite crooked. Unpick it and start again." Louise resumed her reading aloud of the Book of Job.

"I wonder if she'll like us," Amelia whispered to her sister in the undertone that no one but themselves could ever hear. It was the barest movement of their lips as their heads were bent side by side. She began the painstaking task of unpicking her ragged stitches.

"Probably she won't," her sister murmured. "Probably she's like Papa. She'll be busy at court."

"Did you say something, Sylvie?" Madame looked up sharply over her pince-nez.

"No, madame." Sylvie shook her head, gazing innocently over the crumpled scrap of material she was attempting to sew.

The governess looked suspiciously between the two girls. Two identical fair heads bent over their task, two pairs of still-dimpled hands wrestling with needles and thread. "I don't wish to hear another sound until the reading is finished," she pronounced, picking up the holy book again.

Amelia's small foot pressed hard on her sister's. "May I ask, madame, if Monsieur Leo will be coming after the wedding?"

"I have no idea."

Amelia subsided. Monsieur Leo was not a popular subject with their governess.

Louise's lips pursed. She heartily disapproved of the viscount. He made the girls overexcited and indulged them shockingly. But when she'd attempted to point this out to the prince, she'd received very short shrift. She'd been made to understand that it was not her place to complain about her employer's brother-in-law. Louise had interpreted this to mean that Viscount Kierston was to be allowed to spoil the children if it pleased him. It was to be hoped that the new princess would see the folly of this and exert her own influence.

Her mouth grew more pinched. Monsieur Brion, the

majordomo, had not been particularly forthcoming with his information regarding their new princess. Either he really knew very little about her, or he was tormenting the governess. He had said only that he believed her to be younger than his former mistress and that she was an Austrian aristocrat.

The Austrian court was known for its strict adherence to form and ritual. The empress Maria Theresa was known throughout the civilized world as a deeply moral woman who ruled her land by the highest ethical standards and would tolerate no moral laxity at her court. A young woman reared in such an atmosphere would be sure to uphold the highest standards in the schoolroom. She would surely support Madame de Nevry's efforts to turn her charges into model young women who knew their duties, knew to speak only when spoken to, knew to honor and revere those put in authority over them.

Louise had formed an image of her employer's new wife. She had been given no description of the lady and had not been shown the miniature, but wishful thinking and what she believed she knew of her employer's needs and tastes in a wife had informed the picture of a dourly respectable young woman of religious temperament and an absolute sense of duty. Her youth should make it easy for Louise to influence her in schoolroom matters. It shouldn't be difficult to ensure she deferred to a governess who had known her charges since babyhood and could be expected to know what was best for them.

In was late in the afternoon and Louise had enjoyed a substantial dinner. Her head dropped onto her chest and her voice stopped in midsentence. Lulled by these comforting reflections and slightly muzzy after her usual liberal enjoyment of wine at dinner, she dozed. A little snore escaped her, her head jerked on her dropping bosom, and she started upright. She glared at her charges, who were sitting bolt upright opposite, their eyes shining with laughter.

The governess coughed, adjusted her pince-nez, and

began her reading again. The girls dutifully plied their needles, but Louise was uncomfortably aware that they were struggling to suppress their giggles. However, she could say nothing without further loss of dignity. Her voice droned on until the clock struck six.

Amelia and Sylvie immediately looked up and exchanged a glance. It was the hour of the wedding.

Viscount Kierston took his place in the front pew of the king's private chapel in the Hotel de Ville. Organ music swelled to the rafters, saving him from participating in the speculative conversation around him. The talk was all of the prince's bride. None of the wedding guests had been at Compiègne, so no one had yet seen the young woman. Leo had been pestered with questions from the moment of his arrival in the chapel. Was she beautiful? Had the king approved her? How young was she? He had answered briefly, refusing to be drawn into the gossip, and with many disgruntled looks, his questioners had given up.

He closed his eyes against the persistent throbbing in his temples. The rough red wine of the Compiègne tavern had done its work only too well, plunging him into drunken oblivion before dawn. He had woken at noon with a vile headache, nauseated, and in a worse than vile humor.

"Were you in Vienna, Kierston, when the scandal broke about the empress's musician?" A rotund gentleman in crimson and gold velvet leaned over his shoulder from the pew behind, fanning himself indolently as the incense fumes swirled from the censer. "I heard tell the pupil in the business has come to Paris."

Leo forced his dulled wits to focus. Cordelia had firmly dumped the responsibility for Christian in his lap. "Yes, I'm sponsoring him until he can find a patron," he said, knowing that the Duc de Carillac considered himself a foremost patron of the arts. "The young man has a divine touch," he continued. "I'm certain that once the king hears him, he'll need no further patronage."

"Ah." Carillac stroked his chin, his beady little eyes gleaming from their folds of flesh. "But at present he's footloose, you say. You are not offering him patronage yourself?"

"It's not my style, my lord," Leo said coolly. A man needed more than his fair share of pride, influence, and the power of wealth to be a successful patron. By the same token, patrons competed with superficial civility for the artists most likely to succeed. Carillac was one of the most cutthroat competitors in the field, and if his interest could be roused in Christian, then the young musician would be well on the way to establishing himself.

"Good, good," Carillac murmured, nodding to himself. "We'll talk more on this matter."

There was an expectant rustle from the body of the chapel. Leo turned to look toward the door. His aching bloodshot eyes saw at first only a shimmer of gold. As it moved toward him the shimmer became Cordelia, her black hair drawn up beneath a cap of gold thread and a diamond-studded tiara, leaving her face pale and exposed. As she passed him her eyes met his, and they were darkest charcoal with little flickering lights of a smoldering brazier in their depths. Then she stepped forward on the prince's arm, and the organ after a final chord fell silent as they reached the altar.

Christian slipped silently through the door as the service began and made his way around the side of the chapel, keeping to the shadows. He had no invitation, of course, but he felt it was important for him to be there for Cordelia. She had no one else from her past as witness to her marriage. Toinette was still at Compiègne, and the viscount was a new friend who didn't know Cordelia as Christian did. He didn't share their history.

Christian stopped in the shadow of a marble column from where he could see the couple at the altar. The prince was an imposing figure in a rich suit of cream damask edged in silver lace. His shoulders were broad, his belly a distinct presence. He had the appearance of a once muscular, powerful athlete now running slightly to seed. But everything about his bearing exuded the confidence and authority of a man used to power and exerting influence. Cordelia, despite the weight of her cloth-of-gold gown and the glitter of diamonds in her hair, looked fragile, almost insubstantial beside her husband.

The prince had taken her hand and was sliding one of the previously blessed rings onto her finger. As Christian watched, Cordelia did the same for him. It was done. Christian looked across the aisle to where Viscount Kierston sat in the front pew. The viscount's expression was chiseled in stone. He held his body rigid, his hands clasping the rail in front of him. Christian saw that his knuckles were white. This was the man Cordelia professed to love. A man who, she said, would not accept that love because he refused to acknowledge his own feelings. It seemed to Christian at this solemn moment in the dimly lit chapel heavy with incense that Leo Beaumont was acknowledging a depth of feeling that could only be described as anguish.

The bride and groom were returning down the aisle. Cordelia's face was, if possible, even paler than before. Her gloved hand rested on her husband's damask sleeve. This time she didn't so much as glance toward Leo but kept her eyes on the square of light ahead of her. She had tried to close her mind to every aspect of the ceremony, so similar to the one that had taken place in Vienna but so horrendously different. Leo's physical presence in the chapel was so powerful she could almost feel him as an aura around her, and she wanted to weep, to scream at the wrongness of it all, to curse at the unutterable unfairness. But she could do none of these things.

As they emerged into the courtyard from the chapel, the fresh evening air cleared her head of the fug of incense and solemnity. Now she felt detached from herself and her surroundings, hearing the congratulations from a distance, barely registering the eagerly curious eyes, the quick covert assessments of this new addition to the enclosed life of the court of Versailles. She was truly aware only of Prince Michael. He seemed a huge defining presence at her side.

"Princess, pray accept my congratulations."

Leo's voice jerked her back to reality. She looked up at him, aware of the sudden flush on her cheeks. His face was a mask, his eyes flat. He bowed.

Cordelia curtsied. "Thank you, my lord." Her voice seemed rather small, and for a moment a sense of helplessness threatened to overwhelm her. She wanted to fling herself into his arms, demand that he sweep her up and away from this place. That he banish the nightmare reality with the dream of love.

"You will accompany us to the rue du Bac for the reception, Leo?" Prince Michael smiled his thin smile. He looked as pleased with himself as he felt. His bride was quite lovely in her gold wedding dress, and her little hand on his sleeve was quivering with all the understandable trepidation of a virgin. The night to come promised hours of pleasure. He placed his hand possessively over Cordelia's as he issued the invitation.

Leo saw the movement. Bile rose bitter in his throat.

"I beg you'll excuse me, Prince," he said with another formal bow.

"Oh, no, indeed I shall not. You have done me such a service, my dear Leo. Come, Cordelia, add your voice to mine. You owe his lordship much thanks for his kind care of you during your journey. Pray insist that he join us in our celebration so we may thank him properly."

The color now ebbed in her cheeks. She knew she couldn't endure Leo to join such a travesty of a celebration. Every minute, she would be dreading the time when the reception came to an end and her husband bore her away to the marital bed. Leo's presence at that public ceremony would be unendurable.

"I do indeed owe you much thanks for all your consideration, Lord Kierston," she murmured. "But perhaps, sir, his lordship is fatigued after his journey."

"Good heavens, I've seen Viscount Kierston ride to hounds all day and dance all night," Prince Michael said dismissively. "Come now, man, say you'll join us."

For a minute Leo could see no graceful way out.

Then he took Michael's arm and drew him aside with an almost urgent movement. He spoke in a swift undertone. "I must ask you to excuse me, Michael. The occasion . . . a happy one, I know . . . brings me so many memories of Elvira on her wedding day that I will be but poor company."

Michael said grudgingly, "Then I cannot insist. But you will visit us soon?"

"Of course." Leo turned back to Cordelia, who was struggling to eavesdrop while pretending polite lack of curiosity. "I beg to be excused, ma'am. I am engaged elsewhere. But pray accept my congratulations again and my wishes for your every happiness."

She put her chin up and said more strongly than she'd so far managed, "You will come to visit my husband's daughters soon, I trust. You have said so often how attached you are to them."

Leo offered a small bow of silent acknowledgment and was about to leave when he caught sight of Christian, hovering a few feet away. "Michael, permit me to introduce Christian Percossi. He's newly arrived from Vienna, where he was the pupil of the court composer." He beckoned the young man over.

"Christian is a close fr—acquaintance of mine," Cordelia put in, smiling warmly at Christian as he bowed to the prince. She forgot her own concerns for the moment in her eagerness to do something for her friend. "He had some difficulties with Poligny, his master, who stole his work, and now he has need of new patronage. Viscount Kierston has been kind enough to sponsor him." She put out her hand to Christian, drawing him forward.

Michael gave the blushing young man a frigid stare. "You are acquainted with my wife, sir?"

"We were children together," Cordelia said.

"I did not ask you, madame," Michael said icily. "I do not care to be interrupted."

Cordelia flushed crimson under this public rebuke. Hasty words of defense and attack rose to her lips, and it was only with the greatest effort that she contained them. Her eyes darted to Leo, whose expression was grim. Christian was tongue-tied.

"I find it distasteful to think of someone of my wife's position at court consorting with a mere musician, a mere pupil, indeed," Michael continued in the same icy tones. "Viscount Kierston may be sponsoring you, but my wife will not acknowledge your acquaintance." He gave Leo a curt nod, then turned on his heel. "Come, Cordelia." He took her arm and bore her off.

She cast one look over her shoulder at the chagrined and startled Christian and the grim-faced viscount, then said resolutely, "My lord, I must protest at being humiliated in that fashion. I cannot believe it was necessary to take me to task so harshly in front of my friends."

"You will not count people below your status among your friends," he said. "Neither will you interrupt me, nor will you expound you own views without being asked. It is not seemly and I will not tolerate my wife putting herself forward in public. I trust I make myself clear."

They had reached the carriage that would take them to Michael's palace in the rue du Bac. Cordelia was overwhelmed with anger and confusion. No one had ever before spoken to her in such insulting fashion. People listened to her when she talked; she was intelligent and well read and quite amusing on occasion. She was used to thinking for herself, and this man was telling her that henceforth she was to be mute, to have no views of her own.

Oh God, what kind of life was she starting?

Michael handed her into the carriage, his expression

self-satisfied as if he'd just accomplished a serious task. He climbed in after her and took his seat opposite, regarding her with an almost predatory gaze from beneath hooded lids. Cordelia leaned back and closed her eyes. She couldn't bear to look at him, so smug, so . . . so *hungry*.

Chapter Eleven

THE NIGHT WAS still young when the last wedding guests left the prince's palace on rue du Bac. It had been a very restrained, decorous celebration, and Cordelia's fears that she would be escorted to her bedchamber amid raucous ribaldry were unfounded.

She was accompanied upstairs by three elderly ladies, distant relatives of the prince's, who showed no inclination to offer the young bride words of wisdom, caution, or courage. They chattered among themselves about the wedding guests as they went through the motions of preparing the bride for bed, and Cordelia began to feel like an inconvenient hindrance to their gossip.

"Mathilde can look after me perfectly well, mesdames," she ventured, shivering in her shift because the self-styled attendant who was holding her bridal nightgown seemed to have forgotten what she was to do with it, so caught up was she in a detailed analysis of Madame du Barry's coiffure.

Mathilde sniffed and deftly removed the garment from the woman's hands, muttering, "The princess will catch her death in a minute."

Countess Lejeune blinked, seeming to return to her surroundings in some surprise. "Did you say something, my dear?" she inquired benignly of Cordelia, who was pulling off her shift.

"Only that I am most grateful for your attentions, mesdames, but my maid can very well see to everything now. You must wish to be going home before the hour is much further advanced," she mumbled through the tumbling mass of hair, dislodged as she'd dragged the shift over her head.

"Oh, but we must see you into bed, the prince will expect it," the countess declared, nodding at her companions, who nodded vigorously in return. "But I daresay your maid can attend you better than we can, so we'll sit over here to wait until you're in bed."

Cordelia grimaced and caught Mathilde's eye. Her nurse shook her head and pursed her lips as she dropped the heavy lace-trimmed nightgown over Cordelia's head. The chatter from the three women beside the hearth rose and fell in an unbroken rhythm as Mathilde brushed the bride's hair, adjusted the ruffles of the nightgown, and turned back the bed.

"My mistress is abed," Mathilde proclaimed loudly, folding her hands in her apron and glaring at the three women. She might play the subservient servant in the prince's company, but she found nothing intimidating about three elderly gossipmongers.

"Oh, then our work is done," the countess declared comfortably, coming over to the bed, where Cordelia had slipped between the sheets. "I bid you good night, my dear."

"Mesdames." Cordelia turned her head to receive the air-blown kisses as they gathered around the bed. "I am most grateful for your kind attentions."

The ironical note in her voice failed to reach them. They smiled, blew more kisses, and disappeared in a chattering buzz.

"Could have done without that useless lot," Mathilde stated. "Can't imagine what good they thought they were doing."

"I doubt they thought about it." The amusement had died out of Cordelia's eyes now. She lay back against the pillows, her face very pale against the white lawn. "I wish this didn't have to happen, Mathilde."

"Nonsense. You're a married woman and married women have relations with their husbands," the nurse said bracingly. She handed Cordelia a small alabaster pot. "Use this ointment before your husband comes to you. It will ease penetration."

The matter-of-fact statement did more than anything could to bring home the reality of what was to happen. Cordelia unscrewed the lid of the pot. "What is it?"

"Herbal ointment. It will prepare your body to receive your husband and will dull the pain if he's not considerate."

"Considerate? How?" Cordelia dipped a finger in the unscented ointment. Mathilde's advice was important, she knew, and yet her words seemed to exist on some other plane, coming to her from a great distance.

Mathilde pursed her lips. "What happened between you and the viscount would have made the loss of your virginity less painful had he chosen to take it on that occasion," she stated. "But few men think of their wives in these matters. So use the ointment quickly. Your husband will be here soon."

Cordelia obeyed, and her actions seemed to belong to someone else. She couldn't seem to connect with what she was doing. The door opened as she handed the alabaster pot back to Mathilde, who dropped it into her apron pocket before turning to greet the prince with a deep curtsy.

Cordelia could see two men standing behind her husband in the corridor—presumably her husband's ceremonial escort to the nuptial chamber. Michael turned and said something softly over his shoulder. There was a laugh, then the door was pulled closed from the corridor. Michael stepped into the room. He was wearing an elaborately brocaded chamber robe, and when he turned his gaze onto the still, pale figure in the big bed, Cordelia saw the predatory light in his eyes, the complacent, almost triumphant, twist to his mouth.

"You may go, woman." His nasal voice had a rasp to it.

Mathilde glanced once toward the bed. For a second her intent gaze held Cordelia's, then, almost imperceptibly, she gave a decisive little nod before hastening from the room, closing the door quietly behind her. But once outside, she moved into the shadows of the tapestry-hung wall and settled down to wait. There was nothing more she could do to help her nursling now, but she could stay close.

Cordelia stared fearfully as her husband approached the bed. He said nothing but leaned over and blew out the candles at the bedside. Then he reached up and pulled the heavy curtains around the bed, enclosing them in a dark cavern. Cordelia's little sigh of relief in the black silence was lost under the creak of the bedropes as she felt him climb in beside her. He was still wearing his chamber robe.

Nothing was said during the next grim minutes. Her fear and revulsion were so strong, her body was closed tight against him despite Mathilde's lubricating ointment. But her resistance seemed to please Michael. She heard him laugh in the darkness as he forced himself into her, driving into her unwilling body with a ferocity that made her scream. He seemed to batter against the very edge of her womb, plunging, surging, an alien force that violated her to her soul. She felt his seed rush into her, heard his grunting satisfaction, then he pulled out of her, falling heavily to one side.

She was shaking uncontrollably with the physical shock. Her nightgown was pushed up to her belly, and with a little sob she pushed it down to cover herself. The sticky seepage between her legs disgusted her, but she was too terrified of disturbing him to move. She lay trying to stop the shaking, to breathe properly again, to swallow the sobs that gathered in her throat.

The ghastly assault was repeated several times during that interminable night. At first she fought desperately, pushing him, twisting her body, trying to keep her thighs closed. But her struggles seemed only to excite him further. He smothered her cries with his hand, flattened hard across her mouth, and he used his body like a battering ram as he held her wrists above her head in an iron grasp. Blindly, she tried to bite the palm of his hand, and with a savage execration he forced her body over until her face was buried in the pillows and he had both hands free to prise apart her legs while he plunged within her again.

The next time, she had learned the lesson and she lay still, rigid beneath him, not moving until it was over. Again, apart from his short brutal exclamations, he said nothing to her. He breathed heavily, snored during the times he slept, moved over her when he was ready again. Cordelia lay awake, trembling, nauseated, but filled now with a deep raging disgust both for the man who could treat her with such contempt and for her own weakness that forced her submission.

The memory of those moments of glory with Leo at Melk belonged to another life, another person. And she would never know what sensual wonders lay beyond that explosion of pleasure, never know what it was to share her body in love with another.

When dawn broke, Cordelia knew that somehow she must escape this marriage. Even if she couldn't cease to be Michael's wife in name, she must somehow keep her own sense of who and what she was, separate from the violation of her body. She must take her self out of the equation. She must rise above her husband's contemptuous and contemptible acts of possession and maintain her own integrity. Only thus could she keep the self-respect that was so much more important than the mere brutalizing of her flesh.

Michael was now sleeping heavily. Gingerly, Cordelia slid from the bed, pulling back the curtains to let in the gray light of morning. Blood stained the sheet, stained her nightgown, smeared her thighs. Her body felt torn and broken; she moved stiffly like an old woman across to the washstand.

"Cordelia? What are you doing? Where are you?" Michael sat up, blinking blearily. He pushed aside the bedcurtains, opening them fully, then bent his eye on the bedlinen. That same complacent triumph quirked his lip. He looked at Cordelia, standing with the washcloth in her hand. He saw the blood on her nightgown. He saw the trepidation in her eyes as she waited to see if he would rape her again.

"I daresay you need your maid," he said, getting out of bed, stretching luxuriantly. The chamber robe he still wore was untied and fell open as he raised his arms. Hastily, Cordelia averted her eyes.

Michael laughed, well pleased after his wedding night. He reached over and chucked her beneath the chin. She shrank away from him and he laughed again with overt satisfaction. "You will learn not to fight me, Cordelia. And you will learn how to please me soon enough."

"Did I not please you last night, my lord?" Despite her exhaustion there was a snap to her voice, but Michael was so full of his own gratification he heard only what he wanted to hear.

"As much as a virgin can please a man," he said airily, retying his girdle. "I'll not require you to take the initiative in these matters, but you must learn to open yourself more readily. Then you will please me perfectly." He strode to the door, a spring in his step. "Ring for your maid. You need attention." He sounded mightily pleased with himself at this evidence of his potency.

Cordelia stared at the closed door, fighting for composure. Then she dragged off her soiled nightgown and began to scrub herself clean, to scrub as if she would remove the layer of skin that he'd sullied.

Mathilde had kept her vigil all night, and as soon as the prince appeared in the corridor, she stepped forward. "I'll go to my mistress now, my lord?"

"Good God, woman! Where did you spring from? I just told the princess to ring for you."

"I have been up and waiting this past hour, my lord."

"Mmm. So you're a faithful attendant at least. Yes, go to her. She needs attention." He waved her toward the door with another smug smile. His bride had found him a most devoted husband, and he couldn't remember when last he'd been so aroused, so filled with potent energy. Certainly not since he'd begun to suspect Elvira's unfaithfulness.

But that was past history. He had a new bride and a new

lease on life. Cordelia would not disappoint him, he would make certain of it.

Mathilde bustled into the dimly lit chamber. "His lordship looked right pleased with himself."

"He is loathsome," Cordelia said in a fierce undertone. "I cannot bear that he should touch me ever again."

Mathilde came over to her. Her shrewd eyes took in the wan face, the lingering shock in the blue-gray eyes. "Now, that's a foolish thing to say. For better or worse, he's your husband and he has his rights. You'll learn to deal with it like millions of women before you and millions to come."

"But *how*?" Cordelia brushed her tangled hair from her eyes. "*How* does one learn to deal with it?"

Mathilde saw the bruise on her nursling's wrist and her expression suddenly changed. "Let me look at you."

"I'm all right," Cordelia said, "I just feel dirty. I need a bath."

"I'll have one sent up when I've had a look at you," Mathilde said grimly. Cordelia submitted to a minute examination that had Mathilde looking grimmer and grimmer as she uncovered every bruise, every scratch.

"So, he's a brute into the bargain," Mathilde muttered finally, pulling the bell rope beside the door. "I knew there was something dark in him."

"I got hurt because I tried to fight him," Cordelia explained wearily.

"Aye, only what I'd expect from you. But there's other ways," Mathilde added almost to herself. She turned to give orders to the maid who answered the bell. "Fetch up a bath for your mistress. . . . And bring breakfast," she added as the maid curtsied and left.

"I couldn't eat. The thought of food makes me feel sick."

"Nonsense. You need all the strength you can get. It's not like you to wallow in self-pity." Mathilde was not prepared to indulge weakness, however unusual and well justified.

Cordelia would need all her strength of character to survive untouched by her husband's treatment. "You'll have a bath and eat a good breakfast and then you'd best set about making your mark on the household. There's a majordomo, one Monsieur Brion, who's a force to be reckoned with, I gather. And then a governess.

"What about the governess?" Cordelia, as always, responded to Mathilde's bracing tones. She wasn't such a milksop as to be crushed after one wedding night. There was much more to this new life than the miseries of conjugal sex. Time enough to fret about it again tonight, when presumably it would be repeated. She shuddered and pushed the thought from her. She must not allow fear of the nights to haunt her days.

Mathilde turned from the armoire where she was selecting a gown. "Dusty spinster, I understand from the housekeeper. Keeps to herself mostly, thinks she's too good for the servant's hall. Some distant relative of the prince's."

"And the children?" Cordelia's legs seemed to be lacking in strength. She sat on the edge of the bed.

"No one sees much of them. Governess pretty much has sole charge." Mathilde came over to the bed with a chamber robe.

Cordelia slipped her arms into the clean robe. "Do they say whether the prince has much to do with his daughters?"

Mathilde bent to gather up the bloodstained nightgown. "Hardly sees them. But it's his voice that rules in the nursery even so. That governess, Madame de Nevry she's called, is scared rigid of him. Or so the housekeeper says." She glanced sharply at Cordelia. "There's a bad feeling in this house. They all fear the prince."

"With reason, I imagine," Cordelia said. She frowned. "I wonder why the viscount didn't say anything when I asked him about my husband. I gave him every opportunity to tell me the worst."

"Maybe he doesn't know. A man can have one face for

the outside world and another for the inside. And you've got to live in a house to know its spirit."

"But what of Leo's sister—Elvira? She lived here, she must have known these things. Didn't she tell him?"

"How are we to know that?" Mathilde shook her head in brisk dismissal of the topic. "We manage our own affairs, dearie."

Cordelia had always had utter faith in Mathilde's ability to manage affairs of any kind. She didn't always know how she did it, but she hadn't yet come across a situation that stumped her old nurse. The thought gave her renewed strength and courage. "I shall go and visit the nursery as soon as I'm dressed." Forgetting her earlier queasiness, she broke into a steaming brioche from the tray the maidservant had placed on the table. In the small bathroom adjoining her chamber, footmen filled the copper tub with jugs of water brought upstairs by laboring boot boys.

"What should I wear, do you think? Something gay and bright. I want them to think of me as someone cheerful and not at all stuffy."

Mathilde couldn't hide her smile at the quaint notion that anyone might think Cordelia stuffy.

Cordelia eased her body into the hot water with a groan of relief. Mathilde had sprinkled herbs on the surface and emptied the fragrant contents of a small vial into the water. Immediately, Cordelia felt the soreness and stiffness fading away with the throbbing of her bruises. She let her head rest against the copper rim of the bath and closed her eyes, inhaling the delicate yet revivifying scent of the herbs.

Mathilde placed the breakfast tray beside the tub, and after a while Cordelia nibbled on the brioche and sipped hot chocolate as the steam wreathed around her. Her habitual optimism finally banished the lingering horror of the night. It had been hell, but the worst was over because she now knew the worst. And now there were two little girls in a nursery waiting to make her acquaintance. Were they scared? she wondered.

• • •

Madame de Nevry was in a very bad temper. Amelia and Sylvie, well versed in their governess's moods, knew they were in for a miserable day the minute she marched into the nursery soon after dawn and ordered their nurse to prepare cold baths for them.

"But I am already so cold," Sylvie whimpered, standing on the bare floorboards, shivering in her nightgown. It was too early for the rising sun to have taken the chill off the night air that filled the nursery from the perpetually opened window.

"It is your father's wish that you should learn to endure discomfort," Madame stated, pinning the child's hair in a tight knot on the top of her head. The prince had actually said only that his daughters were not to be pampered, but the governess chose to interpret the instruction according to her own mood.

Sylvie whimpered again as her scalp was pulled back from her forehead and the pins dug into her skin. Nurse, looking very disapproving, lifted her and dumped her skinny little body in the tub of ice-cold water. Sylvie cried out at the top of her lungs and received a slapped hand from the governess for her pains. Amelia stood and watched, waiting her turn with rather more stoicism than her sister.

They had heard the sounds of the party the previous evening as they'd lain in bed listening to the confused noises of carriage wheels, shouting linkboys, doors opening and closing in the house far below the nursery, the faint strains of music. They'd imagined the food at the banquet, but since their own diet was plain to the point of tastelessness and had never been anything else, they could only imagine a table laden with the strawberries and chocolates they had sometimes been given by Monsieur Leo, when he could sneak the treat into the schoolroom.

"Come, Amelia." Madame snapped her fingers impatiently as Nurse lifted the still-squalling Sylvie out of the freezing water and wrapped her in a thick towel. Madame's face was thin and pinched, and her lips and the tip of her nose had a blue tinge to them as if they'd been inked with a quill pen. On her cheeks burned two vermilion spots of color. She looked like a paint palette, Amelia thought, raising her arms passively as Nurse drew off her nightgown.

Sylvie's whimpers faded as she huddled in the towel. The goosebumps on her skin went down and her shivers lessened while her twin was doused and soaped and doused again, her lips blue with cold, her teeth chattering.

Even after they were dressed, they were still not properly warm, and a meager breakfast of bread and butter and weak tea did little to improve matters. Madame's blue nose turned pink as she drank her own tea. The girls had noticed it always did when she poured something from a little flask into her cup. And her cheeks grew even redder.

"We will study the globe this morning." Louise gestured to the large round globe with her pointer. "Sylvie, you will find England and tell me the name of the capital city."

Sylvie peered at the bumps and squiggles and lines. Everything looked the same to her. She closed her eyes and stabbed with her forefinger.

Louise put up her pince-nez and examined the spot. If asked to perform the task she had set Sylvie, she would have had difficulty. However, Sylvie's choice appeared to be in a range of mountains, and Louise was fairly convinced that England was not a mountainous land.

It was at this point that the door opened to reveal an astounding vision, shimmering, glowing with color in the drab room.

"Good morning. My name is Cordelia and I have come to make your acquaintance."

The girls stared openmouthed as a black-haired girl in a gown of turquoise silk stepped into the room, her jeweled heels tapping on the oak boards. She was smiling, her mouth red and warm, her eyes so big and blue they seemed to swallow them.

She bent and held out her hand to Sylvie. Leo had said something about hair ribbons, but she couldn't remember which was which. "Are you Sylvie or Amelia?"

"Sylvie. There's Amelia."

Cordelia took both their hands in hers, overpoweringly aware of how small they were. She had never been much aware of children before, but these two, gazing at her with such solemnity, filled her with a strange awe.

"Princess, we were not expecting you." The glacial tones drew Cordelia upright again.

"You must be the children's governess. Madame de Nevry, I believe?" She smiled warmly, reflecting that nothing would be gained by alienating this disagreeable-looking woman.

"That is so, Princess. As I said, we were not expecting you. The prince gave me no instructions as to receiving you." She struggled to hide her dismayed shock at a vision that bore no resemblance to her imaginings of the new Princess von Sachsen. The girl was barely out of the schoolroom herself, and she was beautiful. Even to Louise's jaundiced eye, the vibrant beauty pulsing from the princess was undeniable.

"No, well, I daresay that's because he doesn't know I'm here," Cordelia said cheerfully. "I thought it would be much nicer to meet Sylvie and Amelia without any formal fuss and bother." She turned back to the girls, who still regarded her with openmouthed disbelief. "Shall we be friends, do you think? I do so hope we shall." She took their hands again, holding them in her own warm grasp.

"Oh, yes," they said in unison on a little gasp of delight. "Do you know Monsieur Leo? He's our friend too."

"Yes, I know him," she said, ignoring the preparatory mutterings from the governess. "I know him very well, so we shall all be friends." She straightened again to include the governess in the conversation. "I understand from my husband and Viscount Kierston that His Lordship is a frequent visitor to his nieces."

"That may be so," Louise allowed without moving so much as a muscle. "However, if you'll excuse us, Princess, the children must do their lessons."

"Oh, how drear that they should have to have lessons on the day I arrive." Cordelia's nose wrinkled and she moved closer to the governess on the pretext of studying the globe. "Are you having a geography lesson?"

"We were," Louise said pointedly.

Cordelia nodded as her suspicions were confirmed. The woman smelled like a soused herring, and it was barely nine o'clock in the morning. Surely Michael couldn't know that his daughters' governess drank. But for time being, she would keep the knowledge to herself. She had much to learn about this household.

"Then I'll leave you for the moment," she said amenably. "But I'd like the girls to visit me in my boudoir before dinner. There's no need for you to accompany them." She treated the governess to a dazzling smile. "At one o'clock, shall we say." Bending, she swiftly kissed the children. "We shall learn to know each other soon." Then she was gone, leaving Sylvie and Amelia in a warm daze and their governess as frozen rigid as a stalagmite.

"Practice your writing," she commanded, gesturing to the table and the pens and parchment.

She sat down abruptly by the empty hearth and stared at her reflection in the burnished grate. Surreptitiously, she withdrew the little silver flask from her pocket and took a swift gulp. She could not belive that the prince had countenanced his bride's surprise visit to his daughters. He lived his life by rite and rote and laid down strict orders for the schoolroom as he did for the rest of the household. But what was Prince Michael doing with such a frivolous, volatile, vibrant, unorthodox young bride?

Louise took another gulp. From what she knew of her relative, he wouldn't tolerate those qualities in the girl for very long.

• • •

Cordelia returned to the main part of the palace and descended the curving staircase to the cavernous hall with its marble pillars and vast expanse of marble floor.

Monsieur Brion appeared from nowhere and came to the stair with stately step, bowing low as she reached the bottom. "Is there something I can do for you, Princess?"

"Yes, I should like to be shown around the palace, please. And I should like to meet with the housekeeper and the cook." Cordelia's smile was warm, but the majordomo had the astonishing feeling that his new mistress, for all her youth, was not going to be easy to manage.

"If you have instructions for either the cook or the house-keeper, madame, I will be pleased to relay them for you."

Cordelia shook her head. "Oh, I don't think that will be necessary, Monsieur Brion. I am perfectly capable of giving my own instructions. Please ask them to come to me in my boudoir at noon. Now, perhaps you would like to show me around."

"Cordelia, is there something you wish for?"

She turned at her husband's voice. He stood in the doorway to the left of the hall and, judging by the table napkin in his hand, was presumably in the middle of his breakfast. Her eyes fixed upon his hands. They were square, thick fingered, with clumps of graying hair on the knuckles. Her skin seemed to shrink on her bones at the hideous memory of those hands marking her body. Only with the greatest difficulty did she keep from stepping backward, away from him.

"I was asking Monsieur Brion to accompany me on a tour of the palace, sir."

Michael considered this and could find no fault. "By all means," he said with a nod at Brion. "I shall be in the library in one hour. Perhaps you would join me there, madame."

Cordelia acquiesced with a curtsy and waited until her

husband had returned to his interrupted breakfast before turning back to the majordomo. "Shall we go?"

Monsieur Brion bowed. This was a different kind of bride from her predecessor, unsophisticated, less canny, and yet he thought he could detect a certain strength. In this household one garnered allies wherever one could. "Where would you wish to start, madame?"

An hour later Monsieur Brion showed his new mistress into the library. He was still uncertain about the princess. She had been shockingly informal with the servants they'd met, but the questions she'd asked him about the household had been uncomfortably penetrating, and he was convinced that his earlier assessment had been correct—he had felt the sting of a most powerful will beneath.

Michael carefully wiped the nib of his pen and placed it in perfect alignment with the edge of the blotter before rising from the secretaire when his wife entered.

"I trust you were pleased with what you saw, madame."

Cordelia couldn't bring herself to step further into the room, a step that would bring her that much closer to her husband. "You have a most beautiful palace, sir. I particularly admired the Boucher panels in the small salon." She had to learn to conduct ordinary conversations with this man. She had to separate the daytime husband from the nighttime ravisher. If she couldn't do that, she would be crushed like an ant beneath his boot.

Michael had turned back to his secretaire. With small, precise movements, he sanded the sheet on which he'd been writing and closed the leatherbound book. "Did you notice the Rembrandts in the gallery?"

"Yes, but I preferred the Canaletto." She watched as he carried the book to an ironbound chest beneath the window. He withdrew a key from his pocket, unlocked the chest, and, with the same precision, placed the book inside, then dropped the lid and locked the chest. Cordelia couldn't see what was in the chest, but it struck her as strange that he should have to lock up his writings. But then she reflected that perhaps they were diplomatic secrets and observations. An ambassador was as much a spy for his monarch as he was a diplomat.

"The Canaletto is very fine, but the subject matter is more frivolous than Rembrandt's."

Cordelia didn't argue this point. Her eyes continued to roam the room and fell upon the portrait above the mantel. She knew immediately who it was. The physical resemblance between the woman and Leo Beaumont was unmistakable. Although the woman's eyes were blue instead of hazel, the resemblance was contained in their expression, in the nose, in the quirk of that sensual mouth.

"This is your late wife?" She examined the rich, voluptuous figure with a deep curiosity and a strange little thrill that she knew arose because the act of looking upon Leo's twin in some way connected her with Leo himself.

"Yes. It's a particularly fine Fragonard." The prince's tone did not encourage further discussion of the portrait, but Cordelia didn't move away. She wanted to touch the soft curving white arm, the shining fair hair, so powerfully did the woman's personality come across. Had she also suffered through hellish nights?

"She's wearing my bracelet," she said with a shock of recognition, holding up her wrist in demonstration.

"The bracelet was my gift to Elvira on the birth of her daughters," Michael said, his tone now thoroughly frigid. "It is a priceless work of art and I believed it to be a suitable betrothal gift. There is no need to talk of it further."

Cordelia didn't immediately respond. She examined the bracelet on her wrist and then the one on Elvira's wrist. "She has another charm," she said. "A heart. Is it jade?"

Michael's lips thinned. Was she stupid or stubborn to persist in these observations when he'd made it clear he didn't wish to discuss the subject? "You have your own charm. The bracelet now belongs to you. I wish now to discuss with you the arrangements for our sojourn in Versailles during the dauphin's wedding."

Cordelia touched the delicate diamond slipper. She supposed that by removing the charm dedicated to Elvira and replacing it with one dedicated to the new owner, her husband considered he had been acting with all due consideration. But still, it felt a little peculiar to be wearing the dead woman's jewelry, however beautiful.

"Viscount Kierston said you have an apartment at Versailles." She turned back to the room, her finger unconsciously tracing the shape of the serpent around her wrist.

"Yes, the king has graciously allotted me a suite of rooms on the third staircase. You will find them commodious enough, I believe."

Cordelia knew that apartments at Versailles, thirty miles outside Paris, were greatly coveted and were only allocated to the king's favorites or those with significant influence. "Does Viscount Kierston have an apartment at Versailles?" she asked casually.

"He is much favored by Madame du Barry. He has a small room on the outer staircase through her influence."

That didn't sound too comfortable, but for a bachelor it was probably considered sufficient. Her heart lifted. At least he would be at Versailles also. He had promised to stand her friend.

"I intend to instruct my daughters' governess to bring them to the drawing room before dinner to pay their respects to you." Michael changed the subject, impatient with this question-and-answer session that had nothing to do with the matters at hand.

"Oh, I've already met them," Cordelia said cheerfully. "I visited the schoolroom earlier. They are such lovely children."

"You did *what*?" Michael stared in astonishment.

Cordelia swallowed. Obviously, she'd made a mistake. "I didn't think it would displease you, my lord. I was anxious to meet them."

Michael moved toward her and she stood her ground with the greatest difficulty. "You will not ever take such matters on yourself, do you hear me, Cordelia? I rule this household and you will not *ever* attempt to usurp my rule."

"But ... but how could my visiting the schoolroom be considered usurping your authority?" she protested, forgetting her fear of him in her indignation.

"You will do nothing—*nothing*, do you hear me?—without my permission. No one in this household takes a step without my permission." He had put his hands on her now, and a deep shiver began in her belly.

"But they are servants, my lord. I am your wife," she said. She would not back down. She would not show her fear.

His fingers tightened around her upper arms, bringing back a flood of physical memories of the night. She could smell the muskiness of his skin, almost choking her as it had done during the ghastly hours of darkness. And he was hurting her again. "You are as much under my authority as any servant, my dear." His voice was low but intense. "You will forget that at your own risk. Do you understand?"

Cordelia closed her lips tightly. She averted her face from his, now so close to her she thought she would faint with loathing.

"Answer me!" he demanded.

"You're hurting me." It was all the answer he was going to get.

"*Answer me!*"

"In order for me to understand, my lord, I beg you will explain to me exactly how you would wish me to involve myself with your daughters." She ignored the pain in her arms. She had had confrontations of a like sort with her uncle. She hadn't given way to him; she would not give way to her husband.

"Viscount Kierston implied that it was hoped I would be a mother to them. I cannot do that if I'm permitted to see them only at your command."

With a shock, Michael realized that she was not intimidated. "They have no need of mothering," he said tautly. "Their governess will supervise their education and their day-to-day care. But she has no experience of court circles. You will be responsible for preparing them to move in those circles. You will also begin to prepare them for their betrothals. There will be no need for you to involve yourself in their general welfare. Is that understood?"

"Surely they're too young to be considered for betrothal?" she exclaimed.

"That is no business of yours." He shook her in rough emphasis. "You will keep your opinions to yourself." But he couldn't help adding with cold pride, "I have every hope of making the most advantageous, influential connections for them. It is not unrealistic to look to the highest courts in Europe. There are younger royal sons aplenty who could do worse than a connection with the von Sachsens."

Cordelia had been sacrificed to the pride of lineage. Could she help those two little girls avoid such a destiny? Perhaps—but not by setting herself up openly against her husband. It was time to beat a strategic retreat.

"It is, of course, for their father to decide." She lowered her eyes.

He said coldly, "These displays of defiance will do you no good, my dear. Do you understand that?" He was determined to hear her submission. He remembered the feel of her slender frailty beneath him during the night. Her resistance that he had overcome so easily. She was young. She would make mistakes. It was for him to correct them.

She would not say it. The tense silence was as thick and palpable as a blanketing fog.

A knock at the door made them both jump. His hands fell from her arms, and he swung round with a savage "What is it?"

"Viscount Kierston, my lord," announced Monsieur Brion. Leo entered the library on the announcement with all the informality of an old family friend. He was dressed in black, except for a short riding cloak that this time was lined in peacock blue. He held his lace-edged gloves in one hand, his other resting almost unconsciously on the hilt of his sword. His eyes were sharp and cold as icicles.

Cordelia's heart beat fast and her palms were suddenly damp. Would he be looking for Michael's mark upon her? Would he see some sign of the horrors of that possession? He mustn't know. She couldn't bear him to know.

"Prince Michael. Princess von Sachsen. Your servant." He bowed. Cordelia curtsied. He took her hand and her skin burned with his touch. She raised her eyes for an instant and looked deep into his. She read the question contained in his steady gaze, but she couldn't answer it. With a polite smile she withdrew her hand and stepped back, turning her eyes away.

"Welcome, Leo. You will drink to our wedding as you were unable to do last night." Michael took up a decanter of Rhenish wine on the sideboard. "Cordelia, you will join us in a glass."

It was not a suggestion. Cordelia took the glass of white wine. There was an expectant silence, then Leo raised his glass and said quietly, "To your happiness."

Cordelia drank the toast, the same polite smile fixed to her lips. She knew he was sincere. He would not wish her unhappiness no matter what lay between them.

Michael smiled and drank deeply. "Thank you, my dear friend."

Cordelia couldn't bear it another minute. She put her barely touched glass down. "If you will excuse me, my lords, I have asked the cook and the housekeeper to come to me in my boudoir at noon."

"There is no need for you to involve yourself in the day-to-day running of the household, madame," Michael said sharply. "I have already explained your duties. And they do not include consorting with the staff, who know how to manage their own duties perfectly well."

"You don't consider it necessary for servants to know their mistress, my lord?"

She was defying him again! Michael couldn't believe what he was hearing. But he could do nothing in Leo's presence. He took one menacing step toward her and his eyes blazed. "I have told you what I consider necessary."

Leo saw the look in her eyes as she seemed to withdraw her body into itself. Elvira had had that same shadow in her eyes. The shadow had appeared at the time he'd noticed that her bubbling laughter was heard less often. But whenever he'd questioned her, she'd put him off, changed the subject, and the shadow had been banished as swiftly as it had appeared, so that he'd never been certain that he'd seen it. Now he knew he had. Cordelia was not so adept at masking her feelings.

"It must be as you wish, my lord." Cordelia curtsied, her voice tight. "I bid you good day, Viscount Kierston."

The door closed quietly behind her.

Chapter Twelve

LEO, HIDING HIS concern, remained with his brother-in-law for the best part of an hour. Cordelia had already fallen foul of her husband. It didn't surprise him. Michael had made it clear over the business with Christian that he intended to rule his wife with an iron hand, and Leo knew that Cordelia wouldn't accept that easily. But what had happened between them to cause that shadow of fear in her eyes? And dear God, had he really seen that same look in Elvira's eyes?

But Michael saw none of this disturbed conjecture. As usual, Leo chatted inconsequentially about court matters, snippets of gossip, dropping the occasional juicier morsels into the conversation, knowing that the prince had sharp ears for anything useful either to his own diplomacy or to his personal ambition.

Since Elvira's death Leo had worked hard to give Michael the impression of an idle courtier who loved to play, who knew everyone, was universally liked. A man who could be trusted with Michael's daughters, an uncle who wouldn't undermine their father's authority or attempt to involve himself in decisions concerning them. Michael wouldn't hesitate to ban Leo from the schoolroom if the uncle's interest became inconvenient.

Leo's commitment to watch over Elvira's children as their mother would have done was one of the driving forces of his life. It was the reason he stayed in Paris instead of returning to his native England. Michael had no emotional attachment to his daughters, but Leo knew that he saw them as diplomatic currency, to be sold to the highest bidder. Leo would fight for their welfare when the time came, but in the meantime he played the benign and harmless uncle. When

Michael looked upon Elvira's brother, he saw a smiling mouth, slightly hooded eyes, an elegantly dressed form always relaxed. Unlike Cordelia, he saw little or no resemblance to Elvira, but then, he wasn't looking for it.

And now, Leo thought, he had added Cordelia's welfare to his responsibilities under Michael's roof. "So you will be taking the princess to Versailles for the wedding?" He sipped his wine, idly crossing one silk-clad knee over his thigh.

"I have instructed the majordomo to arrange for our removal in three days' time, when the king's party returns from Compiègne."

"I daresay I'll see you there then." Leo set down his glass. "The king has most graciously insisted that I attend the ceremony. I suspect at the du Barry's own insistence." He laughed lightly, rising to his feet. "His Majesty's favorite is generous with her favors. It was a signal mark of honor that she attended your wedding yesterday."

The prince's expression was dour as he too rose to his feet. "I abhore the fact that in order to rise in the king's esteem, one must court his whore."

"But I daresay you will encourage Cordelia to do so," Leo said with a gentle smile.

Michael shrugged. "She will, of course, be courteous. I see no reason why she should move in the du Barry's circles, however. There is not the slightest need for it."

"Quite so." Leo contented himself with the dry comment. "While I'm here, I'll take the opportunity to look in upon the girls. It's been many weeks since I saw them last."

Prince Michael said coldly, "They are having a busy day, it would seem. Cordelia has already introduced herself to them this morning. I trust their governess will know how much excitement will be good for them."

Maybe that explained the tension between Michael and his wife. He knew Michael well enough to be sure that he wouldn't appreciate Cordelia taking matters into her own hands. "I have noticed that Cordelia has a somewhat impetuous nature," he said mildly. "But her actions are always prompted by the best motives."

Michael looked both surprised and annoyed at this comment. He said stiffly, "I daresay."

Leo let it rest. "Be assured that I shall not overstay my welcome with the girls," he said with an easy smile, and took his leave.

He made his way via the back stairs to the schoolroom to find it inhabited only by the governess, who rose in some agitation at his arrival. "Mesdames Sylvie and Amelia are with the princess," she said, curtsying. "I cannot understand why the princess would not wish me to accompany them. It is most irregular and I cannot believe Prince Michael would countenance such lack of ceremony." For a moment she forgot her animosity toward Viscount Kierston in her eagerness to pour out woeful indignation.

Now what was Cordelia playing at? Leo wondered. He noted the alcohol on the governess's breath and wondered why Michael had never noticed, but probably the prince never came close enough to his employee to detect it. "How long do you expect them to remain with their stepmother?"

"I have no idea." The woman threw up her hands. "I was told nothing, merely to send them to Madame's boudoir at one o'clock. For all I know, they may be dining with her. And what kind of a lesson in consideration is that to teach them? The servants toil up here with the children's dinner, only to find it's not wanted. And what of me? Am I to eat my dinner alone in the schoolroom, I ask you? If I'm to be relieved of my charges for a while, there are better things I could be doing than sitting here twiddling my thumbs."

Leo listened to this impassioned speech with an air of aloof boredom. When Madame had subsided, her cheeks reddening as she realized how she had betrayed herself to one whom she mistrusted and disliked, he said, "I am sure the princess will make her intentions clear to you, madame. You have only to ask her. I have never found her in the least indirect."

The governess's flush deepened. "Well, we shall see what the prince has to say," she muttered.

Leo gave her a cold nod and departed. Cordelia seemed to have created a fair amount of havoc in the short time she'd been in the rue du Bac. She'd made an enemy of the governess, angered her husband, and seemed set upon continuing to do so. She didn't have Elvira's subtlety and sophistication, qualities that would have enabled her to get her own way without causing trouble. She was too young and too straightforward.

But had Elvira managed to avoid trouble? The question lurked uneasily in his mind. It had never before occurred to him that his sister couldn't manage Michael. Leo himself had never liked his sister's husband. He was too rigid and self-serving, but Elvira had accepted the marriage perfectly willingly. She'd laughed at her brother's reservations, maintaining that a high position at the court of Versailles was worth a stuffy husband. Elvira had wanted a literary salon of her own. She had been a close friend of Madame de Pompadour and had been seduced by the power and influence that could be wielded by a clever woman at Versailles. She had seen marriage to the Prussian ambassador as her passport to that influence.

Elvira had never met a person she couldn't manage—in the nicest possible way. And Michael had always appeared a devoted husband. Leo had never had cause to question his treatment of his wife, despite Elvira's occasionally unusually subdued demeanor. She had always had a plausible reason for it. And he'd certainly never seen Michael chastise Elvira as he had done Cordelia. But no doubt Michael saw his second wife as a child, to be formed, educated. Not an unreasonable viewpoint, considering the difference in their ages. But his harshness was disturbing.

He took the main staircase down from the nursery floor, and the girls' voices reached him from a pair of double doors standing ajar along a corridor leading off the first landing.

He knew the room. It had been Elvira's boudoir. He felt a sudden reluctance to enter there. On the occasion of his last visit, his sister had been vibrant and alive. He could still hear her laughter, feel her goodbye kiss on his cheek. When next he'd seen her, she'd been in her coffin, barely recognizable, skeletal against the white satin, her once rich golden hair thin and straggly. What dreadful curse could have wreaked such devastation in such a short space of time?

He forced himself to the doorway. Both girls were talking at once, their voices rising excitedly as they competed for attention. Leo smiled involuntarily. He couldn't remember hearing them chatter with such uninhibited gaiety before. Without further thought, he stepped through the open door.

Cordelia was sitting on a low stool, the girls kneeling on the floor beside her. They were playing cat's cradle, and one exuberant child was trying to transfer the complicated net of wool from her own tiny dimpled hands to her sister's.

Cordelia looked up as she sensed Leo's silent entrance. Her color ebbed, then returned. She smiled at him over the children's heads, and the nakedness of the smile made his heart turn over. It was filled with warmth and promise and longing, brimming with the love she had so often expressed. And it was a smile paradoxically so vulnerable and so full of danger that he wanted to shake her into awareness of reality. Either that, or turn and run.

"Monsieur Leo!" Amelia, or so he assumed from the hair ribbon, saw him first. Both girls jumped to their feet, then stood awkwardly, curtsying, Amelia's hands still occupied with the cat's cradle.

"Viscount Kierston." Cordelia also rose and curtsied. "This is an unexpected pleasure." Her voice was a honeyed caress, her eyes deepest sapphire. There was no sign of the earlier shadows.

"I wished to visit the children," he said, struggling to sound cool and matter-of-fact in the face of that over-powering sensuality. "They were not in the schoolroom and Madame de Nevry told me I would find them with you."

With relief he dropped his gaze from the burning intensity of Cordelia's and bent his eye on the two small faces staring anxiously up at him. "And how are my little mesdames?" he inquired with a smile.

"Very well, thank you, sir," they said in unison, curtsying again. They seemed to be waiting for permission to move. Cordelia wondered whom they expected to give it. They were looking over their shoulders at her, their eyes wide in appeal, and she finally realized with something of a shock that in the absence of their governess she was the authority in question.

"Amelia and Sylvie and I were getting to know each other," she said, coming over to lay her hands lightly on their shoulders. "But you and they are old friends, of course."

"Oh, Monsieur Leo's been our friend since our mama died," Amelia confided, losing her stiffness. She put her hand in Leo's.

"We were only babies then. How could he have been our friend?" Sylvie scoffed, edging forward to put her hand in Leo's other one. "Babies can't be friends with people."

"Yes, they can. Can't they, Monsieur Leo?"

Leo laughed. "I don't see why not."

"I told you so!" Sylvie declared in triumph, giving her sister a little push.

Amelia pushed back, her cheeks pink with annoyance. "Well, I say they can't. Babies don't talk. Of course they can't be friends with people."

"Who wants to see what I have brought?" Leo interrupted this escalating argument, dropping their hands to reach into his pockets.

The girls crowded around him, gasping with excitement as he gave them each a tiny tissue-wrapped packet.

"Oh, mine's a pony!" Sylvie held up a china miniature. "For our collection, Melia."

Amelia's fingers trembled as she tore off the paper to reveal a miniature cat. "Oh, she's so pretty. I shall call her kitten." She held it up to her cheek, crooning softly.

"They have a collection of china animals," Leo told Cordelia quietly.

"They seem to have little else to play with," she returned. "Will the dragon lady approve?"

Leo grinned involuntarily. "I can't say I give a damn whether she does or not."

Cordelia touched his hand. He withdrew it with a jerk. For a moment they were silent. Then Leo spoke, his voice soft beneath the children's prattle.

"I wonder if it's wise of you to set yourself up against your husband so soon."

Cordelia said nothing immediately. She stared straight ahead, frowning at the painted panels on the door as if she were trying to identify the flowers depicted there. Then she said, "I must do what I think right. He doesn't wish me to be a mother to the children, but I know that I must be their friend, whether he wishes it or no."

"It does you credit," he said quietly. "But you should proceed with caution."

Cordelia suddenly shuddered. It was an involuntary movement and again he saw the shadow flicker across her eyes. Then she shrugged with an assumption of carelessness. "I'm not afraid to do what's right, Leo." But the disturbing shadow deepened.

He changed the subject. "I understand Michael will be escorting you to Versailles for the wedding."

"Shall we meet there?" She responded to the change with a note of relief that she couldn't disguise.

"I shall be at court."

"Will you be able to do anything for Christian, do you think?" Her eyes kept sliding away from his as if she were suddenly afraid to meet his gaze. But Cordelia was never afraid to look a person in the eye.

"I have a possible patron in mind. The Duc de Carillac," he replied in a neutrally conversational tone that covered his unease.

"Monsieur Leo, will you take us for a ride in your carriage if Madame de Nevry permits?" The shy approach of Amelia and Sylvie, each clutching her china miniature, brought a welcome diversion.

"If *I* give you permission, then of course you may go," Cordelia said. She glanced up at Leo, her chin lifted unconsciously as if she challenged him to argue with her.

"Are you more important than Madame de Nevry, then, madame?" They gazed up at her in wonderment.

Cordelia considered this, and her eyes began to twinkle with a return of her usual spirit. "Well, I think I am," she pronounced. "Since I am your stepmother. And you must not call me madame. My name is Cordelia."

Leo cleared his throat. "I think what they call you should be left up to Prince Michael. He will have his own intentions."

Cordelia frowned at the warning. But she couldn't fault it. If she were to achieve her own goals where the girls were concerned, she should choose her battles.

"Perhaps Monsieur Leo is right," she said. "We will discuss it with your papa."

"But we may go for a ride in your carriage, sir?" Elvira's eyes, twinned, gazed appealingly up at him.

"I haven't brought my carriage today, but I will do so next time."

"And then we may *all* go for a ride," Cordelia declared. "Yes?" She turned as someone scratched on the open door.

The footman bowed. "Madame de Nevry wishes to know if Mesdames are to dine abovestairs, my lady."

Cordelia hesitated but Leo said swiftly, "Yes, of course they must go immediately." He bent to take their hands in his, kissing them with laughing formality. "Mesdames, I am desolated to bid you farewell."

The girls' disappointment dissolved in giggles, but they remembered their curtsies, their stiff skirts billowing around them as they took their leave of their stepmother and uncle.

Cordelia picked up her fan from the side table, tapping

the delicate painted sticks in the palm of her hand. "He wants me to prepare them for their betrothals," she said. "He doesn't want me to love them, or befriend them."

Leo's lips tightened as he thought of Michael's cold indifference to the children. But he controlled the urge to discuss his own careful involvement in his nieces' affairs. "Michael has very strict notions on how matters in the schoolroom should be conducted. If you wish to improve their lives, you will do so only by inches. If you allow your customary impetuosity to rule you, Cordelia, you will gain nothing in this household."

"Is this advice based on your sister's experiences, my lord?" Idly, Cordelia unfurled her fan, hoping her eagerness for his answer wasn't obvious in her voice. What did he know of Elvira's life in this house?

"My sister's marriage has little to do with yours, Cordelia. I'm offering the advice of a friend. One who has known your husband for several years."

It wasn't much of an answer. But she couldn't believe he would knowingly have let her walk into this prison. Perhaps Michael had been different with Elvira. She'd been older, wiser, more experienced than Cordelia. Presumably, it had affected his conduct toward her.

Leo came toward her, drawn as if to a lodestone. He knew that the closer he came to her, the greater his danger, but he had promised to stand her friend and he could not desert her simply because he was afraid of his own feelings. He took her hand in both of his, saying with quiet sincerity, "I wish only your happiness, Cordelia. The reality of marriage to Prince Michael may not match up to your fairy-tale fantasy, but it has many advantages if you learn how to take them. Versailles and its many pleasures await you. If you don't antagonize your husband, you can find much to enjoy in this new life."

"Yes, of course," Cordelia said, averting her eyes. She withdrew her hand from his and tucked a loose ringlet behind her ear.

Leo took her hand again, turning it over to examine the purpling bruise on her inner wrist. "How did this happen?"

Cordelia tried to pull her hand free. "I knocked it on the edge of the bath this morning. I slipped as I was getting out. The soap ... or ... something ..." She stopped. She'd always had a tendency to expand fibs, and Mathilde had long ago told her that the best lies were the simplest. Not that she ever lied to Mathilde, only to her uncle.

Leo's frown deepened but he released her wrist. "I must go now. I'll set up a meeting with Christian and the Duc de Carillac without delay."

He was rewarded by a vibrant smile, a return to the lively Cordelia that he knew. "Oh, that would be wonderful. I knew you would be able to help him."

"Your faith is touching," he said lightly. "I'll see you at court, Cordelia."

She nodded and kept on smiling through the forlorn knowledge that once he'd left her, she'd be alone again. Without friends or support in this house. Except for Mathilde. She had Mathilde, and Mathilde's support was worth more than an army of foot soldiers.

The thought buoyed her as Leo left the boudoir. Sitting on the deep cushioned window seat, she looked out onto the courtyard below the window. The palace flanked the courtyard on three sides, the great iron gates to the street occupying the fourth side. Leo emerged from the main doorway to her left. He stood for a minute at the head of the flight of steps leading down to the cobbles, slapping his gloves into his palm in a gesture so familiar that a wave of insuperable longing broke over her. She had endured a hellish wedding night, filled with pain and mortification, and she yearned for what the act of love could bring. Now she wanted Leo with a naked lust that at this moment had nothing to do with love, let alone friendship. She wanted his body, the feel of his skin, his smell in her nostrils, his taste on her tongue. She wanted him inside her, each powerful thrust touching her womb, his flesh filling her, possessing her as she took him into her and made him part of her self. She had never experienced the wonders of such loving, but in her blood she knew they existed.

The need was so strong, a soft groan broke from her lips. Her forehead pressed against the cold windowpane and she touched the glass with her tongue, imagining she was stroking the smooth planes of his belly. She could almost feel the hard contours of his thighs molded beneath her palms, the throb of his erect shaft against her fingers. He would bring her such pleasure, a pleasure that would eradicate the dreadful violations of her husband's possession.

"Is there something of particular interest in the courtyard, madame?"

She started violently, turned, and stared at her husband, who stood in the doorway, his expression glacial. Her erotic dream vanished into the black clouds of reality. This man was reality, not the man now mounting his horse in the courtyard.

"I was daydreaming, my lord."

"A bad habit," he said. "You have many, I am discovering." He came into the room, banging the door shut behind him. "I understand from Madame de Nevry that you have again disobeyed my orders with regard to my daughters."

Cordelia stood up, feeling slightly sick. Michael had a strange look to his eyes. He was angry, but there was also a curious satisfaction, a hungry anticipation that sent cold shudders through her belly. "I wish only to befriend them, my lord."

"But I gave you instructions that you were to see them only with my permission. Instead of which, you deliberately disturb their routine, bring them down from the schoolroom, encourage them to disobey their governess—"

"No, indeed I did not," she protested.

"Do not interrupt me," he said icily, and that dreadful anticipation in his eyes seemed to strengthen. "Did you or did you not disobey my direct instructions regarding my daughters?"

There seemed nothing for it. Cordelia put up her chin and met his glare with a steady stare. "If you say so, my lord. But I consider that I was merely fulfilling my duties as stepmother."

"Those duties will be defined by me, not by you, as you must learn. Come." He crossed the room to the door to Cordelia's bedchamber. "Come," he repeated, the word a whiplash in the tense silence. He opened the door.

"What do you want of me?" She couldn't help asking, even though her voice shook, and she knew the question betrayed her fear.

Again that terrible satisfaction flared in his eyes. "I want a wife who knows her place, my dear. And I intend to have one. *Come!*" He held the door open.

Cordelia walked past him into her bedchamber. He followed her in and she heard the key turn in the lock.

Leo rode along the left bank of the Seine toward the Belle Etoile, where he had told Christian to put up.

As he turned away from the river, however, he spied the musician hurrying down the street toward him with an abstracted air.

"Christian?"

Christian stopped in his tracks. He looked up at the horseman, blinking, clearly trying to come back from whatever astral plane of genius he had been inhabiting. "Oh, Viscount Kierston." He smiled, with an air still somewhat bemused. "I was thinking of Cordelia. I'm so worried about her."

Leo swung down from his horse. He looped the reins over his arm. "There is a pleasant little tavern on the next street. Let's quench our thirst and talk in private."

Christian fell in beside him. "Have you seen her, sir? That man . . . her husband . . . the prince . . . he seemed so severe.

To talk to her in such manner and in such a place. I haven't been able to sleep for worrying."

"I think she worries as much about you," Leo said casually, wondering why he was reluctant to share his own concerns with the musician.

Outside a tavern on the rue de Seine, Leo handed his horse to a waiting urchin and politely stood aside as his companion dipped his head to pass beneath the narrow lintel. Inside, it was dim, the air musty, sawdust on the floor. It didn't strike Christian as a pleasant place at all, whatever the viscount said. But then, he wasn't to know that it had a very special reputation among those in the know.

"Wine, mine host!" Leo waved a hand toward the apron-clad tavernkeeper standing at the stained bar counter. "My usual." He brushed off a chair and sat down, swinging his sword to one side. He drew off his gloves and placed them on the table, saying with a smile, "You might find it hard to believe, but Raoul here has as good a cellar as any house in Paris. And I mean *any* house. There isn't a lord or prince of the blood whose cellar is more extensive."

Raoul, grinning, put a dusty bottle on the table. He wiped two glasses on his less-than-clean apron, plunking them beside the bottle. "Aye, that's right, milord. But don't ever ask where I gets it from." He tapped the side of his nose with another suggestive grin before drawing the long cork. His expression was reverential as he sniffed the cork, held it for Leo, then passed his nose across the neck of the bottle. As reverently, he poured a measure into one glass, swirling it around until the sides were coated, then he handed it to Leo.

Leo sipped and closed his eyes on a blissful sigh. "Manna."

Raoul nodded and filled both glasses to the brim. "I'll fetch a bite of cheese and some bread. It's no quaffing wine."

"Raoul is a sommelier who could teach the stewards at Versailles a thing or two." Leo took another sip of wine, then sat back, crossing his legs at the ankles. He didn't open the conversation until the tavern keeper had returned with a crusty loaf of bread and a round of cheese.

Christian controlled his impatience as best he could. He was indifferent to wine, and the ceremony and the savoring struck him as a complete waste of time. He broke a piece of bread, cut a piece of cheese, and ate with relish. Food was a different matter. He seemed always to be hungry.

"Have you heard of the Duc de Carillac?" Leo finally began.

Christian nodded. "He's well known even in Vienna for his patronage."

"Well, I think he might be interested in offering you his support." Leo refilled his own glass after casting a glance at his companion's barely touched one.

Christian looked up from the cheese that he was cutting into again, and his eyes sparkled. "Really? Really and truly, sir?"

"Really and truly," Leo said, smiling. "I promised to bring you to him this afternoon . . . if you're free, of course."

"Oh, but of course I will be . . . whatever else could I be doing?" Christian stammered. "You are too kind, sir. I hate to think that I might have caused you trouble. I would never have asked for such a favor myself, but . . ."

"But Cordelia has no such scruples," Leo finished for him with another dry smile. "She's a most loyal friend, I believe."

"And I would do anything for her," Christian said, his delight fading from his eyes. "I don't like that husband, sir. He makes me uneasy."

And me also. But Leo didn't say that. He nibbled a crust of bread and said carefully, "Prince Michael is more than thirty years older than Cordelia. It's inevitable that he should feel a need to mold her to his—"

"But Cordelia cannot be molded." Christian interrupted passionately, banging his fist on the table in emphasis. "Surely you must know that, sir. You've spent time with her. She's her own person." He pulverized a bread crumb with his fingertips against the stained planking of the table.

Leo put a protective hand on the bottle as the table continued to shake. "Yes, I understand that," he said quietly. "But she will have to adapt in some way, Christian, surely you accept that."

"Why would her husband forbid us to talk to each other?" Christian took another tack. "I know I'm a humble musician, but I have some status. If I have the duke's patronage, I shall be at court. I shall play at court. Why should we not be able to talk to each other?"

"Prince Michael is very conscious of his social status," Leo said lightly. "It's a Prussian characteristic. But Cordelia, I'm certain, will win him over, once he's become accustomed to her and she to him. Until then . . ." He paused, picking his words carefully, "Until then, it would be wise of you to keep your distance. For your own sake as well as Cordelia's. Carillac is a close friend of Prince Michael's. You don't want to ruin your chances there."

"Have you seen her since her marriage?" Christian raised his head from his gloomy contemplation of the table. He'd asked the question once already but hadn't received an answer.

"This morning." Leo drank his wine, keeping his voice calm and matter-of-fact.

"Is she well?"

"Perfectly. And looking forward to going to Versailles."

Christian still looked doubtful. "I wish I could speak to her myself. Do you think I could write to her?"

"Give me a letter and I'll see she gets it." Leo wondered ruefully why he would suggest playing postman. Except that he knew how it would please Cordelia to be able to communicate with her friend.

Christian's face lit up. "Then, if you'll excuse me, sir, I'll go back to the inn and write at once. I can give it to you when I see you this afternoon."

Leo inclined his head in acknowledgment. "I'll come for you at three o'clock."

Christian, burbling his thanks, hastened away, leaving

Leo staring into space. He couldn't shake his own uneasiness, despite his dismissal of Christian's fears.

"Raoul!" he bellowed across the noisy taproom. "Another bottle. And drink it with me. I've a wine thirst this afternoon and a need for company."

Chapter Thirteen

IT WAS LATE morning when Cordelia stepped out of the carriage in the great court of the palace of Versailles. They had left rue du Bac before dawn, and the thirty miles from Paris had taken hours as the long procession of carriages had wound its way single file along the narrow road. Half of Paris, it seemed, had come to see the dauphin wed. Burghers, merchants, even tradesmen mingled in the court with elegantly dressed courtiers, the women sporting plumed headdresses and skirts so wide they needed at least six feet of space around them.

The palace of Versailles was a city in itself, its doors ever open to the populace who wandered freely through the great rooms, uninhibited by the careless dismissal of courtiers and the haughty glares and commands of powdered liveried flunkies. The people of Paris regarded their king in the light of a father, and his palaces and entertainments were as much for their benefit as his. A royal wedding was a party to be enjoyed by everyone.

Cordelia listened to the buzz around her as she waited for Monsieur Brion, who had accompanied his employers, to summon carriers and footmen to deal with their luggage. The people of Paris had fallen in love with the dauphine, it seemed. They talked of her sweetness, her beauty, her inevitable fertility that would provide for the succession with a line of healthy sons.

Cordelia repressed a shudder as her husband came up behind her and only with the greatest difficulty kept herself from flinching when he put his hand on her shoulder. She knew now that any show of fear excited him, just as the merest hint of rebellion brought hideous punishment.

He punished her with his body in the dark cave of the bed-curtains, subduing her resistant flesh with a savagery that seemed to feed on itself. Only when she was reduced to a disgusted, pitiable quiver of mortification would he achieve his climax, and then, smiling smugly, he would leave her and return to his own bedchamber.

But this morning Cordelia sensed that he was preoccupied by much more than the perverted pleasures of ruling his wife. "We must get out of this crush." He raised a pomander to his nose with a fastidious sniff. "The people stink. Brion will direct you to our apartments, where you must wait until it's time for us to go to the chapel. I must go immediately to the Cabinet du Conseil to pay my respects to the king." He turned and vanished into the throng, the pomander still held to his nose, liveried flunkies clearing a path for him with shouts and swinging staffs.

"This way, my lady." Monsieur Brion set off for the flight of steps leading into the palace. He walked slowly so that Cordelia on her high heels could keep pace as he cleared the way for them. He knew full well that if he lost sight of the princess, it might take hours to find her again, and she would quickly become lost in the warren of staircases and passages in the vast palace. Newcomers were generally issued maps and could be seen scurrying along the corridors from one function to the next, their eyes glued to the parchment.

The prince's apartments were spacious and elegant, located on the north staircase, very close to the royal apartments. They looked out over the sweep of gardens at the rear of the palace, where myriad fountains played in the soft air and the parterres were massed with color. In honor of the occasion, a series of trellised arches ran along both sides of the canal. They were decorated like Venetian windows, and Cordelia could see the little lanterns that would illuminate them at night.

Two bedchambers, each with a dressing room, opened

off the salon—a square, comfortable room with a dining alcove at one end. There was even a small kitchen where their own cook could prepare meals if the prince and princess were not dining elsewhere. The servants' quarters consisted of cubbyholes at the rear of the kitchen, furnished with sleeping pallets and very little else.

Mathilde arrived in a very few minutes under the escort of a footman, who carried on his shoulder the ironbound leather chest that Prince Michael kept in his library in the rue du Bac.

Mathilde was panting after the long haul up the stairs. "Goodness me, I must have walked miles." She plumped herself down onto a chair, fanning herself with her hand. "What a place. And the crowds! Everywhere. A body can't move. I can't think what the empress would have to say." It was clear her comparison of the orderly Schönbrunn with the chaotic magnificence of Versailles was not favorable.

Cordelia murmured a companionable agreement, watching as Frederick, the footman, under orders from Monsieur Brion, staggered with the chest into the prince's dressing room. His papers must be of vital importance if they had to accompany him everywhere, she reflected.

"We'd best touch up your dress," Mathilde said, finally dragging herself to her feet. "Your hair is coming loose too."

It had been four in the morning when Mathilde had dressed Cordelia for the wedding in a sacque gown of crimson damask open over a petticoat of ivory silk sewn with pearls. A pearl tiara glimmered in her black hair, pearls encircled her throat and nestled in her earlobes. But the long carriage journey had inevitably caused some disarray.

"I would kill for a cup of coffee," Cordelia declared. "Can it be arranged, Monsieur Brion?"

The majordomo hesitated. It went against the grain to admit that he couldn't fulfill his employer's every wish, but on this occasion the cook and the servants had not yet arrived or were still struggling to make their way through the crowds.

"I don't know if the kitchen is ready for use, madame."

"Oh, you leave it to me. Just show me the way, monsieur." Mathilde brushed off her hands with an air of unmistakable competence.

Monsieur Brion had decided early on that Mathilde should be left to her own devices. She was no ordinary servant and he sensed that his customary authority wouldn't wash with her; in fact, they were all just a little frightened of the princess's abigail, although she was always perfectly pleasant and never put on airs, but sometimes there was a look in her sharp eyes that gave a man the chills.

Cordelia wandered into the bedchamber that by its feminine hangings was clearly intended for herself. She wondered if Elvira had used it, if it was the same now as it had been in Elvira's time. Or whether the prince had had the delicacy to change the decorations. That thought brought a grim turn to her mouth. Delicacy was not one of Prince Michael's hallmarks.

She explored her own dressing room and then on impulse pushed open the connecting door that led to the prince's. The chest stood beneath the small, high window. She stepped hesitantly into the room. Even though Michael hadn't entered it as yet on this visit to Versailles, it felt as if she were trespassing. She hadn't set foot in his bedchamber in the rue du Bac, not that she could ever imagine wishing to. She grimaced in disgust.

She bent over the chest, examining the small padlock, then with a shock realized that it hung loose in the lock. Had Michael forgotten to lock it the last time he'd used it? Or had it broken open on the journey? Unable to help herself, with a sense of almost delicious terror, she lifted the lid and gazed at her husband's secrets laid out before her.

A key, presumably a spare one for the padlock, lay on top of a purple bound book. She picked up the key and tried it in the padlock. It was a perfect fit. An idea nibbled at the back of her mind. She picked up the purple bound book and stared at the title. *The Devil's Apothecary*. Whatever could it mean? She flipped open the pages and her jaw dropped. It was a poisoner's manual. She flicked through the book, hardly aware that she had almost stopped breathing. There were enough poisons to do away with an army in any number of ingenious ways. Each substance was meticulously described, its various dosages and effects analyzed with a chilling objectivity.

What on earth was Michael doing with such a book? Did he have some intellectual interest in the poisoner's art? She knew enough history to know herself how fascinating it could be. Lucrezia Borgia ... Catherine de Médicis ... they'd rid themselves of their enemies with abandon and incredible ingenuity. Poisoned gloves, lip salves, perfumes. But historically poison was a woman's weapon. It was an odd interest for a man like Michael.

She put the book down and examined the contents of the chest again. The identical spines of a series of volumes faced upward. They all bore the date of a single year. She picked out the most recent. It fell open on the previous day's date, marked with a purple ribbon bookmark. It was a daily journal. She read the entry, then the preceding one. His dealings with her were meticulously, sickeningly described right down to a description and rating of the strength of his climax. His pleasure was directly related to the degree of pain and humiliation he inflicted upon his wife. Cordelia had suspected as much, but it had seemed too perverse to consider seriously. And yet it was here, written with cold objectivity, as if it were some clinical analysis in a medical report.

She dropped the book with a shudder of disgust. What else was contained in this daily record of her husband's life? In here, she would find out about Elvira. She would discover whether he had treated Elvira as he treated her.

"Holy Mary, child! What are you doing?" Mathilde's shocked tones brought her swinging round with a cry of alarm. The woman stood in the door, clutching a breakfast tray.

"I couldn't help it." Cordelia flushed to the roots of her hair. "I know it's despicable to spy, but . . ." With a sudden movement, she bent over the chest, replaced the book she'd been reading, and picked up the tiny key. She darted across to the washstand, and pressed it into the cake of soap on the dish. "I'm mad, I know. It's a dreadful thing to do, but there're things I must know, Mathilde." She was muttering this rushed torrent almost to herself as she wiped the key clean of soap and put it back in the chest.

Mathilde continued to stare at her as if her nursling had indeed run mad. "If the prince finds you in here . . ." she began.

"Don't even think of it." Cordelia shivered. "Quick, let's go back." She darted into her own dressing room and closed the door to Michael's. Her heart was hammering against her ribs, her palms were slippery with sweat. Gingerly, she put the cake of soap on the washstand. The imprint of the key was clear and deep.

"Do you know how to get a key copied, Mathilde?"

"Now, what in the name of mercy are you up to, Cordelia?" Mathilde set the tray down and stood, arms akimbo, frowning fiercely. "That man would flay you alive if you gave him the excuse." Her eyes were bitter, her mouth thin. She had not yet worked out a way to deal with Prince Michael that wouldn't in the end make matters even worse for Cordelia. The man enjoyed giving pain, it was inextricably bound up in his sexual pleasure, and he would relish the slightest pretext to punish his wife in the darkness of the bedcurtains.

"I know, but I won't let him break me, Mathilde." Cordelia spoke with fierce determination. "He has secrets in that chest, and maybe they'll help me. It won't hurt to find out everything I can about him, will it?"

Mathilde shook her head doubtfully, but she took the

cake of soap and wrapped it carefully in a linen hand-kerchief before dropping it into her apron pocket. "I'll get the key cut and then we'll see," she stated noncommittally. "Now, let me do your hair."

She gestured brusquely to the tray where sat a pot of coffee and a basket of fruit and pastries that she had somehow conjured out of the air. "You'd best eat something. It's noontime and there's no knowing when you'll have the chance to eat again before the banquet." She busied herself with adjusting Cordelia's coiffure.

"I wonder how Toinette is feeling," Cordelia mumbled through a mouthful of almond cake. "Monsieur Brion said she arrived here at half past ten this morning, but the queen's bedchamber is not renovated as yet. Something to do with repairs to the ceiling. Anyway, they had to put her in another room. They seem to be as disorganized here as at Compiègne. I wonder if the other royal palaces are the same."

"I daresay the archduchess is well enough." Mathilde removed the last pin from her mouth and drove it into the mass of black curls. "I just hope they remember to make sure she eats. When she gets excited, she forgets all about it, and we don't want her swooning at the altar."

Cordelia wished she could be with her friend at this moment. It would be especially hard for Toinette to have no intimate companion with her as she was dressed for her wedding. Cordelia felt years older than her childhood friend. True, Toinette was fourteen and a half to her own sixteen, but their age difference had never mattered in the past. Now she seemed separated from Toinette by much more than eighteen months.

Half an hour later, Prince Michael entered the apartment. Cordelia was standing in the salon, careful not to disturb her dress now that she was once more in perfect order. The prince's first thought, however, was not for his wife. "Brion, is my chest here?"

"In your dressing room, my lord."

The prince strode into the dressing room. Cordelia crept forward. She watched curiously through the open door as he bent over the chest. Then he let loose a bellow of fury. "Brion! Brion! Who's been tampering with my chest?"

"Oh, Your Highness ... no one ... what could you mean ... what has happened?" Brion, his eyes round as saucers in his plump face, came racing from the kitchen.

The prince was raging. "The chest is unlocked! Look at it! The padlock is hanging loose!" He raised his cane and Brion cowered against the wall, all vestiges of his dignified major-domo persona vanished.

"Your Highness, I haven't touched it. I haven't been near it since Frederick brought it in from the coach," he babbled, creeping backward to the door.

"Where's Frederick?" The cane came down across a chair with a violent but harmless crack.

Cordelia darted to the window and stood gazing down into the gardens with every appearance of utter deafness.

Brion bellowed for Frederick, radiating relief at finding an alternative victim for his master. The footman came racing from the kitchen. "What is it? What have I done?"

Brion gestured with his head to the prince's dressing room, and Frederick nervously approached, the majordomo following him. Cordelia turned again, positioning herself so that she could see what was going on. It was not a pretty sight. The prince in a wild fit was belaboring the hapless footman with his cane, bringing it down over the man's shoulders even as Frederick protested his innocence.

Then the fit passed almost as quickly as it had arisen. The white-faced servants emerged from the dressing room and scuttled away to the relative safety of the servants' quarters, and silence emanated from the dressing room. Cordelia crept closer. Michael was kneeling before the chest, examining it so closely his head was almost inside. Her heart began to hammer again. Had she disturbed something, left some telltale sign of her intrusion?

Finally, Michael raised his head. He dropped the lid, locked it, and pocketed the key. He returned to the salon, his face wiped clear of all emotion, a beating pulse in his temple the only lingering sign of the fearsome rage of a few minutes earlier.

"The dauphine is to be conducted to meet the royal family in the Cabinet du Conseil at one o'clock. We must take up our positions in the Salon d'Hercule immediately." He examined his wife critically as he spoke.

"Is there some significance in the Salon d'Hercule?" Cordelia lifted her chin. She knew perfectly well that no fault could be found with her appearance and couldn't help resenting his scrutiny.

"It's the station immediately before the chapel. We will follow the royal party into the chapel. It's a great honor," he told her, frowning. That lifted chin was disagreeable. One of these days he could cure her of it, but now was not the moment. Tight-lipped, he offered his arm.

The Hall of Mirrors was lined on both sides by glittering courtiers, already awaiting the royal procession. Michael walked sedately between the lines, smiling and bowing to some, loftily ignoring others who tried to catch his eye. Cordelia's eyes darted from side to side as she tried to absorb the scene.

They continued through the long series of linked rooms that made up the state rooms, these also lined with men and women perspiring freely in the heat, packed too close together to wield their fans to good effect. The Salon d'Hercule, immediately before the royal chapel, was less crowded, and Cordelia guessed positions here were by royal command only. Her husband proceeded to the very head of the room. In this salon he acknowledged with a small bow everyone who caught his eye, and Cordelia, taking her cue, curtsied in her turn.

Viscount Kierston was one of the honored few. He was dressed in emerald green thickly embroidered with silver thread. The color deepened his eyes, accentuated the hazel glints. He was standing with Madame du Barry across the salon from Cordelia and her husband. He raised his eyes and bowed. His gaze was both troubled and intently questioning. The king's mistress smiled and dropped a slight curtsy. Cordelia responded in kind.

She had seen Leo twice since her wedding. On the second occasion, he'd brought her a letter from Christian and with obvious reluctance had taken her answer back to Christian. On that second time, she'd stood away from the light of the window, her fingers nervously adjusting the fichu at her neck. The bruises beneath the muslin were large and dark, despite Mathilde's ministrations and a liberal dusting of powder. She had not encouraged him to prolong his visit, and she'd seen how her behavior had puzzled and disturbed him.

Now Cordelia closed her gloved hands tightly, her nails digging into her palms, and forced herself to smile nonchalantly into his questioning gaze. Leo must not know. But she could see that he was not at ease. There was too much tension in his jaw, in the gripped mouth, in the set of his shoulders. She glanced sideways at her husband. The thin mouth, the slightly fleshy face, the cold eyes. She could feel his hands, clammy on her body, the weight of him when he fell onto her, satiated, before rolling sideways to snore until he'd recovered his strength. She closed her eyes on a graveyard shudder.

A herald's trumpet sounded. There was a stir around them. People leaned forward slightly, looking back down the series of rooms. The royal party was approaching.

Toinette was tiny. A slender, almost childish figure smothered in diamonds. But she looked around her, acknowledging the homage of the court with a grace and dignity that belied her childlike appearance. Beside her walked the dauphin, who seemed much more ill at ease than his bride. There was a moment when Toinette caught

Cordelia's eye, then she had passed and Cordelia wasn't sure whether the gleam in the round blue eyes had been laughter or tears.

During the wedding, gaming tables were set up in the chain of state rooms, with cards and dice for the king and his courtiers to while away the remainder of the day until the banquet. Roped barriers kept the witnessing crowds from getting too close as they gawked at the court at play. It had begun to rain heavily, sending the masses inside from the gardens, and the smell of wet cloth pervaded the air already heavy with scented candles.

Cordelia saw her husband and Leo at the king's table playing lansquenet. The ladies of the court, including the dauphine, were also at cards. Cordelia strolled among the tables, trying to decide whether to dice or join the card-players. As she passed her husband, the king looked up from his cards. "Princess von Sachsen. Pray take a seat at our table. If you don't play, then you may bring your husband luck." He beamed with great good humor.

"Oh, but I do play, Your Majesty." Cordelia's eyes suddenly sharpened. Lansquenet, a game of German origin, had been played a great deal at the Viennese court. She and Toinette had perfected their somewhat dubious skills at the tables and had become adept at defeating the archdukes.

She took the chair held for her by a footman, arranging her skirts of crimson and ivory with a deft hand, her dazzling smile embracing the table.

Leo recognized that look. That mischievous, calculating, gleeful gloat. He had seen it in the carriage as they played dice to pass the time, and he had seen it over chess one memorable night. And now he was seeing it again, only she was at the king's table in the state rooms of Versailles, surrounded by courtiers and gaping spectators.

He shot her a warning look, but she smiled sunnily and took up her cards. He said, "I doubt you have so many bystanders at Schonbrunn, Princess? The Austrian court is less open to the world."

"Oh, I am accustomed to playing under the most watchful stares, my lord," she said with the same radiant smile.

Leo ground his teeth. He glanced at Michael, who seemed indifferent. He would expect his wife to play. Everyone gambled. It was a social skill.

The king held the bank. "We play high, Princess," he warned with a jocular smile. "But I daresay your husband will stake you. A wedding gift, eh, Prince?"

Michael's smile was tight, but he drew a leather purse from his coat pocket and handed it to his wife with the patronizing comment "If you play at all competently, my dear, that should cover you for a few hands."

"I believe you will discover that I play competently, sir," she said serenely, opening the purse. She placed a golden louis on the table and fanned out the cards in her hand with an expert flick of her wrist.

Leo groaned to himself and took up his own cards. Apparently there was nothing he could do to avert catastrophe.

But catastrophe seemed long coming. Cordelia won steadily. She played intently, her expression utterly serious, except at the end of a hand when she would gather up her winnings with that little crow of triumph that he remembered so vividly. She beamed around the table, and even the king chuckled and told her she was a fine card player but a shameless winner.

Michael, however, looked blacker and blacker. He was losing to his wife, his golden louis piling up at her white elbow, and her triumph was a thorn in his side. It was directed at him. She threw it at him with every smile. She had the upper hand and she was relishing every minute of it. Even the thought that later he could have his revenge didn't help the sour taste of defeat in the face of her gloating. Had she been meek and modest, he could almost have borne her success, but this blatant exultation was intolerable.

Leo tried to see how she was doing it. He watched her hands, the slender white beringed fingers. Her sleeves reached only to her elbow, so the obvious hiding place for cards was denied her. She made no sudden distracting movements, and when he thought she had become blinded to danger by her success, she averted any possibility of suspicion by calmly losing the next three hands.

She had a purpose, more serious than mere winning, and it took him a while to see it. She lost when it seemed sensible to do so, but she never lost to her husband. She outbid him, outmaneuvered him, took every louis he had with him. And she smiled with such artlessly shameless satisfaction that, even though Michael was clearly livid, everyone at the table laughed and shared her pleasure, her husband obliquely becoming the butt of their laughter.

And when she sweetly offered to lend her husband some of the money he had so kindly given her to play with, the table rocked with amusement. "She's got you there, Prince," the king boomed. "Such a pretty little thing, butter wouldn't melt in her mouth, but sharp as a rapier. If you ever need to repair your fortunes, just send your wife to the tables."

Michael smiled thinly and Leo wondered if he was the only one to feel the hostility and tension surging beneath the apparent bonhomie at the table. Finally Leo threw in his cards, laughingly admitted defeat, pushed his last coins across to Cordelia, and begged the king for permission to leave the game.

"I was always taught that a wise gamester knows when to close his game," Cordelia said swiftly. "Would Your Majesty excuse me also? I feel my luck is about to turn."

"You would deny us our revenge?" chuckled the king. "But we will have it another time, my dear Princess." He tossed his own cards to the table. "Ladies, gentlemen, I shall retire before the banquet."

His fellow players rose, as did the rest of the tables. The king passed through the salon, offering his arm to his new granddaughter-in-law. "Come, my dear."

Cordelia's head ached after the intensity of the game, but she was filled with jubilation. She would pay for it later, but it had been worth it. She scooped her winnings into her reticule under cover of the king's departure and left the table before Michael could summon her back.

Her initial impression of the palace had been of a succession of glittering mirrors, gleaming marble floors, rich tapestries, exquisite paintings. But there must be more to the place than that.

She moved unobtrusively through the series of rooms, keeping to the court side of the roped barriers. The massive Hall of Mirrors was disorienting, and she stopped, almost blinded by the reflections of the great candelabra in the vast expanse of looking glass. The crowded scene of glittering, jeweled courtiers and the massed throng of spectators were doubled by their reflection, and she felt as if she'd strayed into some infernal scene by Hieronymus Bosch. The acoustics in the gallery threw the noise up to the ceiling, where it bounced back in a discordant racket of voices, rattling dice, and above it all the gallant strains of a trio of musicians.

Cordelia reached the end of the gallery and turned aside into an anteroom. It was quieter here, with only a few people standing around looking out at the rain-drenched garden and discussing whether the evening's firework display would have to be postponed. Beyond the anteroom was a long windowed corridor that she guessed would lead downstairs and to some garden exit. She started toward it.

Leo broke off his conversation as he caught sight of the distinctive crimson and ivory figure crossing the anteroom. "Excuse me." He strolled casually in pursuit, waiting to catch up with her until they were out of earshot of the people in the anteroom.

"What the *hell* did you think you were playing at?" he demanded, catching her wrist, spinning her to face him.

"Lansquenet," she retorted, her eyes still sparkling with excitement. "Wasn't that what we were all playing, sir?"

"How did you do it?" He refused to respond to her mischief, unable to think of anything but what could have happened if she'd been discovered.

"I won," she said. "It was as simple as that."

"Damn you, Cordelia! Tell me how you did it!"

"Oh, don't be cross, Leo." She put a hand on his arm. "Nothing bad happened and I squashed Michael like a bug. Didn't I?" Bitter triumph laced her voice, glittered in her eyes, curled her lip.

Leo was shocked by the bitterness. It was as unexpected in Cordelia as malice would have been. She was wickedly mischievous, but never spiteful. She was determined, candid, frequently outrageous, but embittered . . . never.

"He was livid, could you tell?" she continued in the same tone. "Wasn't it wonderful? They laughed at him and I *beat* him." Her lovely mouth tightened. "I will not let—" Abruptly, she stopped, remembering who she was talking to, realizing that she had dropped her guard.

"Won't let what, Cordelia?" Leo asked quietly. He took her hands, holding them tightly. "What are you talking about?"

She tried to laugh, to avert her gaze. "I was just rattling on. I do when I get excited; it's a terrible habit. You know how I love to win—it just goes to my head."

"Are you in trouble, Cordelia?" His gaze was piercing, intent.

She shook her head. "Of course not. How should I be? No one guessed what I was doing."

"That's not what I'm talking about, and you know it. Something is wrong. What is it?"

"Nothing is wrong. Of course it's not. At last I'm here, in fairyland. How else would you describe this place, Leo? It's even more fantastic than I'd imagined. I can't wait to explore the gardens and—"

"Stop it!" he interrupted sharply. "What are you trying to hide?"

If Michael had treated Elvira as he treated his second wife, she had not told her brother. Cordelia was now convinced of it. Leo's concern was as puzzled as it was genuine. He had loved his sister dearly; it would be unbearable now, after her death, to suspect that she had suffered at her husband's hands.

There was one sure way to deflect him. "I'm trying to hide that I love you," she said simply. "I'm married to one man and I love another. That's what's the matter, Leo. Nothing else. Just what you've always known. I'm torn apart. I have to pretend with my husband, all the time. *All* the time," she added with pointed emphasis. "In bed, in—"

"That's enough," he snapped, wanting to close his ears to the words, his mind to the images they created. He dropped her hands. "If you cannot resign yourself to reality, Cordelia, you will only store up misery for yourself. Don't you see that?"

She raised a sardonic eyebrow. Nothing could be more miserable than the reality of life with Prince Michael. "Is Christian settled with the Duc de Carillac?"

It was such an abrupt change of subject, he was taken aback. But it was easier to talk of Christian than to talk of futile love. And if that was all that was troubling Cordelia, then he could do nothing to help her.

"I believe Carillac made him a generous offer," he said neutrally. "I daresay Christian will be at Versailles at some point during the wedding festivities. Carillac will want to show him off."

"I wonder how we can contrive to talk," Cordelia mused. "Michael must have ceremonial duties, meetings and levees and things to attend. He can't watch me all the time." She shook her head suddenly and offered him a bright smile. "Forgive me, I have need of the retiring room."

She glided away in the direction of one of the rooms set aside as a tiring-room for the ladies, but her smile seemed to remain, hovering in the air, bright, and as brittle as crystal.

Leo went over to one of the long windows looking down on the gardens. He stared out into the rain. Why did she think Michael watched her? Husbands weren't spies. She had been keeping something from him, lying to him. But why?

Chapter Fourteen

"WHERE'S MATHILDE?" CORDELIA stared at the red-cheeked girl in her bedchamber. The girl was bobbing curtsies, her cheeks growing redder by the minute.

"I don't know, m'lady. Monsieur Brion said I was to look after you. Shall I help you with your gown?" Nervously, she came toward the princess, who continued to stare at her as if she were some unknown member of the animal kingdom.

Cordelia spun on her heel and marched into the salon, which was lit only by two candles on the mantel. "Monsieur Brion!" She called for him at the top of her lungs. And when he didn't immediately materialize, she yelled again. She paced the Turkey carpet, from window to door, her hands gripped together so tightly that her knuckles were white.

"Princess. Did you call?" Brion appeared from the kitchen. He was still fully dressed in livery and would remain so until the prince had gone to bed. He looked anxiously at the princess.

"Where's Mathilde? What's that girl doing in my chamber?" She rapped out the questions, so filled with dread that her voice was a high-pitched staccato rattle, bearing almost no resemblance to her own.

The majordomo pulled nervously at his chin. "The prince told me to summon Elsie to attend Your Highness," he explained.

"*Where is Mathilde?*" She took a step toward him and involuntarily he edged backward.

"The prince said Mistress Mathilde had to go somewhere." Brion was wringing his hands apologetically as the white-faced Fury, eyes ablaze, advanced on him.

"*Where? Where has she gone?*"

Unhappily, he shook his head. "The prince didn't say, my lady."

"But Mathilde. She must have said something." It was unreal to imagine that Mathilde would disappear without a word.

"I didn't see her, my lady. She was in your bedchamber last I knew, then the prince came up before the banquet and spoke with her. I haven't seen her since."

Cordelia was beginning to feel as if the world had tilted into insanity. This couldn't be true, it couldn't be happening. "Her belongings. Has she taken them?"

"I don't believe so, madame." To his relief, he saw that the princess was beginning to calm down. The light of madness was slowly dying in her eyes, and her voice had resumed its normal pitch and volume.

"Have you been told to send them on anywhere?"

He shook his head. "Not as yet, my lady."

Cordelia nodded slowly. "Very well. Thank you." She turned and went back to her own room, closing the door quietly behind her.

Elsie still stood where she'd left her in the middle of the room, gazing anxiously at the door through which her mistress had disappeared—and now reappeared.

"Should I help you now, my lady?"

Cordelia didn't appear to hear. She resumed her pacing, nibbling at a loose thumbnail. Why would Michael send Mathilde away? How had he done it? Mathilde would not have abandoned Cordelia willingly or easily. He must have come up here before the banquet had begun, after she had defeated him so soundly at the card tables. And he'd said nothing to her the whole evening.

The banquet in the opera house had not begun until ten o'clock and had dragged on interminably into the early hours of the morning. Michael had sat beside her, saying nothing to her, confining all his conversation to those around them. They were all strangers to Cordelia, and because her husband didn't address her, neither did anyone else, leaving her feeling as if she were sitting invisible in a freezing void. Once the dauphin and his bride had been escorted from the opera house, the prince had said in a cold undertone that she now had his leave to return to their own apartments, where he would join her at his pleasure.

Cordelia didn't make the mistake of assuming she had a choice. She had simply curtsied and left. She had come up to bed and found Mathilde gone, just as Michael had planned it.

Her head began to ache anew and her body throbbed with weariness. She had been up and wearing court dress for almost twenty-four hours, and the heavy weight of damask and the constriction of her corset was a torment in her fatigue. She was too tired tonight to deal with this. She wanted Mathilde. And the thought of what Michael might have done to her nurse buzzed in her brain like a tormenting bee. She had never believed anyone could defeat Mathilde, could force Mathilde to do anything she didn't believe was right. So how had he compelled her departure?

"Should I help you, madame?" Elsie ventured again. She knew what she was supposed to do but didn't know how to respond when she was prevented from performing her tasks. Experience, however, had taught her that if she failed to perform those tasks, she would be blamed regardless of the reason.

"Yes . . . very well, yes, you may assist me," Cordelia said vaguely.

Relieved, Elsie ran forward to unbutton, unhook, unlace with reverent hands. Cordelia stood stock-still, offering little help, too absorbed in her own thoughts to be really aware of what was happening. She shrugged into the white velvet chamber robe that Elsie held for her, and sat on the dresser stool, beginning to unpin her hair.

"Oh, I must do that for you, madame." Elsie leaped forward. "I've never waited on a lady before," she confided, pulling out pins hastily. "So I hope I'm doing things right." She picked up the ivory-backed brush and began to draw it through the rippling blue-black cascade falling down Cordelia's back.

Cordelia didn't respond. She was still thinking furiously. Mathilde would come back. She would come to her even if she'd been forbidden by the prince. If she was physically capable of doing so.

The door opened behind her and her heart jumped into her throat. She looked at him in the mirror in front of her. He stood in the doorway. He had removed his sword, but apart from that was still dressed in his wedding finery, the gold emblem of Prussia pinned to his sash.

She drew the folds of her chamber robe tighter around her as she rose to face him. "Where is Mathilde, my lord?" She spoke without inflection, but her eyes were filled with anger and contempt. Not a shadow of fear. She had gone beyond fear.

"She has been replaced as your abigail." He smiled his asp's smile. "I told you that you had need of a woman with more experience of the duties of a lady's maid at Versailles than some elderly nursemaid."

"I see." Still her voice was flat. "Elsie informs me that she has no previous experience of an abigail's work anywhere, let alone Versailles. But I daresay you assume that she comes by the required knowledge in some other way. Perhaps she breathes it in, or it comes to her in dreams."

Michael's pale eyes became opaque. For a minute he couldn't believe what he was hearing. This cold, derisive sarcasm from a chit of a girl, and in front of a servant to boot. Then a muscle twitched in his cheek, and the pulse in his forehead began to throb, and his eyes became cold and deadly.

Cordelia knew that she had not aroused his anger to this extent before, and despite the desperation that fueled her defiance, sick tremors of fear started in her belly. She fought them down, forcing herself to meet the threat in those terrible eyes. What could he do to her worse than he had already done?

"Get out of here!" He spun round to the petrified Elsie, who with a little gasp dropped the hairbrush and fled the room, ducking past the prince in the doorway.

Michael flung the door closed. He came across to her and she stood her ground, still meeting his eye, her chin held high.

"By God," he said softly, "I will break you, madame. I will break you to the saddle like any self-willed filly." He took the sides of the velvet robe and threw them open. His eyes dropped to her body, white, naked, its perfection marred only by the traces of his previous possessions.

An hour later he left her. He was humming to himself as he went into his dressing room, where his valet still waited to put him to bed. He had not removed his clothing beyond what had been necessary to achieve his purpose and now, still humming softly, allowed the man to undress him and hang up his clothes in the armoire. The valet assisted the prince into his chamber robe and then stood waiting, his hands folded, to see if his master had further orders for him.

"Bring me a glass of cognac and then go."

The man obeyed, bowed a good night, and soundlessly left the room, thankful for his dismissal. He had found it impossible to close his ears to the ugly sounds coming from the princess's bedchamber.

Michael drained the cognac in one gulp. Taking from his pocket the key that he'd automatically transferred from his suit coat, he went over to the chest, unlocked it, and took out the present journal. He refilled his glass, then stood leafing through the daily entries. He sipped from his glass, his mouth taut. Had the lock been opened deliberately that morning? He couldn't believe that it had been anything but an accident. Nothing appeared to have been disturbed, at any rate. It was extraordinary that he could have been careless, but it seemed the only explanation—he must not have secured the padlock properly the previous night. He had perhaps been overly anxious to get to his wife.

He walked into his adjoining bedchamber and placed the journal on the secretaire. Then he returned to the chest. He drew out the volume for 1765. His mouth grew thinner, his frown deeper, as he read through the entries. Throughout, his comments indicated that Elvira bloomed, daily increased in beauty. How much did that beauty owe to her triumph at cuckolding her husband?

He snapped the book closed and drained his glass once again. He replaced the journal in the chest and went back to the secretaire. Dipping quill in the inkstand, he began the day's meticulous entry. It was long, containing as it did a detailed description of the wedding, the demeanor of the royal party, and the subsequent celebrations. Only then did he describe the last hour with his wife.

He placed his pen on the blotter and stared unseeing at the doodling pattern of dripping ink. Cordelia was bidding fair to become as unsatisfactory a wife as Elvira had been. But he had failed with Elvira. He would not fail with this one. He would master this one in life.

Cordelia lay naked on the bed, curled into a tight ball, her body convulsed with violent shivers, dry sobs gathering in her throat. It had been worse . . . much, much worse than usual. If he had hurt her in rage, she thought, it would have been easier to bear. But he had used her, inflicting pain with an icy deliberation that had negated her very self, had reduced her to an animal, soulless, spiritless, worth no more than a clod of earth.

She knew she had cried out during the worst of it, although she had sworn to herself that she would keep silent. Now her weakness filled her with self-disgust. Perhaps she deserved such treatment. Perhaps she'd invited it with her cowardly cringing. A wave of nausea rose invincible and she rolled off the bed with a moan, reaching for the chamber pot. She could see herself in her mind's eye, crouched on the floor, vomiting helplessly with shock and self-disgust, a trembling, fearful, beaten animal.

But as the heaving of her stomach quieted and cold sweat misted her skin, her brain seemed to clear. The vomiting had somehow purged her spiritually as well as physically. She rose unsteadily to her feet, looking around for something to cover her chilled nakedness. The robe he'd torn from her lay on the floor, and she pulled it on, huddling into it. She looked around the dark room, where the shapes of the furniture stood out gray against the gloom. The window was a black square, but beyond she could see the faintest lightening at the edges of the darkness.

She could not sleep. She could not get back into that bed. She wanted Mathilde, with the deep, overpowering, speechless need of a wounded child for its mother.

Without any clear thought, she left the bedchamber, crossed the salon, and let herself out into the corridor. Candles in wall sconces lit the deserted expanse, and as the door to the apartment closed behind her, a great wave of relief and release broke over her. She was free. Out of the stifling, shackling darkness of her prison. Where she was going or what she was doing were questions that didn't even pose themselves. She clambered painfully onto a broad windowsill overlooking an inner courtyard, gathered the robe securely around her, rested her head on her drawn-up knees, and waited for daylight. Waited for Mathilde.

Leo left a card party just as dawn streaked the sky. He was mildly the worse for cognac. Cards, cognac, and companionship had seemed the only distractions from the niggling unease that made sleep an impossibility. He couldn't separate Cordelia from Elvira for some reason. He was bound to them both by ties whose similarity he couldn't explain to himself. Elvira was his sister, his twin. He loved her unconditionally. Her welfare was his responsibility. And now he was haunted by the idea that perhaps he had failed to meet that responsibility.

Cordelia was a young girl whose life had touched his by chance for a few weeks. He lusted after her. If he was truly honest, he could admit that to himself. But pure lust and a passing responsibility didn't account for what he felt toward Cordelia.

The confused yet obsessional thoughts continued to tumble in his head amid the brandy fumes as he made his way to his own humble room on an outside staircase in the north wing. On an inexplicable whim, he deviated from his course, taking a side stair that led into the corridor outside the von Sachsen apartment. The closer he came to the door, the greater his unease. It was almost like a miasma filling the marble-floored passage.

He walked past the double doors. Turned and walked past them again. Then with an impatient shrug, he swung on his heel and started back the way he'd come. And then he stopped. Slowly, he retraced his steps. A crouched figure huddled on the deep windowsill. The figure was so still he hadn't noticed it at first.

The lustrous blue-black river poured down her back. Her face was turned from him, resting on her knees.

"Cordelia?" He laid a hand on her shoulder.

With a start she turned her head. Her eyes were almost vacant, dark holes in a face whiter than her robe. "I'm waiting for Mathilde."

Leo frowned. "In the corridor? Where is she?"

"I don't know. Michael sent her away. But she won't leave me. I know she won't."

He saw the shadow of the emerging bruise on her cheekbone. And he knew what he had been trying so hard to deny. Gently, he moved aside the robe at her neck. Finger bruises stood out against the smooth white skin. The well of rage was bottomless. Wave after wave broke over him. He saw Elvira, he saw the shadow in her eyes. He saw Cordelia, bereft, her spirit, her courage, her laughter vanquished.

Bending, he lifted her from the windowsill, cradling her in his arms. She said nothing as he carried her away.

He carried her through the quiet corridors and up deserted staircases, his heart filled with rage. She curled against his chest, her arms around his neck. Her eyes were closed, the thick lashes dark half-moons against the deathly pallor of her cheeks, and he thought she slept. Her breathing was deep and regular and he could feel her heart beating against his hand.

At the head of a steep stone staircase, he opened a narrow wooden door onto a small chamber. It was simply furnished with a bed, an armoire, a washstand, two chairs, and a round table beneath the narrow window that looked out onto the Cour de Marbre. It was very much a bachelor apartment.

Leo laid Cordelia on the bed and her eyes opened. They were startled, then frightened, then slowly her gaze cleared and he saw with a surge of relief that she was fully aware, the vacant look in her eyes displaced by knowledge and recognition.

He bent over her and unfastened the velvet robe, slipping a hand beneath her to draw it away from her body. His mouth was tight, his eyes grim as he examined her closely, gauging how badly Michael had hurt her. The marks on her body were not severe, but he knew that the real wounds had been to her self, to the determined, courageous, effervescent spirit that made her what she was.

Cordelia lay still beneath his gaze, her own eyes, fearless now, gazing up at him. She was warm at last and the dreadful shaking had stopped. But Leo's rage and pain were a palpable force in the room. His hands as he raised her arms, her legs, turned her over, were as gentle as a dove's wings, but his eyes were fearsome.

"I don't expect he did this to Elvira," she said softly. "She was different from me. Perhaps she didn't provoke him. I can't seem to help provoking him."

He was not surprised that Cordelia had guessed the

source of his mental agony. He had noticed how insightful she was when it came to her friends. He touched her cheek with a fingertip and she smiled.

"It was because I beat him at cards," she said, reaching up to hold his wrist, keeping his hand against her face. "He sent Mathilde away because I made people laugh at him." She turned her face against his hand and kissed his palm. "Please hold me."

Leo sat down and lifted her into his arms. She was fragile, almost insubstantial, reminding him of a skeleton leaf. Her bare skin was soft and warm beneath his hands, and he slid one hand around to cup the roundness of her breast. She moved against him, raising a finger to pull loose his cravat. She kissed the pulse at his throat, and her breath was a sweet rustle of need and longing against his skin.

"I need you to show me how it can be," she whispered with soft urgency. "I need to know that it doesn't have to destroy. It doesn't have to be vile. Once you showed me a little of what it could be like. Show me now, Leo. Please." It was a heartfelt plea, no hint of mischief or seduction.

"Make me whole again," she whispered, raising her head to kiss his mouth, her body lifting slightly on his lap. His hands moved over her of their own accord, tracing the contours of her form, the narrowness of her rib cage, the swell of her breasts, the flat belly.

She seemed to be coming alive under his touch; her body filling again with the vital spirit that made her who she was, opening again like a weather-torn bud under the rays of a sudden sun.

Slipping his hands free, he gently circled her neck, his fingers light as featherdown smoothing away the rough marks of Michael's imprints. He knew that what he was doing was right. Only by vanquishing Michael's prints upon her body could he heal her. "Are you sure you want this now, sweetheart?" he asked quietly. "It's so soon after he hurt you. Are you sure you're ready?"

She could feel her own pulse beating rapidly against his

fingers. His eyes were now dark and unreadable, but they seemed to swallow her whole.

"Please," she said again. Her voice was a plea, the residue of her pain and fear lingering, but the need in her eyes could not be denied. It was a need not for passion but for tenderness, for the healing touch that would close the wounds of violation.

He moved his hands to cup her face, tracing the curve of her cheekbones, the line of her jaw. He was terrified of hurting her, of making the wrong move, of frightening her. He passed his hands over her in a delicate caress, almost hesitantly brushing his fingertips over her nipples, looking into her eyes for the first sign of dismay, of withdrawal. And when he saw none, he bent his head to kiss her breasts, taking her nipple into his mouth, suckling, grazing, until he felt the crown of her breasts harden under his tongue.

Cordelia's head fell back against his shoulder, her naked body lying across his lap. She felt herself open and vulnerable, an offering for his eyes, his mouth, his hands, and she yet knew that to feel open and vulnerable here, with Leo, was safe, an essential part of the wonder of loving. Only once had she come close to understanding that wonder, but she knew with every breath she took that at Leo's hands tonight she was going to understand it fully.

He moved his mouth from her breasts to the hollow of her throat. "I'm so afraid of hurting you. I want to touch you, sweetheart, but I need you to tell me if I may."

"Please," she whispered. "Please touch me." She didn't seem able to move, her body was as languid as a cat's in the sun, and yet beneath the surface her blood flowed swift.

Leo's fingers moved between her parted thighs. Again, he hesitated, expecting her to tighten against him, but she remained open, passive, and yet there was nothing passive about the heat of her body or the swift rise and fall of her breasts or the sudden hardening of the sensitive bud that rose under his dancing touch. He watched her face. Her eyes were closed tight, but her lips were warm and red, and there was a translucent glow to her cheeks.

"Sweetheart?"

Her eyes opened. She stirred beneath his arousing touch. "I love you, Leo."

He smiled, moved his damp hand up over her belly, shifted her on his lap so that her head fell into the crook of his arm. He kissed her, this time with a touch of his own urgency, his tongue pressing against the barrier of her lips, asking, not demanding, entrance. Her lips parted immediately and his tongue explored the sweet cavern of her mouth. She moved beneath him now, and her own tongue joined tentatively with his.

It seemed to Cordelia that she had abdicated responsibility for her body. It seemed to know all on its own what to do, how to respond. She was aware of something building deep in her belly, a liquid fullness growing in her loins, and now she turned in his arms to press her nakedness against him.

Leo stood up, lifting her with him. She looked up at him and smiled slowly. "Is it time?"

"Only if you wish it," he said quietly, holding her against him, searching her expression. She reached up to touch his mouth with her thumb, running the pad across his lips in an unknowingly sensual gesture that was all the answer he needed.

Leo laid her on the bed again, then swiftly stripped off his clothes. Cordelia hadn't seen a naked man before. She gazed at the lean, powerful frame, the flat belly and narrow hips, the erect shaft jutting from the nest of curly black hair, the long hard thighs. And for an instant her body closed tight, shrinking in upon itself as if in defense against the intrusion of a violent trespasser.

Leo sat on the bed, his hand stroking her belly until he felt her relax again, her body become fluid beneath his touch. He was waiting for a sign and she gave it to him. She reached to touch his erect flesh, her eyes half closed as she felt him, learned his shape, his texture. Making of his strange flesh something she knew and understood. When she guided him within the moist portal between her thighs, she knew that she wanted this man inside her, making her whole as he joined with her in flesh and in spirit.

He gazed intently down into her eyes, looking into her very soul as he held himself at the very edge of her body. "Tell me how you feel, sweetheart."

She knew he wanted to pull something from her, something more than the responses of her body. He wanted to hear her say how much she wanted this. How much she needed it. That without it, she could never be healed, never be whole again.

"I need you so much. I love you so much," she replied, her eyes candid, her tongue lightly moistening her suddenly dry lips. "I want you inside me, Leo."

He drew her legs up onto his shoulders, running his hands down the backs of her thighs, cupping the curve of her buttocks. Then he entered her fully with one long, leisurely, deep movement.

And as she felt him moving within her, Cordelia fell from some great and miraculous height. She tumbled over and over, light as a thread of silk, through a golden ether. Her mouth was dry and she could hear little sobbing cries that on one plane she knew were her own, and when she landed and the liquid rush of her pleasure flowed from her she clung to her lover as he moved again within her, and again, taking his own pleasure now, savoring the glorious tightness of her honeyed sheath, until he withdrew from her and let his own climax cascade over him, his seed spilling warm and wet on her belly and thighs.

She stroked his back as he lay breathless upon her. Her legs had fallen to the bed in an ungainly sprawl, her heart was thudding, her body as limp as a newborn kitten's.

Finally, Leo rolled sideways, relieving her of his weight. He lay on his back, one hand flung across her belly, the other over his eyes. He waited for the guilt, the sour remorse, the biting self-contempt, but he felt only a wondrous joy as if he had both given and received a priceless gift.

"I can endure anything if you love me," Cordelia whispered, stroking his hand as it lay heavily on her belly. "You've made me strong again, Leo. You've given me back myself."

He stared upward at the molding on the ceiling, his joy and confidence seeping from him like lifeblood from a wound. If he loved her, how could he endure that she should go back to Michael?

"I will take you away from Michael," he said. "But I have to plan. If we act in haste, it won't work. It will be too easy to pursue us, and Michael has every legal right to do as he wishes with a runaway wife. Do you understand, Cordelia?" He sat up, caught her beneath the arms, and drew her up facing him. He cupped her face. "Do you understand what I'm saying?"

Cordelia nodded and smiled trustfully. "Yes. I will wait. And I will endure." She touched his face. "I swear to you that it won't be so bad now that I have you to love me. Nothing can touch me now, Leo. Nothing."

He shook his head almost impatiently. He had less faith than Cordelia in the power of mere emotion as shield and buckler. "You must go back now," he said heavily. "I will work as fast as I can to get you away, but for now . . ."

"Yes, I understand." She smiled, the same vibrant smile he had learned so reluctantly to love. "If only I could find out what happened to Mathilde." Her smile was wiped clean from her face and she stared in horror. "He couldn't have had her killed . . . or . . . or imprisoned, could he?"

"Of course not," Leo said with a confidence he didn't feel. Michael wouldn't resort to murder, he was certain, but an oubliette in some dark French prison wouldn't be hard to arrange for an errant servant.

Hurriedly, he threw on his clothes, while Cordelia shrugged into the robe. Her color had returned and the white velvet now accentuated her radiant beauty instead of drowning her deathly pallor.

"Let me carry you. Your feet will freeze on the floors." Marble and stone were hard on bare feet, and Cordelia didn't demur as he swung her easily into his arms. She felt very different this time. Stronger, firmer, more supple, no hint of leaflike frailty.

"I can defeat Michael," Cordelia said into his ear. "I am stronger than he is. I don't need to prey upon people in order to feel powerful. I will beat him at his own game, Leo."

"And what happened the last time you tried that?" he asked dryly. Much as this return of the vital Cordelia delighted him, he was only too painfully aware of the dangers.

"I'll be careful," she said after a minute. "I won't make the mistake of gloating again."

They turned onto the corridor that housed the von Sachsen apartments, and Leo felt Cordelia tense in his arms. His mouth tightened. The thought of putting her back into that hellhole filled him with revulsion, but he could see no alternative. Not for the immediate future.

As they approached the door a figure emerged from a corner of lingering shadows not yet pierced by the early light.

"Mathilde?" whispered Cordelia, almost in disbelief. Then she was struggling in Leo's hold. He set her down and she ran barefoot toward the woman who held out her arms to receive her.

"There, baby, there, baby," Mathilde crooned, stroking her hair, her back. Her eyes, sharp and bright and shrewd, looked over her nursling's head at the viscount. She seemed to read everything she needed to know in his face, because she nodded and a grim little smile touched her mouth.

"What did he do to you, Mathilde?" Cordelia straightened, pushing her hair out of her eyes, her retreat into babyhood passed. "Did he hurt you?"

"Bless you, no, dearie," Mathilde said briskly. "But he's

turned me off without a character, without a sou, just the clothes on my back. But never you fret, Cordelia, he'll not keep me from you."

"But what will you do? Where will you go? I can give you money, of course, but—"

"There's plenty of places for a body to lie quiet in this palace," Mathilde told her. "The place is a small city, with staircases and nooks and crannies everywhere. I'll be around, dearie. I'll be watching you even if you don't often see me." She didn't say that the prince had given her a choice of leaving quietly, or of being arrested on a charge of theft and spending the rest of her natural life in the Bastille, her nursling lost to her forever. The threat still hung over her if the prince ever laid eyes on her again.

She didn't say this, but Cordelia made a good guess. She looked at Leo, a question in her eyes.

"I'll take care of Mathilde," he said, turning to the elderly woman. "Cordelia will need you until I can get her away from her husband. I'll hide you and we'll contrive somehow that you should see her often."

Mathilde looked shrewdly at Cordelia, then again at the viscount. Then she nodded, but this time with brisk satisfaction. "Well, that's as it should be," she said obliquely. "I always knew it had to be. The little one will only love once. Just like her mother."

She drew Cordelia to her again and kissed her. "I'll get you something that will give you some respite from that brute of a husband, don't you worry now."

"What kind of thing?" Cordelia was immediately curious. Mathilde was as devious as she was clever, and she knew many strange arts. If she were pitted against Michael, Cordelia would put her money on her nurse anytime.

"Never you mind."

"Listen to me, Cordelia." Leo spoke urgently. He didn't have Cordelia's faith in Mathilde's ability to draw Michael's teeth, and even if he did have, the woman was offering no immediate solution. "You must promise me that you won't provoke him again."

"I can't let him think he's beaten me," she said fiercely.

"Swallow your pride for a while. Just until I can contrive something." He tipped her chin, forcing her to look up at him.

"I'll be very careful," she conceded.

"Not good enough! Do you love me?"

"You know that I do."

"And you have put this hideous situation in my hands. Haven't you?"

"Yes, but—"

"Therefore you will do as I tell you. I cannot help you if you don't do as I say. Is that clear, Cordelia?"

She hesitated, wanting to agree but knowing that her spirit would not allow her to give Michael even the illusion of victory. Then footsteps sounded from along the corridor behind them. Heels taptapping on the marble. Voices came closer. One of them belonged to a courtier acquaintance of Michael's. Cordelia had vanished like a white wraith through the door to their apartment and Mathilde had melted into the shadows, before Leo could move.

Leo swore under his breath. She had not promised. Didn't she understand that she had laid upon him the heaviest burdens a man could bear—her trust and her love? He had carried those burdens for Elvira too, but he had dropped them. He would not fail Cordelia in the same way. But dear God in heaven, how was he to protect her when she deliberately courted danger?

Cordelia closed the door to the salon. Monsieur Brion stood in the kitchen doorway, his expression startled as he stared at the barefoot princess in her chamber robe. Cordelia looked across the room and met his gaze steadily. She knew he and all the servants knew what went on at night behind her bedchamber door. Just as she knew how Michael misused them when it pleased him. Now, with her clear-eyed gaze, she offered the majordomo an alliance.

Monsieur Brion bowed. "Good morning, madame." Casually, he adjusted an ornament on a side table before saying, "His highness has not yet rung for his coffee."

Cordelia smiled. "Thank you. You may send Elsie to wake me with my chocolate in ten minutes."

Monsieur Brion bowed again, and Cordelia went into her own room. She threw off the chamber robe and climbed into bed. The sheets were cold. She pulled up the coverlet and smiled to herself. She would not break. *Now* she would not break. She had the love of her life. She knew what love was. And knowledge was power. The knowledge of love would protect her.

Chapter Fifteen

CORDELIA LAY ABED until ten o'clock that morning. She was filled with a great lassitude although no desire to sleep and could see no reason to get up when lying dreamily in bed was so pleasant. However, at ten o'clock she received a summons to attend the dauphine. Indolence vanished at the prospect of some private conversation with her friend after the stiff formality of the past weeks. She was also intensely curious about Toinette's experiences and impressions of her own new husband, the dauphin.

In dishabille she hurried into the salon to inform her husband of the summons. He was sitting at breakfast and looked up as she entered. His eyes slowly ran over her and she knew he was looking for the marks he had left upon her the previous night. He could see the blue bruise on her cheekbone, the series of finger bruises on her neck where he'd held her down. And she saw the triumphant satisfaction spark in his eyes.

She returned his scrutiny with a cool contempt and, to her own satisfaction, saw puzzlement replace the gratification in his gaze. She was supposed to be cowed, bruised, defeated. And she wasn't. If anything, she was stronger than she'd ever been, and she knew that strength radiated from her.

After a long minute, she curtsied deliberately. "Good morning, my lord." She held out the written summons. "I am to visit the dauphine this morning. I thought you would wish to know."

He took the paper from her and cast his eye over the message before commenting frigidly, "It is good that you remain in her favor. I would not wish you to become a member of her household, that would occupy you too much at court, but you will ensure that she continues to regard you with goodwill."

"She is my friend, my lord. Such friendships are not at the whim of politics." Her eyes flashed, her chin lifted. She loathed and despised him, and she would let him see it.

His brow darkened. "Have you not as yet learned the unwisdom of arousing my anger, Cordelia?"

"There are some things I find it difficult to learn, sir," she retorted, with another insolent curtsy.

He rose from the table and came to stand over her and with grim triumph she saw the frustration in his eyes. "You will learn," he said softly. "Make no mistake, my dear."

"Did Elvira arouse your anger, sir?" She regretted the words the instant they were spoken. She had promised Leo she wouldn't deliberately provoke Michael to violence, but it was too late now. He struck her mouth with the flat of his hand.

"You try my patience, madame."

The slap had not been hard enough to do any damage, but the shock and sense of violation still rocked her to her core. She couldn't keep the distress from her eyes, and she knew that he'd seen it. She had no choice but to leave him in possession of the field.

"If you will excuse me, my lord, I will prepare myself to wait upon the dauphine."

Instead of answering, he turned from her and returned to the table. Cordelia left the room.

In the privacy of her chamber, she touched her lips fleetingly with her fingertips as she examined herself in the glass. There was no swelling or bruising, but the bruise on her cheekbone was very noticeable. Would it be best to try to cover it, or to leave it and invent some lie? Toinette would be bound to ask.

"What gown should I put out, my lady?"

Cordelia jumped. She'd forgotten Elsie. The girl seemed to fade into the wallpaper when she wasn't actually doing something. She stood now behind the armoire, her hands twisting in her apron, radiating anxiety to please. Cordelia forced herself to smile. It wasn't the girl's fault that she wasn't Mathilde.

"Let me see." She went herself to the armoire, riffling through the contents. She needed a gown that would cover her throat. The prevailing fashion was for extreme décolletage, but she found a *robe à l'anglaise* of saffron muslin over a green satin petticoat. The gown had a wide lace ruffled collar and a muslin fichu that could be used to conceal a multitude of sins.

Elsie took the gown reverently. "Will you be powdering your hair, m'lady?"

"No, it's not a fashion I care for," Cordelia said. "On state occasions it has to be done, but not for every day."

"How tightly should I lace you, m'lady?" Elsie approached with a corset.

Cordelia bit back a sigh. "I'll tell you when to stop. But fetch my stockings first."

"The white silk ones."

"The white silk ones," Cordelia agreed. She didn't have any other kind of stockings, but presumably Elsie was not familiar with the contents of her wardrobe and dresser.

It took an hour of fumbling and innumerable questions before she was ready for the day. Elsie had volunteered no comment on Cordelia's bruises, but she had produced the hare's foot and box of powder without being asked. Cordelia brushed it lightly across her cheekbones. It didn't conceal the bruise completely, but as long as the marks on her neck and upper arms were invisible, she could find an excuse for a bruised cheek.

Monsieur Brion awaited her in the salon to escort her to the dauphine's temporary apartments on the ground floor of the palace.

She hadn't seen him since their strange, silent encounter that morning. She smiled quite naturally and wished him good morning. He bowed and a tiny conspiratorial smile touched his usually solemn mouth. "I trust you slept well, madame?"

"I find one sleeps much better knowing who one's friends are, Monsieur Brion."

"Quite so, my lady." He held the door for her.

Toinette was still in dishabille and jumped up from her chair when Cordelia was announced.

"Oh, Cordelia, how I've missed you. Come into my boudoir where we can talk privately." She cast her mentor, the Countess de Noailles, a look, half defiant and half appealing, as she said this. For all her newfound status as the wife of the dauphin of France, she was still awed by this stiff-necked arbiter of court ritual.

"You have but half an hour, madame, before you must be dressed for the opera."

"It's *Perseus*, isn't it?" Toinette wrinkled her small nose. "It's such a serious piece, and the music is tediously boring."

"It is His Majesty's choice," the countess stated, and that was the end of the discussion, at least in front of her.

"Maybe he did choose it, but I still think it a tedious and heavy piece," Toinette declared with a chuckle as she closed the door of her boudoir and at last they were alone. She flung her arms around Cordelia. "I have been so desperate to talk to you. What do they say about me? Do you hear anything?"

"You've been the cynosure of every eye," Cordelia said, happy to give her friend the information she wanted. "Everyone talks of your beauty, your composure, your grace. They say Louis-Auguste is a most fortunate man."

Toinette plumped down on a chaise longue. "What happened on your wedding night, Cordelia?"

Cordelia sat beside her. Not a comfortable question to answer. "The same as on yours, I imagine," she said noncommittally.

Toinette shook her head. "*Nothing* happened! Absolutely nothing. My husband kissed me on the lips at the door of my bedchamber and went away. He never came back."

Cordelia stared with incredulity at her friend. "Your marriage has not yet been consummated, Toinette?"

"No." The dauphine shrugged helplessly. "What am I to do?"

"Your women know this, of course."

"Of course. And my husband's gentlemen. I assume someone will tell the king. But was it *my* fault, Cordelia?" Toinette seized Cordelia's hand. "What did you do to entice your husband? I must have a child, you know that."

"I didn't need to do anything to entice my husband," Cordelia said on an acid note. "He was enticed enough."

"Then I do not appeal to my husband," Toinette wailed.

"Nonsense," Cordelia said briskly. "Even if that were the case, he would still bed you to get you with child."

"I suppose so. So what *is* the matter?"

"I can't imagine," Cordelia said. "Perhaps he's a virgin and he's scared."

"Perhaps I should write to *madame ma mère*?" Toinette considered. "But it's so embarrassing, Cordelia. I feel I'm lacking in some way."

"You are not," Cordelia reassured with the same briskness. "If anyone is lacking, it's Louis-Auguste."

"Oh, hush!" Toinette put her hand over her mouth to suppress a giggle. "You mustn't say such things about the dauphin."

Cordelia grinned. "Between ourselves, we can say anything."

"Don't ever leave me." Toinette grasped Cordelia's hand tightly, all laughter banished. "I feel so alone. I don't know how I'm to find my way. The Noailles is no help at all. She preaches and prates and sniffs and looks down her nose at me. She's so starched I think she must spend all day at the laundress."

Cordelia hugged her, hearing the tears in her voice beneath the attempt at humor. "All will be well, you'll see."

"It will be once my husband beds me and I conceive," Toinette said with grim truth. For all her childishness, she knew why she was married to the dauphin. She was in France to breed, to produce the children who would cement the alliance between Austria and France—the children who, for the people of France, would justify burying the age-old enmity between the two countries.

"So, what of you? Tell me about your husband." The dauphine, with one of her swift mood changes, turned her attention fully on Cordelia. "Oh, what happened to your cheek? Did you knock it on something?" She touched the shadow of the bruise with a gentle finger.

Between themselves they could say anything. "Since you ask," Cordelia said decisively, "I knocked it against my husband's hand."

"What do you mean?" Toinette looked aghast. "Is he cruel to you?"

Cordelia shrugged. "Let's just say that if Prince Michael showed no interest in the marriage bed, I should be a happy woman."

"Oh." Toinette took hold of her hand and held it tightly. "Shall I tell the king?"

"Oh, no, of course not!" Cordelia cried in horror. "The king wouldn't involve himself in such a matter. A man is entitled to treat his wife as he sees fit, you know that. If the king said anything to Michael, I don't know what he'd do."

"But it's terrible." Toinette glared fiercely at a crystal vase of hothouse orchids on the table beside her. "We have to do something. What about the children? Is he cruel to them too?"

"No, I don't think so. He leaves them to their governess." She frowned. "That's the other thing, Toinette. He has forbidden me to make friends with them. I'm to teach them about society and prepare them for their betrothals, but I'm not to love them or play with them."

"You aren't to be their mama?" Toinette was indignant. Her own mother had been the most important person in her life, and in many ways still was.

Cordelia shook her head. "They're so lovely, too,

Toinette. They're completely identical and they have such funny ways. I know they like to laugh, but there's nothing for them to laugh about in that ghastly mausoleum with that prune-faced Nevry woman."

Toinette's eyes suddenly brightened. "I have an idea. Why don't we bring them here?"

"Here? To Versailles? Michael would never permit it."

"But I'm the dauphine. The first lady at Versailles," Toinette declared with a haughty little toss of her head. "I can command anyone, even your husband."

"What are you suggesting?" Cordelia asked, her own eyes now glowing with anticipation.

"I shall tell your husband that I would like to meet his daughters. I'll say that you've told me so much about your new stepdaughters and for friendship's sake I wish to make their acquaintance."

"Tell him to bring them to Versailles, you mean?" Toinette was not usually the ingenious one in their relationship, but she was doing very well this morning.

"Precisely."

"Toinette, you're brilliant." Cordelia flung her arms around the dauphine and kissed her soundly. "It just might work."

"Of course it will work," Toinette declared with the same mock haughtiness. "And since the king loves me, I'm sure he'll give me his support if I ask for it. I'll write the command immediately and you may take it back with you."

"That might not be such a good idea," Cordelia reflected. "I don't relish being the bearer of ill tidings. He's going to hate the idea and he certainly won't care to receive a direct command from you at my hands; it will hurt his pride."

"Yes, I suppose it might." Toinette was deep in thought, then she clapped her hands. "I have it." She was flushed with excitement. "At the opera, I'll ask for you both to visit me in my box, and then I'll casually bring up the subject of the children with the prince, and then have my wonderful inspiration. How will that be?"

"Perfect." Cordelia nodded her satisfaction. "You're a true friend, Toinette."

"But isn't there anything I can do to help *you*?" Toinette asked passionately. "How can you stay married to a man who likes to hurt you?"

Her friend's distress was genuine and Cordelia knew it would torment Toinette. She almost told her that everything was really all right, that she could endure anything now. That Leo would take her away from her bondage when he could. But she didn't dare share that secret with anyone.

"It might get better," she said vaguely. "Let's not talk of it anymore, it'll only depress us."

"Oh, very well," Toinette agreed, stating with another lightning change of subject, "I am determined that I shall not acknowledge Madame du Barry."

"Why ever not?"

"She's a whore. The empress would never permit such a one at court and I don't see why I should be insulted by her presence." Toinette looked proudly at Cordelia and she was suddenly her mother's daughter.

Cordelia could see that Toinette was going to get herself into trouble. "The du Barry *is* the king's favorite. By slighting her it could be said you were slighting the king."

Toinette shook her head, her pretty mouth taking a stubborn turn. "She is an immoral woman and the king is living in sin. He cannot make confession while he keeps a mistress, and it's my God-given duty to help him change his ways."

Cordelia stared incredulously. She knew that Toinette could take strange notions into her head and become obsessed by them. She knew that the empress had imbued all her children with strong faith and religious conviction. But Maria Theresa, despite her high moral tone, was also a pragmatist. Such foolish opposition to the king would make Toinette a laughingstock.

"I think you should consider this very carefully," she said. "There's more to this than simple immorality."

"I know my duty," Toinette stated, folding her lips

together. "I know what my faith requires of me. I will not acknowledge that vulgarian whore."

Cordelia sensed she would get no further at this point. Perhaps during the wedding celebrations over the next few days Toinette's attitude to the king's mistress would not be noticed.

"Madame, it is time for you to dress." Countess de Noailles appeared unannounced.

Cordelia rose to her feet. "I'll see you later, Toinette." She kissed her, then stepped back and dropped a low curtsy. "I beg leave to depart, madame."

Toinette chuckled, much to the countess's disapproval. "You're supposed to curtsy three times to the future queen of France."

Cordelia did so, backing out of the dauphine's presence. Her eyes, alight with mischief, held Toinette's, who adopted an arrogant tilt of her head, until her ever ready laughter got the better of her.

Cordelia, thoughtful but still smiling, left the royal apartments. She glanced around the thronged hallway, where courtiers gossiped and servants scurried. She could see no sign of Monsieur Brion. He had said that since she presumably had not yet learned her way around the palace, she could summon any flunky to escort her back to the prince's apartments on the imperial staircase. Was it safe to suppose that for this moment she was out of her husband's observation? Surely he wouldn't have spies in the crowd. It was worth the risk.

But could she remember the way? It would have been easier if she'd walked it herself, but Leo had carried her. On the way to his apartment, she had been almost unconscious, and on the way back, she had been aware only of his arms around her, his closeness, her mind and body filled to over-flowing with the memories of his bed.

She made her way through the throng to a footman standing at the foot of a staircase. He bowed as she approached him.

"Do you happen to know where Viscount Kierston is lodged?"

"On one of the outside stairs, madame."

"Can you be more precise?"

The man's eyes sharpened. He had no idea whom among the hundreds of unfamiliar wedding guests he was talking to, but his service at Versailles had taught him to smell out an intrigue. "I could escort you, madame."

"That will not be necessary. Just give me directions."

She listened attentively. It sounded relatively straight-forward, and if she became lost, she could always ask someone else. With a nod of thanks, she disappeared into the crowd, leaving the curious footman to his speculations.

Once Cordelia had left the state apartments, she found herself traversing long marble corridors, climbing wide, shallow marble staircases, meeting only servants and the occasional hurrying courtier. Everyone at Versailles seemed to be in a tearing hurry, which, given the vast distances they had to travel and the frequent events they were required to attend, was perhaps understandable.

By the time Cordelia reached the staircase where Leo's apartment was situated, she felt as if she'd walked miles, but she'd recognized certain landmarks on the way and was certain she could find her way back to her own apartments.

Cordelia raised her hand to knock on the narrow wooden door, then decided against it. Boldly, she lifted the latch and pushed open the door. The room was empty. She stepped inside, closing the door quietly behind her. Then she took a deep breath of relief. For the moment, she was safe from prying eyes. She looked around the small chamber with a sense of wonder. Everything was just as she remembered it. The room was filled with Leo's presence. She could almost smell his own special scent in the air. She touched the bed, the pillow, looking for the indentation of his head, his body, remembering the crispness of the sheet against her back as he held himself above her.

She opened the armoire and stroked his clothes, taking secret guilty pleasure in the feel of the garments that had touched his skin. She rested her cheek against a velvet coat that she remembered him wearing at Compiègne.

"Cordelia, what in the devil's name are you doing here?"

She jumped, spun round. Leo stood in the door.

"What's happened?" He kicked the door shut behind him and came toward her.

"Nothing." She ran to him, flinging her arms around his waist. "Nothing's happened, but I had to find out if it was real. Did it really happen? Do you really love me, Leo?" She looked up at him, her head tilted against his breast. "Tell me I didn't dream it all."

"You didn't dream it all," he said wryly. "But you shouldn't be here, Cordelia."

"No one saw me." She released his waist and stood on tiptoe to kiss him. "Prove that it wasn't a dream, love."

The passion in the sapphire depths of her eyes was purely erotic, and Leo felt his bearings slip. She came into his embrace with a little sigh, her face lifting for his kiss, her eyes wide open, her lips parted eagerly, a soft flush on her cheeks.

He took her mouth with his, felt her lean into him, yielding every muscle and fiber to his hold so that if he dropped his arms from around her, she would sink to the floor.

He bore her backward to the bed. She fell in a tangle of skirts, her arms around him, pulling him down with her. She wouldn't release his mouth, her hands clasping his head as she drank greedily of his mouth as if it were a goblet full of the sweetest hippocras.

He grabbed her wrists behind his neck and broke her grip as he pushed himself up onto his knees. She lay beneath him, her skirts lifted in a tent on the wide hoop. She gazed up at him, her tongue moistening her lips, her eyes wild with excitement, her cheeks pink. He threw her skirts up to her waist, baring her long creamy thighs encircled by lace-edged garters, the thick curly bush at the base of the smooth white plane of her belly, the sharp pointed hipbones, the tight whorl of her navel.

He feasted his eyes on the sight as she lay ready and waiting, her hips shifting eagerly, her thighs parting to reveal the faint dew of arousal on their satiny inner slopes.

Her fingers were busy on his britches, unbuttoning him, as he knelt above her, her breath coming swift and hot from her parted lips. His hard flesh sprang forth. She enclosed him in her fist, holding him, feeling the blood pulsing in the thick corded veins. Her thumb brushed over the tip of the shaft where the moist drops of his own arousal gathered. She smiled up at him, raised her hips, and guided him inside her. It was as if she had always known how to do this.

The current of joy at their joining leaped through them, so explosive they both cried out. Leo held himself above her, his weight on his flat palms; his mouth came down on hers, stifling their cries. He moved slowly within her, trying to prolong the moment yet knowing it was hopeless. There was too much spontaneous excitement in this coupling and no way he could control his own arousal let alone Cordelia's rippling convulsions of pleasure.

"No . . . no," she whispered urgently against his mouth, sensing that he was going to leave her. "Stay with me."

He wanted to stay forever in the heavenly chamber of her body. He wanted to feel her joy against his flesh as his own burst from him. But caution prevailed. He kissed her again, holding himself on the edge of her body as the wave broke over her, then he withdrew from her just as his own climax ripped through him. He fell heavily upon her, tossed and tumbled in the sea of sensation, his heart beating wildly against his ribs so that Cordelia could feel its pounding against her bosom as if his heart was trying to break through flesh to join with hers.

She stroked his hair, her eyes closed on a warm red darkness. She was at peace, as if she had come home. Her body's pressing hunger had been for the moment assuaged, and the love she felt for this man had found expression. And she knew with the deepest joy that his for her had been contained in the loving of his body.

Slowly, Leo raised his head, pushed himself back onto his knees, and looked down at her.

She smiled impishly. "I think I'm learning this business very quickly, don't you?" She raised her arms above her head and a ray of sunshine caught the serpent bracelet encircling her wrist. The diamond slipper glittered against her white skin.

He took her wrist, turning it over as he examined the bracelet. The serpent who tempted Eve. Eve who tempted Adam.

But Leo had bitten the apple with full knowledge of its consequences, and now this woman was in his heart. He would love her and he would protect her.

"What are you thinking? You look very stern." Almost shyly, she touched his mouth.

He smiled. "I was thinking of the burdens of love," he said lightly. "Come, get up and tidy yourself. You must leave quickly."

Cordelia swung herself off the bed, straightening her skirts. She tidied her disordered hair in the mirror. Her skin was translucent, her lips reddened, her eyes glowing. "I do look wanton," she said in some awe.

Leo came up behind her. He placed his hands on her shoulders and looked into her eyes in the mirror. "You must not take risks, Cordelia. Do you understand me?"

"I won't take unnecessary risks," she promised. "Did you find somewhere safe for Mathilde?"

"She's with Christian at his lodgings in the town," he said shortly. "I will contrive a meeting for you later."

"You're cross again," Cordelia accused, turning from the mirror. "I hate it when you're vexed with me."

"Then do as I tell you," he said as curtly as before. "You are a very frustrating child."

"No child," she said with another impish chuckle. "Children don't know what I know." She reached up to kiss him again. "Children can't do what I can do." She whirled to the door, blew him another kiss over her shoulder, and vanished, leaving him shaking his head at empty space.

Chapter Sixteen

MICHAEL WAS WAITING for her when she returned to their apartments. "Just where have you been?" His face was dark and she felt the barely controlled threat behind his words. It was not difficult to heed Leo's warning. However much she was prepared to defy Michael, she couldn't bear him to strike her again.

She curtsied politely. "I was summoned to the dauphine, my lord. As I told you."

"You left the royal apartments over an hour ago," he stated, coming toward her. "I sent a footman to inquire and to escort you back here. He was told you had already left."

It seemed she was always to be under observation. "After I left Her Highness, I went for a walk in the gardens, sir. There was no time to view them yesterday."

Michael didn't know whether to believe her or not. She was looking a little disheveled, her hair looser than it should be, the ruffles on her sleeves turned back. "You are untidy, madame. It does not suit my pride for my wife to be seen abroad looking as if she had slept in her clothes."

It was such a wonderfully apt comparison in the circumstances that Cordelia wanted to laugh despite herself. However, this situation did not warrant amusement. "The wind was brisk, sir. And when I realized that I had been out overlong, I hurried back. I imagine that's why I'm somewhat disordered."

Despite her politeness, her formal curtsies, Michael was not convinced that he had finally subdued her. There was something beneath the surface of those brilliant blue eyes that disturbed him.

Elvira had taught him to be alert to all the tricks and wiles of a beautiful woman. To know that when they plotted deceit, they were at their most innocent.

"If you would excuse me, sir, I'll go my bedchamber to tidy myself." She executed another perfect curtsy.

Michael regarded her coldly. She looked up and met his gaze with a stare as unflinching and penetrating as his, and he knew he'd been right. She was far from subdued.

"Go. We leave for the opera in half an hour." He turned away with a contemptuous gesture of dismissal. Cordelia went into her own bedchamber to summon the hapless Elsie.

When she returned to the salon, Prince Michael was at the secretaire, writing. Cordelia paused in the doorway. She didn't think he was yet aware of her. She watched, almost holding her breath. Was he writing in his journal again?

Suddenly, he turned, his expression as dark as before. "Why are you creeping around?"

"I wasn't. I just entered the room. I didn't wish to disturb you."

He turned back to sand the sheet and closed the book with a snap. Cordelia took a step closer. It was a ledger. "Do you keep track of the household accounts, sir?" She was so surprised that the question popped out before she gave it due thought.

"When I feel the need," he said, and she could see that he was coldly furious, but for once not with her. "When I sense some discrepancy in my wine shipper's bill. When the wine I drink doesn't match with the wine I've bought." He snatched up the ledger, locked it in the drawer of the secretaire, and strode across to his dressing room. The door banged shut behind him.

Was Monsieur Brion robbing his master? All servants did it as a matter of course. A few bottles here and there would go unnoticed in most aristocratic households. But surely Brion wouldn't have been stupid enough to leave traces for the prince? Perhaps Michael just suspected it. If so, he'd look for proof.

Michael returned, his expression as cold and remote as before. He offered her his arm and they left the apartments to join the throng hurrying to the opera house in order to be at their places before the royal party arrived.

In every bay in the colonnaded opera house hung a half chandelier against the surface of a mirrored backdrop so that the reflection offered a complete illuminated piece. The auditorium was ablaze with light from fourteen massive crystal chandeliers suspended on blue rope to match the cold cobalt blue of the theater hangings. Cordelia was accustomed to magnificence, but she had no words to describe this scene. The courtiers of both sexes seemed to scintillate as their jeweled garments and rich adornments caught the light. The buzz of voices rose to the exquisitely painted ceiling, drowning out the strings from the orchestra pit as the members of the orchestra tuned their instruments.

The prince was responding to greetings as they made slow progress to their own box. Cordelia curtsied, murmured her own salutations, her eyes missing nothing.

Their companions in the box were already seated, but the two front seats had been left for the prince and princess. She sat on the low cushioned stool specially designed to accommodate her wide hoop, arranged her skirts, opened her fan, and looked around. Michael was in conversation with their companions, so for the moment she was unobserved.

She saw Christian strolling through the pit, and her heart jumped. She leaned over the velvet-padded rail of the box, fanning herself indolently, the painted chicken skin of the fan facing her husband so that he couldn't see her face. Christian looked up and she signaled frantically with her eyes. His own lit up and he began to push his way toward her box. Just in time he remembered and stopped in his tracks. His eyes, filled with frustrated rage, moved to her husband. Cordelia realized with a start that her gentle-tempered, pessimistically fatalistic friend was ready to do murder. Presumably he knew the full truth if he now shared a roof with Mathilde.

Embarrassment flooded her. How could she bear that people should know of her nightly humiliations? She who had always been so unfailingly optimistic, so self-confident, so much the stronger partner in her friendships. But Christian was not people, she reminded herself. Toinette was not people. They were her friends and there was nothing shameful about depending on friendship for comfort and support. She didn't always have to be the strong one; she could show weakness too.

She mouthed a message to Christian and he nodded with a quick ducking movement of his head. Then he turned and pushed back into the pit.

Leo Beaumont stepped into a box opposite. He turned and said something to a lady in a crimson turban, sporting peacock feathers with diamonds and turquoises for the eyes. She laughed and Cordelia could hear her high-pitched whinny as she tapped the viscount's wrist with her fan. Leo merely smiled and settled into his seat. Punctiliously, he bowed toward Michael's box. Michael returned the salute; Cordelia bobbed her head. She could feel Leo's tension on every current of air that crossed the space between them.

Michael, however, seemed quite unaware that there were two men in the opera house prepared to challenge him to the death. Casually, he took a snuffbox from his pocket. Cordelia had spent her life at court and knew that court rules forbade any public enmity between courtiers. It would be an insult to the king. Men met socially, always the epitome of courtesy, while murderous hatred frequently simmered beneath the affable surface.

The arrival of the royal party put an end to these reflections as she rose with the rest of the audience. The king and his family took their places in the royal box, the court sat down again, the music began.

It was a tedious opera, the music heavy and boring. The chandeliers were kept alight throughout so that people-watching rapidly became the chief entertainment as the performance lumbered along on the stage. Toinette was looking very bored, fidgeting in her chair, whispering to her companions.

Cordelia allowed her thoughts to run along their own channels until the interlude of ballet at the end of the first act. Toinette, who adored dancing, also sat up, leaning forward to watch attentively.

It was a charming piece, but Cordelia was particularly struck by one young dancer's solo. The girl was exquisite, dainty, and an excellent ballerina. Cordelia leaned over the edge of the box. Christian was sitting rapt in the first row of the pit, just behind the orchestra. Cordelia recognized the tilt of his head and knew that he was lost to the world, every fiber of his being concentrated on the music . . . and perhaps also the stage.

Could his attention also be held by the dancer? she wondered with a surge of interest. It would be a wonderful partnership. Christian's music and the girl's inspired dancing. Maybe more than a working partnership, she caught herself thinking. Christian needed someone to care for him, to love him for his genius and his gentleness and shake him out of his pessimistic glooms. And she wouldn't always be around to do it. Not if Leo took her away . . . Her fingers curled into her palms and she breathed deeply for a minute.

"Do you not find that dancer very talented, sir?" she observed to the man sitting behind her. "Does she dance often for the court?"

"She's been fortunate enough to catch the king's eye," the Duc de Fevre told her.

His duchess chuckled behind her fan. "And we all know what that means. The little Clothilde is on her way to a nice little billet in the Parc aux Cerfs."

The king's private bordello—that would not suit Cordelia's tentative plans at all.

"She comes of a very respectable and devout merchant family, I'm told," Prince Michael remarked. "I understand her father is very resistant to her appearing on the stage, and one can only imagine how he would view her residing in the Parc aux Cerfs, even with the king as lover."

"But dare a man defy his sovereign?" the duke said. "Droit de seigneur ..." His rather squeaky titter was unpleasant.

"Aren't the girls selected by Madame du Barry?" Cordelia inquired, her eyes wide over her fan.

"The king usually states a preference, madame," the duchess informed her.

Cordelia could tell that Michael wasn't too happy with the tone of the conversation. He moved restlessly in his seat, his mouth pursed and tight. "Do you enjoy the ballet, my lord?" she inquired, trying for a demure little smile.

"I find I prefer the opera," he said as pleasantly as behooved a man who knew appearances must be maintained.

"*Perseus* in particular, sir, or opera in general?" She plied her fan.

Michael's answer was lost as a footman arrived in the box. "Her Highness the Dauphine requests the pleasure of the company of Prince and Princess von Sachsen."

Michael looked for once approving. Cordelia rose, reveling in the mischievous thought that he might approve of his wife's influence when it came to the notice of the dauphine, but when he heard where else it had led, he was going to be *very* discomposed. But he wouldn't be able to blame her.

She placed her hand on his proffered arm, and they proceeded to the royal box, the flunky clearing the way for them with booming shouts of "Make way for Prince and Princess von Sachsen." On stage the ballet continued with or without the attention of its audience.

The king greeted Michael amiably and offered his hand to Cordelia with a cheerful "Ah, the other little Viennese. Princess von Sachsen, the card player par excellence. You should know that I find myself very well pleased with those who come from Schonbrunn." Cordelia curtsied and kissed his hand. The dauphin greeted her with a stiff nod that denoted ill ease rather than arrogance. Toinette gave her her hand to kiss.

"I heard how thoroughly you carried the day at lansquenet the other evening, my dear friend. You must teach me some of your skills." Her eyes sparkled.

"I believe you are as skilled as I, madame," Cordelia said, hiding her grin.

Toinette's eyes went meaningfully toward Cordelia's silk reticule, hanging from her wrist by a ribbon. Cordelia nodded. They both knew about the tiny mirror it contained. A mirror that could be concealed in the palm of a hand that might be casually resting on the arm of another player's chair.

"How do you enjoy the opera?" Toinette changed the subject.

"It is a most solemn, weighty piece, madame," Cordelia said gravely, her own eyes dancing.

"That is hardly an answer to Madame the Dauphine's question," the king said with a guffaw. "Do you find it as tedious as everyone else appears to?"

"Perhaps I am not a good judge, monseigneur." Cordelia curtsied again and was rewarded with another hearty guffaw. "I can see from your eyes, madame, that you tease me. Shame on you. Prince Michael, did you know you had taken such a tease for your bride?"

"The princess has a very pleasing humor, sir."

It must have been a real effort to get that out, Cordelia reflected. The words probably scorched the back of his throat. She smiled at him over her fan. "My husband is too kind."

"Tell me, Prince, about your children." Toinette demanded in her clear bell-like tones. "Before we left Vienna, Cordelia and I had much talk over her role as a mother. Are they pleased to have a new mother?"

Michael bowed, clearly taken aback by this unexpected

topic. "My daughters are dutiful, madame. They will respect their stepmother."

"I would dearly like to meet them," Toinette said artlessly. "Could it be arranged that they could come to Versailles during the remainder of the wedding celebrations?" She turned rapidly to the king before Michael could marshal his senses. "May I invite them, *Grandpère*? My very first guests to the palace."

The king was well on the way to adoring his new granddaughter-in-law. He patted her cheek. "Yes, indeed. A capital idea. There's nothing like children at court. Send for them at once, Prince. We should be delighted to notice them."

The notice of the king was a signal honor as much for the children's father as for themselves. Michael bowed and murmured his gratitude. Cordelia exchanged a wink with Toinette.

"You must send for them directly, Prince," Toinette declared. "In fact, perhaps you should fetch them yourself. We shall look after your wife in your absence." She smiled radiantly, with the air of one who knew she was being wonderfully generous. "Is that not the best idea, *Monseigneur Grandpère*?"

"If you wish it, my dear," the king said with a benign beam. "And I shall look forward to getting to know Princess von Sachsen. You must have her more in your company."

"That would please us both," Toinette said.

"It would please me immeasurably, madame." Cordelia curtsied. Beside her, Michael struggled to hide his own feelings. Somehow, in five minutes he had been temporarily dismissed from court and his wife elevated to the side of the dauphine and the particular attention of the king. The honor to his wife reflected upon him, but he had been manipulated in some way. He looked suspiciously between the dauphine and his wife and caught the exchange of a conspiratorial smile.

If Cordelia became an intimate of the dauphine's household, she would be beyond his observation for long periods of time. He could not follow her into those circles and he could not forbid her to obey a royal command. She would effectively be beyond his jurisdiction except at night.

Was his youthful bride cleverer than he could have imagined? Cleverer even than Elvira? A chill ran down his spine.

The arrival of other visitors to the royal box was their signal to leave. Toinette squeezed Cordelia's hand in private communication while saying graciously for the benefit of the prince, "Do pray come to me in the morning, Cordelia. We can plan amusements for your stepdaughters when your husband brings them to us."

Cordelia curtsied and murmured acquiescence. Toinette had gone a step further than they'd planned, but she had no fault to find with the prospect of being husbandless for a night or maybe two.

Michael stiffly escorted her back to their box as the orchestra began tuning up for the second act. "Will you excuse me for a minute, my lord? I have need of the retiring room," she murmured as they reached their box, slipping her hand from under his arm.

He was looking thunderous, but she couldn't imagine how he could blame her for the dauphine's command, backed by the king's cheerful approval. Even if he suspected she had had a part in it, he could never be certain, and he couldn't openly object. He didn't respond to her polite excuse, merely marched into the box, leaving her behind.

She slipped away into the crowded theater foyer, where people lingered, chattering, obviously preferring this entertainment to what was on offer on the stage. Christian was waiting for her beside the tapestried screen that half concealed the entrance to the ladies' retiring room.

She came up to him without giving him so much as a glance and began to examine the embroidery on the screen with every appearance of interest.

"How are you?" Christian whispered, staring out over the

crowd, his lips barely moving. "That bastard . . . I cannot bear to think of it, Cordelia."

"I can endure it," she reassured. "While I have my friends, love, I can endure anything. You and Leo, and Mathilde." Her voice shook for the first time. "Taking Mathilde from me was the worst, Christian. Without her I feel so alone in that hellhole."

"She sent a letter." Christian's hand went behind him. "And this."

Cordelia moved her own hand casually and received a small glass object and a folded sheet of parchment. Something hard was inserted into the fold. "What is it?"

"I don't know. I expect the letter explains. What can I do, Cordelia?" His whisper was anguished.

"Don't worry. I'm just so happy that you're close by." With determined cheerfulness she changed the subject. "What did you think of the solo dancer?"

"Divine," Christian responded promptly, his large brown eyes for a minute losing their melancholy softness.

"She's called Clothilde. Her father's a merchant in the town. Why don't you contrive an introduction? I'm sure someone in the musical community will know her."

"But what could interest her about me? She's exquisite and I'm just a musician under patronage. I'd bore her."

"*Idiot!*" Cordelia scoffed with an affectionate smile. "You have more to offer than anyone I know and—"

"Go into the retiring room!" His urgent whisper interrupted her and without a moment's hesitation she slipped behind the screen and vanished into the chattering crowd of women.

Christian ducked sideways, losing himself in a group of courtiers. Prince Michael stood at the entrance to the foyer, the opera house at his back. He was scanning the throng, frowning. Cordelia had been gone a long time for a simple visit to the retiring room. Folding his arms, he leaned against a pillar, watching for her.

Cordelia pushed through the crush of women waiting to

use one of the two screened commodes and found a quiet corner in the lavishly appointed salon, its mirrored walls doubling the number of its occupants. She opened Mathilde's note and, as she had guessed from the feel, a small padlock key fell into her palm. She dropped it into her reticule with a tiny thrill of excitement. Now all she needed was opportunity. She ran her eye over the contents of the note. She was to put three drops of the liquid in the glass vial into her husband's cognac before he came to her bed. He would sleep soon and heavily.

Cordelia dropped the vial into her reticule with the key and casually held the note to a candle flame. It caught, curled, fell to the tabletop in a scatter of gray ash. She drew several curious looks but she smiled serenely, as if she had a perfectly good reason for playing with a candle, and made her way to the door.

She saw Michael the minute she emerged. The little sick tremors started in her belly again. Had Christian's warning been in time? Forcing a social smile, she moved toward him. "There were a great many women waiting for two commodes, my lord."

A flicker of distaste crossed his eyes at the indelicacy of this blunt statement. "Come," he said curtly. "It's discourteous to leave our companions alone in the box."

For the remainder of the afternoon, Cordelia's fingers curled around her reticule, feeling the hard shape of the vial. If its contents put Michael to sleep, she wouldn't have to endure more than one assault at night. And she had the key too. For the first time in days, she had the sense of regaining control over her own life. She had the power now to take charge; she didn't have to be a defenseless victim.

And she and Leo would leave Versailles. . . .

But how? She was no ordinary citizen who could pack up and disappear without question. They would need passports to cross France, unless they stole away like thieves in the night. But they could be pursued. Adultery was a crime. It was a crime for a wife to leave her husband, and a crime for anyone to aid and abet her. If they were caught, Michael could kill them both with impunity. Or he could kill Leo and devise some other even more ghastly punishment for his errant wife.

The thoughts swirled in her head through the remainder of the dreary performance, and she rose with the same alacrity as those around her the minute the last chord had died away.

"I will escort you to our apartments, then I am engaged to meet with some friends," Michael state coldly.

"I can make my own way without escort, my lord. There's no need to trouble yourself," Cordelia said—a little too eagerly.

"It will be no trouble, madame," he said distantly. "I don't care for you to be roaming around the palace unattended. There will be no repetition of this morning."

Cordelia bit her lip. It was as good as a promise to put a guard on her. She said nothing, however, and having seen her inside the door, he left her with the curt injunction that she was to remain within until he returned in an hour's time.

Cordelia rang for Monsieur Brion, who appeared almost immediately. "Is there something I can do for you, my lady?"

Cordelia turned from the window where she'd been looking out somewhat wistfully. It was a fine soft evening and the gardens looked most inviting. "Yes, bring me tea, would you?"

"Immediately, madame." He bowed and turned back to the kitchen.

"Oh, and Monsieur Brion?"

"Madame?"

"I believe it might be wise of you to check your inventories and accounts," she said casually. "As soon as possible. Particularly those pertaining to the wine cellars."

He looked sharply at her, a spot of color appearing on his cheek, a touch of fear in his eyes. She merely smiled. He cleared his throat. "I'll see to it at once." A short pause. Then he bowed. "Thank you, my lady."

"One good turn deserves another, Monsieur Brion," she said serenely, turning back to the window.

"Indeed, madame. I'll bring the tea at once." The door closed behind her.

Cordelia smiled to herself. Making allies was a deal more satisfying than making enemies. And under Prince Michael's punishing rule, every member of his household must know who their allies were.

Chapter Seventeen

"WHAT IT IS to have influential friends," Cordelia announced jubilantly as she closed the door of the dauphine's boudoir the following morning. "Michael has gone to Paris and I'm free for at least twenty-four hours. That was such a clever idea to send him for the children."

"Wasn't it?" Toinette said smugly. Then her expression sobered. "I wish I could send him away altogether, Cordelia It's so terrible to think of him misusing you. Why can't I tell the king?"

"You know why." Cordelia curled onto the end of the sofa, kicking off her slippers. She was in dishabille and it was blissful to be without hoop and corset. "The king would be furious at being told something so distasteful. You know he doesn't like to hear anything unpleasant." She plucked a grape from the bunch on a side table.

"I assume he's heard about my husband's reluctance . . . failure . . . oh, I don't know what to call it, Cordelia." Toinette cut a handful of grapes with a small pair of silver scissors. "But I'm so embarrassed. Everyone must be whispering about it. And if he doesn't get me with child, they could annul the marriage and send me home again." She munched glumly for a minute. "Can you imagine being sent home to Vienna in disgrace? A failed wife? It doesn't bear thinking of."

"No," Cordelia agreed. "But it won't happen because someone will discover what's wrong and fix it."

"But what if it's me that's wrong?" Toinette wailed.

"How can it be? You're beautiful, you're an empress's daughter and an emperor's sister. You're young, you're charming. The whole country is half in love with you already, and the king adores you."

Toinette brightened considerably. "Yes, it does seem to be so, doesn't it?" Cordelia smiled slightly. Much as she loved her friend, she wasn't blind to her vanity. It was always easy to coax Toinette out of the doldrums with a few well-placed compliments.

"Was your husband very angry about having to go and fetch his daughters?" the dauphine asked, restored to her customary cheerful self.

"Yes, but he didn't take it out on me for once." Cordelia leaned forward to pour coffee into two shallow cups. "In fact, he didn't come to my bed at all."

"Ah." Toinette looked knowing. She took the cup Cordelia handed her. "I heard that the king gave permission for some of the courtiers to go to the Parc aux Cerfs for amusement last night. Perhaps your husband was one of them?"

"Perhaps," Cordelia mused, sipping her coffee. In the Parc aux Cerfs, Michael could have exhausted as many harlots as he needed in order to exorcise his rage. Maybe he had thought that taking it out on his wife when she had an early morning appointment with the dauphine might be unwise. "Where did you hear that?"

Toinette pinkened slightly. "I overheard Madame du Barry telling Noailles."

"You were eavesdropping? Shame on you!" Cordelia exclaimed, laughing. "You won't even recognize the du Barry with as much as a nod, and yet you listen in on her conversations."

"At least I don't cheat at the king's table," Toinette retorted. "I don't know how you dared, Cordelia."

"Well, ordinarily I wouldn't have done. But the temptation to get even with my husband proved overpowering." She selected a gingersnap from the tray and dipped it in her coffee.

"You used the mirror trick?"

"Yes and it worked beautifully. Not even Viscount Kierston could guess how I was doing it."

"Why should he?"

"He caught me a couple of times on the journey," Cordelia confessed. "With the notched dice. And he was most unpleasant about it."

"You are outrageous, Cordelia!" Toinette exclaimed.

Cordelia laughed merrily. She was feeling extraordinarily lighthearted, much as if she and Toinette were back in their own private parlor in Schonbrunn. Toinette's chuckle joined hers and neither of them heard the door open.

"What a delightful sound."

They both leaped to their feet. The king stood in the doorway, an indulgent smile on his face. The Countess de Noailles behind him looked far from indulgent.

"Monseigneur ... I ... I ... wasn't—You do me too much honor." Stammering, Toinette curtsied. Cordelia was already in a deep curtsy, wondering if she could unobtrusively catch her discarded slippers with her toes. To appear before the king in dishabille was unheard of. Barefoot added insult to injury. True, they hadn't been expecting him, but there was no way of knowing whether His Majesty would take that into account.

"Princess von Sachsen, how charming you look. Rise ... rise." The king accompanied the command with an illustrative gesture. "You will excuse us if I have a private word with Madame the Dauphine."

Thankfully, Cordelia curtsied her way backward, grabbing up her slippers as she slid from the room. She caught sight of Toinette's alarmed expression. The king didn't ordinarily visit even his granddaughter-in-law unannounced.

She hurried from the royal apartments. Her informal morning gown of peach muslin was very pretty, but it was clearly time to dress herself for the day. Gathering her skirts into her hand, she ran up the flight of stairs leading from Toinette's apartment, enjoying the freedom of movement, the ability to stride instead of glide. She whirled around a corner at the head of the stairs and bumped headlong into Viscount Kierston. She flung out her arms as if to steady herself.

"Oh, I wasn't looking where I was going!" Her arms had found their way around his waist. "But how very fortunate that it was you who saved me." She looked up at him, still clutching him tightly. "Would you believe I've just been barefoot in the king's presence?" Her eyes brimmed with the laughter that bubbled in her voice, and Leo saw again the carefree, mischievous girl who'd thrown roses at him in Schonbrunn. But underneath, he now detected the dark currents of experience, and he was filled with a great sadness. Cordelia would never again be that girl. She had had too many illusions shattered in too short a time ever to recapture her carefree girlhood.

"For pity's sake, Cordelia, let go of me!" he demanded, laughing, glancing over his shoulder. The corridor was for the moment deserted.

"No," she said with another chuckle. "You're my proxy husband again and it's your duty to catch me when I fall."

"What are you talking about?" Despite himself, he grinned down at her. She was utterly enchanting and her body was unconstrained, warm and fluid beneath the thin muslin gown.

"Michael has gone to Paris at the behest of the king and the dauphine," she informed him, her eyes shining. "They sent him to fetch the girls so that the king might notice them. Oh, you should have seen his face. He had to say how honored he was, of course, but you could see he was grinding his teeth in rage. And now I have no husband, so I must rely upon my proxy as escort at all the functions. Oh, and at the hunt in the morning," she added. "I can't wait for that, it's been an age since I've been on horseback."

Her arms still encircled his waist. Her breath was warm and sweet carrying the excited gush of words. He could see himself reflected in the turquoise pools of her eyes as he looked down into her face.

"I could come to you tonight." Her voice was now low, throbbing with sensual anticipation. "We could have all night, Leo. May I come?"

He fought to get his bearings. She was talking in riddles but all he could see were those huge brilliant eyes singing their siren's song, inviting him to lose himself in her sensual tempest. But one of them had to be sensible. Half laughing, half exasperated, he seized her hands at his back and tried to break her grip. "For God's sake, Cordelia, remember where we are. Let go of me, girl!"

"I haven't got my balance yet," she said wickedly, linking her fingers tightly to resist him. "And anyway, as my proxy husband, it's your duty to support me."

Leo glanced around again. Two courtiers appeared at the far end of the corridor. A door stood ajar on an empty antechamber across the passage. "Come here!" With a final tug, he succeeded in breaking her clasp, seized her wrist, and jerked her into the room, kicking the door shut behind him. "You are an impossible creature."

Cordelia chuckled. "We're quite safe here, though, aren't we?" With a swift movement, she darted behind him and turned the key in the door. "There, now you can relax. Nobody is going to come upon us unawares."

He didn't reply but his lips twitched. She was leaning against the door, eyes sparkling, lips parted. "I love you," she mouthed.

"And for my sins, I love you, you dreadful girl!" He pulled her into his arms, kissing her hard, before setting her back against the door. "Now, would you just begin at the beginning, please?"

"What room is this?" Mischievously ignoring his request, Cordelia looked around with every appearance of fascination. "It's like a junk room."

Leo massaged the back of his neck and found himself absently examining his surroundings. Cordelia's description had been accurate. Piles of furniture and boxes, covered paintings, and massive gilt frames littered the dusty marble floor. It looked as if the room hadn't been used for years. But Versailles was full of such places, even along the most populous corridors and staircases.

He pulled himself back to the issue at hand. "Never mind where we are, Cordelia. Just explain what the devil you were prattling about in the corridor?"

"I wasn't prattling," she protested. "I *never* prattle. I have got rid of Michael for a while and the girls will be here soon. And we can have a whole night together!"

She plunked down on the faded striped chintz, setting up a cloud of dust.

"Where has Michael gone?"

"To fetch the girls." She told him of Toinette's clever scheme. "And while they're here, I intend to make a lot of changes in their lives," she finished. "If the dauphine and the king take an interest in them, then they'll have to have my escort rather than the Nevry's, won't they?"

Leo frowned. "In theory. But I don't know how Michael will react in practice. Did he say how long he'd be gone?"

"No, but it can't be less than twenty-four hours. He hasn't said anything to me since the opera. I don't know where he was last night, but he didn't come near me, and Monsieur Brion said he left at dawn this morning." She jumped up again. "We'll have the whole night together."

"Brion will know that you're not there."

"Ah, but Brion and I are allies," she said with a decisive little nod of her head. "I am building my defenses, you should know."

His gaze sharpened. "Explain."

Succinctly she gave him the details of her unspoken alliance with the majordomo. "I am becoming adept at political scheming, my lord," she finished with another little nod.

He couldn't help laughing at her smugness, but neither could he hide his admiration. Cordelia was very young, but she could be remarkably sophisticated.

"Come to my room at midnight," he said with an apparent nonchalance that concealed the heady rush of arousal. He would plan for a night that would live in Cordelia's mind and body until her dying day.

"I won't be able to endure the waiting," Cordelia said with a catch in her voice. "How can I wait until midnight? It's but eleven in the morning now."

"You will learn, my sweet, that anticipation has its own rewards," he replied. His eyes were golden fires, ablaze with promise.

Abruptly, Cordelia sat down again. Her legs seemed to have gone to butter and she was not prepared for the abrupt change of topic, when he said coolly, sitting down beside her on the dusty sofa, "For the moment we have other matters to discuss.

"If you leave your husband with my escort, you will be going to a life of exile. Every court in Europe will know the scandal and we will be received nowhere. And you will always be in danger of recapture by your husband. Do you understand these things, Cordelia?"

"Yes, of course. I've thought of it myself. But we could live privately, couldn't we? As private citizens on your estates, or something? You do have an estate in England, don't you?"

"Yes, of course. But I don't think you understand what such a life could be—"

"Oh, but I do," she interrupted eagerly. "A life with you, loving you. Just the two of us. I can't think of anything more blissful."

Part of him wanted to agree, but he owed her the knowledge of reality. Love's first raptures didn't last forever. And how could he be sure that Cordelia's passionate convictions could survive a lifetime of their consequences? "My sweet child, you must consider." He was very grave now. "You're only sixteen years old. A life of a disgraced exile buried in the English countryside will pall very quickly. If we have children, they will be illegitimate. Have you thought of that?"

"No, I hadn't." She was frowning now, the light gone from her eyes. "But if they had us to love them, then—"

"While they're children, yes. But to carry that stigma for all their lives? Just consider, Cordelia."

"Then perhaps we shouldn't have any children," she suggested. "We'll have the girls, won't we? We can't leave them with Michael." She spoke the thought as it popped into her head. Everything had happened so fast, she hadn't had a chance to think further than this all-consuming love. But of course the children had to be a part of that love, of the future of that love.

Leo had had plenty of time to think. He took her hand. "No, I can't leave them with Michael. Not knowing what I do about him. They are Elvira's children and I am self-sworn to protect them."

"Yes, of course, I understand that," she said impatiently. "That's what I said—"

"Cordelia, listen!" He took her other hand. "To take a man's wife is one thing. Michael might agree to divorce you so that he would be free to take another wife. It's not impossible. But if I take his children—that's a crime punishable by death. Michael will *never* willingly give up his children."

"Then we'll have to go somewhere far away and take on other identities," she said simply.

Leo was silent, frowning down at the floor, absently noticing tiny footprints in the thick dust. Mice presumably.

Cordelia swallowed uncomfortably as the silence lengthened, then she drew a deep breath and said, "Do you not wish to take me away, Leo? Have you thought better of it? I understand, of course I do. The children are your blood. They must have first consideration."

"No, I haven't changed my mind," he said, raising his head. "I was merely trying to point out to you the difficulties. I'm no fairy godmother, sweetheart. I don't have a magic wand."

"I understand that," she said in a small voice.

"You cannot go back to Vienna—"

"No, of course I can't!" she exclaimed. "My uncle would simply send me straight back to Michael."

"As I was saying," he said repressively, "you cannot go back to Vienna. If I can procure a passport for you, you could perhaps travel incognito to England. My sister and her husband would take you in." His frown deepened. Lizzie was an impulsive creature with a head full of romance. She'd throw herself heart and soul into such a scheme, but her husband, Francis, was less impetuous. He might well fight shy of sheltering an adulterous relationship under his roof, particularly when the woman was sought across the Continent by an outraged husband and her own family. Cordelia, the goddaughter of an empress and the wife of a prince, was much less of a private citizen than he himself.

"You wouldn't come too?" she ventured.

"Not immediately. It would be suspicious if we disappeared together."

"And what of the girls?"

"Until I can find a way to get them away from Michael, I must be able to see them. Therefore I must stay close by."

"Yes, I see." She swallowed. Leo loved her. He loved her enough to save her from her husband. But his love and responsibility for his sister's children must take precedence. She understood that. She wouldn't argue with it. Loyalty to one's friends and loved ones was an imperative she could never deny. Leo had to find a way to handle the conflicting demands of two such loyalties. She could think of only one way to help him.

She sat up very straight, facing him across the separating length of the sofa. "I told you that as long as I have your love, I can endure anything, Leo. I can stay in this marriage, if I have you near me. If I know that I have my friends. Mathilde and Christian and Toinette, and *you*." Her eyes were bright with tears and the light of conviction. "I will stay with Michael until we can develop a plan that enables us to take the children with us. If you don't desert me, Leo, I can endure *anything*."

And again he thought bitterly that while love might make endurance easier for Cordelia, it made it impossible for him. He would send her to Lizzie as soon as he could arrange it. And then he would worry about the children. But since Cordelia would resist being sent away, he must make his plans in secret.

"I'll work something out," he said confidently. "But I do want you to think about the realities of life as it will be. Think very carefully, love, because once done, it cannot be undone."

"I *know* that. Do you think I don't?" she said, gripping his hands tightly. "I won't want it undone, Leo. *Never.*"

"Never is a very long time," he said, his smile disguising his racing thoughts. There was a whore in the Parc aux Cerfs whose brother-in-law was the chief of police on Ile de la Cité in Paris. For the right consideration, passports could be acquired. He could have Cordelia out of Paris within the fortnight.

And in the meantime, they had a whole night ahead of them. Deliberately, he allowed his mind to dwell on the images already building. As yet half formed, most of them, but the picture of the coming night was painting itself in sinuous silhouette.

"If you wish, this afternoon I'll conduct you to Mathilde." His voice was as calm as the Dead Sea, and he knew Cordelia couldn't begin to guess his erotic thoughts.

"Oh, that would be wonderful," she said. "I so miss her." She leaned into him, placing her flat palm against his cheek. "We'll make it work, Leo, I know we will."

The conviction of idealistic youth? The conviction of an incurable optimist? He turned his head to plant a kiss in her palm. "Come to me after the stroke of midnight." He tipped her chin and kissed her mouth, the delicate fluttering eyelids, the tip of her nose. "Now you must go."

He stood up, drawing her with him, unlocked the door, and stepped behind it, out of sight of the corridor. "Go, and don't look back."

He waited five minutes before stepping out himself, strolling casually down the corridor, blending with the crowd of courtiers hurrying to the king's levee. A tall slender man in a charcoal gray suit lined with crimson silk mingling easily with the scurrying throng. And behind the amiable smile exquisitely erotic dreams warred with the facts of a grim reality.

Prince Michael, arms folded across his chest, sat back in the cumbersome coach as it lumbered over the narrow road from Versailles to Paris. At his feet rested the leather chest. He was glowering in the dim interior of the vehicle. The leather curtains covered the windows, protecting the occupant from the curious stares and insolent observations of passersby on the carriage's frequent enforced stops at crowded intersections.

Two outriders attempted to clear the roadway ahead of the carriage, but often enough their whip-cracking orders were ignored by sullen-eyed peasants driving their cattle or produce to market. They stared at the gilded coach with the von Sachsen arms emblazoned on the panels, and one or two surreptitiously spat into the ground beneath the large painted wheels of the aristocratic conveyance.

Michael swore under his breath as the carriage slowed yet again. He still found it difficult to believe that he was driving to Paris to act as nursemaid for his children in the middle of the wedding celebrations. He could not believe that he had been manipulated by a schoolgirl—by *two* schoolgirls. That arrogant chit of a dauphine had definitely played her part. He could still see the complicitous glance she'd exchanged with Cordelia. They had been laughing at him. But he who laughs last laughs loudest, he told himself grimly.

He had no choice but to obey the king's orders, but if he could remove Cordelia from Versailles, then, of course, his children would have no reason to remain. He would have all three of them back in the palace on the rue du Bac, and he would make damn sure that they stayed there. His wife must become indisposed. An accident that would force her removal from Paris. A concussion, such as might result from a fall from a horse. Easily arranged if one knew the right people.

The coach lurched forward again. It was only a temporary solution to the problem of Cordelia. She was in her way every bit as unsatisfactory a wife as Elvira had been. For the moment, he still enjoyed bedding her, but that would pall eventually. He needed a son, and once she had supplied him with the child, he would be free to dispose of her. If he could arrange to leave Versailles, return to Prussia, he could concoct an accusation of adultery and banish her to a convent. It would be a neat solution and a very appropriate punishment for such a willful and flighty creature. It would take time to arrange his transfer out of France. He would have to petition his own sovereign, and Frederick the Great was not known to heed the personal wishes of his servants if they went against his own. But he could set the process in motion.

He closed his eyes, his foot unconsciously resting on the chest as the carriage jolted in a pothole.

It was midafternoon when he reached the palace on the rue du Bac. The household had been alerted by a runner of the master's impending arrival, and when he entered the cavernous hall, even his most critical eye could see nothing amiss. Monsieur Brion remained in Versailles, but his second-in-command was bowing respectfully even before the prince set foot in the house.

"When would you wish to dine, my lord?"

"Later," the prince said with an irritable gesture. "Bring claret to the library and send for Madame de Nevry immediately."

The majordomo went off to inform the harassed cook that he'd better delay the spit-roasting ducks, and sent a footman posthaste to the schoolroom.

Louise was nursing a cold, her head wrapped in a turban,

a blanket around her shoulders, a tisane, heavily doctored from her silver flask, in her hands. The little girls sat at the table, laboriously copying their letters. There was a lowering silence in the room to match the overcast sky beyond the shuttered window.

"My lord commands the governess to attend him in the library," the footman intoned from the door in a tone of studied insolence. The governess was ill liked in the household and treated with scant respect.

The children looked up, curiosity mingling with anxiety in their bright eyes. Louis sniffed and stared at the footman. "Prince Michael is at Versailles," she said thickly.

"No he's not. He's in the library and he demands your presence immediately." The footman sneered. The smell of brandy in the room mingled unpleasantly with the powerful distillation of herbs that the sufferer was periodically inhaling to relieve her congestion. He offered a mocking bow and departed, carelessly leaving the door ajar.

Louise rose to her feet in a flurry. The blanket dropped to the floor, her fingers scrabbled at the tightly wound turban. "Oh my goodness. What could have brought the prince here so unexpectedly? How can I go to him like this? Where's my wig? Oh my goodness, in my old gown, too!"

The girls watched, sucking the tips of their quills, their eyes shining with enjoyment at their governess's frantic antics. Their father's unexpected arrival meant little to them except that they would probably have to endure one of the dreaded presentations in the library that evening.

Fluttering, complaining, Louise crammed her wig onto her sparse gray hair. "I mustn't keep his lordship waiting, but, oh dear, how can I go to him in this old gown? What will he think?"

Her audience didn't venture an opinion, just continued their bright-eyed observation of the spectacle. Finally, Louise's mutterings faded as she scurried down the corridor, frantically smoothing her skirt, wondering if the mud on the hem of her petticoat was too noticeable. She'd worn it in the rain the previous day, but linen was expensive to launder and it hadn't occurred to her that she would see anyone but her charges for the next few days.

Amelia and Sylvie threw down their pens, simultaneously leaped to their feet, and did a silent dance around the gloomy room, celebrating their moment of freedom. It was a ritual they performed whenever they were free of observation.

"Do you think Madame Cordelia came with Papa?" Out of breath, Amelia fell in a panting heap into a chair.

"Yes, yes, yes!" squealed her sister excitedly, still dancing like a dervish in the middle of the room. "And Monsieur Leo too!"

Amelia jumped up again, grabbed her sister's hands, and they twirled in a circle, skirts flying, hair escaping pins, chanting the names of the two people who lightened their daily drabness.

"If she did, she'll come to see us soon." Amelia, a little less robust than her sister, collapsed onto the floor in a puff of stiff tarlaton skirts.

Sylvie dropped beside her, her legs sticking out in front of her like thin sticks from beneath her own ruffled skirts. "I wish," she said. "I wish wish *wish*!"

"I wish wish *wish*," her sister repeated fervently and they both sat still, closing their eyes tightly.

"What are you doing on the floor?" The outraged tones of their governess destroyed their dream. They both scrambled to their feet, guiltily brushing down their skirts, standing, hands folded, to gaze penitently at their governess.

Louise looked as if she'd suffered an acute shock. Her wig was slightly askew and two bright spots of color burned on her powdered cheeks. "Sit down at the table," she snapped, "and continue with your lesson." She turned back to the open door and called shrilly, "Marie . . . Marie . . . where are you, girl?"

"Here, madame." The flustered nursery maid came running.

"Pack Mesdames Amelia and Sylvie's best clothes and all necessities for a journey."

The nursery maid stared, mouth ajar. The prince's daughters had never left the palace on rue du Bac except for sedate walks in the park with their governess and the occasional drive with Viscount Kierston.

"What's the matter with you, girl? You look like a halfwit. Do as you're told."

"Yes, madame." The girl bobbed a curtsy and scuttled away.

"Where are we going, madame?" Sylvie gnawed at her fingernail, too absorbed by the momentous occurrence to notice the bitter paste.

"Never you mind," the governess snapped, taking perverse delight in keeping them in ignorance. "Get on with your lessons or there'll be no supper tonight."

The girls dutifully bent their heads over their copying, but their eyes met across the table, brimming with excitement and questions. What could be happening?

Louise unscrewed her little flash and took a swig of the contents hearty enough to have done justice to a drover after a hard day's work. She was in shock.

Summoned to Versailles for the children to be presented to the king and the dauphine! It was an astounding prospect. The prince had been very unforthcoming about the circumstances that had led to the summons, but it was clear to the governess that he was seriously displeased. He had made it clear that the children's conduct would reflect entirely on her care of them but that she could expect to keep to the palace rooms assigned to them for the most part. The princess would take responsibility for her stepdaughters when they were to be seen in public.

It was the princess's doing, of that the governess was convinced. That interfering, unorthodox, frivolous girl had created this disruption in Louise's carefully ordered world. She had a horror of crowds and public appearances. The children's routine would be destroyed, the princess would encourage them to misbehave, and then the governess would be held accountable. It was appalling, terrifying. And so inconsiderate when she was as sick as she was. The prince hadn't even seemed to notice her sniffles and watery eyes. She certainly needn't have worried that her appearance might cause unfavorable comment; her employer had barely looked at her throughout the interview. He'd drunk his wine and stared at the wall above her head while he'd rapped out his orders.

She began to wind the turban around her head again, quite forgetting that she still had on her wig. Sylvie gave a snort of laughter and buried her face in her arms. Amelia kicked her sister under the table.

Louise looked across at them, frowning, her mouth pursed tight. She caught a glimpse of herself in the mirror above the empty grate and hastily pulled off the turban and the wig. She glared at the girls who were now solemn faced, bent studiously over their papers, their little legs swinging beneath the table.

Muttering, the governess rewound the turban and took up her flask. Sylvie and Amelia, flushed with laughter and excitement, exchanged another gleeful look.

Chapter Eighteen

ON THE STROKE of midnight, Cordelia yawned delicately behind her fan and murmured to her dance partner that she was utterly exhausted. Her coach was about to turn back into a pumpkin if she didn't seek her bed without delay.

He smiled a little pityingly. To be exhausted at midnight was rather pathetic at the height of the wedding festivities, but the princess had been a less than exhilarating partner, so he was perfectly ready to escort her off the floor. He bowed punctiliously and left her at the double doors of the ballroom.

Cordelia glanced casually around the throng swirling and swaying beneath the brilliant light thrown by hundreds of massive crystal chandeliers. There was no sign of Leo. Had he left already? Was he waiting for her? He'd said she was not to go to him before midnight. Presumably, he'd been present at the king's couchée—an absurd ceremony, Cordelia thought. The king in his nightgown retired to his ceremonial bed surrounded by his courtiers, then as soon as they'd left, he got up again and went off into the town, or even to Paris, or simply to the card tables in his private apartments. It was the same at the morning levee. Most mornings, the king had been up and dressed for hours, before returning again to the state bed to be ceremonially and publicly dressed by his gentlemen of the bedchamber.

But at least once the ceremony of the couchée had been observed, the court was freed from royal observance for the remainder of the evening, so it had some useful purpose.

Cordelia slipped out of the salon and glided away from the bright, noisy scene. The antechamber was much quieter, containing only a few card players being entertained by a group of musicians. Christian had played for the king earlier in the evening. It was a mark of great honor and the king had been visibly impressed; the Duc de Carillac, Christian's patron, had beamed with pride and pleasure. Christian's once uncertain future was looking assured, Cordelia thought. But her satisfaction was tinged with the wry reflection that while Christian's future was now assured, her own and Toinette's, once so certain, had developed some distinct hiccups.

But all such distracting thoughts vanished as she sped down the quieter corridors and up the narrow stairs of the less fashionable parts of the palace, each step drawing her ever closer to Leo.

His door at the head of the stone staircase was ajar. Cordelia paused, glancing behind her down the stairs. There was no one around. The other doors along the passage that stretched from the stairs were all closed; a few candles flickered dimly in wall sconces. Cordelia lightly laid her fingers on the door. Why was it open? Had Leo perhaps gone somewhere? If so, it couldn't have been far. He wouldn't leave his door open if he was expecting to be gone long. Perhaps his servant was in the room. But Leo was expecting her. He wouldn't summon his servant. She pushed and the door swung soundlessly inward.

She stepped into the chamber. It was empty. A curtain fluttered at the open window. Fresh candles burned brightly on the dresser and the mantel. A decanter of wine stood on a table, a half-full glass beside it.

"Leo?" She took another, this time tentative, step, feeling like an intruder. Her heart skipped. Her scalp crawled. She had the sense that she was not alone.

Something flashed across her eyes. Then she was staring into a soft, velvety blackness.

"Leo?" she whispered again as the blindfold was drawn tight and tied at the back of her head. She heard the door close quietly.

"Don't be afraid." There was a depth to his voice, a potent current of lust.

"I'm not," she said truthfully, standing very still, trying to orientate herself in this private darkness. Her mounting excitement mingled now with the sense of entering some dangerous and unknown territory.

She could feel him standing in front of her, and she put out her hands to touch him. He was naked. Her heart beat faster. She was fully dressed, buttoned, hooked, laced into corsets, hoops, three petticoats, and a heavy gown of thickly embroidered ivory taffeta. She became conscious suddenly of every garment on her body, of her garters fastened at her thighs, of her silk stockings, of the lace edging to the stays that pushed her breasts up over the low neck of her gown. Of the shape and texture of her flesh and bone beneath.

Her hands moved over him, an eye in every fingertip. Deprived of sight, she found that her fingers were extra sensitive. They saw as they touched, they absorbed every little bump and ripple on his skin as she stroked his chest, finding his nipples. Delicately, she licked her fingertips and caressed his nipples with the damp tips, feeling them lift and harden. She listened to his breathing, more aware of every sound in the stillness than she'd ever been before. The tiny hiss of a spurting candle, the rustle of her feet on the woven rug, the sudden catch in his breath when she slid her hands down over his rib cage into the concave space below. She played in his navel with a dampened fingertip, clasped his narrow waist between her hands.

He put his hand on her head, not hard but with an urgency, pushing her down. She slipped to her knees, her skirts billowing in an ivory corolla around her. Her hands gripped his buttocks, her thumbs pressing into the hard pelvic bones, and she nuzzled blindly against his belly, stroked with her tongue, before gathering his erect flesh on her tongue and drawing him into her mouth.

She moved her mouth up and down the hard pulsing stem, keeping her hands where they were, using only her face and her mouth to hold and caress him. She inhaled deeply of the scent of his arousal, savored the saltiness of his flesh on her tongue.

Leo looked down at her from the plane of his own bliss. Her upturned face was radiant, somehow made even more so by the black velvet scarf that prevented him from seeing the soul in her eyes. Her head was back, her throat a graceful white curve, as she pleasured him with an all-absorbing concentration. He knew as he looked down into her blind face that she was aware of nothing but his body so close to hers, of the taste, the scent, the feel of him, and his blood thrilled with a strange deep power.

Cordelia was lost in her own sense of power, the power she had to give him such pleasure. She could feel his joy in her fingertips, feel it on her tongue, at the back of her throat. She adored his body, reveled in what she was doing to him, gloried in the moment when she knew the merest flickering caress would cause him to plunge over the edge . . . gloried in the moment when it happened and his jubilant cry filled the room, his fingers twined in her hair, holding on as if she were his only rock in the storm that promised to sweep him away.

His grip loosened finally, but she remained on her knees, resting her head against his belly. His legs were braced as if he needed to withstand some force, but his hands on her face were gentle, stroking the curve of her cheek, lifting her chin to caress the soft tender flesh beneath. Then he took her hands and drew her firmly to her feet.

"Do you wish me to take off the scarf?"

Cordelia shook her head. "Not unless *you* wish to."

Leo smiled and kissed her, tasting his own salt essence on her lips. "What a wonderfully compliant lover you are, my sweet."

Cordelia smiled. "Do you?"

"No, I have a few other ideas up my sleeve." He drew her farther into the room and she clung to his hand, taking hesitant little steps, afraid to trip over something. "There, now stand quite still."

She felt him move away from her and was suddenly lost, but it was only for a moment. Then he was behind her, his fingers on the hooks at the back of her gown. She kept very still as he stripped her with unhurried movements, leisurely loosening each hook, each button, each tie, until she stood in her chemise, corset, stockings, garters, and shoes. She blinked behind the velvet blindfold, aware of the cool night air on her bared skin, seeing herself in her mind's eye as if she were looking at her image in a mirror.

She waited for him to untie the laces of her corset, and then caught her breath as she heard the snip of scissors and the garment fell from her.

His hands moved down her, pressing the thin chemise to her body, molding her breasts, the curve of her bottom. He kissed her throat, drew his tongue along the line of her jaw, traced the shape of her ear. Cordelia quivered, waiting for the unbearable yet exquisite moment when his tongue would delve into her ear. He knew the sensation drove her wild, but he teased for long minutes, his teeth nipping and tugging gently on her earlobe, his tongue stroking behind her ear, little darting thrusts within, withdrawn as soon as he felt her begin to shrink and shudder. Her blindness accentuated every sensation and every instant of anticipation. She couldn't see him, could only feel him, couldn't guess when the tantalizing would stop.

He clasped her head firmly between both hands, and she knew it was coming, was already wriggling and squirming. Then his tongue was ravaging her ear, sending her into helpless paroxysms where the line between torment and entrancement was so fine she couldn't possibly have drawn it.

He laughed as he held her still and his breath mingled hot with the dampness of his probing tongue. Cordelia tried to squiggle away, laughing even as she begged and pleaded for him to stop. But her excitement grew with every fruitless wriggle, and the sensations were all becoming mixed up so that she no longer knew which part of her body was responding.

When at last he took pity and raised his head, she sagged against him, exhausted by her struggles, weak with laughter and the pulsing arousal in her loins.

"I'd like you to finish undressing." His voice was almost shocking in her velvet darkness, banishing laughter. He spoke softly but definitely and she felt him step backward from her so that she was standing in her own cool space.

She kicked off her shoes and the carpet was coarse beneath her stockinged feet. She lifted the hem of the chemise and untied her garters. She rolled her stockings carefully to her ankles and drew them off her feet. Every movement was exaggerated by her sightlessness. She knew his eyes were upon her, watching every movement, but she could only imagine his gaze.

She dropped the stockings to the carpet and straightened. Where was he? Was he behind her, to the side, or facing her? She stood very still, trying to feel his presence. She couldn't even hear his breathing, couldn't sense the warmth of his skin. She turned slowly, moving her hands through the air. And encountered only air.

"Take the scarf off if you wish." The voice came from behind her. She spun around.

"No . . . no, I don't wish to. But I didn't know where you were."

"Why don't you wish to?" There was a low languorous note to his voice, a deep caressing invitation to enter a world he was creating for them both.

"I want to find out what happens," she replied without a moment's hesitation. "I feel so different . . . everything's different, new . . . I'm experiencing everything as if it's for the first time."

"Take off your chemise."

Cordelia caught the hem of the thin garment and drew it up her body and over her head. She tossed it aside and stood naked, the breeze from the open window cooling her heated skin.

"Turn around."

She obeyed, standing with her back to him, hands at her sides, every inch of skin alive, waiting, wondering when and where he would touch her. There was utter silence. Utter blackness.

Leo waited, forcing himself to keep still as he gazed upon her; the narrow back, the sharp pointed shoulder blades that he longed to touch with his tongue, the line of her spine, carved deep into her back, the indentation of her waist, the flare of her hips, the taut round cheeks of her bottom. He waited, knowing that as she stood there, her body, already aroused, was working its own magic under the orchestration of imagination.

When he touched her shoulder blades with a brush of a fingertip, she gave a startled little cry. He steadied her with a hand on her shoulder, then languidly traced the line of her spine with the pad of his thumb. His flat palm stroked over her bottom, then slid between her thighs. Cordelia quivered and again he steadied her with a hand on her shoulder while his fingers reached for her, dancing, probing, feeling her readiness as they slid inside her.

His tongue stroked upward along the grooved nape of her neck, then his hand left her shoulder, slipped round to clasp one breast, teasing her nipple as the hot moist caress on her neck continued and his fingers opened inside her while his thumb played on the hard nub of her sex.

Cordelia no longer knew which part of her was responding to which exquisite caress. The hard lines of her body were fluid, and she seemed to be adrift in a world without physical boundaries. Her eyes were now centered inward on herself, and she could almost see the blood moving through her veins, her soft nether lips pink and swollen with joyous need, the pulsing of her thudding heart.

And yet the explosion took her by surprise. It was as if she were consumed in a roaring conflagration; her skin was on fire, her blood was molten lava as the searing bliss devoured her.

The flames were still roaring in her ears when Leo toppled her forward. She felt the soft arm of the sofa under her belly, her arms stretched out in front of her, her toes touching the carpet. Holding her hips he entered her while the conflagration still raged and the new sensation of his hard driving flesh added fuel to the flames. She no longer knew who or what she was, aware only of flesh and blood united, the point where Leo's body was separate from her own blurred beyond definition.

Leo felt as if he had limitless staying power. He felt as if he were drifting godlike above the two joined bodies, capable of bringing them both to the extremes of physical bliss. He was filled with the burning need to take his lover to the top of her mountain, to the absolute pinnacle beyond which there was only infinity. And he would do this not once but many, many times during the next hours. He wanted to brand her with his lovemaking so that nothing and no one would ever erase the glorious memories of this night.

Where Michael had violated her, exploited her weakness, he would show her the perfect joy of surrender. He passed his flat palms up her bent back, pressing his thumbs into the vertebrae. Her back arched in response, her inner muscles tightened around him. He scribbled a path with his nails down her back and over her bottom. Her body rippled around him. He drew back for a second, then plunged deeply, and she convulsed around him. He remained inside her, his own responses now well in control.

Cordelia sobbed her pleasure into the sofa cushions, and then he began to move again inside her. His hand slid beneath her belly, reaching down to touch her so that the muscles of her belly tightened and the pleasure built again, rippling through her in little rivulets that gradually swelled to a full stream. The instant before the stream burst its banks, he slid from her. He turned her over on the sofa, rested his bent knees on the arm, drew her legs high onto his shoulders, and entered her again.

Cordelia existed in her own darkness, every nerve centered on the one part of her body that seemed truly alive. She thought she couldn't bear another dissolution, another moment of this intense pleasure, but she found she could. Not once more but many more times during the next hours. She was mindless, sightless, insatiable.

The stars faded, the sky lightened, red streaks of dawn filled the sky outside the window. Neither of them noticed in the reckless world of their own entrancement. But eventually Leo could hold back no longer. Cordelia sat astride his lap on the end of the bed, her hands on his shoulders, her lips parted, head thrown back, as she held him tight within, moving only her inner muscles.

The instant before the wave broke, Leo fell back on the bed, holding her tight against him as he rolled sideways, finally separating their joined bodies.

Cordelia lay bathed in sweat, prostrate, unable to move or think. When Leo moved her head sideways and unfastened the blindfold, she protested weakly, so accustomed was she now to her own private darkness that the intrusion of the visible world was a violation. Her eyes closed against the unfamiliar light, and she was immediately unconscious, sleeping the sleep of total exhaustion.

Leo's right hand rested on Cordelia's breast, the fingers splayed; the other hand was flung around her waist. His body felt hammered into the thick feather mattress, and even the growing light in the room and the knowledge that they were moving into a dangerous time couldn't prevent him from sleeping.

He awoke soon enough, fully alert, his heart hammering as he listened to the sounds in the corridor outside. People were talking and moving around. From the courtyard below came the clarion call of a herald's trumpet as the night guard was changed.

"Hell and the devil!" he muttered, pushing himself onto

an elbow, looking down at the unconscious figure beside him. Despite his anxiety he smiled, brushing a tangled ringlet from her cheek. She was so beautiful. And dear God in heaven, what a partner in love. Not once had she fallen behind, not once had she pleaded exhaustion, not once had she failed to divine what he wanted of her.

She had woven such chains about him, gossamer chains of love that were nevertheless adamantine. How had it happened that in a few short weeks this young girl had bewitched him out of all rational sense?

His eye flickered to the bracelet that he didn't think he'd ever seen her without. Elvira had always worn it too, he remembered. It was a curious piece of jewelry, undeniably beautiful but with something almost repellent about it. And yet both its owners had rarely taken it off. But surely it must symbolize marriage to Michael? A bondage to a loathsome man. Cordelia daily struggled against those bonds. Had Elvira also? Had Elvira suffered in the same way? Had the bracelet symbolized bondage for her too?

Cordelia stirred, her eyelids fluttered up. She caught his expression as he looked down at her before he had time to banish the dark thoughts. "What is it?" She reached up a hand to touch his face. "Were you thinking of Elvira?"

Her intuitive insight was uncanny. He caught her wrist, bringing it down so that he could examine the bracelet. "Why do you never take this off?"

Cordelia frowned. "I don't know. I didn't realize that I don't. Don't you care for it? It belonged to Elvira, I know. I saw it on her wrist in the portrait in the library on the rue du Bac."

"She never took it off either," he commented. "And no, I don't like it."

Cordelia examined it closely. "It's unique, I'm sure there's not another one like it in the world. The jeweler at Schonbrunn said as much. But it is a little sinister, I suppose."

"The temptations of Eve," he said. "But why would you

wear a present that Michael gave you to mark a betrothal that has brought you nothing but suffering?"

Cordelia's frown deepened. She had never thought of the bracelet in that way. Somehow it just seemed to belong on her wrist. "I won't wear it if you dislike it," she said slowly. "But don't you think Michael might wonder if he noticed that I had suddenly stopped wearing it?"

"Yes, I'm sure," he said with a careless shake of his head. "It's of no consequence, Cordelia. I was just struck by its curious design." He swung himself off the bed. "What is of consequence is getting you back to your own apartment without drawing attention to yourself. The entire place is awake."

Cordelia peered blearily at the discarded heap of clothes in the middle of the room. "I can't put those on again."

"I don't see much choice." He swung himself off the bed. "Come, let me help you."

Cordelia got gingerly off the bed. "I'm sore," she complained. "How did that happen?"

Leo couldn't help laughing. "Use your imagination. If it's any consolation, you're not the only sufferer."

"I don't think I could sit on a horse," she said with a mock grimace, coming over to him, slipping her arms around his neck, pressing her naked body against his. "And we're to go to the hunt this morning."

Leo glanced over his shoulder at the window, where it was full daylight. "In less than an hour," he said ruefully, reaching behind him to break her hold. "Be good now, Cordelia." He picked up her chemise and dumped it in her arms. "Hurry."

"Oh, Lord!" Cordelia groaned. There were clear penalties for a night of unbridled lovemaking. She pulled the garment over her head. "I won't bother with stockings and garters, no one will be able to tell under my skirt. . . . What about my corset? I can't wear it if the laces are cut." She stepped into her first petticoat.

"I'll get rid of it." Leo shrugged into a dressing gown as he went over to the window. The court below was abustle, horses, wagons, soldiers going about the business of the new day.

Cordelia balled up her stockings and garters in her fist. She sat down to manipulate her shoes over her bare feet. "There, now I'm as dressed as I'll ever be at this point. Shall I just go?"

"No, wait." He went to the door and opened it, holding up an arresting hand as he looked down the stairs, then backward along the corridor. "All right, hurry!"

Cordelia darted to the door, reaching up to kiss him. He was prepared for a light farewell embrace, but she threw her arms around his neck, palming his scalp, pulling his head down to hers with all the passionate fervor of the night. He wanted to yield, but knew that they couldn't. He still held the door open and broke her hold almost roughly. "For pity's sake, Cordelia! We have less than an hour." He pushed her through the door and closed it briskly at her back.

Cordelia chuckled and danced down the stairs. Despite a sleepless and extraordinarily energetic night, she was filled with vigor and energy. A whole day in Leo's company stretched ahead, even if it was on the back of a horse. She grimaced at a prospect that ordinarily would have filled her with delight. Mathilde would know how to soothe the soreness, dissipate the stiffness. But instead of Mathilde, she had only the gormless if well-meaning Elsie.

But she would make the best of it, she told herself firmly. Mathilde would expect it of her, and this miserable situation wouldn't last forever. They would defeat Michael.

As she turned into the corridor leading to her own apartments, a scurrying maidservant bobbed a curtsy, looking a little curiously at the disheveled lady in her evening dress tottering on her high heels in the early morning. Cordelia gave her an airy smile but waited until she passed before opening the door to her own apartments.

The salon was deserted. She'd told Elsie not to wait up for her, and if Monsieur Brion was aware that she hadn't returned overnight, he was discreetly ensuring that she returned unobserved.

She slipped into her own chamber, threw off her clothes, bundling them into a corner, dragged a nightgown over her head, and jumped into her cold, unrumpled bed. Reaching out, she hauled on the bell rope, then lay down, pulled the covers up, and closed her eyes tightly.

"I need a bath, Elsie," she declared when the maid arrived somewhat breathlessly a few minutes later, bearing a breakfast tray. "I'm to join the hunt within the hour and I need hot water." She threw aside the bedclothes as she spoke, leaping to her feet. "Hurry, girl."

Elsie bobbed a curtsy and disappeared. Cordelia poured hot chocolate into a cup and hungrily attacked her breakfast.

She was as ravenous as if she hadn't eaten in days. She slapped thick slices of ham between hunks of rye bread and wolfed it down while Elsie laboriously filled a porcelain hip bath from steaming brass jugs of water.

Cordelia rummaged through Mathilde's pouches of herbs, trying to identify by scent the ones her nurse used to relax muscles in a bath. "These should do." She scattered the herbs on the surface of the water and sank into the tub with a little shudder of pleasure. "Oh, that's better. Put out my riding habit, Elsie. The emerald green velvet one, with the tricorn hat with the black feather."

Forty-five minutes later, feeling immeasurably restored, Cordelia joined the hunting party assembling in the outer courtyard. Her groom held Lucette. Leo, already mounted, was drinking from the stirrup cup presented by a footman.

"Good morning, Princess. I trust you slept well."

"Very well, thank you, my lord." She smiled serenely, putting her booted foot in her groom's waiting palm.

"Isn't it wonderful to be riding to hounds again, Cordelia?" Toinette's excited call came from the royal party gathered a few feet away. "You must come and ride with us."

Cordelia shot Leo a ruefully disappointed look and obeyed the dauphine's summons. The king greeted her pleasantly, the dauphin with a dipped head and averted eyes. Toinette was radiant.

The huntsman blew the horn, and the crowd of gaily dressed riders moved out under the early sunshine with a jingle of silver bridles and a flash of spurs into the thick forest surrounding Versailles.

Chapter Nineteen

THE BROAD RIDE stretched through the trees, dappled with green and gold as the bright sunlight shone through the new leaves. The scent of the earlier rain rose from the turf, crushed beneath the hooves of a hundred horses. The lean, elegant deerhounds ran yapping ahead of the hunt, their huntsmen on sturdy ponies following. Beaters crashed through the bushes, driving up birds for the archers' skill, scaring doe and rabbit into the path of the dogs.

For the first hour, Cordelia rode with Toinette in the king's party, but when the dauphin had drawn alongside his bride and begun a stilted conversation, Cordelia had discreetly excused herself and dropped back. The dauphin, it seemed, needed all the encouragement he could get to increase his acquaintance with his wife. And Cordelia needed no encouragement to join Leo, who was riding just behind.

He greeted her with a doffed hat and a formal "I trust you're enjoying the ride, Princess."

"Immensely, it's such a beautiful day," she replied in like manner. "And I've already shot two pheasants," she added with the ill-concealed triumph that usually followed her gambling wins. But she certainly hadn't cheated with her bow. The arrow had flown clean and swift to its target, bringing the bird down dead and unmangled for the dogs to fetch and the keepers to bag.

"So I saw," Leo said, amused. "You're a fine archer, if a trifle immodest."

Cordelia chuckled and fitted another arrow to the bow that rested across her saddle. She held the reins with one hand, the bow and its arrow with the other, with an air of assurance that bespoke both experience and skill. Her voice dropped to a conspiratorial whisper. "Leo, can you think of any reason why the dauphin should not have consummated his marriage as yet?"

"*What?*" He was incredulous.

"It's true. Poor Toinette is at her wits end. Every night he leaves her at her door. One of his gentlemen must have told the king, because yesterday he spoke to her about it. That was why he came to her boudoir when we were in dishabille and I had no shoes on. She said he was very delicate and gentle, but it was *so* embarrassing to admit that she didn't know what was wrong."

"Good God! Poor child, what could she possibly know of such things? Maybe he needs a physician."

"Yes, she said the king was going to order an examination. So she's waiting on tenterhooks to see what happens. She *has* to conceive."

"Of course," Leo agreed wryly, the realities of the marriage no more lost on him than they were on the lowest members of the Paris stews.

What if Cordelia already carried Michael's child? It was a question he had tried to ignore, but no longer. If Cordelia gave Michael a son, perhaps, just perhaps, Michael might be prepared to surrender his wife in exchange for his male heir. In a fantasy land, perhaps he would be prepared to surrender his wife *and* his female offspring in exchange for an heir. But how could Cordelia give up her own child? How could either of them contemplate leaving an infant in the hands of such a man? But Michael would move heaven and earth to reclaim a male child. There would be no safety, no peace, ever, unless they lived outside of society in a world where the children would be deprived of their birthrights, unable to claim their rightful place in the world, and therefore unable to make even the ordinary choices of adulthood, like whether or whom to marry. They would be dispossessed. How could he condemn helpless innocents to such a future? But how could he condemn Cordelia to a living death at the hands of Prince Michael?

First things first! He reined in the galloping thoughts before they bolted from him. If she was pregnant, they would cross that bridge when they came to it.

The cavalcade turned onto a broader thoroughfare, where a group of carriages awaited them. Madame du Barry sat prettily at the reins of an open landau, her ladies beside her. The king drew rein and greeted her. The dauphin bowed to his father's mistress. The dauphine looked the other way.

"Oh, Toinette, you're behaving so stupidly," Cordelia said in low-voiced exasperation, cutting into Leo's absorption.

"Why? What's she doing?" Leo was suddenly aware of the ripple of whispered awareness around him.

"She refuses to acknowledge the du Barry. She says it would be countenancing immoral behavior at court. Look at her, sitting there like some prissy nun at an orgy!"

Leo shook his head and quietened his shifting horse. He looked down to see what had upset the animal and saw a small ragged boy sidling up against the horse's neck.

"What are you doing?" he demanded sharply.

The lad shook his head. "Nuffink, milord. I jest likes 'osses." He looked pathetically up at Cordelia. His gaunt, hollow-eyed, dirt-streaked little face had an almost elderly cast, wizened with malnutrition.

"Are you hungry?" Cordelia said impulsively.

The child nodded and wiped his encrusted nose with a ragged sleeve.

"Here." Cordelia leaned down to put a coin into his filthy palm. Clawlike fingers closed over it and he was off, weaving his way through the horses, ducking and dodging shifting hooves and whipcracking huntsmen.

"Poor little mite," Cordelia said. "Do you ever look at their faces . . . the people's, I mean? They look so lifeless, so hopeless. I never noticed it so much in Austria."

"Or in England," Leo replied. "There's poverty, of course,

but the ordinary folk are not downtrodden in the same way."

"I wonder if Toinette notices it," Cordelia mused. "Oh, she seems to be beckoning me. I hope she won't expect me to ride with her all day." She walked her horse to where Toinette sat somewhat to the side of the still-chattering group around Madame du Barry's carriage.

"Talk to me," Toinette said in an urgent whisper. "No one's taking any notice of me, they're all talking to that whore!"

"That whore is the king's mistress," Cordelia reminded her mildly. "She happens to have more influence at court than you, my dear friend."

"Oh, go away," Toinette said petulantly. "If you're going to scold, I don't want to talk to you."

Cordelia knew that the flash of bad temper would dissipate rapidly and her friend would be all remorse and apologies within minutes, but she merely nodded and rode away, determined to leave the dauphine to her own reflections.

"Psst. Milady!"

The whispering hiss came from a stand of trees to the side of the clearing. Cordelia drew rein and the urchin of before darted out. "Me mam's mortal sick, milady," he said. "Will ye come an' 'elp 'er."

"I'll give you some money—"

The child shook his head vigorously. "Not money, milady. She needs 'elp."

A beggar turning down money! It was extraordinary. Curiously, Cordelia signaled that he should lead her, and she followed him into the trees. He trotted along just ahead of Lucette, who was picking her way delicately through the thick undergrowth. Suddenly, the lad was no longer there.

Cordelia drew rein and looked around. She called, but the only sounds were the tapping of a woodpecker and the cawing of a rook. The tree cover was dense, the sunlight barely managing to filter through the thick leaves, and the air was heavy with the smell of damp moss and rotting leaves.

Cordelia began to feel uneasy. Lucette seemed to feel it too and began shifting restlessly, raising her elegant head to sniff the air. "Come on, let's go back. I expect he was playing a trick." Cordelia nudged the mare's flanks to turn her.

The two men came out of the trees at her so fast she barely had time to draw breath. One of them had seized Lucette's bridle, the other had hold of Cordelia's stirrup. Lucette was too well schooled to rear without orders, but her nostrils flared and her eyes rolled.

Not a thought passed through Cordelia's head. The bow was in her hand, the string drawn tight, and the arrow loosed in one fluid series of movements, so quick it was hard to separate them. The man at Lucette's bridle bellowed and fell back as the arrow quivered below his collarbone.

The second arrow was as swift and true as the first. The man holding her stirrup dropped his arm and stared stupidly at the arrow sticking out of his bicep.

"Up, Lucette, *now*!" Cordelia instructed, and the Lippizaner rose on her hand legs, her front feet pawing the air. The two men fell to their knees, terror writ large on their broad faces, their eyes wild with pain as Lucette towered over them.

"Dear God in heaven!" Leo's hunting knife was already in his hand as his gelding pounded across the forest floor toward them, tearing up the ground, loam and debris flying from beneath his hooves.

"What the devil!" Leo hauled on the reins and Jupiter came to a stamping halt. Cordelia brought Lucette onto four hooves again.

"Footpads," she said, her voice shaky now that the crisis was passed. "That little boy brought me here, then he disappeared. I suppose they were going to rob me."

"I saw you leave the hunt." Leo dismounted and stood over the two cowering men.

"Leave us be, yer 'onor?" the older one begged. "They'll 'ang us fer sure."

"A merciful death compared with what you presumably had in store for the lady," he said coldly, running a gloved finger over the blade of his knife.

"No, we wasn't goin' to kill 'er, yer 'onor! Jest get 'er to the ground, like." The spokesman inched backward as if he could escape the icy stare of the tall, slender Englishman.

"Leave them, Leo."

He turned in surprise. "Leave them? God knows what they were going to do to you."

"They're starving," she said flatly. "Their families are starving. That wretched child probably belongs to one of them." She reached into her pocket and drew out a leather pouch. "Here." She tossed it down to the ground between the two men, who merely stared at it as if they couldn't believe their eyes.

Which seemed an entirely logical reaction in the circumstances, Leo reflected. He sheathed his knife and remounted. An arrow hole was no light wound, so they weren't exactly escaping scot-free. "Next time, I suggest you curb your philanthropic urges," he said to Cordelia as they emerged from the trees. "Ragged children have a sting in their tails."

"It's not their fault," she said flatly.

He looked across at her, thinking that she had so many unexpected sides. She was as many faceted as a diamond. And as precious. When he thought of what could have happened, his blood turned to ice. But Diana the Huntress also seemed supremely capable of looking after herself. However, she was rather pale, and he noticed that her hands on the reins were a little unsteady.

"Let's return to the palace."

"And not rejoin the hunt?" She looked surprised.

"I think you've had enough excitement for one day."

"I'm not such a milksop," Cordelia protested indignantly. "I was a little shaken, but not anymore. And I'm not in the least hurt. Come. I'll race you. We'll hear the horns soon enough." And she was off at a gallop down the ride.

Leo hesitated for a minute, then went after her. She seemed unhurt, but something about the whole incident niggled at him. Footpads who preyed upon the king's hunting party in the forest of Versailles were asking for the hangman's noose. And hunters would offer slim pickings—there was little need for money or jewels when chasing deer. No, there was something distinctly odd about the whole business.

Amelia, Sylvie, and Madame de Nevry traveled in a coach that lumbered in the wake of the prince's. The girls were so excited they could barely control themselves, and only their governess's grim visage and threats to report their behavior to their father kept them from kneeling up on the seat to look out of the window at the fascinating scenery and people they passed. They sat side by side, clutching each other's hand, their legs swinging with the motion of the coach, their eyes brilliant with excitement.

At last the governess dozed off, and they scrambled onto the seat to gaze outside, their thrilled whispers so low they couldn't possibly disturb the snoring Louise, who didn't awaken until the carriage turned through the great gilded gates into the outer court of Versailles.

She sat up and with fluttering hands adjusted her wig, which had slipped sideways. The girls were sitting innocently opposite her, hands in their laps, their bright blue eyes gazing steadily at her. She coughed, took a quick nip from her flask, and looked out of the window. She had never seen Versailles and gazed awestruck at the magnificent spread of golden buildings, their red roofs and shutters glowing in the evening sun.

The girls tumbled from the carriage as soon as the footstep was lowered, ignoring the steadying hand of a powdered footman. They stared around. Sylvie's hand crept into her sister's. She felt like an ant she'd once watched crawling laboriously across the schoolroom floor. Amelia squeezed the hand tightly, totally terrified by the size of the court stretching ahead of them toward the massive golden palace.

The prince's carriage had arrived first and he stood a little way away from the children, in conversation with Monsieur Brion, who'd been alerted to his master's arrival by a runner.

Michael glanced over his shoulder at his daughters. They looked absurdly tiny and frightened, as they should, he reflected. This was no place for a pair of small children.

"Take them away," he said to Brion. "I assume rooms have been set aside for them."

"Yes, indeed, my lord. The princess has supervised the arrangements herself with the dauphine's approval."

"I trust the princess finds herself in good health?" Michael took a pinch of snuff, his tone bland.

"Perfectly, I believe, my lord."

Michael sneezed abruptly. He dusted his nose with his handkerchief. "I understood she was to ride to hounds today."

"Indeed, my lord. I gather she had a very good day."

He controlled his furious disappointment with difficulty. "Is the king returned from the hunt?"

"An hour ago, sir."

"Then I shall attend him at once." Michael stalked off without a backward glance at his daughters and their bemused governess.

The court was gathered in the state apartments, talking about the pleasures of the day's hunt over the gaming tables. The king looked up from his favorite game—lansquenet— as the prince bowed before him.

"Ah, Prince, you are back from your errand, I see. You have brought your children? Madame the Dauphine is most anxious to make their acquaintance."

"They are with their governess at present, monseigneur, but will wait upon the dauphine at her pleasure."

"Oh, yes, of course. Well, I daresay you wish to find your delightful wife. She accompanied us on the hunt, splendid archer. We were most impressed . . . brought down at least two birds." He nodded amiably and the prince took his dismissal.

He strolled through the rooms, acknowledging acquaintances, listening for interesting morsels of gossip. A man could get out of touch in as little as a day in this hotbed of scandal. There was no sign of Cordelia at the tables, although the dauphine was playing animatedly with her ladies. He took a glass of wine from a footman's tray and wandered over to the long windows overlooking the gardens. The lights on the mock Venetian windows along the canal had just been lit.

Bungling idiots! The plan had been foolproof. They had not been required to think of anything themselves, just to identify their quarry from an unmistakable description and follow the prince's orders to the letter. A simple fall, a blow to the head, a few hours lying on the forest floor until she was missed and a search party was sent out for her. How could they have failed?

"I imagine my nieces are very excited at their new lodgings."

Michael spun around. Leo was smiling his amiable smile. *Damned fool,* Michael thought savagely. He probably thought the palace was a perfectly good place for his nieces. Besotted idiot didn't give a moment's consideration to the deleterious effect of distractions and such a violent break in their carefully ordered routines. He had no patience to exchange inane pleasantries about a situation into which he'd been blatantly manipulated, even if he couldn't blame Leo for it. He bowed, said tightly, "I trust their governess can curb unseemly excitement." And he stalked off.

Leo's blood raced with savage fury. Michael was clearly not a happy man, and he would be bound to take out his unhappiness on Cordelia. He glanced at his fob watch. Five o'clock. The women in the Parc aux Cerfs would be preparing for the evening. But as yet, they wouldn't have visitors. Now would be a good moment to discover if Tatiana had had a chance as yet to talk to her brother-in-law about acquiring a false passport.

Michael, seething with cold fury, made his way to his own apartments, where he presumed he would find his wife, unharmed and as stubborn and defiant as ever. He found her sitting at the mirror in her dressing room peering intently at her image. She rose immediately at his entrance and curtsied. "Good evening, my lord."

He ignored the cool greeting. "You attended the hunt this morning?"

"I had some success with my bow and arrow," she offered, taking her seat at the mirror again, folding her hands in her lap, with an air of demure attention that did nothing to conceal the insolence behind it. "The king was pleased to compliment me."

"Nothing untoward occurred?" His pale eyes were pinpricks as he watched her for a reaction.

Cordelia decided rapidly. If she told him of the attempted robbery, he could well institute a search for the footpads, and he would show no mercy if they were found. Even if he didn't care a fig for his wife, his pride would not endure that a crime against his family should go unpunished.

She shrugged. "Nothing out of the ordinary, my lord."

A flash of vicious frustration darted across the pale surface of his eyes. He spoke with caustic satisfaction, "Hunting is not a safe activity. I am beginning to think that you should give it up."

Cordelia stared at him, her expression as dismayed as he'd hoped it would be. "Give it up, my lord?"

"If you are with child, it is unwise," he said with a grim little smile. "I would not risk my heir."

Cordelia didn't know whether she was pregnant or not, but she did know that he was tormenting her and enjoying it. She could defeat him only by not giving him the satisfaction of seeing her unhappiness. "I'm sure you know best, my lord," she said with an indifferent shrug. "The children are settled in their apartments. Would you wish to see them?"

It was a successful deflection. Michael flushed angrily. "I would not. I also intend that they should remain with their governess except when they're summoned by a member of the royal family. On those occasions, you will accompany them, but you will also be escorted by a guard."

"A guard, my lord?" Her eyebrows crawled into her scalp. "What danger could they be in at Versailles?"

"You will do as I say, is that understood?"

"Of course, my lord." She rose and curtsied again, radiating insolence, so that he took a step toward her, his mouth tight, his hand raised.

Then he stopped and his asp's smile flickered thinly. "I will deal with this further when I come to you tonight, madame. Be prepared." On which note he turned on his heel and marched out.

The familiar sick tremors fluttered in her belly, but Cordelia squashed them resolutely. She had Mathilde's little vial. Michael always took a glass of cognac before he came to her. He would have it in his hand when he stood by the bed, looking down at her as she lay waiting for him, struggling to hide her fear. Struggling and so frequently failing.

But never again. From now on he would never detect so much as a quiver of fear. And tonight she would use Mathilde's potion.

❀

Chapter Twenty

MICHAEL ENTERED HIS dressing room just after midnight. He locked the door behind him, then locked the door communicating with his wife's dressing room.

He unlocked the brass padlock of the ironbound chest and took out the book with purple binding—a startling contrast to the somber bindings of the daily journals. He turned the volume between his hands, running his finger over the gold lettering on the spine. *The Devil's Apothecary.* A most useful volume. If accidents failed, he could find something in here to cause his wife a serious indisposition. Enough to ensure her removal from Versailles. It was always better to do things for oneself, he thought. Relying on bumbling idiots to carry out even the simplest instructions was clearly futile.

He didn't want an illness that resembled Elvira's in the least degree. Something more like food poisoning, perhaps. Not fatal, just distinctly unpleasant. But neither must it be something that would endanger a possible pregnancy.

He closed the book with a snap, returned it to the chest, turned the key in the padlock. Then he unlocked the doors to his dressing room and rang for his valet. There was silence coming from his wife's dressing room. He had insisted she be escorted back to the apartment as soon as the royal family had left the evening's concert, so he knew she would now be abed, after Elsie's less than expert assistance. Abed and waiting for him, knowing that she had offended him earlier. Knowing what she must expect. His loins stirred.

"Cognac!" he demanded with a snap of his fingers as his valet appeared.

He drank deeply and the fiery spirit calmed him. Once he had Cordelia out of Versailles, the rest would be easy. He must separate her from all her friends, all who had known her before. And most particularly the dauphine. He would be able to censor her correspondence very simply, and when she was completely isolated, then he would be free to do with her as he pleased.

He frowned suddenly. Leo Beaumont might prove awkward. He could well ask inconvenient questions if Cordelia was suddenly incommunicado. But Leo could be handled. He was only really interested in the children. Michael would throw him a distracting sop or two regarding the girls and ensure that whenever he saw Cordelia it was only in her husband's company. The man was gullible; he could be managed.

Cordelia, lying wide-eyes and wakeful, heard Michael's bell, and her skin seemed to shrink on her bones. He would be with his valet for fifteen minutes, maybe twenty, and then he would come to her. Her hand shook slightly as protectively she buttoned the high neck of her nightgown. A pointless gesture, she knew, but an involuntary one.

When she'd seen Mathilde the previous afternoon, her nurse had said the sleeping draught would take a half hour, maybe three quarters, to work. Michael was a big man.

But a half hour was more than enough time for him to inflict punishment, Cordelia thought grimly. But what couldn't be helped must be endured. He would only be able to assault her once tonight, and if she concentrated on that, she could bear it. It could be no worse that what she'd endured before.

But the tremors in her belly intensified as she listened to her husband and his valet moving about next door. Her palms were slippery with sweat, her heart pounding. But when the door to her chamber opened and her husband's powerful shape was for a moment outlined in the doorway, illuminated by the shaft of light from the room behind, a great calm swept over her. Her fingers curled around the little vial, finger and thumb gently easing off the stopper.

Michael stepped into the room, closing the door at his back. Cordelia slipped from bed as he crossed the room carrying his brandy goblet. She stood beside the bed, a frightened smile trembling on her lips. "Welcome, husband."

Michael looked startled. He was a man of habit and ritual, and Cordelia was supposed to await him in bed. Then his lip curled. This show of fear and penitence was presumably a plea for leniency. A foredoomed plea, but nonetheless gratifying for that.

He came up to her and stood over her. She dropped her eyes before the cold, ruthless cruelty of his gaze. A quiver went through her, and the silence in the room stretched into infinity as he watched her dread grow with each moment. He set his glass down on the bedside table, caught her hair on either side of her head, twining his fingers painfully in the ringlets, crushing her mouth beneath his in a smothering, assaulting travesty of a kiss.

But for the moment he only held her head. Cordelia struggled to keep her mind clear as his heat and musky odor enveloped her. Her hand moved sideways, blindly. She had registered the position of the glass in her mind's eye. Her fingers located the rim. She estimated three drops but couldn't be certain exactly how many had fallen in. Mathilde had said the potion was tasteless and odorless, but that was with three drops. If she'd added too much, maybe he would notice. But she couldn't afford to add too few. Her fingers fumbled with the stopper and then her hand was back at her side, the vial hidden in the folds of her nightgown as she now gave him what he wanted—resistance. She struggled to breathe, to free her hair from the vicious tugging of his fingers.

When he abruptly raised his head, spun her around, and hurled her facedown across the bed, she held her breath. He planted his knee in the small of her back, holding her down as he drained the contents of his glass in one swallow. Her hand with the vial was trapped beneath her. When he threw up her nightgown and drove into her, she closed her eyes tightly, her teeth closing over a fold of the coverlet, biting down as she fought to keep back the cries of pain and mortification. Soon it would be over. . . .

Half an hour later, Cordelia lay listening to her husband's breathing. His heavy frame weighed down the mattress beside her, so that she had to hold herself stiffly to stop rolling into the deep trough against his body. She could swear that his breathing had changed. It had been lighter before, but now it deepened, became stertorous. She could feel that his body had somehow changed, become heavier, more inert. Tentatively, she touched him. His skin was clammy. He didn't move. She pulled aside the bedcurtains, letting in the moonlight from the window. Still he didn't move. She propped herself on an elbow and leaned over him, examining his face. It was a mask, showing not a flicker, not a twitch. She touched his mouth. No reaction.

Her heart in her mouth, she slipped from bed. Still he didn't move. She snaked her hand beneath the mattress on her side of the bed and felt for the key to his chest. Her heart was pounding so loudly it was astonishing that it didn't penetrate his sleep. But Mathilde had done her work well.

The little padlock lay on the palm of her hand as Cordelia stepped back from the bed, her gaze still riveted to the form on the mattress. With a sudden heave, Michael rolled over onto his side, burying his face in the pillows. She felt sick.

His snores deepened yet again, reverberating around the room. She stood immobile by the bed, turning the key over in her hand, looking down at Michael, his face still buried in the pillow. Even muffled, his snores still reverberated. He wasn't going to wake for hours.

If she was going to do it, it had to be now. Cordelia flew across the room, through her own dressing room, and let herself into Michael's. She closed the door and lit the lamp, turning the wick down low, then dropped to her knees before the chest. The key fitted the brass padlock with oiled ease. She turned the key, heard the little click as the padlock opened. She lifted the lid. The contents looked just as they had done on the last occasion—the book of poisons on top of the series of journals.

Her hand went unerringly to the journal for 1764—the year before Elvira's death. With trembling fingers, she opened it at the first page.

The book fell to the carpet with a thump as a loud bellow erupted from her bedchamber, a howl almost like an animal in pain. *He knew. He knew that his chest had been violated.* But how could he?

Dear God! She waited, frozen, for him to burst through the door to confront her. He would kill her. Another bellow crashed onto her ears, but he didn't come.

Slowly, she managed to move. She managed to stand up, although her legs were trembling so much they could barely carry her as she crept to the door to the bedchamber, opened it a crack, and peered around, her dread so profound she thought her heart was going to stop with fright.

Michael was sitting up in bed, his chest bare, his chamber robe fallen open to the sides. His eyes were wide open. They stared at the door, seemed to fix her on the dark points of his pupils. Cordelia trembled, her teeth chattering, nausea rising in her belly as she waited for him to do something. But he just sat there, staring. And slowly, very slowly, it dawned on her that he couldn't see her. His eyes were open, but he couldn't see her. He wasn't awake, he was in the grip of some ghastly nightmare.

Her relief was so great she almost collapsed to the floor. Mathilde's potion obviously did more than put a man to sleep. It must arouse the demons in the sleeper's soul. And Mathilde had chosen such a draught for such a man.

Again Cordelia shivered. Mathilde had a long reach and an uncanny instinct for appropriate punishment.

She returned to Michael's dressing room, picked up the fallen journal, and settled down on the carpet, leaning against the opened chest, to read. The ticking of the clock, the rustle of the pages as she read were the only sounds in the room. Slowly and in growing horror, she read through the events of 1764.

Her husband's documentation was meticulous. In February of 1764 he had begun to suspect Elvira of unfaithfulness. Each little detail was recorded, each hint of suspicion, each moment of conviction. His nightly attempts to dominate her were described with all the nauseating attention to detail Cordelia remembered from reading his description of her own ordeals. Elvira had suffered, but if Michael's entries were to be believed, she had taken her revenge with a lover.

The case against her was built up, pebble by pebble, day by day. Reading the journal was a horrifying excursion into the mind of a man obsessed to the point of dementia by his belief that his wife was making of him a fool and a cuckold. And yet, Cordelia could see no utterly incontrovertible evidence. Michael had seen it . . . or had he in his mad jealousy invented it?

Cordelia had forgotten the time, the place, all sense of danger. She replaced the volume for 1764 and withdrew the next year's. And she read about Elvira's death. Disbelief and then horror seeped cold and dreadful into the very marrow of her bones. Each stage of Elvira's decline was documented, the vomiting, the weakness, the loss of her once beautiful hair, the blurring of her vision, the dreadful bodily pains that racked her beyond even the help of laudanum. The descriptions of her symptoms were as cold and dispassionate as the descriptions of what had caused them—the poison and its relentless administration.

Each dose Michael had given to his wife was recorded. Three times a day right up to the hour before her death. Her death was simply stated. *At 6:30 this evening, Elvira paid for her faithlessness.*

Cordelia closed the book and stared sightlessly into the empty grate. The wick in the oil lamp flickered faintly, the oil almost gone. She replaced the journal and took out the book of poisons. With growing repulsion she flicked through it, looking for and yet dreading to find a description of the poison that had killed Elvira. But disgust became too much for her. She closed the book with another shudder of horror. Her hands felt dirty just by touching it. She felt soiled through and through by this journey into the dark vindictive soul of a murderer.

Only one thought filled her head now, as she replaced the book, checked with a cold pragmaticism that everything was in its right place, and closed and locked the chest. She had to get herself and the children away from Michael. Whatever the danger they faced in fleeing, it would be as nothing compared with the danger they all faced every minute they spent under the prince's roof. And all Leo's scruples about the kind of future they would have vanished in a puff of smoke when compared with the prospect of no future at all.

She cast one last look around the dressing room before turning out the dying lamp and creeping back to her own bedchamber. Michael was lying down again, on his back, his eyes once more mercifully closed. Cordelia slipped the key back beneath the mattress and drew the curtains around the bed again.

It was dawn. Leo and the male members of the court would be heading out into the forest for a boar hunt. Michael had been intending to join them, but she wasn't going to try to waken him. Part of her almost wished that she had given him an overdose of the potion, one that would ensure he never woke up. But he was sleeping too noisily for near death.

She wrapped herself in a chamber robe and curled up in an armchair, waiting until it would be a reasonable hour to summon Elsie and Michael's valet. Her mind was as cold and clear as a marble tablet on which every word she had read was engraved. And her problem was simple. How was she to face her husband when he awoke? How could she act as if she didn't know what she now knew? The least suspicion and he would kill her too.

•   •   •

Michael awoke to brilliant sunlight. His body felt leaden, clammy, his head thick as if he'd indulged too heavily the night before. For a moment he didn't know where he was. He blinked at the brightness of the light. Then he realized that he was in his wife's bed. He must have spent the entire night with her. He turned his head. The pillow beside him was vacant. He was alone in the bed.

He sat up ... too suddenly for his head, which felt swollen, assaulted, as if it were a boulder being attacked by pickaxes. His eyes were raw, his mouth dry and foul tasting. He'd been drinking brandy freely before coming to bed. But surely no more than he was accustomed to. He buried his head in his hands, trying to think.

"You are awake, my lord." Cordelia's voice interrupted his desperate musing. "Are you ill, sir? You look most unwell." There was no hint of concern in the cold voice.

He raised his head painfully. Cordelia, in a pale negligee, her hair loose on her shoulders, stood at the end of the bed.

"What's the time?"

"Past nine. You have slept long."

"*Past nine!*" He had never slept that late.

"I think perhaps you are ill, my lord." Cordelia regarded him dispassionately. "You look a little heated. Could you have caught a chill?"

"Don't be absurd, woman. I've never had a day's illness in my life." He thrust aside the covers and stood up. Immediately, the room pitched violently and his legs refused to hold him. He sat down heavily on the edge of the bed and wondered if perhaps Cordelia was right. Could he be ill?

"I'll call your valet." Cordelia pulled the bell rope.

"What happened?" Michael demanded thickly. "Last night? What happened?" He had a vague sense of dread that permeated his mind. He didn't know where it came from, but he felt as if something dreadful had happened, leaving him clothed in sticky, cold strands of apprehension.

"Why, nothing out of the ordinary, my lord." Cordelia came back to the bed. "Except that you fell asleep afterward." She couldn't keep the contempt out of her voice, but somehow she knew that at the moment her insolence would pass with impunity. Michael was too wrapped up in his own ills to hear her tone.

He shook his head slowly. Something was wrong. Badly wrong. His valet knocked and entered. "Is something amiss, my lord? You were to join the hunt this morning, but you didn't ring for me."

The.hunt. How in the devil's name could he have slept through the dawn? Missed one of the king's hunts? He'd never done such a thing in his life.

"Give me your arm," he demanded harshly. He stood up, leaning on the valet's stalwart arm, his face set in lines of grim determination to defeat this mortifying weakness. "I'll take a hot milk punch and a plate of sirloin. Then I'll have the leech to bleed me." He drew the sides of his robe together. He cast a look of bemused frustration at his wife, then staggered from Cordelia's room, supported by his valet.

Cordelia smiled grimly. She must discover from Mathilde how long Michael's weakness would last. If he was forced to keep to his bed for a while, then matters would be easier to arrange.

As she rang for Elsie the clock on the mantel struck the half hour. The men would return from the boar hunt at around ten. Four hours of that brutal sport was enough even for the king, who lived for the hunt.

"Put out the gray gown, Elsie," she instructed as the maid scurried in, looking as usual as if she'd run a marathon to get there. Her cheeks were scarlet, and her hair was escaping in a frizz from beneath her cap. She curtsied and smiled nervously as she set Cordelia's breakfast tray on the table. "Will that be the one with the heather-colored petticoat, m'lady?"

"Yes, the one you mended yesterday," Cordelia said

patiently, dipping her brioche into the wide, shallow bowl of coffee.

"And you wear the blue silk shoes with it," Elsie announced triumphantly.

Cordelia couldn't help smiling. "Precisely."

With a pleased beam, Elsie filled the basin with hot water from the ewer and bustled over to help her mistress out of her nightgown, asking with an air of importance, "How will you be wearing your hair today, m'lady? Should I heat the curling iron?"

Cordelia shook her head hastily. Elsie's last attempt with the curling iron had produced a few singed ringlets. "I'll wear it loose, with a ribbon."

At ten o'clock she went into the salon, where Monsieur Brion was arranging the newest periodicals on a console table. "How is the prince?" she inquired casually, casting a quick checking look at her reflection in the mirror above the fireplace.

"I have sent for the physician, my lady. He keeps to his bed, I understand," Brion replied without a flicker of an eye.

"If he should inquire after me, perhaps you would inform him that I am waiting on the dauphine. She will expect me to escort Mesdames Amelia and Sylvie to her later this morning."

"As you say, madame." He bowed. Cordelia smiled. They both gave a half nod, then the majordomo moved to open the door for his mistress.

Cordelia moved as fast as her high heels and wide hoop would permit down the grand staircase and out into the garden. She strolled along the gravel walks and through a side gate that led to the stable courtyard. It was here that the hunt would return.

Within five minutes the first huntsmen clattered onto the cobbles, the king at their head. They were splattered with mud and blood. Blood clotted on their britches and their gloved hands, streaked their faces. The grooms accompanying them carried their weapons, the knives and spears that they had used in the last fierce tussle with the boar. A hand-to-hand fight to the death, with the maddened deadly animal cornered by dogs and men, all out for its blood.

Women did not go on boar hunts. They were considered too dangerous, too bloody. The death toll among dogs and horses was frequently horrendous, and many a huntsman was crippled for life by a slashing tusk.

The morning had clearly been successful. A group of beaters carried a massive boar slung on two poles, blood dripping from its slit throat. Hounds limping and slavering crowded around, waiting for their share of the prize. The stench of blood was almost overpowering, and even Cordelia, who had been riding to hounds ever since she could walk, was sickened by it.

Leo came in with the second party. He too was blood spattered, his leather boots coated with mud. Presumably, he was one of those who had to be in at the kill, facing the beast, eye to eye. It didn't surprise her. What did surprise her was her wish that he would leave the risky reckless bravado to others and stay safely on his horse at the kill.

"Princess von Sachsen." She turned swiftly at the king's unmistakable hail, curtsying deeply. He beamed at her from atop his horse. "What a beautiful morning we've had. But we were expecting your husband?" He raised an inquiring eyebrow.

Cordelia swam gracefully out of the curtsy. "My husband is indisposed, monseigneur. He sends his deepest regrets."

The king frowned. "Indisposed? Not seriously, I trust?"

"No, indeed not, sire," she said swiftly. Indisposition in the king's presence was frowned upon, death was forbidden. It was an absolute rule that a dead body should never lie under a roof where the king was in residence, and if anyone had the bad taste to expire in the night, they were removed with unseemly haste before the king got to hear of it.

"Then I will expect to see him this evening," His Majesty declared, accepting the hand of an equerry to dismount.

Cordelia curtsied again and slipped away from the royal

notice. Leo was standing to one side, respectfully bare-headed in the king's presence, tapping his whip in the palm of his hand.

"What's the matter with Michael?" he asked in a low voice as she came to stand beside him.

"Mathilde's potion. But I must talk to you at once. It's most dreadfully urgent, Leo." She tried to keep her eyes on some distant spot across the yard, tried to keep the panic from her voice, tried to appear if she were merely passing the time of day.

But Leo wasn't fooled and his gut knotted with apprehension. It wasn't like Cordelia to panic. He glanced around, then said, "Make your way to the laurel maze; I'll meet you there."

"But soon, Leo. You must come quickly." She hurried away, leaving him in a turmoil of anxiety. He looked down at his filthy hands, his torn and blood-streaked coat and britches. Splashes of mud had dried hard on his face. He had to change. He would draw unwelcome notice if he appeared in the gardens in such a state.

Cordelia waited half an hour at the entrance to the laurel maze. It was in a secluded uncultivated part of the landscape, on a grassy knoll that gave a clear view over the parterres and fountains of the formal gardens below. They would see anyone coming while being concealed themselves within the maze.

But where was he? And how was she to tell him what she'd discovered? How was she to tell him that his beloved twin had been murdered? How could he bear such knowledge, bear to know that he had done nothing to help her?

She saw him climbing the knoll toward her. He was dressed in ivory satin, the lining of his coat peacock blue. He was bareheaded, wearing neither wig nor powder. And despite the dreadful business that had brought them here, a current of desire jolted her loins, curled her toes. He was so beautiful. And he loved her. She ducked backward into the maze, out of sight of anyone who might chance to look up from below. She was too far away to be immediately identifiable, but any risk, however small, was one too many.

Leo stood at the top of the rise and looked casually around, shading his eyes with his hand, as if taking stock of his surroundings. Then, in a leisurely fashion, he strolled into the maze.

"What is it?" he asked quietly. His face was pale, his eyes steady, his voice even.

Cordelia twisted her hands into impossible knots. However hard she'd tried, she hadn't been able to come up with the words. "Michael poisoned Elvira," she blurted finally. "I'm sorry, I didn't mean to say it like that."

His face was a dreadful mask, his eyes lightless caverns, the planes and contours of his skull suddenly standing out in harsh relief. "What did you say?"

Cordelia moistened her lips. She reached for his hands, but he jerked them away with an impatient rejection that hurt even though she understood it. "Last night I read Michael's journals. He is meticulous in his daily entries. I think there's a volume for every year of his adult life. I read about Elvira. . . ." She stopped, her hands outstretched, palms up in a gesture of helplessness.

"Tell me," he rasped. "Everything you can remember."

"I can remember everything," she said painfully. "I have one of those memories that retains everything I read on a page. It . . . it . . . it's very useful for studying." She swallowed, realizing how stupid such burble sounded.

"Get on with it." He began to pace the narrow aisle between the high laurel bushes as she recited word for word the pages from Michael's journal. And when she fell silent, he continued to pace, and the profound quiet seemed a black chasm into which they slowly slid.

"Could . . . could Elvira have been unfaithful?" Cordelia could bear the silence no longer.

Leo's dead eyes sprang into life. "Possibly," he said curtly. "But what has that to do with murder?"

"Nothing . . . nothing, of course. I'm sorry."

"Poison!" he spat suddenly. "Of all the vile instruments. A weak, cowardly, *woman's* weapon!"

Cordelia had no urge to defend her sex at this point. She didn't know what to do or say. Leo was completely unapproachable. Every line of his body held her away. She was the bearer of ill tidings, and messengers always suffered. But her heart ached for him and she longed to touch him, to offer him some comfort, but she knew there was nothing she had that was strong enough to overcome his grief and anger. Not even the power of her love.

"Leave me!" It was a curt order and he didn't look at her as he issued it.

Cordelia melted away, down the hill, blending with the glittering butterflies of the court strolling under the sun, between the fountains.

Leo spun on his heel, his eyes blinded with tears as he retreated into the cool seclusion of the maze. He wanted to scream his rage and grief to the skies but instead he paced the narrow alleys between the high laurel hedges, slamming one hand into the palm of the other in a futile expression of his despair.

He blamed himself. He should have known. All their lives, he and his twin had been inextricably bound together. They had understood each other's thoughts before they were spoken. As small children, even when apart they had occasionally had uncanny flashes of knowledge about the other's doings or feelings. When Elvira had been sick of scarlet fever, Leo had been at school, but the night when the fever hit its peak, the moment when his twin had hovered between life and death, he had woken and found himself staring into a strange internal landscape. A dark tunnel with a soft warm light at the end. He had struggled, finding it hard to breathe, as he'd fought to refuse the invitation of that light. His whole body seemed to be at war, wrenched from side to side by opposing forces, and then the light had receded and he'd woken fully, drenched in sweat, as exhausted as if he'd been fighting a pitched battle for many hours.

He had fought that battle against death hand in hand with Elvira across the distance that separated them. But when she lay dying at her husband's hands, he'd been frolicking in Rome and had experienced not a twitch of unease.

How could he have abandoned her? How had it happened, when had it happened, that the spiritual tie between them had loosened and flown apart?

Tears poured unrestrained down his face as he moved deeper and deeper into the maze. Tears of guilt and of unspeakable grief. They had both known that they were drawing apart, that the connections of twinship were giving way to the independence of their separate lives. They had accepted it, acknowledged it. But now Leo felt again, for the first time since Elvira's death, that old spiritual connection. Now he knew that he had truly lost a part of himself, and he felt that loss in his blood, in his bone, in his sinew.

Chapter Twenty-one

AT THE FIRST birdsong of the dawn chorus, as the king's hunting party were leaving for the boar hunt, Amelia had nudged her sister awake. Sylvie opened her eyes and sat up all in the same movement. "Where are we?" She gazed bemused at the strange bedchamber with its blue velvet hangings and gilded ceiling. A fresh, fragrant breeze blew through the long open windows.

"In the palace, stupid," her sister whispered, sitting up beside her. "We're going to meet the king."

Sylvie's mouth opened on a round O as memory flooded back. "With Cordelia." Only in the presence of others did they give their stepmother the courtesy title of Madame.

"Yes, and not with Madame de Nevry." Amelia stuffed the pillow against her mouth to stifle the excited giggles bubbling irrepressibly from her chest. "Change places, Sylvie." She wriggled over her sister.

"We can't do that *here*," Sylvie protested. "What about the king?"

"He won't know," Amelia said matter-of-factly. "No one ever does." She shoved against her sister, pushing her over to the other side of the bed.

Sylvie continued to look doubtful. The trick they played in the nursery and schoolroom at home was all very well, even when their father was their dupe, but to play it in the king's palace, in front of the king, was very different. "What about Cordelia?"

"She won't know either," Amelia stated, hiding her own doubts now under a show of bravado. "No one will know, 'cept us. Like always."

Had Sylvie been able to persevere in her doubts, she

would have won over her sister; however, the door opened to admit their governess, still in dishabille, and the nursery maid.

Louise brandished the two hair ribbons and without so much as a morning greeting had labeled each twin while they were still in bed and she thought she could be certain which was which. She gave orders to the nursery maid through compressed lips and communicated with the children with little pushes and pinches, lacing them into their gowns as if they were insensate dolls, scraping back their hair, thrusting pins into the tight braids, retying the ribbons until they both felt as if their scalps were about to split.

When their little corsetted bodies were clothed in the formal, heavy brocaded gowns over stiff damask petticoats and wide swinging hoops, their governess shooed them ahead of her into the small salon next to the bedroom. She sat them side by side on a slippery chintz sofa, their feet on footstools so that they were in no danger of sliding off, and told them dourly not to move a muscle. They were to wait there until the princess came to fetch them for their state visit to the dauphine.

Amelia glanced at her sister, whose mouth turned down with dismay. The hands on the pretty gilded clock on the mantel meant nothing to them, but they knew it was still very early and Cordelia had said the previous day that she would come for them at eleven in the morning. The dauphine was not an early riser.

Louise instructed the nursery maid to watch them and make sure they didn't ruffle so much as a hair, and went off to her own chamber to dress.

"Are we to have no breakfast?" Sylvie asked timidly as her stomach grumbled beneath the stiff panel of her bodice.

"I don't know, madame," the nursery maid said. She too was hungry and lost in this vast palace. There was no kitchen attached to the children's apartments, and she slept on a thin mattress in a small closet in the corridor outside. She didn't know how to order food or fuel or water and felt as powerless to look after her own wants as any prisoner in the Bastille.

Louise returned in half an hour, a suspicious pink tinge to her cheekbones, her pale watery eyes as usual slightly yellow and bloodshot. She glared at the little girls.

"Are we to have no breakfast, madame?" Amelia this time inquired.

"We're very hungry," Sylvie added.

Madame was hungry too, but she was no more *au fait* with the workings of Versailles than the nursery maid. Supper had been brought to them the previous evening without any effort on her part. But how to initiate the production of a meal was beyond her. She wasn't about to admit that to her charges, however, let alone to the anxious nursery maid.

"You will wait," she declared loftily. "A little self-denial is good for the soul."

The children's dismay increased as they understood that their governess hadn't the faintest idea how to feed them. For four interminable hours, they sat side by side on the sofa, not daring to move a muscle, while their governess took nips from her silver flask to subdue her own hunger pangs, and dozed in between whiles. The nursery maid tidied the salon and the bedchambers, then stood miserably by the door. From beyond the closed double doors came sounds of life: hurrying footsteps, murmured voices, the occasional shout. There were smells too, food smells. In the courtyard below their window, horses clattered over cobbles, iron wheels clanged, military voices bellowed, trumpets sounded. Everyone, it seemed, in this vast place, was oblivious of the four newcomers huddling in a small salon on an outside staircase.

Until the door opened to admit Cordelia in her gray gown and heather pink petticoat, her hair cascading in loose ringlets as black as night to her creamy shoulders. "I give you good morning," she declared, bending to take the girls' hands in both of hers and kissing their smooth round cheeks. Her eyes were haunted but her smile was as warm as apprehension and anxiety would permit.

"Oh, but you're so cold!" she exclaimed. "How can you be cold on such a beautiful day?" She looked almost accusingly at the governess, who had risen, blinking, from her chair. "They're frozen, poor darlings. They must have some tea or something to warm them."

"We're hungry!" they announced in unison.

"Hungry? But have you had no breakfast?"

Louise sniffed audibly. "The prince believes his children should exercise self-discipline on occasion."

"I'm sure that's very laudable," Cordelia said acidly. "But I cannot believe he would expect them to starve." She examined the woman in frowning silence for a minute, then cast a swift glance at the pale nursery maid. "Could it be that you didn't know how to order breakfast?" she murmured wonderingly. She whirled around to pull the bell rope by the door. "This bell rings in our own apartments. It will bring Frederick from our own household. You may order whatever you wish from him."

"I am aware, madame," the governess said, pursing her lips. "But as I said, it's good for children to—"

"It is *not* good for children to face the day on empty bellies," Cordelia interrupted vigorously. "They have a long and tiring day ahead of them, and they look like ghosts. How long have they been sitting there?"

"Since early morning, madame," the nursery maid put in, emboldened both by her own hunger and the governess's clear discomfiture.

Cordelia spun round on Louise. "You exceed your authority, madame." Her voice was ice, her eyes were blue flame. "As I understand it, you are paid to care for the prince's children, not to torture them!" She turned back to the opening door in a gray and pink swirl of skirts. "Frederick, bring chocolate and brioche and jam for the children, and show the nursery maid where she may break her own fast."

Silence fell in the wake of the footman's departure with the maid. The governess fulminated, her chest swelling like an outraged bullfrog's. The children, eyes bright with curiosity and excitement, still sat on the sofa, but their gaze never left Cordelia's face. Cordelia paced the small salon, her brain working furiously. She had broken one of her rules in this new life and declared war on the governess, instead of offering an alliance. But the woman was so odious, how could she bear to court her?

She paused in her pacing for a minute, her eyes resting on the children. Something wasn't right with their appearance. But what could possibly be wrong?

"Princess, I must protest your tone." The governess finally gave voice to her anger. "My kinsman, Prince Michael, has entrusted his children to my care and authority since their infancy and—"

"Ah, here's Frederick." Cordelia brusquely interrupted this seething beginning. "Frederick, set the tray down there." Having thus reduced the governess to the status of a piece of furniture, she issued a stream of orders to the returning footman, who set his laden tray down and scurried around, placing two chairs with extra cushions, lifting Amelia and Sylvie onto the chairs, pouring hot chocolate, shaking out napkins, passing a basket of brioches.

Cordelia hovered over the table, breaking the brioches, spreading jam, encouraging the children, who required little encouragement, to eat their fill of this succulent feast, so vastly different from their usual fare of weak tea and bread and butter.

When Louise realized that she was excluded from this meal, she stalked out of the room to her own chamber, banging the door behind her. Cordelia stuck her tongue out at the door and the twins choked on their hot chocolate, splattering drips across the table.

"I've spilled it on my dress!" Amelia wailed, rubbing fiercely at a spot of chocolate on her bodice, all desire to laugh vanished at this disaster.

"Oh, it's nothing much." Cordelia spat on the corner of a napkin and dabbed at the mark. "No one will notice." She stood back to examine the tiny stain, and that same puzzled frown drew her arched brows together.

"But ... but ... we're to see the dauphine," Sylvie breathed, shocked at this insouciance.

"Toinette knows how easy it is to spill something," Cordelia reassured, shaking off the moment of puzzlement.

"But ... but what of the king?" Their eyes, twinned, gazed at her across the table.

"What of the king?" came a voice from the door.

"It's Monsieur Leo!" they squealed in unison. "Did you find us?"

"It certainly looks that way," he said solemnly, closing the door behind him. "I am sent by the king, who wishes to make the acquaintance of my nieces." This last was directed more at Cordelia than at the girls.

His expression was calm, his manner easy. Leo was a past master at the courtly art of dissembling. Only in his eyes could the truth be seen. They were no longer lightless, but they burned with a dreadful rage, akin to despair, and Cordelia's scalp lifted with cold dread. He was blaming himself. She had known that would be his first response, and she had no idea how to reach him in that bitter slough of self-denunciation. Even to attempt ordinary words of comfort would be insulting, especially since she had not known Elvira.

Michael was presumably still keeping to his bed, but he knew that she would be escorting the children to Toinette, so there was no danger of falling foul of him at this point. He could hardly expect her to refuse to obey a royal summons while she waited for him to recover.

"Then we should not delay," she said neutrally. She didn't look at Leo, because she knew that her eyes were filled with compassion and her own fear, and to see that would only add to his burdens. She wiped chocolate from one child's mouth and turned to the jam on the other's fingers.

The door to the governess's chamber opened, and Louise stood glaring in silent accusation in the doorway.

Leo said with cold authority, "I have been sent by the king to escort your charges to his presence. Perhaps you would make certain their dress is in order."

"The princess has made it clear that my services are not required," Louise said spitefully, with downturned mouth. "The princess believes she can tend to her stepdaughters without assistance. Even though I've been doing it to the prince's satisfaction for close on four years."

Leo didn't deign to reply, he merely looked through her as if she were some transparent insect. Cordelia said curtly, "Whatever grievance you may have, madame, this is not the place to air it." She lifted Amelia and then Sylvie from their chairs, smoothing down their skirts, adjusting their muslin fichus.

Amelia, still troubled by the faint spot on her bodice, surreptitiously scratched at it with a fingernail while casting anxious glances toward the governess.

"Come." Leo took their hands. "We mustn't keep the king waiting."

Louise didn't move from her spot by her door until they had all left the room. Then she came over to the table. Her mouth was pursed, her eyes sharply speculative. Greedily, she began to eat the remains of the children's breakfast, cramming brioche into her mouth as if she hadn't eaten in a week, swallowing jam by the spoonful in between sips of the now cold chocolate remaining in the jug.

She would appeal directly to the prince. He must surely regard an affront to her authority as an affront to his own. It was common household gossip that he ruled his young bride with the same rod of iron he held over the rest of his staff.

She brushed crumbs from her lips with the back of her hand, heedless of a smear of jam that transferred itself to her gown. She took a long nip from her flask and sat down beside the empty grate. It was obvious that the princess was hand in glove with the viscount, which made the situation even more intolerable but would act in her favor with the prince. An alliance between stepmother and uncle would not be tolerated by the father. Prince Michael ruled alone.

"I know what it is!" Cordelia exclaimed suddenly as they began to walk down the corridor. She stopped and looked down at the children, stepping away to get a better look. "Amelia's wearing Sylvie's ribbon, and Sylvie's wearing Amelia's."

"What?" Leo dropped their hands and looked in astonishment at the twins, who were now covered in confusion, giggling behind their hands, their faces crimson. "How can you tell?"

"Well, I couldn't at first, but Sylvie has a beauty spot on the back of her neck." She touched the almost invisible mole on the supposed Amelia's neck. "I'm right, aren't I?" The child nodded, still convulsed with giggles.

"I'll be damned!" Leo shook his head. "How often do you play such a trick?"

Neither child answered, but they covered their faces with their hands.

"It must be such fun to fool everyone like that," Cordelia said, much struck by the possibilities of the masquerade. "Don't you agree, Leo?"

For a moment the shadows retreated. Leo couldn't help smiling at the thought of the governess, not to mention, Michael, never knowing which child they were talking to. The game must have lightened their dreary days.

"How many times have you deceived me?" he demanded.

"Oh, never," they assured him in unison. "*Never!*"

"Somehow I doubt that," he commented wryly. "But you'll not do it again, thanks to your observant stepmother."

His smile faded as they renewed their walk through the thronged corridor, he and Cordelia each holding a child's hand. "I will have passports for you and the children within two days." His lips barely moved as he spoke in the direction of her ear. "I must find a way to get the girls out of Versailles on some pretext. Something that will give you a few hours' start."

"Mathilde will come with us," she returned in the same almost soundless murmur, responding as if this were merely the continuation of a long previous discussion. Of course, there was no choice, no decisions to be made apart from the when and the how. And she didn't have to be told that Leo would not come with them. Michael might suspect his involvement, but he mustn't be given proof. It would be for her to ensure the girls' safety.

The children, hanging on their hands, gazed wide-eyed at the magnificence around them, their little feet taking the tiny gliding steps they'd been taught. The king's audience chamber was crowded with courtiers, but a word from Leo to one of the king's chancellors secured them clear passage to where the king sat with the dauphine and her husband. Amelia and Sylvie were engulfed. They saw only legs and hoops as they were wafted through the crowd, their cheeks brushing against rich silks and velvets, their tiny slippered feet barely touching the marble floors. They clung desperately to the supporting hands of their escorts, terrified that if they came adrift, they would be lost in the sea of gowns, drowned beneath the rising waves of noise way above them.

They had so little experience of the world outside their shuttered apartments on the rue du Bac that they were tongue-tied, staring at their feet, when they reached the king. They only remembered to curtsy when they saw Cordelia sweeping into a deep obeisance at the king's feet.

Toinette leaned forward in her chair, beckoning them to her. "I have some sweetmeats," she said warmly, gesturing to a flunky holding a silver salver of cakes and pastries. The children looked up at Leo and Cordelia, too shy to move a muscle. The king laughed, selected two marzipan roses from the salver, and gave one to each child, then with great good humor turned to Madame du Barry, signaling that the audience was over.

Toinette rose from her chair. "Let us walk with the children, Cordelia. Do you accompany us, Viscount Kierston?" This last was a trifle imperious, breaking into Leo's conversation with Madame du Barry, who stood at the king's right shoulder.

Leo smiled politely but his eyebrows lifted a little as he bowed to the young woman, whose nose was definitely in the air, her eyes studiously averted from the king's mistress. "I am yours to command, of course, madame."

"Then I command that you accompany us," Toinette declared, now trying to sound lighthearted and teasing. But the attempt was too late to reverse the effect of her outright snub to Madame du Barry, who stood glaring, her mouth pinched, her cheeks white beneath the rouge. The king was looking most displeased, but Toinette appeared not to notice.

"I do not believe *madame ma mère* would expect me to mingle with whores," she said in a defiant undertone as they moved away from the circle fawning at the king's feet.

"I imagine the empress would expect her daughter to behave with courtesy," Leo said. Despite his own wretchedness, he couldn't stand aside and see the child make such a dreadful mistake. "If you make an enemy of the du Barry, madame, you will play into the hands of those who would use you to cause trouble at court. That will not please the king."

"I follow my conscience, my lord," Toinette declared loftily. "And my conscience is answerable only to God." She gave a short nod of her head in punctuation. "Let's go into the gardens and show Amelia and Sylvie the peacocks and the fountains."

The girls, who were beginning to recover from the ordeal of the king's audience and to examine their exotic surroundings with more interest, exclaimed with delight at this prospect, tugging on Leo's hands.

Leo bowed with more than a hint of irony and gave up. He had far more pressing concerns. "If you'll excuse me, madame." He strode away.

Toinette seemed barely to notice. "I am having a concert this afternoon, Cordelia; you must bring the children. Signor Percossi is to play for us. And there's to be a dancer too."

"A dancer?"

"Yes, she's called Clothilde, I believe. He requested it most specifically."

"Oh." Despite everything, Cordelia smiled with pleasure. Christian must have summoned up his courage to approach the dancer. "Do you have music lessons, Sylvie?"

Sylvie's nose wrinkled. "Madame de Nevry teaches us."

"But we don't think she can play," Amelia interjected. "She makes a terrible noise."

"Yes, all thumps. It doesn't sound a bit like music," her sister continued. "And she makes us go up and down the keys." They both ran their fingers over an imaginary keyboard, singing out the scales in their high and not very tuneful voices.

"Oh, how unpleasant." Cordelia grimaced sympathetically, but her mind was racing as a plan took shape. "I'll have to see if I can't arrange a better music teacher for you. All girls must learn to play, isn't that so, Toinette?"

The dauphine nodded in fervent agreement. "And sing and dance too. You'll see how amusing it can be."

The girls didn't look convinced, but they had reached the gardens now and all thought of music lessons vanished in the pleasures of the outdoors.

"His Highness is not receiving today," Monsieur Brion haughtily informed the governess, who stood in the corridor outside their apartments. He held the door at his back, effectively barring her entrance.

"And when will the prince be receiving?" Louise put on all her airs. She was a relative of the prince's, not to be put off by a mere servant.

"He hasn't said. I suggest you return to your own quarters, madame, and he will send for you when he is so inclined." Brion stepped back into the room and began to close the door.

"You will tell him I wish to speak with him?" Louise pleaded desperately as the door closed against her nose. There was no response.

She lurked in the corridor, muttering to herself. She didn't trust Brion to pass on her message, or at least not in a timely fashion. And it was vitally important she tell her tale to the prince as soon as possible. She would tell him that if her authority was to be flouted after all these years, then she must hear it from his own lips. Of course, she would bow to the prince's commands, but he would understand her position. The princess was so young; she was playing at the novelty of motherhood. Soon she would become bored, and court pleasures would seduce her from the schoolroom. And the governess would be left with fractious, disappointed, spoiled children.

She hovered outside the door, rehearsing her speech under her breath, trying to look assured, as if she had good reason to be where she was, becalmed on the tide of scurrying servants and chattering, fan-flourishing courtiers whose jeweled heels taptapped on the marble floors as they hurried past. Everyone was in a hurry and no one cast a sideways glance at the red-nosed, watery-eyed governess with her unfashionable wig and dowdy gown.

Louise glanced anxiously at her fob watch. It was nearing one o'clock and the children had been gone for two hours. She should return to her own quarters, but she kept hoping that the prince would emerge. Just because Brion said he wasn't receiving didn't necessarily mean that he wasn't.

Brion was a malicious beast and would enjoy her discomfiture, she thought with compressed lips.

A servant walked by with a pair of spaniels straining at a leash. The dogs stopped and sniffed at the governess's shoes, the hem of her gown. In one disdainful glance, the man-servant appraised Madame de Nevry, put her down as a charity case, a poor relation, maybe even an upper servant, although her dress was a trifle dowdy for the upper echelons of a servants' hall in any powerful household. He let the leash go slack and a wet nose pushed up beneath Louise's petticoat. The servant stared indifferently around, making no attempt to drag the animals away, as if the governess were merely a tree trunk for the dogs' convenience.

"Oh, go away!" she squeaked, backing against the wall.

The servant grinned. "They're only being friendly," he said.

"Take them away!" She brushed at them, trying to straighten her skirt. "Horrible little animals."

"Don't you let His Grace of Burgundy hear you say that. Dear me, no." The man shook his head in mock reproof. "These two are more precious to the duke than his own children."

He was making game of her and she could do nothing about it, backed up as she was against the wall with the slobbering snuffling dogs at her ankles. Tears of frustration pricked behind her eyes. She knew she was the butt of kitchen jokes in the rue du Bac, but why some complete stranger should pick upon her she couldn't imagine.

"Madame de Nevry!" The princess's voice chimed from behind the odious footman. "Did you wish for something? For goodness sake, man, pull those dogs off. Can't you see that Madame has a dislike of the animals?"

The servant, recognizing the voice of authority, tugged his forelock and dragged the dogs away. Cordelia surveyed the red-faced governess with a raised eyebrow. "The children are with the nursemaid. They should have dinner and a rest before they attend the dauphine's musical entertainment this afternoon."

The princess's coldly arrogant tone was a timely reminder of Madame's grievances. She drew herself upright, her pursed mouth almost disappearing. "I understood that you had taken responsibility for the children, Princess. You made it very clear that I was not needed."

"And you were perhaps going to discuss that with my husband?" Cordelia asked softly, her eyes narrowed.

Louise almost flinched. "I wish to clarify matters with my cousin."

Cordelia stood in frowning silence for a minute.

"Walk with me awhile, madame." She took the governess's arm and marched her away down the corridor before Louise had time to recover from her astonishment. "Listen carefully," Cordelia continued in a conversational tone of voice that passed unnoticed among the chattering crowds. "I can only assume that my husband hasn't noticed that you reek like a pickle barrel, but I assure you that everyone else is aware of it. Myself, Viscount Kierston, Monsieur Brion, every member of the household right down to the potboy."

Louise gave an outraged gasp and tried to pull her arm free, but the princess for all her slenderness was more than a physical match for the governess. "I will not be spoken to—"

"Tush!" Cordelia interrupted. "You will listen, madame. I intend to involve myself in the children's welfare, and in every aspect of their education. You will say nothing of this to Prince Michael, and you will make no attempt to thwart me. If you do, then I promise you that the prince will know that a drunken sot has charge of his daughters. I leave you to imagine the consequences for yourself."

Louise was winded. She gasped like a gaffed fish, her face gray. It had never occurred to her that her numerous dips into her little silver flask left any trace. She had no idea she smelled of brandy. No idea that her bloodshot eyes and sometimes unsteady gait and her frequent dozes gave her away. She had thought herself perfectly safe from detection in the schoolroom with two tiny children.

"Do we have an understanding, madame?" Cordelia demanded crisply, plying her fan with her free hand. She smiled and curtsied to an acquaintance as she continued to march the governess along. "Your silence in exchange for mine."

Louise's head reeled. More than anything, she wanted a nip from her flask to clear her thoughts. "I . . . I will deny it. How dare you talk to me in such fashion," she managed to say.

Cordelia gave a short laugh. "There are too many witnesses for a denial to pass muster, madame. And I can safely promise you that they will step forward if I ask it of them. You are not very popular, you know," she added almost cajolingly, suddenly switching tactics. "And I have only the children's best interests at heart, as I am sure have you. We will work together to make them happy."

Louise's only response was an inarticulate moan, but Cordelia judged she had won the day. "We will start tomorrow," she said cheerfully. "I will introduce the girls to a musician friend of mine. A very influential friend," she fibbed, "who will undertake their musical instruction. And since I'm certain they'll make great progress under his tuition, their father will be very pleased. And, of course, you will take all the credit."

She stopped where two corridors branched, the left one leading to the children's quarters. "So, do we have an understanding?"

Louise was now flushed, but she could think of nothing to say. She ducked her head in a gesture that could have been agreement, pulled her arm free of Cordelia's, and scuttled away.

Cordelia nibbled her bottom lip, wondering if she'd over-reached herself. She'd offered both blackmail and bribery.

Would it be enough to keep the governess silent and turning a blind eye for the necessary time? Leo had said he would have passports within two days. If she could get the children into the town to Mathilde in Christian's lodgings without Michael's being aware of it, then they would have taken an important step. Just as long as Louise would keep quiet about a supposed music lesson.

She turned and thoughtfully made her way back to her own apartments. Michael was sitting in the salon, looking pale and drawn, when she entered.

"The king was very pleased with your daughters, my lord," she said almost indifferently. "The dauphine walked with them in the gardens, and they are bidden to attend her at a concert this afternoon."

Michael glowered. The leech had taken copious amounts of blood, and he felt too weak to take exception to her tone. "I will accompany you myself," he stated, taking a deep draught of the hot milk punch that he hoped would put blood back in his veins.

Cordelia curtsied. "If you feel well enough, my lord."

"Damn you! Of course I'm well enough!" He stared at her and the horrendous suspicion popped into his head that perhaps she had done this to him. Witchcraft? Could she be a witch? Absurd thought. But it wouldn't leave him. Something had drained all the strength from him while he'd been sleeping. While he'd been unconscious, something had filled his head with those ghastly images, those fearful premonitions that still haunted him in the bright sunlight of a new day.

His wife? His child bride? That willful, defiant, intractable chit?

Under his fixed stare, Cordelia felt pinned like a rabbit mesmerized by the fox. She couldn't imagine what thoughts could produce such dreadful menace. Had he looked at Elvira in that way? When he'd decided to kill her?

O God, help me. The prayer went round and around in

her head. She who put little faith in prayer. With a supreme effort of will, she smiled into those terrible pale eyes and excused herself. And in her deserted chamber, she hung over the commode, dryly retching as if she could rid herself of her terror.

Chapter Twenty-two

THE FENCING MASTER dropped his point and stepped back as the buttoned tip of Viscount Kierston's foil met his shoulder. "That was too quick even for me," he conceded, wiping his brow with a lace-edged handkerchief. "You have wings on your feet today, Milord Kierston."

Leo shook his head in disclaimer and mopped his own brow. It was early afternoon and warm in the gallery over the stables where courtiers tried their foils against the skill of Master Leclerc. Leo was a regular here, dueling with the master several hours a day whenever he had the opportunity. But today there was a deadlier purpose behind his practice than mere sport, and it showed in every muscle of his body, in his lethal concentration, in the ferocity beneath the impassive surface of his eyes.

"You are planning a duel, milord?" Leclerc never beat around the bush and he knew from years of experience how to read the signs.

Leo merely laughed and picked up the water carafe from the low stone sill behind him. He drank thirstily, then tilted back his head and poured a cool clear stream over his face. His hair was drawn tightly back from his face, accentuating the clean lines of the set jaw, the high cheekbones, the broad expanse of forehead.

"I pity whoever it is who's fallen foul of you, milord," Leclerc said phlegmatically, taking the carafe that Leo now offered him. He drank. "Another bout? Your footwork on the lunge is occasionally just a minuscule beat off perfection." He illustrated the gap with finger and thumb.

The dauphine's concert was not until three o'clock. Leo raised his point, saluted the fencing master, and the clash of blade on blade, the soft pounding of stockinged feet, were once again the only sounds to be heard in the long gallery.

As they fought, others arrived, ready to try out their skill against the master. Several pairs began a match of their own; others gathered to watch the master and his opponent. Leo was peripherally aware of the audience. Deliberately, he blocked them out, concentrated until he saw only the opposing blade, flashing, flickering, always looking for an opening. He reduced his opponent simply to a blade, as he knew he must do when this practice became reality. Then he would be watched, and by an audience much less disciplined that these fellow fencers. There would be rustling skirts and whispering women, languid comments from the fops and dandies who preferred the less active pursuits at court. All of those he must block out.

And all thoughts of Cordelia.

His blade faltered. Monsieur Leclerc slipped beneath Leo's guard, and the slender foil bent in a graceful arc as the button pressed into his ribs. He dropped his point, held out his hand. "Well fought, monsieur."

"Something happened in your eyes, milord," the master said simply. "Only you know what."

Leo gave a brief nod and picked up his coat from a chair. He responded casually to the greetings of friends and acquaintances, mopped his brow again, put on his shoes, then rested for a moment perched on the windowsill, his long legs, ankles crossed, stretched out in front of him.

No one looking at him taking his ease, watching the swordplay, would guess at the hot red anger in his soul at his mistake. An anger that had its roots in fear. Fear of his own death. He could defeat Michael only as long as he allowed nothing to interfere with his concentration. The prince was a superb swordsman, renowned throughout the Prussian army for his skill. He was older and heavier now than in his youth, when he'd dispatched ten of his fellow cadets to their deaths on the dueling ground in as many months. But he was still almost matchless. He still practiced religiously. And he could kill.

But he must put all thoughts of Cordelia from him. He must ensure that she and the children were safely out of the way. If he fell to Michael's sword, then Cordelia and the children would be defenseless unless they could disappear into thin air. His sister would hide them if they could reach England, and they would be safe for a while. At least until the immediate hue and cry had died down.

He must put from him the knowledge that if he succeeded in killing the prince, Cordelia would be free.

Elvira would be avenged; Cordelia would be free; Elvira's children would come under his own protection. All three goals achieved with one thrust of a rapier. But he must concentrate only on avenging Elvira—on punishing her murderer as was his legal and moral right. If he allowed himself to think beyond that, to a future—a life of love with Cordelia, where their children could grow in love and security—then he risked losing the concentration that was as great a weapon as his sword. A concentration that was all that stood between him and Michael's death cut.

"I was watching you fence, Lord Kierston."

Leo glanced up. Christian Percossi was smiling somewhat tentatively. He was still rather shy of the viscount. "I don't mean to be impertinent, but you seem very ferocious, as if it was not sport."

Leo pushed himself off the sill. "How observant of you. Walk with me awhile. There are some matters I need to discuss."

Christian, gratified at such in invitation, accompanied Leo from the gallery. But now the viscount's face was dark and closed, his eyes hard as iron, and those who glanced up as he passed felt a cold shiver as if an icy wind gusted in his wake. And Christian's blood stirred with foreboding.

They strolled along the gravel paths between the fountains, two courtiers engaged in conversation like any of the other couples around them. But this was no ordinary conversation.

"I intend to challenge Cordelia's husband under the ancient law of trial by duel," Leo was saying, his voice perfectly calm although the subject matter was incendiary. "It has to be a public accusation before the king, and a public trial. Cordelia must not be there. If I should lose, she will be in immediate danger from her husband and must be in a position to flee France with her stepdaughters."

"You would accuse him and fight with him because he mistreats Cordelia?" Christian asked hesitantly. Surely such a statement would immediately give rise to speculation about the relationship between the viscount and the prince's wife.

"No," Leo said flatly. "I will accuse him of murder. Of murdering his first wife, my sister."

Christian paled, his jaw dropped. "He did such a thing?"

"Yes." Leo plucked a rose from the trellis of the arbor under which they now walked. "He did such a thing. And I will claim my family right to avenge the death of a sister."

"But ... but surely it would be simpler ... less uncertain ... to accuse him before a court of law?" Christian stammered.

"Maybe. But he took the blood of my sister, and I will take his." Both voice and face were expressionless, and it seemed to Christian that the viscount was encased in ice. An ice sculpture far from the reach of ordinary human contact. A man contained by a most terrible rage.

"What ... what would you have me do?"

Leo's response was succinct, his voice still without expression. "In the event of my death, I would like you to escort Mathilde, Cordelia, and my nieces to the coast and there arrange passage for them on a packet to Dover. You will be pursued by Prince Michael, but you'll all have correct papers and passports, you'll need to be disguised in some way, and you'll need to travel warily. Do you think you can undertake such a task for Cordelia?"

"Yes, yes, of course I would try," Christian said. "But

Cordelia will want to make all the arrangements. She always does." He looked stricken at this admission, as if he was in some way failing Leo, but the viscount smiled for the first time. It was a fleeting smile, but it somewhat reassured Christian.

"Yes, I'm sure she will. But I need to know that you'll assist her in whatever ways are necessary."

"You have my word on it." Christian impulsively stuck out his hand. Leo took it in a firm, dry clasp.

"Good. Thank you, my friend." He shook the musician's hand briefly, then dropped the rose he'd been holding to the gravel. With a short nod, he turned and strode away in the direction of the palace.

Absently, Christian bent to pick up the fallen rose. He sat on a low stone bench in the arbor, inhaling the flower's delicate scent. He would have to get a leave of absence from his patron, who might well be displeased, since Christian had been such a short time in his service. He couldn't tell the Duc de Carillac the truth, of course, so he'd have to invent some foolproof tale. But when was the viscount intending to drop his bombshell? Christian kicked himself for not asking. He didn't know whether he had a day or a week or a month in which to prepare.

He glanced at his fob watch and leaped to his feet with an exclamation of horror. It was just after half past two and he was to play for the dauphine at three o'clock. He couldn't possibly be late. He set off at a run, arriving breathless and sweaty in the small oval music room off the Hall of Mirrors.

Mopping his brow, he examined the harpsichord. It was an elegant instrument, with glowing inlaid wood and soft ivory keys. The disturbing conversation with the viscount faded into the background of his mind as he sat down on the blue velvet stool and played a few chords, his head tilted as he listened to the notes.

"I trust the instrument is to your satisfaction, Signor Percossi?"

"Yes, thank you," he replied absently to the hovering

footman, only vaguely aware of the activity in the room behind him as servants arranged little gilt chairs in rows and set out decanters and platters of fruit, tarts, and sweetmeats.

"If you wouldn't mind moving for one minute, sir, we need to roll up the rug," an apologetic footman murmured.

Christian looked startled, but he stood up and moved aside obligingly as the Turkey carpet was rolled back to reveal the smooth oak floorboards. "Why are you doing that?"

"For the dancer, Mademoiselle Clothilde, sir."

Oh, yes. How could he have forgotten? Christian smiled involuntarily. He had arranged for Clothilde to dance this afternoon through the influence of his patron. The girl's father had been delighted at the honor done his daughter and was inclined to look upon young Signor Percossi with a favorable eye. Christian was not as yet sure how Clothilde viewed him; she was as timid as a fawn. But Christian had discovered in himself all the patience of a skilled hunter.

He moved away from the harpsichord and went to look out of the long window opening onto a flagstone terrace. The scene was as tranquil as always, the lawns and pathways dotted with bright-plumaged figures, hooped skirts swaying gracefully, the silks and satins of their escorts glowing like so many jewels under the late afternoon sun.

It was all so rich and artificial, Christian thought. Life centered around frivolities; no one had a serious thought in his head. Hunting, gaming, feasting, dancing, and the endless gossip occupied them from the moment they opened their eyes on the day until the last courtier had vanished from the marble corridors with the first birdsong.

A shiver ran down his spine as he remembered Leo's face, heard his voice again. There was nothing artificial or superficial about the viscount's deep, cold, contained rage, and his vengeance would shatter this peaceful, orderly world as effectively as a hurled boulder would smash one of the great mirrors in the gallery. And there was nothing playful, no hint of fantasy, about the responsibility he had laid upon

Christian. A life-and-death responsibility to save Cordelia and two small children from a murderer.

The last time he'd seen Cordelia had been in his lodgings when she'd come to visit Mathilde. He knew then that something definitive had happened between her and the viscount, and he had known then that the situation was so fragile that something would have to break. Leo, Cordelia, and Mathilde had been drawn together, forming an intent circle from which he had felt excluded. They seemed to share a knowledge, an experience of an evil that had not touched him directly. But now he had been touched by it. Now he was no longer excluded. And he would play his part. The fire of determination smoldered in his belly, giving him courage and the exulting sense of being someone he wasn't. Of breaking through some barrier of his character.

"Your pardon, sir, but . . . but I wondered what music you would be playing?"

Christian turned at the timid voice behind him. A slight brown-haired girl stood there in a simple gown of white muslin, her hair drawn back to reveal the pale oval of her face. "Why, Clothilde." He smiled with pleasure and was infused with a wonderful sense of his own strength and experience beside this fragile young creature. He was a man with a mission.

"Good afternoon, sir." She curtsied gracefully.

"There's no need to be frightened, child." *Child.* He relished the sound of it on his tongue. He tipped her chin, lifting her face, and smiled down at her. What a little thing she was. So young, so timid, and her eyes were filled with awe as they fixed on his face—the face of an acknowledged genius, one who had played for royalty across the continent.

"I've never danced privately for royalty, sir," She confided, curtsying again, her tiny slippered feet peeping from beneath the hem of her gown.

"There's nothing to be afraid of," he said from the vast wealth of his own court experience. He'd been playing for imperial audiences since childhood. "What would you like me to play?" He took her hand gently, drawing her over to the harpsichord. "What do you intend to dance?"

"Anything that you wish, sir," Clothilde said, still as tremulous as before. Christian felt himself growing, expanding like some tall protective tree that would shelter this shy woodland creature.

He sat down at the harpsichord, took her hands between his, and drew her beside him. "Let me play a little of a ballet by Cavalli and see if you know it."

Clothilde listened her head on one side as he played. Her smile was radiant. "I know it well, sir."

"Then we shall entertain the company with Cavalli," he said with another flashing smile. "How old are you, Clothilde?"

"Fourteen, sir."

The same age as the dauphine, Christian reflected. But this child seemed so much younger, so much more innocent.

A stir came from the anteroom adjoining the music room. Christian stood up as the dauphine entered on the arm of the dauphin, their entourage flowing behind them. He bowed, Clothilde curtsied, and the dauphine acknowledged them with an inclination of her head before seating herself in the first row of chairs.

Cordelia, dressed in canary silk, topaz circling her neck, glowing in her ears, entered the room on her husband's arm, the two little girls walking just behind them, their eyes sometimes fixed on their feet, sometimes gazing more boldly around at the glittering throng.

Toinette beckoned Cordelia, calling in her clear high voice, "Come and sit with me, Cordelia. And the children too."

Cordelia glanced up at her husband. His face still had a gray cast to it, and beads of perspiration stood out on his forehead, but his eyes were as pale and cold as ever. "You will excuse us, my lord," she said punctiliously before escorting Amelia and Sylvie forward.

They settled excitedly on footstools at the feet of their stepmother and the dauphine. The dauphin shifted uneasily on his little gilt chair, nodding briefly to Cordelia when she curtsied. It seemed an unfriendly acknowledgment, but she guessed that he was still ill at ease in his wife's company. They certainly didn't appear close, exchanging not so much as a smile or a touch as they sat stiffly side by side. The poor boy must be aware that his lack of interest in the bedchamber was now the talk of the court.

Michael took a seat two rows behind the royal couple. He could see the back of his wife's head, the dusky ringlets piled atop the slender alabaster column of her neck. He looked sharply at the musician, recognizing him as the young man whom Cordelia claimed as a childhood friend. His mouth tightened. He had to get Cordelia away from Versailles, but he felt too damnably ill to gather together a coherent plan. But ill or not, he wouldn't let her out of his sight. He folded his arms grimly and stared fixedly ahead.

Leo entered the music room a few minutes later. He stood at the back, leaning against the door, his gaze flickering over the scene. The sight of Cordelia with the dauphine and away from Michael brought him some comfort, although he knew it was spurious. She was never in danger from her husband in public.

"I thought you would wish to sit apart from your husband," Toinette said in an undertone.

"Call Signor Percossi over," Cordelia whispered. "I wish to say something to him but my husband has forbidden me to speak with him."

Toinette obliged without demur. She knew that Christian and Cordelia had been friends at Schonbrunn.

Christian came over, bowing low. "Your Highness, you do me too much honor."

"Not at all," Toinette said with a smile. "We are always delighted to support our friends from the past." She turned to her husband. "Monseigneur, may I present Christian Percossi. He was a most particular protégé of my mother's."

Christian flushed with pleasure. The dauphin accorded him a short nod and a movement of the lips that could have been interpreted as a smile. Christian turned to bow to Cordelia.

She smiled at him from behind her fan and gave him her hand. He bowed over it, receiving the slip of folded paper in his palm with all the discretion of an experienced conspirator. Then he returned to the harpsichord.

The audience stirred and settled like so many birds coming to roost in a spinney. With considerable address, Christian greeted them and introduced the dancer. Smiling warmly, he drew her forward to make her blushing curtsy. "Clothilde is a little shy, my lords and ladies," he said. "But I know you will be entranced by her performance."

He began to play, and he played for the girl who danced. Every note was a note to inspire, to enable her to lose herself in the magic of the music. For the first time in his life, he was not playing simply for himself and Cordelia, who had listened to him so many times, listened to his private self-critical practices, his agonies of creation. Now Clothilde brought an extra dimension to his art. It flowed from his fingers, shone in his rapt eyes, and his audience was spellbound, entranced by the exquisite dancer who seemed to fly on the notes he played, an embodiment of the music.

For a moment Cordelia could forget Michael's steady gaze on the back of her neck. Only when Christian's hands finally came to rest on the keys did the sense of danger return, lifting her scalp. She knew Michael was plotting how to hurt her, as he gazed at the vulnerable, exposed column of her neck, and it was all she could do to keep her seat. She couldn't flee yet. The plan was not in place and every detail had to be worked out if they were to avoid the horror of recapture.

She felt him come toward her and stiffened. Instinctively, she placed her hands on the girls' shoulders as they still sat at her feet. "I trust you enjoyed the recital, madame." Michael spoke with cold indifference.

"Very much so," she returned blandly, rising from her seat.

"Mesdames, the king's daughters, have expressed a desire to meet my children," the prince informed her. "You had better take them over and perform the introductions." He took a pinch of snuff, regarding his daughters with the same dispassion as they rose hastily at his approach and now stood attentively hand in hand. "Much as I disapprove of children in adult company, I suppose one must indulge a royal whim."

Cordelia dropped an ironic curtsy, took the children by the hand, and led them away to where Mesdames de France, the king's unmarried daughters, were gathered in a circle before the window, sipping champagne and nibbling savory tarts from a tray held by an immobile footman. He might just as well have been a stuffed dummy as far as the royal princesses were concerned. They turned in unison as Cordelia approached with the children.

"What dear little things," Princess Adelaide declared. "Such perfect identical little dolls. Have a sugared almond." She took two sweetmeats from the salver and popped them into the girls' mouths. Sylvie and Amelia looked startled but gratified. It seemed that since they'd arrived in this enchanted palace, they were always being fed sweetmeats from royal fingers. They sucked the sugary nut with solemn pleasure and received the shower of compliments from the princesses in wide-eyed silence, remembering to curtsy whenever it seemed required.

"Goodness me, how do people tell you apart?" Princess Sophie exclaimed, clapping her hands in exaggerated astonishment.

"With difficulty." Leo answered the question with light amusement. "Mesdames." He bowed to the royal sisters. "And my little mesdames." He offered the same courtesy to the children, who giggled, before turning to Cordelia. "The dauphine wishes to speak with you, Princess. May I escort you?"

"Leave the children with us while you talk with the

dauphine," Princess Sophie insisted. "Come, my dears, would you like to see my songbirds?"

"And I have a pet monkey," Princess Louise put in. "A most amusing little thing, you'll love him."

It seemed that the princesses, always on the lookout for new amusements, had decided to vie for the attention of Prince von Sachsen's identical twins. The novelty probably wouldn't last long, but Michael couldn't object to Cordelia's leaving his daughters to bask in the royal competition to amuse them.

She put her hand on Leo's arm and allowed him to lead her away. "I have a plan," she said in a low voice. Large groups were ideal for exchanging secrets so long as one kept one's expression bland and one's voice an undertone. No one took a blind bit of notice of what anyone said anyway, unless it was the juiciest morsel of gossip. "I will bring the children to Christian's lodgings in Versailles on the pretext of their taking a music lesson. The Nevry woman will cooperate. I gave Christian a letter explaining the plan; I'm sure he'll agree to do what he can to help."

"Good. I want you and the children to leave the palace tomorrow afternoon. Take nothing with you and go directly to Mathilde and Christian. They will know what to do."

"But what are *you* going to do?"

They had reached Toinette, and Leo didn't answer; instead he said, "Madame, I bring the princess to you, as commanded."

"Oh, good, I wish to play piquet, Cordelia." Toinette flourished a pack of cards. "It's been ages since we played together."

"I wonder if you cheat each other as well as everyone else," Leo commented carelessly, drawing out a chair for Cordelia at the card table.

"What calumny, Lord Kierston," Toinette declared, quite pink cheeked. "Whatever makes you say such a thing?"

"A long journey in the company of the princess," Leo responded with an amused smile.

"As it happens, Toinette and I never have the slightest need to cheat with each other," Cordelia said with a dignified tilt of her head, slipping easily into the role he was dictating. Light, slightly flirtatious banter was enjoyed by everyone at court. "We developed the strategy, as I told you, to combat the underhand dealings of others. Fight pitch with pitch, my lord." She glanced over her shoulder as she said this, and her eyes held a very different meaning. Leo merely smiled, bowed, and moved away into the main body of the room.

Tables were being set up for gaming. The children seemed to have vanished with the royal sisters. Michael was sitting at a whist table. It seemed to Leo that the man was having difficulty sitting up straight in his chair. His shoulders kept slumping. For the first time, Leo remembered Mathilde's potion and how Cordelia had said it had kept Michael from the boar hunt. So many momentous things had happened since then, he'd completely forgotten.

There were as yet only three people at the table just behind Michael's. Leo went over. "May I join your rubber? Or are you waiting for someone?"

"Not at all, dear fellow. But all means, sit." A snuff-stained whist player waved jovially at the empty chair. Michael glanced over his shoulder and acknowledged Leo's smiling greeting with a stiff bow. He looked ghastly, Leo thought. And then he thought grimly that if Michael was ill, he couldn't be expected to fight a duel. Leo would be expected to hold his challenge until his opponent was fit and well.

But he could still issue it. Once the challenge was issued, Cordelia would be beyond danger. The matter would fall under the king's jurisdiction until it was resolved.

He picked up his cards and sorted them. He intended to make his accusation in the most dramatic way possible. The following afternoon, after the play, on stage, he would speak out. He had his speech prepared and it would create a stir that would live in the memory of this court into the next generation.

He laid an ace of spades on top of the ten and took the trick. A hand touched his arm. A tiny dimpled hand.

"Monsieur Leo."

He looked down at the twins, standing together at this chair. They curtsied as his eyes fell upon them, and then they gazed at him solemnly, as if a little unsure of their welcome. "Madame Cordelia said we could come and pay our respects, sir. We have something most particular to ask you."

"These are your nieces, I understand, Lord Kierston." A dowager duchess put up her lorgnette and examined the children, who were so fascinated by the ostrich plumes in her powdered mountain of hair that for a moment they stared unabashed as the feathers bobbed perilously close to the rim of a glass of champagne.

"Make your curtsies," Leo reminded them softly, and they did so hastily.

"May we watch?" Amelia inched closer against his arm, gazing up at him with Elvira's eyes, where appeal and mischief mingled.

"If no one else objects," he said, glancing at Michael's back at the next table. He didn't seem to be aware of his daughters' somewhat unorthodox arrival.

"Not in the least," the duchess said airily. "Have a comfit, *mes petites*." She selected two chocolate dragées from a silver dish. The girls, experienced now, opened their mouths to receive the sweet and smiled politely at their benefactress.

"What's a passport, Monsieur Leo?" Sylvie asked when she'd swallowed her chocolate.

Leo's hand froze in the act of scooping up his new hand. "Why do you ask?"

"You said to Madame Cordelia that you were going to get us one," Amelia put in. "Is it a present?"

"I don't know what you're talking about, Amelia," Leo said with a slight, dismissive laugh, examining his cards. "And children with big ears certainly aren't given presents."

They both looked crestfallen, but that couldn't be helped.

"Go back to your stepmother now," he instructed. "You're disturbing my play."

They curtsied disconsolately and scurried off, but recovered sufficiently to take strawberry tarts from a salver that a footman obligingly held down to them.

"Pretty little things," the dowager duchess said. "So like their mother. The same eyes." She leaned sideways and bellowed at Michael's averted back. "I was just saying, Prince. Your daughters . . . such pretty little things . . . the image of their mother—may she rest in peace," she added piously, crossing herself.

Michael looked over his shoulder. His eyes were blank. "How kind of you to say so, madame." He turned back to his cards.

Chapter Twenty-three

MICHAEL TOOK A glass of burgundy from a passing footman and drank deeply. It was his fourth glass in an hour, but contrary to medical opinion it didn't seem to strengthen him after the bleeding he'd undergone that morning. He still felt weak and his hands had an uncharacteristic tremor to them.

"I trust you are feeling better, my lord." His wife spoke at his elbow. Her eyes were more gray than blue this evening, reflecting the almost opalescent misty gray of her gown. The side panels of the gown were drawn up over her hoop to reveal an emerald green undergown sewn with seed pearls. A tiara of emeralds nestled in the black hair, a matching collar was clasped at her throat, and on her wrist she wore the serpent bracelet; the diamond slipper, the silver rose, and the emerald swan caught the candlelight whenever she moved her gracefully rounded forearm.

Elvira had worn the intricate bracelet with its strange, almost sinister medieval design with flamboyance. She had worn it constantly and flourished it as she flourished the male admiration that flowed over her. Admiration that she had played up to with all her seductive wiles. Cordelia was also never seen without the bracelet. She touched it frequently but almost absently, as if it were a kind of talismanic ritual.

Whenever he looked at the bracelet, he became superstitiously convinced that some dreadful mischance had brought it into his life. Both women who wore it with such constancy were corrupt. Both were as devious, as faithless, as manipulative as the Eve it represented.

A wave of dizziness washed over him, and he grasped the back of a chair.

"You are unwell, my lord. Perhaps you should retire." Cordelia spoke again, not that she gave a damn whether he was on his deathbed. One thing was certain, he was not going to come to *her* bed tonight, not in his present state. The relief made her want to sing.

And then he looked at her and the familiar nausea and tremors began anew. He loathed her. The malice in his eyes was worse than she'd ever seen it. He seemed to look right through her, into the darkest corners of her soul. "I will retire in my own good time, madame," he said. "And I will come to you in my own good time. You will await me."

Cordelia turned away, unable to bear those eyes. She didn't think he was capable of hurting her tonight, but she was no longer certain of it.

Michael's mouth twisted. He moved around the chair he held without releasing his grip and sat down heavily. *Passports.* The child had prattled to Leo about passports. A promised present from her uncle.

Leo Beaumont had escorted Michael's wife all the way from Vienna. Twenty-three days in her company. More than long enough to form a liaison. Had she since confided the dark secrets of her marriage? Of course, she would have confided in a lover. And the impulsive lover would scheme to take her away.

The fat maggots of suspicion writhed in Michael's head as they had done since he'd overheard his daughter's question that afternoon. Elvira had been deceitful. Elvira had been unfaithful. Why should her brother be any different? Michael had never liked Elvira's brother. He had made use of him, but he had never really trusted him. And most particularly not since Elvira's death. There was a slyness to him. And definitely something peculiar about his besotted attention to a pair of infants. What grown man without an ulterior motive would be so attentive to such unrewarding objects?

Suspicion once aroused grew and grew as it had done

over Elvira. Michael's head became filled with it, a great gray mass of twisting, gut-churning suspicion that in a few hours had become conviction. It was perfect logical reasoning.

Leo was planning to kidnap his sister's children, and he was going to run off with Michael's wife. Michael knew he was right. He'd been right about Elvira. He was always right to trust his instincts. He knew in his blood when something threatened his habits, his choices, his dignity, his very self. He had known since he was a small child when someone or something menaced his chosen path. And even as a small child, he had known how to fight back.

He was always right to act upon these instincts.

His wife had been virgin on her wedding night, he would swear to it on his mother's grave. But if she had not kept exclusively to his bed since then, she could even now be carrying Leo Beaumont's child. He would not give his name to another's bastard. He wanted an heir, and there must be not the faintest taint of suspicion as to its lineage.

Tonight he would make sure of it. Then he would make sure of Elvira's brother. His eyes closed, his head pounded mercilessly. He leaned back against the chair, resting his head, but the tormenting images of his wife's pale body moving against Leo Beaumont's sinuous flesh wouldn't leave his mind. They seemed to take him over, fill him with an all-consuming rage, so strong he thought he would vomit. His fingers curled over the arms of the chair.

"Prince, you seem unwell."

Michael opened his eyes. One of the king's equerries was examining him with an air both concerned and displeased.

"His Majesty noticed," the equerry said in explanation. The message was clear. Either the prince became his usual lively and diplomatic self, or he removed his feeble and offending carcass from the king's sight.

Michael rose, unable to disguise the effort it cost him. "I find myself a little fatigued," he said. "I beg His Majesty to excuse me." He walked toward the door of the salon, concentrating on putting one foot in front of the other.

Had that deceitful wife put a curse on him? He couldn't lose the suspicion however firmly he told himself it wasn't rational. But witchcraft wasn't rational, and it was still a fact. That woman of Cordelia's—that Mathilde. There was a witch if ever he'd seen one. Perhaps she'd put the evil eye on him when he'd dismissed her. He'd find her. She had to be around somewhere, starving in some alley in the town. She couldn't have gone far.

He staggered into his own apartments, summoned Brion to bring him cognac, and shut himself up in his dressing room. He had some preparations to make before his wife came upstairs.

Leo, frowning, had watched Michael's departure from the salon. The man was clearly still far from strong, and Leo found himself cursing Mathilde's potion. Paradoxically, since without it, he wouldn't be contemplating Michael's destruction. A destruction he couldn't effect until the man was well and strong again.

Could Michael have heard Amelia's burble about passports? The child had spoken quite softly, and why should Michael have broken the habit of a lifetime and actually listened to her? It would be the supreme irony that a man who never paid the slightest attention to his daughters' verbal forays should have heard the one thing he didn't need to hear. But if he had . . .

There was nothing to be done about it. After the play tomorrow afternoon, it wouldn't matter.

"Leo, Michael's gone." Cordelia spoke breathlessly at his shoulder. "I can't believe he would leave me unwatched, but he has."

"I saw." He looked at her and he wanted to hold her. To snatch her up and taste the warm sweetness of her mouth, feel the supple slenderness of her body, inhale the fragrance of her skin. She read his eyes and her own filled with hungry longing.

"Where can we go?"

He almost laughed, it was so typical of Cordelia. No pre-liminaries, no forethought, just the simple question that she assumed he was asking himself. But the time for laughter and lovemaking had passed, and would not come again until their future was assured.

He shook his head and saw disappointment vanquish desire on her open countenance. "My sweet, we can take no risks now. Stroll with me along the gallery." He offered his arm.

Cordelia took it, swallowing her disappointment. "You have a plan," she stated, as they moved among the crowds. "For tomorrow. Tell me about it."

He paused by a deep window embrasure and looked out attentively, murmuring into the air ahead of him. "Tomorrow afternoon I want you to take the girls and go to Mathilde and Christian, as I said earlier."

"But why?"

"To see if it can be done," he said simply. "A trial run, if you like." He ticked off items on his fingers, his voice quiet and authoritative. "We need to be certain that we have the governess's cooperation. We need to be certain that you can all leave the palace without drawing comment. And we need to be certain that the children don't make difficulties when it comes to the real thing because they don't understand what's happening." He turned his head. "Is that clear enough, Cordelia?"

"I suppose so," she said a little doubtfully. Why did she have the feeling he was hiding something from her? She looked up at him. "You wouldn't lie to me, would you, Leo?"

"Why would I do that?" He raised an eyebrow, his voice slightly sardonic.

Cordelia shrugged. "I don't know." But she still wasn't satisfied.

Leo resumed the stroll. He had been racking his brains

for a way to ensure that Cordelia and the children didn't attend the play the following afternoon. The children must never ever gain so much as a hint of what their father had done to their mother, and he couldn't risk Cordelia's presence. One impulsive move when she understood what he was doing could reveal their liaison and totally discredit his challenge to her husband. Once the challenge was issued, the arrangements for the duel in place, then she and the children must start for England with Christian's escort . . . just in case anything went wrong. . . .

But it wouldn't. Desperate determination sent a grim jolt to his belly.

Cordelia took her hand from his arm. "You *are* lying to me," she accused, barely raising her voice above a whisper. "I can feel it. I can see it in your eyes."

He shook his head. "You're tired, Cordelia. You had little if any sleep last night and it's been a long and emotional day."

All of which was perfectly true. And yet she knew she was right. "If you don't trust me, there's nothing I can do about it." Hurt glistened in her eyes. "I'll do as you ask because I happen to trust *you*. I'll bid you good night, my lord." She curtsied and walked away.

Leo swore under his breath, wondering if he could have handled that any better than he had. Cordelia was so damnably intuitive.

A great wave of weariness washed over Cordelia as she walked away from Leo. Weariness, disappointment, and now loneliness. She wanted Mathilde with a piercing, tormenting need. She wanted to go to bed and have Mathilde bring her hot milk, and put a cool, lavender-soaked cloth on her forehead, and tuck her in, and tell her everything was going to be all right.

Instead there was only Elsie. Well-meaning but clumsy, who didn't know how to brush Cordelia's hair with the soothing strokes that took all the tension from her scalp;

who didn't have the clever fingers that unknotted the tight muscles in her shoulders and neck.

Oh, she was being childish! Cordelia took herself roundly to task. Leo was right. She'd had no sleep the previous night and the day had been overloaded with emotional tensions. She would go to bed and sleep off this presentiment of doom, this ridiculous sense of injury. Of course he hadn't been lying to her. Why would he do that? She was imagining things because she was exhausted and overwrought.

With sudden decision she turned aside toward the staircase leading away from the state apartments. At least tonight she was safe from Michael, and poor little Elsie did her best.

She greeted the girl with a determined smile as she entered her bedchamber and fell back onto the sofa. "Help me with my shoes, Elsie dear. I can barely move a muscle."

"La, madame! Whatever have you been doing to yourself?" Elsie rushed over solicitously and, despite much fumbling and self-recrimination, finally managed to ease her mistress out of her heavy court dress, unlace her corsets, and help her into her nightgown. "Shall I brush your hair, madame?"

"Yes, but very gently." Cordelia sat at the dresser. Her scalp felt tight and sore with tiredness. Elsie tried but she couldn't emulate Mathilde, and after a minute Cordelia took the brush from her and finished the task herself.

She climbed into bed with a sigh of relief, her body sinking into the deep feather mattress. "Blow out the candles, Elsie, and pull the curtains."

The maid had barely done so when Cordelia fell into a black and dreamless sleep.

Michael waited, dozing in the armchair in his dressing room. He needed his wife to be asleep because tonight he wasn't strong enough to overpower her without restraints and she would fight him. With Elvira, he had administered the initial doses of poison in the burned champagne that she enjoyed so much. After a couple of days, when the mixture had started its work and she was too weak to resist even if she'd known what he was giving her, he'd administered it neat. But she still hadn't guessed what he was doing to her. Not until those last hours, when he'd seen some dawning realization in her hollow eyes.

But there was no reason to conceal from Cordelia what he intended for her. In fact, he had no desire to do so.

He was beginning to feel that his draining weakness was abating as the hour approached two o'clock. Each time he awoke from a short doze, he felt stronger and more confident, and to his great relief the dizziness seemed to have disappeared. His head no longer swam when he stood up. He must have caught some minor infection, he decided. It was absurd to have contemplated witchcraft. The infection had weakened his brain.

The palace was quiet, his own apartments absolutely silent, the servants long gone to their beds. Cordelia had been in bed for an hour. She would surely be asleep now.

He picked up the four lengths of thinly braided rope, testing them between his hands. They would hold Cordelia's slight frame despite her supple strength. He looped them over his arm, then took up a shallow silver cup waiting on the dresser. He sniffed its contents. A bitter smile touched his lips. The juice of the herb savin. Not for nothing was it nicknamed Cover Shame in the underworld of procurers and midwives. It was well known as a "restorative of slender shapes and tender reputations," and it would suit his purposes this night.

He walked softly through Cordelia's dressing room and turned the handle on her door. The room was in darkness, relieved only by the faint moonlight from the open window. He padded to the bed and soundlessly drew the bedcurtain aside at the head of the bed. Cordelia was a still shape within the white covers, deeply asleep on her back, her arms thrown most conveniently above her head.

He moved behind the bed and had secured her right wrist to the bedpost before she awoke.

Cordelia struggled up from a deep sleep as the sense of something terrible forced its way through her unconsciousness. She was only half awake, disoriented, struggling to discover what was wrong, when the rope went around her other wrist. It was fastened to the bedpost before she could open her mouth to scream.

"Scream if you must. No one will pay any heed." Michael's cold voice came to her as if from some long tunnel. She struggled, writhed, and then he came into view. He stood looking down at her and his eyes were filled with indescribable menace.

Oh God, what was he going to do? He was going to kill her.

She pulled frantically at her imprisoned wrists, brought up her legs to kick at him. He grabbed one ankle and laughed, a harsh rasp of satisfaction, and she knew she was giving him what he wanted. Bitter experience had taught her that her resistance heightened his pleasure.

"*No!*" The scream of protest burst from her as he pulled her leg straight and fastened her ankle to the post at the end of the bed. "*No!*" But he had secured her other leg before the cry had died in the air, and she lay spread-eagled on the bed, shaking with terror, staring up at him, her eyes dark with fear.

"Now, my dear." He sat down on the bed at the head. "I am going to give you something to drink. The sooner you drink it, the sooner this unpleasantness will come to an end."

She shook her head, her tangled hair framing her face, blackest black against the ghastly whiteness. *He was going to kill her as he'd killed Elvira.*

She tried to scream again, but the sound was thick and somehow curdled in her throat, so great was her terror. She tried to turn her head aside as he brought a shallow silver cup toward her.

He leaned over her and pinched her nostrils between

finger and thumb. She gasped for breath, her mouth opening. And he poured the contents of the cup straight down her throat. She choked, swallowed before she drowned. It was bitter, herbal, medicinal.

He held her nose until he was certain she had swallowed every drop, then he let go and stood up. "You'll not breed a bastard," he said cruelly. "Whatever you're carrying, you'll lose before morning. And then, my deceitful whore of a wife, you'll lie beneath me night and morning until you carry and deliver *my* son."

Uncomprehending, she stared up at him, the horror of what she had endured, of what she feared, indelible in her eyes. "I'll leave you now to your reflections." He unfastened the ropes that held her, then stood looking down at her with his asp's smile. "I doubt you'll pass a comfortable night, my dear, but I believe the punishment is appropriate to the offense."

He walked away. She heard him lock the door to the salon, then he left through her dressing room. The door clicked shut behind him and the key turned from the outside. She was alone.

Merciful God, what had he given her? She fought to control the panic that threatened to overwhelm her, to banish all rational thought. What had he said? "You'll not breed a bastard."

Now she understood what he'd done. He had given her something to abort a pregnancy. A bastard pregnancy. He must have discovered her relationship with Leo. But how? And she didn't even know if she was pregnant, and, oh God, the final irony. If she was carrying a child, it would be Michael's. Leo was too careful.

She sat up, looking around the familiar room. When would it begin to work? What would it do to her? The thought that some alien substance was working within her to cause damage and destruction was so terrifying that the black mists of panic this time nearly engulfed her, but she pushed them away with every fiber of her being.

What would happen if she screamed? Nothing. He'd locked the doors, taken the keys. And besides, the servants were accustomed to the sounds that came from this chamber during the long hours of the night. And they were far too terrified of their master to intervene. Her alliance with Brion didn't encompass his risking his livelihood.

She closed her eyes on the bitter tears and tried to empty her mind so that she could sleep. Even ten minutes would be ten minutes gone of this interminable night.

The cramping began just before dawn. She groaned, curling onto her side over the pain, trying to ease the muscles in her belly. The pain was more violent than her customary monthly terms, and the flow of blood felt stronger. She was suddenly too debilitated to move, to examine what was happening to her. The sheet beneath her was soon soaked and sticky, and the great waves of lassitude broke over her, rendering her almost immobile.

She was going to bleed to death, helpless on this bed.

Cordelia opened her mouth and screamed. She screamed and screamed until her throat was sore. And now there were sounds from the salon. Voices, footsteps. The handle turned, met the resistance of the key. She screamed again.

The door to the dressing room was flung open. Michael strode in. "Stop your caterwauling, whore!" He flung back the sheet and stared at the red mess beneath her. Then he looked up into her face and said with quiet satisfaction, "You'll be breeding no bastards."

Cordelia had little strength left, but she screamed again. It seemed it was the only thing she knew how to do. She screamed in pain, in fear, and in hatred.

Michael looked down at the blood again. There was surely too much. He didn't want her to bleed to death. He hadn't finished with her yet. He flung open the salon door and bellowed, "Brion, fetch the physician."

Cordelia hauled herself onto one elbow. Her eyes fixed on him through the tangle of hair. "If you don't want me to die, fetch Mathilde." She spoke slowly, with an effort, the words dragged from her. "Mathilde will know how to stop it," She fell back again.

Michael hesitated. He didn't want her to die. He wanted to hurt her. To punish her. To tear from her any life that might not be of his own blood. But he wasn't finished with her yet.

"Where is she?"

Even through the agony, Cordelia knew that by divulging Mathilde's whereabouts, she was putting all their plans in danger, but she did not want to die. And only Mathilde could help her. It was possible Michael was tricking the address out of her, but it was a risk she had to take. "In the town. At the sign of the Blue Boar." She closed her eyes against the tearing pain in her vitals.

When next she opened her eyes, her blurred gaze fell onto Mathilde's face, and unstoppable tears spilled down her cheeks. Mathilde bent and kissed her cheek. "It's all right, my babe. It's all right."

"Am I going to die?"

"Bless you, no." She smiled, but the smile didn't diminish the grimness in her eyes. "It's slowed now."

"How?"

"I have my ways, child. Sit up and take some of this." She slipped an arm beneath her and lifted Cordelia up against the pillows.

The sheets were clean and crisp beneath her, her nightgown freshly laundered. There was no sign anywhere in the chamber of that blood-soaked, pain-filled terrifying horror of the night. Except for the red liquid Mathilde was holding to her mouth.

"What is it?" With instinctive revulsion she tried to push it away.

"Drink it down. You need your strength."

"Is it blood?" She looked in disgust at her nurse.

"And a few other things."

Cordelia closed her eyes and tipped the warm, evil-smelling liquid down her throat. Curiously, it didn't taste bad at all. Didn't taste salty like blood.

"You'll drink some more in an hour." Mathilde took the cup away.

Cordelia lay back against the pillows, feeling warm and sleepy. "Mathilde?"

"Yes, dearie?" Mathilde came back to the bed.

"Was I? I mean did I lose . . . ?"

"If you were carrying, my dear. it was too soon to tell," Mathilde said briskly.

"Where's Michael?"

"That bastard son of a ditch-born drab!" Mathilde was not given to swearing, but her face was as harshly savage as her words. "I've not finished with him yet."

"Is he here?"

"No. He's gone to the king's levee, and I'm to be out of here before he returns," she said dourly.

"Did he say anything else to you?"

Mathilde shook her head. "Just told me he believed you were miscarrying and I'd better do something about it."

"He gave me something to make it happen," Cordelia said dully. "I don't know what it was. But he must know about Leo."

Mathilde looked up, and her eyes, bright, black, and utterly unreadable, rested on Cordelia's face for a minute. Then she nodded once and, with the same inscrutable expression, returned to her task. She was packing things in the leather bag that accompanied her everywhere. Over the years, Cordelia had grown to trust the contents of that bag as she trusted the woman who administered them. "That girl?" Mathilde gestured with her head toward the dressing room. "Is she as gormless as she seems?"

A weak smile flickered. "Yes, but she's very willing and good-hearted."

Mathilde clucked crossly. "Well, I'd best tell her what to give you and when."

"Tell me. I feel quite strong now."

"You lost a power of blood," Mathilde stated. "And you need to put it back." She flourished a jar of the red liquid. "Take a glass of this every hour until it's finished."

"What is it?" Cordelia asked again.

"Marrow, ground liver and heart, salsify, ginger . . . Oh, a host of things that you needn't trouble yourself about." Mathilde placed the jar on the bedside table. "Now, if the bleeding becomes heavy again, more than your usual terms, send the girl for me."

Cordelia nodded. "Mathilde, Leo wants the children out of the palace this afternoon. Their governess believes they're going to a music lesson. I gave Christian a note yesterday afternoon, asking him to notify the Nevry woman formally that he will be giving them a lesson at three o'clock this afternoon in his lodgings in the town. I was going to escort them myself, but I don't think I can. Will you make sure they get there?"

"Aye, leave it with me." Mathilde bent over her again, brushing her hair from her face. "Tell me where to find them in this warren."

Cordelia gave her precise instructions, Mathilde nodding her comprehension. "I'll see to it, child. You've a bit more color in your cheeks now. How are the pains?"

"Just the usual dull kind of ache."

"Rest in bed for today and you'll be right as rain tomorrow." She kissed her nursling and patted her cheek. "We'll come through this, never you fear."

Cordelia's smile was a trifle wan. Mathilde's complete lack of reaction to Michael's part in all this was surprising, but Mathilde was often surprising. Now the nurse gave her another brisk kiss and bustled away into the dressing room.

Cordelia heard her giving slow instructions to Elsie as if the girl was in possession of only half her senses.

She would not come through this unless she could escape her husband. Cordelia knew this as she had never known it before. There was nothing that Michael would not do if he felt in his vile, twisted mind that it was necessary.

And Leo was planning something. He had *not* been giving her the entire reason why he wanted her out of Versailles this afternoon. She had tried to convince herself that he had told her the whole truth, but she knew that he hadn't. She closed her eyes again, thinking. There was to be a play in Madame de Pompadour's theater at four o'clock. Toinette had been thrilled with the exquisitely designed and decorated theater, eagerly reliving the theatricals of their childhood in the little theater at Schonbrunn where all the royal children had entertained visiting dignitaries as well as members of the royal household.

There was the play. And nothing else until the usual evening festivities.

But why would Leo not want her to attend the play?

"Is there something I can get you, milady?" Elsie bobbed a curtsy beside the bed, and Cordelia opened her eyes.

"Yes, pour me some of that foul mixture in the jar," she said. If she was to get herself out of bed and to the play, she was going to need all the strength she could muster.

When Prince Michael returned at noon, he found his wife peacefully asleep. The nurse had done her work well and had then disappeared as ordered. He surveyed Cordelia. She looked almost herself, her cheeks slightly pink now against the white of the pillow. If the woman had failed, she would have ended her days in the Bastille. But she had succeeded. He would reward success in this instance. For as long as she kept out of his sight, he would leave her be.

Cordelia's eyes fluttered open and for a moment fear stood out naked in their blue depths as she saw her husband's frowning regard.

"You are better, I see."

She nodded weakly. The frailer he believed her, the more likely he was at this point to leave her alone.

"You will keep to your bed," he declared, then turned on his heel and left the chamber.

She would keep to her bed until close to four o'clock. Then somehow she would drag herself to the theater.

❈

Chapter Twenty-four

"WHERE'S CORDELIA?" CHRISTIAN sprang up from the spinet as Mathilde with Amelia and Sylvie entered the room in the lodgings at the sign of the Blue Boar. "The viscount said she would be coming with the children." He ran a hand through his hair, looking as distracted and anxious as he had felt since the viscount had taken him into his confidence and laid such a heavy charge upon him.

"She's keeping to her bed today," Mathilde said, bending to untie the children's bonnets.

"Is she ill?" Christian sounded almost panicked. "The viscount said I was to keep her here until this evening."

"Not ill, just a touch of the female complaint," Mathilde responded stolidly, ignoring Christian's sudden flush. "Now, stop your fretting and meet the girls."

Christian pulled himself together. Somehow, in Mathilde's company it was impossible to indulge his anxieties. He turned his attention to the two little girls, who were regarding him solemnly.

"We saw you at the concert with the dancer," one of them said.

"She was so pretty," the other said. "I wish we could dance like that. Cordelia said we can have lessons."

"This is Amelia and this is Sylvie." Mathilde touched each child in turn.

The children looked at each other, startled. They had done their morning switch and had only met Mathilde once or twice before. How could she get them right without knowing?

Mathilde's smile was tranquil. "You'll not fool me, m'dears."

"Oh," they said in unison.

Christian looked bewildered, but he took their hands and shook them earnestly. "I'm to give you music lessons."

"Yes." Their twinned noses wrinkled simultaneously.

"Don't you care for music?" he asked, incredulous. At their age he was already composing and was an accomplished player on both harpsichord and spinet.

"Madame de Nevry says we're very bad at it," Sylvie confided.

"But *she's* very bad," Amelia put in. "She plays but it doesn't sound like music at all."

"Come." Christian beckoned them over to the spinet. He sat down. "Listen to this and tell me if it sounds like music."

He played a light air, but for once the music didn't soothe him. Cordelia was supposed to be here too. How could he fulfill his responsibilities to the viscount if the plans changed? The viscount had said he didn't think they would need to leave Versailles this afternoon, but he was to hold himself ready for anything. A coach and fast team were ready to start at a word. Mathilde had arranged boys' clothes for the children, and a groom's britches and jerkin for Cordelia. Christian had the passports and papers.

But there was no Cordelia. They couldn't leave without Cordelia. He was confused and dismayed. The entire operation was risky enough without unexpected hitches.

He brought his hands down on the keys in a final chord and sat staring at a crack in the wall above the spinet, talking sternly to himself. Mathilde didn't seem concerned. And this was only supposed to be a trial run. When it was time to go, Cordelia would be here. Everything then would go according to plan. And if he couldn't control his anxiety on a trial run, what good would he be when it came to the real thing?

He swung around on the seat and regarded the children, standing hand in hand behind him. "Well, did that sound like music?"

They nodded in unison.

"Would you like to learn to play like that?"

Another vigorous nod.

"Then sit down, you . . . Sylvie, is it? You first."

"I'm Melia."

"Oh. Well, you go first, then. Show me what you've learned so far."

Mathilde bustled around putting the room to rights as Christian stood listening with a pained frown to the girls' plunking. Mathilde's expression was placid, showing none of the grimness of her internal monologue. Leaving Cordelia alone again in the clutches of that monster had been one of the hardest things she had ever done. But she too was in the viscount's confidence, and she knew that Cordelia could not disappear too early from her husband's roof. Not until the duel was an established fact would it be safe for her to go. Weak as she was now, she couldn't have left her sickbed this afternoon without arousing suspicion.

Mathilde's mouth tightened. She knew of only one thing that could bring on early and severe menstruation: savin. The prince had forced Cordelia to take the juice of the herb savin.

Mathilde had attended many a miscarriage and there was usually some sign of the lost embryo. She had found nothing in the detritus that morning, but Prince Michael would pay a hefty price for that act of pointless brutality.

Cordelia stood in the darkness at the back of the theater that Madame de Pompadour had built in the palace to entertain her royal lover. She leaned against a pillar, wishing she could sit down, but if she was to keep her presence a secret then she had to keep to the shadows of the auditorium. The play itself no more interested her than it did the courtiers, jaded after the week of wedding festivities and in need of something more stimulating than a play to amuse them. Even the king was seen to nod off now and again, and the bridal couple appeared bored and dissatisfied.

Cordelia moved forward a little so that she could see more of the audience. Her husband sat with friends in a box in the first tier, opposite the royal box. He had his eyes closed and was clearly indifferent to the stage. Cordelia wondered if she would ever again be able face him without fear. Last night he had broken her and he knew it. The recognition brought a fresh wave of weakness, and her knees turned to water. She grabbed hold of the pillar, resting her cheek against the cold stone, until the wave passed. As soon as the play was over . . . as soon as she discovered why she wasn't supposed to be here . . . she would be able to return to bed.

She had seen Leo sitting in the pit, in the front row, laughing and talking in the interval to his companions. He didn't glance once in the direction of Prince Michael and behaved as if he hadn't a care in the world. Did he know what had happened to Cordelia? Or did he assume she was with the girls in Christian's lodgings as he'd directed? She was beginning to feel queasy with an anticipation tinged with premonition.

The play's finale received desultory applause and the audience was preparing to leave when Leo made his move. He rose in an almost leisurely movement, then sprang lightly onto the stage.

Cordelia's heart banged wildly against her ribs, and for a dreadful minute she thought she would faint. She clung to her pillar, her eyes fixed almost painfully on the lean, dark-clad figure on the stage.

Leo walked to the very edge of the stage and bowed to the king in the royal box. "Your Majesty, I make petition according to the law." His voice was clear and carrying. The audience stopped fidgeting, was riveted. The king looked astounded. Courtiers petitioned him constantly, for favors, pensions, advancement for relatives, but always in private, and always through his ministers.

"You puzzle us, Viscount Kierston." He rested his beringed hands on the blue velvet rail of the box. "Are we to be treated to a third act of the play?" He smiled at his little pleasantry and those around him politely chuckled.

"In a manner of speaking, Your Majesty," Leo responded, without so much as a flicker of an eyelid, a twitch of a muscle. "I claim the ancient right of a brother to avenge the murder of a sister by public trial of arms."

The gasp that went around the audience was almost synchronized. People turned to look at each other, but no one said a word. It was for the king to speak.

"Surely you jest, Viscount." His voice was heavy with displeasure. Lack of harmony at Versailles was forbidden by royal decree.

"No, monseigneur. I do not." Leo turned and looked directly up at Prince Michael. "With a warrant for search and seizure, I can lay hands on evidence that Prince Michael von Sachsen poisoned Lady Elvira Beaumont, his first wife."

The collective gasp this time reverberated from the rafters. All eyes swiveled to Prince Michael's box. He was deathly pale, unmoving.

In the shadows, Cordelia struggled to clear her mind. What did Leo mean? What was a public trial of arms?

"What does this evidence consist of, Lord Kierston?"

"Prince von Sachsen's own words, taken from his daily journals."

At these words Michael jerked as if he were a puppet on a string. Involuntarily, he stared, horror-struck, at the king, who looked across at him, the royal expression cold with distaste.

"If such a warrant were issued, sir, would you have any objection?" the king demanded harshly in the deathly hush. All eyes remained fixed upon Michael. He had the attention of everyone in the theater; people unaccustomed to paying attention to the most sublime music, the most eloquent poetry, the most majestic prose, were stunned to silence.

Michael half rose from his chair. He moistened dry lips. He fought for words. On the stage below him, his accuser remained still against the scarlet and gold backdrop of the theater.

The silence in the theater was absolute. Then the king said with the same cold anger, "You could direct our investigators to this evidence, Lord Kierston?"

"I could, monseigneur. But I claim the ancient right of trial by combat."

Once more Leo looked up at Michael, and the icy triumph in his golden eyes chilled the prince to the bone.

"Prince von Sachsen?" The king spoke crisply now. "Do you accept Viscount Kierston's challenge?"

Michael rose. He bowed to the king. He bowed to Leo. "I will prove my innocence according to ancient law, Your Majesty."

"As the defendant, the choice of weapons is yours."

"I choose rapiers, monseigneur."

Cordelia gripped her hands tightly together, the nails biting into her palm. Her head buzzed. She wanted to scream. She wanted to fall on Leo and pummel him to the ground. How could he do such a thing? Risk everything? His life, their future. The children. What kind of vengeance was it when the sword could as easily be turned upon the avenger?

No wonder he hadn't wanted her to witness this suicidal, prideful challenge.

"The public trial of arms will take place in the town square at sunrise tomorrow," the king announced. "You will both remove yourselves beyond the gates of Versailles until such time as this affair is settled and we make our pleasure known."

The king swept from his box, the dauphin and his bride on his heels. The silent court stood bareheaded until the royal party left.

Cordelia, still numb with shock and horror, stumbled

blindly to the exit amid the tumult erupting in the auditorium after the king's departure. She had to get back to her own chamber, back into bed, before Michael returned. For the moment, she had to play the innocent whatever he suspected, while she tried to decide what to do.

Leo was abandoning her. If he died at Michael's hand, she was condemned. But as she hurried on shaking legs through the corridors to her own apartment, the angry turmoil of betrayal began to smooth out. Leo had wanted her and the children out of the palace before this whole business exploded. That way they were poised for flight. But what good was flight to her if there was no end to it? She could contemplate waiting for Leo for a year is she had to. But if he was dead on the dueling ground, there would be no future. By issuing this challenge, he *was* abandoning her. He was abandoning their own happiness for a personal vendetta.

Her mind was filled with the image of Leo's body limp on the ground, bleeding from her husband's rapier. Maybe Leo would win. But she could tolerate nothing but certainty, and there was no certainty in a duel.

She entered the apartment, breathless with haste and weakness. Monsieur Brion looked at her, first in astonishment and then in concern. "Madame . . . is something the matter?"

"Send Elsie to me." She stumbled across the salon and into her own chamber. She caught sight of her image in the glass and understood why Brion had looked so shocked. Her eyes were almost wild in her white face, her hair tumbling from its pins. She looked as if she'd seen and run from a ghost.

She began to undress with feverish haste, her fingers, slippery with sweat, fumbling with the hooks and buttons.

Elsie hurried in. "Oh, madame, I knew you shouldn't have got up," she said, wringing her hands. "You're not well enough. Shall I fetch the physician?"

"No, just help me back into bed."

In five minutes Cordelia was lying back against the pillows, praying her heart would slow its painful, nauseating banging against her ribs. She was exhausted, still conscious of the steady flow of blood from her body. But mercifully, it didn't seem to have worsened despite all the standing and running.

The door to the salon banged shut, and Michael's voice, harsh, savage, rent the waiting quiet. "Brion, pack a valise and send Frederick with it to the Coq d'Or in town. He's to await me there. At once, man! Don't stand there looking at me like a half-wit."

Cordelia held her breath, waiting. Then the door burst open and Michael strode in. "Get out!" He jerked a hand at Elsie, who, with a frightened gasp, curtsied and ran from the room.

Michael came over to the bed. His face was white, with a whiter shade around his drawn mouth. He looked at her, through her, with his cold pale eyes. "What do you know of this, whore?" His voice was surprisingly soft.

Cordelia said nothing. She turned her head away.

With a foul oath, he bent over her, wrenching her face back toward him. "Did you plot this with him? How did he know about the journals?"

His fingers squeezed her chin and it was all she could do not to cry out. But she was determined she would not show him her fear. "I don't know what you're talking about, my lord. I have been abed. You made certain of that."

"You can't fool me with your deceitful tongue," he spat, bringing his face very close to hers, so that she could smell the sourness of his breath, the muskiness of his skin. "I will kill your damned lover, and then, by God, whore, you will never escape me until I decide it's time for you to meet your death. Do you understand me!" His mouth was almost touching hers now in a vile simulation of a kiss. "*Do you understand?*" His spittle showered her face.

"I understand you," she managed to say through the

waves of disgust. "And you understand, husband, that you will *never* break me. I will die first."

He laughed and abruptly released her chin. "I've broken you already, my dear wife. Don't you realize it?" He stood up. "You and my daughters will journey immediately to Paris. You will await me in the rue du Bac. When I have killed your lover, I will come to you."

Cordelia pulled herself up against the pillows. She wiped her face with a corner of the sheet. "And just how do you plan to kill him, my lord?"

He stared at her with an arrested expression. "You don't know?"

"How should I, my lord?" She met his stare calmly and had the satisfaction of seeing uncertainty scudding across his countenance.

"At sunrise tomorrow I will spit him on the end of my rapier," Michael articulated slowly. "I'm sorry you won't be there to see it, my dear, but I want you safely put away. Thanks to your damnable lover, we will be persona non grata at court after the duel until the king is prepared to forget this distasteful disruption." Michael's lip curled as he mimicked the king's austere euphemism for the duel unto death that would take place in his presence. "The dauphine will offer you no protection now, madame."

He waited to see if she would react, but she remained still, regarding him almost indifferently until his uncertainty grew. Then he spun on his heel and left by way of her dressing room.

Cordelia wouldn't have believed it possible to feel such hatred for a fellow human being. But Michael did not fall into that category, she thought. He was a devil, a monster from the pits of hell. And he would return to the fires that had given him birth. Leo would pitchfork him right back into the inferno. She would not allow herself to consider the alternative. She had to plan. She had to prevent Michael from sending her back to Paris. She had to stay here. She had to be here when it happened. And the children. They must be taken to safety tonight. Mathilde would have to go with them because she couldn't go herself. Not now.

She was running through her plans when Elsie returned, her eyes reverently fixed to the letter reposing on a silver salver. The wax bore the dauphine's seal. "A messenger brought this from Her Highness, madame." She proffered the salver, too awed to touch the august paper herself.

Cordelia took it and slit the wafer. The message was short and she knew that Toinette had written it at dictation. Presumably by the Noailles: *Dear Princess von Sachsen, I very much regret that I will be unable to receive you until His Majesty permits. Maria Antonia.*

Cordelia nibbled her lip, gazing at the cold words that meant the official end of friendship. Then she saw that a corner of the paper had been folded over. She opened it. *Dearest, I can't help it. But I will always love you. T.*

Cordelia touched the message to her lips in a brief, symbolic farewell. When this was over, she would find a way to correspond with Toinette. There were always unofficial channels.

Elsie still stood by the bed, wide-eyed with the momentousness of events. Her gaze was filled with sympathy for her poor mistress. To lose a pregnancy and then face the prospect of being widowed in the morning. It was a dreadful thing. "Everyone says what a magnificent swordsman the prince is, madame," she offered in misguided reassurance. "They say he's never been defeated in a duel before and he always fights to the death. He killed ten men in ten months once . . . although he was a lot younger then."

That presumably explained Michael's confidence, Cordelia thought bitterly. How many duels had Leo fought? How many men had he killed?

"Bring me some tea, please, Elsie." She had to get rid of the girl with her inarticulate sympathy and hand-wringing before she burst into tears.

Monsieur Brion was her next visitor. He stood awkwardly in the doorway of the chamber. "The prince has instructed me to escort yourself and Mesdames Sylvie and Amelia back to Paris immediately, madame. Would you be good enough to instruct your maid to help you rise?"

"Monsieur Brion, I am not returning to Paris tonight," Cordelia declared. "And neither are the children."

"But, madame!" He looked astounded.

"You will not suffer, I promise you," she said. "If the prince survives this duel, then I will give you sufficient funds to free you from his service." She pushed aside the covers and rose somewhat shakily to her feet. She went to the dresser and opened her jewel casket. "Here. Payment in advance, monsieur." She held out to him a sapphire ring. "You will know how to sell it?"

Brion nodded, slowly taking the ring. He had contacts in Paris who would give him a good price and ask no questions. He could get enough for the bauble to set himself up in a snug inn in the little village in Cognac, where he'd grown up. He'd be set for life.

"What would you have me do, madame?"

"Simply inform the prince that all is in order for our departure. Have the coachman drive through the town. Make sure that the coach is seen to leave, make sure that you are seen to leave with it. Oh, and you'd better take Madame de Nevry," she said in afterthought. "Tell her that on the prince's orders you're fetching the children from their music lesson and taking them with her to Paris. When you drive through the town, if possible, drive past the inn where the prince is staying, but too fast for him to hail you. Whether you choose to go on to Paris with the governess, to return, or to get off somewhere else, is your business and I shall not inquire." She sank into an armchair, weakened by the effort to gain this vital support.

"Very well, madame." Brion bowed low. "And may I say it's been a pleasure to serve you."

Cordelia smiled in surprise and caught a flickering response from the majordomo. "Thank you, Brion."

"May I wish you the happiest outcome tomorrow," he said.

"Thank you," she said again. He left and she sat back, regaining her strength, certain that he would do his part. She was safe from Michael for the moment.

And now she had to go to Leo. Tell him what she had done. Arrange for the children's departure. She closed her eyes again.

How could he have done this thing? How could he sacrifice their love, their future?

Must she believe that that love and that future took second place to his love for his murdered sister?

Chapter Twenty-five

"WHERE'S CORDELIA?" LEO asked as he entered Christian's lodgings at the Blue Boar. He didn't need to look to know that she wasn't there. He didn't need eyes to detect that vibrant presence.

"Monsieur Leo!" The girls bounced up from the spinet stool. "We're having a music lesson. We're learning lots, aren't we, sir?" They turned confidently to Christian, whose teaching methods concentrated on praise rather than criticism. As a result he had two utterly devoted pupils.

For once, their uncle had neither smile nor greeting for them. "Where is she?" he demanded again.

"She's kept to her bed today, my lord," Mathilde informed him with customary placidity.

"Is she ill?"

"Woman's trouble," the woman returned. "She needed to rest."

Leo stared at her, trying to absorb this and the implications of Cordelia's absence from his carefully laid plans. He had ridden with Cordelia, loved with her, spent days in her company, and not once had she suffered from "woman's trouble." Or at least not so that he was aware of it. "She's been in her bed all day?" Harsh anxiety rasped in his voice.

Mathilde nodded. "As far as I know, my lord. I've been here with the little ones since early afternoon."

"Did you do it?" Christian asked, almost hesitantly.

Leo nodded curtly. "The king has ordained sunrise tomorrow. I want you to take the children and Cordelia away now. They will have a good twelve hours' start."

"But we don't have Cordelia," Christian pointed out.

"Mathilde, go and fetch her. The prince has been banished from court, as have I, so he won't be in the palace." *But supposing he had taken her into exile in the town with him?*

"Hell and the devil! Why does Cordelia never cooperate!" he exclaimed, unjustly he knew, but his frustration was beyond all bounds. He became aware of two pairs of bright blue eyes regarding him solemnly and with a degree of injury.

"Isn't that a bad thing to say, Monsieur Leo?" Sylvie—or at least he assumed it was Sylvie—asked.

"Isn't what?"

"Hell and the devil," Amelia supplied.

"Melia!" exclaimed her twin, and they both dissolved in giggles.

Leo raised his eyes heavenward.

"Here's Cordelia."

Leo strode to the window where Christian was looking down on the street. Cordelia had just turned the corner of the street below. She wore a dark cape over her riding habit, and a capuchin hood drawn close over her head. Relief flooded him. Now he could act.

But when she pushed open the door and entered the parlor, her pallor, the deep black shadows under her eyes, that beautiful mouth drawn with suffering, her obvious frailty, brought him forward with a cry of dismay. She looked as she had done when he'd found her on the windowsill waiting for Mathilde. That night seemed to have happened in another lifetime and yet, incredibly, was no more that a week past.

"Sweetheart, you are ill." He took her hands. "What are you doing running through the streets?" He forgot how he needed her here, forgot everything but the pain radiating from her.

"I am not ill!" she said with a vigorous impatience that belied her appearance. "At least, not so it matters. What have you done, Leo?" She hadn't meant to reproach him, but the words tumbled forth regardless. "I was there," she said fiercely. "I saw you. I heard you."

"I'll be taking the children into the garden," Mathilde said, with a significant nod at Christian, who needed no prompting. They left the room without Cordelia or Leo being aware of it.

Leo released her hands and moved back to the window. "I asked you not to be there."

"You deceived me." She wanted to weep. She hadn't meant this to be bitter, but suddenly all vestige of understanding was leached from her.

He stood by the window, the evening sun falling across his left cheek, his strong white hands resting on the sill behind him. Angrily, with shaking fingers, she untied the strings of her hood and threw it back. The turquoise silk lining contrasted with the black hood and cape, framing her face, accentuating her pallor and the blue-black shadows beneath her hollowed eyes.

"I did not deceive you, Cordelia. I asked for your trust," he said flatly. "I could not have my challenge compromised by anything that you might have done or said."

"And you would not take me into your confidence?" Her voice was as bitter as aloes.

"I *could* not," he said simply.

"Because I would have said to you then what I'm saying to you now." She stepped toward him. "You cannot do this, Leo. You can't fight Michael. You might not *win*." She held out her hands in appeal, her eyes desperate. "You *cannot*, Leo. Surely you see that."

He didn't take her hands. He said simply, "It's what I'm going to do, Cordelia. I will be avenged upon my sister's murderer."

"But you won't be if he kills you!" she exclaimed, grabbing his arms, all possibility of dignity, of graciousness, of understanding vanquished under this desperate need to keep him with her. "You'll be dead, and Elvira will be dead, and Michael will go scot-free." She tried to shake him, but it was like shaking an oak tree.

"This is the way I have chosen," he said, his voice suddenly cool and dispassionate, distancing her. "And I will take my chance."

Her hands dropped from his arms. "Why couldn't you have simply enacted a warrant, had his journals seized in evidence? Why couldn't you have let justice take its course?" But she heard the defeated note in her voice.

"I could not," he said simply.

"I don't understand."

"We're all a mystery to others, Cordelia. I don't expect you to understand how I feel. It's enough that Elvira would know and understand." Elvira would applaud it too. He could almost see her little nod of comprehension and approval. They had always understood each other's motives, even when they hadn't shared them.

Cordelia's eyes were dark with emotion. *So she must believe that their love and their future took second place to his love for his murdered sister.*

"You don't love me," she stated quietly.

He felt her dreadful hurt, but for the moment he could do nothing to help her understand. "I love you," he said flatly. "But I must avenge my sister's death. Once that is done, we will have everything."

"We will have nothing if you die."

It was hopeless and they both knew it. Leo moved into the room again, and now his voice was even, brisk. "You and the children will leave with Mathilde and Christian tonight. You will be long gone by the morning."

"The children may go. I will not."

"Cordelia, for God's sake!" He took a step toward her.

"You expect me to accept your needs, my lord. You must accept mine. If I have to, I will watch you die." She turned from him, drawing up her hood. "Christian and Mathilde can escort the children. Michael assumes that the children and myself have gone to Paris, so they will have an even longer head start. And if Michael lives, then it matters not what happens to me." She shrugged. "If I can run, I will. If that will make you die easier, my lord."

She left without another word.

Leo turned back to the window, watching for her to re-appear in the street. His heart was a black void. He had drained all possibility of emotion, of feeling, from his soul. He had been so afraid it wouldn't be possible, but in the end it had been simply a matter of mentally returning to the fencing school. There he had trained himself to see only one thing, his opponent's blade. He had trained himself to be aware of his opponent only as a thinking weapon. He had learned to close out all else from his sight, both physical and mental.

He had closed out Cordelia. He could hear her words in his head, the power of her love behind them, but they existed as mere words. They had no connection for him with the woman who formed them. Thoughts of Cordelia, thoughts of any possible future, would not now intrude in the fight for his life and Michael's death. There would be no muddying of the purity of his motives and his purpose. Only thus could he accomplish Elvira's revenge.

As Cordelia was going downstairs, Mathilde came in from the garden, Christian and the children behind her. Cordelia's face was ghastly in its pallor, her eyes large holes filled with pain. "Oh, my babe!" Mathilde ran forward to embrace her. "It will be all right. I promise it will be all right."

Cordelia shook her head. "I . . . I thought he loved me. I couldn't see how . . . I still can't see how . . . I could love him so much and he could be untouched." She raised her head, a face a mask of bewilderment and hurt. "He was so cold, Mathilde. So cold. How could he not feel as I do, Mathilde?"

"A man with a mission, dearie, is not an easy man for a woman to understand." Mathilde caressed the back of Cordelia's neck, stroked her back.

"Have I just been a fool?" Cordelia asked bleakly. "A

naive, self-deluded fool?" She pulled out of Mathilde's embrace, her expression now stark. "You and Christian must take the children away tonight."

"You'll be staying here?" Mathilde knew the answer already. "Then I'll be staying with you, child."

"No, you must go with the children." Cordelia turned to where Christian stood, with an air both stricken and helpless, in the doorway behind her, the two little girls staring solemnly at the scene. "You have papers, Christian?"

"Yes, yes, of course. But you must come too. The viscount said you must." He tried to sound authoritative, but it was not a role he had ever played with Cordelia, and he knew it was doomed before he began.

"Leo knows I'm staying. But the children must go."

"Where are we to go?" piped Sylvie.

Cordelia came over to them. She bent to take their hands, bringing her face to their level. "On an adventure," she said. "You're to go and visit your mama's sister in England. Your aunt Elizabeth."

"Does our father know?" Amelia was scared; her lip trembled, her eyes glistened.

"Yes," Cordelia said firmly. "And I will be coming with you later. I'll catch up with you before you go on the ship."

"On a ship?" Some of the alarm faded from their eyes.

"An adventure," Cordelia affirmed, smiling. "It'll be so exciting and there's nothing to be frightened of. Is there, Christian?"

The children immediately looked up at Christian, their eyes demanding confirmation.

"Of course not," he said with an attempt at joviality. "It'll be fun, you'll see."

"And Mathilde will be—"

"I'll be staying here," Mathilde interrupted stolidly. "The young man can manage for the first stage. We'll be catching up with him soon enough."

"But Mathilde—"

"I've work to do here," the elderly woman declared through compressed lips. "And I'll be off about it now. You get yourself back to bed, Cordelia, and don't expect to see me until the morning." She marched out of the inn without a backward glance.

"Oh dear." Cordelia rubbed her temples. "I'm sorry, Christian, you'll have to start out on your own."

"But . . . but, Cordelia, I'm no nursemaid!" he exclaimed, running a distracted hand through his crisp curls. His soulful brown eyes were filled with dismay.

"You have to do it," she said. "The children won't be any trouble. Will you?" She smiled reassuringly at the twins, who shook their heads in vigorous agreement. "They'll be dressed as boys, so they won't have all those laces and buttons to worry about. You'll be their tutor, taking them on a journey to visit relatives. No one will be looking for such a party, and no one will suspect your involvement. It's safer than if we all traveled together."

She turned back to the children before Christian could respond. "How would you like to dress up as boys? Boys have much more fun than girls. I've always thought so. And their clothes are so much easier to wear. You can run and jump and climb trees in britches."

Their mouths dropped open at this catalog of unimaginable activities.

Cordelia took Christian's hands in a tight grip. "Please, Christian. In the name of friendship."

It was not an appeal he could resist. And her reasoning was impeccable. No one would be looking for a tutor and two small boys. "Get them dressed," he said. "Their clothes are in Mathilde's bedchamber. I'll summon the coach and get the papers together."

She stood on tiptoe to kiss him. "I'll catch up with you at Calais. But don't wait there if there's a favorable wind and you can get immediate passage. Wait for me at Dover." Somehow she and Mathilde would get there if they had to.

And the two of them could travel much faster than Christian and his young charges.

Christian nodded grimly. If he had to sail to England, his career as protégé of the Duc de Carillac would be over. He could explain a journey to Calais and back, but a sea voyage? However, in this catastrophic situation, personal considerations must be ignored.

Half an hour later, a tutor and two silent but wide-eyed little boys left the town of Versailles in an unmarked coach drawn by a team of swift horses.

Cordelia returned to the palace to wait for sunrise.

In the kitchen of the Coq d'Or, Mathilde sat comfortably beside the range, chatting with the cook, whose acquaintance she had made some days earlier after her banishment from the prince's household. Her previous association with that household made her a welcome guest this evening. The entire town was salivating at the events of the day and the prospect of the morrow's duel. The merest tidbits of gossip were received as holy gospel, and Mathilde could spin a tale when necessary with the best of them.

Frederick, the prince's valet, was also in the kitchen, his opinions also much in demand. There was much juicy talk about the poor princess and how she suffered nightly at the hands of a brutish husband.

"Such a poor young thing," the cook declared, slapping a rolling pin over the pastry dough on the scrubbed pine table. "Only sixteen, you say, Mathilde."

"Aye." Mathilde obligingly stirred the contents of a soup kettle on the hob beside her. "And as pure and innocent as a lamb."

"But she stood up to the prince," Frederick stated, raising his nose from a foaming tankard of ale. "Old Brion said it was a treat to see it."

There were renewed sighs and murmurs around the

warm, fragrant kitchen, its vaulted ceiling blackened with wood smoke. "What we'll be doing if the viscount kills him, I don't know," Frederick commented dourly. "It's a fair bet he hasn't remembered us in his will." He gave a crack of sardonic laughter at such a novel idea.

Mathilde merely smiled and stirred her pot.

In a private parlor upstairs, Prince Michael was eating his dinner when the landlord knocked and entered the room. "Is everything to your satisfaction, my lord?" His little eyes gleamed with curiosity and the satisfaction of having such a celebrity under his roof. His taproom was doing better business this night than it had in months.

"Well enough." Michael took a forkful of his mutton chop braised with onions and artichokes. "But bring me another bottle of that claret."

"Yes, my lord. At once, my lord." The man picked up the empty bottle. "Will you require anything else tonight?"

"No, just bring me the bottle and tell my man to wake me at four o'clock with beef and ale."

The landlord bowed with some respect. The prince's legendary dueling record was clearly not exaggerated. It took a supremely confident man to face death on a dueling field with a full belly.

He went downstairs to relay these instructions to Frederick, who received them with a taciturn grunt. The kitchen would be up and running an hour before then, so he was in no danger of missing the call.

Mathilde settled back in her chair and prepared to doze the hours away.

Michael poured the last of the claret into his glass. He drank slowly, staring into space. His eyes were clear, his head was clear—he felt no effects from the two bottles of wine. But he hadn't expected to. He always drank deep before a dawn meeting. It relaxed him. His gaze roamed the room, rested on the leather chest that had so nearly proved his downfall. He still couldn't guess how Leo had read the journals. But it didn't matter now. The prideful fool had passed up the opportunity to condemn his sister's murderer by choosing such a ridiculously uncertain path to retribution as a trial by arms.

His gaze moved on, fell upon the long tooled-leather case standing against the wall beside the chest. *An uncertain path for Leo Beaumont, but not for his opponent.* Michael smiled slightly, took another sip of wine. He was not prepared to put his life in the hands of his own skill, however highly he regarded it. Leo was younger, lighter, possibly with more stamina. Even if he wasn't as good a swordplayer, those could prove decisive advantages, and Michael was not going to play against uneven odds.

Setting his glass down, he rose from the table and went to the case. He opened it and drew out the two rapiers it contained. Deadly blades of chased tempered steel, their hilts plain silver. No jewels or engraving to dig into the hand. Just smooth, cool metal. He weighed them in his hands, flexed them, lunged with each one, touched the wicked points with the pad of his thumb.

The grace and speed of his movements were unaffected by the wine he had taken, and he smiled with satisfaction. As the defendant, he would have the advantage of fighting with a familiar blade. Leo had never handled these weapons. He would have to become accustomed to the weight, the feel of the hilt in his hand. But even that advantage wasn't sufficient.

After five minutes of exercise, Michael laid one rapier down carefully across the table. The other he propped against the wall. He bent to the leather chest, opened it.

When he straightened, he had a small vial in his hand. He set it down and bent again to the chest, bringing out a pair of kidskin gloves. He drew them on, flexing his fingers to get a tight fit. Then he turned again to the rapier on the table.

He unscrewed the top of the vial, picked up the rapier in his other hand, and dipped the point into the vial. His face was closed, intent, his eyes like pale quartz.

Curare. The smallest amount inserted through a cut would bring paralysis and death. One nick was all it would take, and Leo would begin to falter. His movements would slow, and as it seemed he was tiring, his opponent would administer the coup de grâce. It would be a clean fight. There would be no suspicion of foul play. The prince would have lived up to his reputation and the viscount have proved himself the lesser swordsman. And Michael would have proved his innocence of all charges in the ancient way. There would be talk, of course. The king would not receive him for some time. But he could wait. He would have Cordelia. Alone, unprotected. *His.*

He took a piece of thread from his pocket and tied it around the hilt of the clean rapier, leaning against the wall. Then with his gloved hands, he very carefully replaced both weapons in the case and softly clicked the case shut.

He went into the next-door bedchamber, removed his boots, and lay down fully dressed upon the bed, his hands behind his head. The smile was still on his face, but his pale eyes were still as cold and hard as quartz.

Downstairs, in the kitchen, the only sounds were the occasional crackle from the banked fire, the ticking clock, and the guttural snores from Frederick, asleep on the settle, his head pillowed on his bundled cloak. Mathilde was now awake and refreshed after her nap. Her eyes were on the clock. One more hour before the prince was to take his beef and ale.

The scullery maid arrived first, blinking sleepily from her pallet in the pantry. She lit the oil lamps, then bent to rake over the coals, bringing the fire to blazing life. Other servants appeared, yawning, cursing. Frederick awoke, yawned, stretched, and went outside to relieve himself.

When he returned, the cook gestured to the tray on the table. "There's the prince's breakfast."

Frederick peered at the tray. He knew his master's preference and he didn't relish having the tray broken over his head. The plate of sirloin was red enough, the bread crusty, the ale had a good head to it. He shouldered the tray and went to wake the prince.

Mathilde leaned into the fire and threw a screw of paper into the flames. There was a hiss as the residue of the fine white powder it had contained hit the flames. Then she strolled out of the kitchen into the graying light of dawn, through the town nestling at the gates of the palace, across the great outer courtyard of the palace and inside.

Cordelia was up and dressed when Mathilde came in. She hadn't summoned Elsie but had dressed herself in a simple morning gown of blue muslin. She had no need of court dress for this occasion. She was persona non grata at court, and if anyone saw her, they would ignore her. She splashed cold water on her face from the jug on the washstand, then brushed her hair and plaited it, fastening the braids in a coronet around her head. She did all this like an automaton. Her mind and spirit were with Leo, preparing himself in this chill hour before dawn. How she wished she could be with him. But she knew he didn't want her. Where she saw Leo as an absolute, intrinsic part of her life, her very soul—felt she had never existed properly before he had become her life—he had a life that didn't include her. A past on which she had no claims. She laid out her past for him, offered it to him as part of her gift of her self. Leo couldn't do that.

She turned with a jump as Mathilde entered. "Oh, where have you been?" She fell into Mathilde's arms with a sigh of misery. "I have been so lonely."

"I know, dearie, but I had something to do." Mathilde stood her up and examined her critically. "How's the bleeding?"

"Almost stopped." Cordelia frowned. She was accustomed to Mathilde's placidity, but she seemed even more phlegmatic than usual on this ghastly morning. She almost didn't appear sympathetic to Cordelia's agony of mind.

"Come along, then." Mathilde wrapped a cloak around Cordelia's shoulders. "You'll be needing this. It's nippy in the dawn air."

The town square was packed with townsmen. Hawkers moved among them, selling pies and mulled wine against the dawn chill. Tiers of benches had been set up overnight for the court, all of whom, even the most diehard slugabeds, were present. The royal party were gathered under a velvet canopy. Cordelia drew the hood of her cloak over her head, and she and Mathilde pushed through the throng, inching into the front row below the first tier of courtiers.

Michael stood at ease in the square. Beside him two guardsmen were handling the rapiers. They wore gloves to protect themselves from the fine-honed blades and deadly points. But they didn't know how deadly one of them was as they examined them for evenness of weight and keenness of edge.

A general shifting and murmuring ran through the crowd. Viscount Kierston stepped into the square. He had no guardsmen as escort. He came alone. He bowed to the prince, who returned the salute. Both men removed their coats, then they stepped up to the royal canopy and bowed before the king.

"May God be in the hand of the righteous," the king declared. "And may God forgive the wrongdoer."

Cordelia looked steadily ahead into the middle of the square. She seemed paralyzed. Unable to move so much as a muscle. Unable to blink, to move her mouth, barely able to breathe. She lost all sense of the crowd around her, seemed to be existing in a cold void.

They began slowly after the formal salutations. They moved around each other on the new-raked sand of the square, watching, assessing, biding their time. Michael was in no hurry to deliver the first cut that would ensure his final victory. Assured of success, he could play with his opponent, entertain the crowd.

The sun was a diffused ball reddening the horizon. Leo had become the dancing point of his rapier. He was a single eye and single will focused on the flashing silver of the opposing weapon. He had no fear. He felt nothing. He knew he had to tire his enemy. The older man would tire before he did, so he must keep him on the move, play him constantly, press him but not engage too closely.

It took Michael a few minutes to realize what was happening. He thought he was controlling the dance, but suddenly he understood that he was reacting, not initiating. It had happened insidiously, but now he felt himself pressed, as if he was being backed against a wall, yet he knew that they had the entire town square for their arena. He parried, feinted, thrust. But Leo had jumped back and the rapier merely skimmed his shirt.

Leo was breathing easily. His eyes glittered like the point of his rapier. Michael came in close, too close. Leo lunged, his foot slipped, and he went down to one knee. A murmur broke the concentrated silence in the square. Michael's rapier sliced through the sleeve of Leo's sword arm. But Leo was up and back with the agility of a hare. He had switched his blade to his left hand almost without Michael's being aware of it, and suddenly the prince was fighting a new opponent—a left-hander whose moves could not be easily parried.

Leo was not as quick or as sure with his left hand as with his right, but he knew it gave him an advantage, at least until Michael had become accustomed to the change. He must use those minutes.

Michael pressed forward. Had his blade sliced the skin? He could see no blood, but a nick was all that was needed. The sun seemed to be in his eyes and he blinked, feinted, backed away, trying to turn his opponent into the sun. His eyes were blurred; he wanted to wipe them with his sleeve, but he didn't have the chance. Then he had his back

to the sun, and he blinked again to clear his vision. But the
film remained. Leo was a dancing shape, his blade a flashing
blur, and Michael realized he was fighting by instinct. Fear
crept slowly over him. He shook his head, trying to dispel
the haze, praying for the moment when Leo would falter,
would slip. Surely he had nicked the skin? *Please God, let
there be a bead of blood.*

Then his vision miraculously cleared. But the clarity and
light were almost as blinding as the haze had been. Something was the matter with his eyes. Unable to help himself,
he dashed a hand across them.

Cordelia, still petrified as rock, felt Mathilde's slight shift,
her tiny exhalation of breath.

As Michael fought to banish his fear and confusion, Leo
lunged, his blade at full extension. Michael, in the last
minute before his vision clouded again, saw his chance. He
brought his rapier in for a *froisse*, an attack that if delivered
with sufficient power would disarm his opponent. But Leo
moved with the agility of a gymnast, and their blades
clashed ineffectively. Michael's arm was at full extension. He
had a second to recover his balance, and in that second,
Leo's riposte took his blade beneath Michael's arm, burying
itself deep between his ribs. Slowly, Leo stepped back, withdrawing his point.

Michael's blade fell to the sand. He dropped to his knees,
his hand clasped to the wound. Blood pulsed between his
fingers.

There was utter silence in the square, barely a breath.
Cordelia didn't move. It had happened so fast that her terror
was still mounting even as Michael fell to his knees in the
sand. Leo stood over him, the point of his rapier dark with
blood.

Then, as the first moment of reaction stirred the rapt
crowd, she stepped into the square and ran to the two men.

"Don't!" Leo said as she raced toward him, her eyes wild
with joy. The command was spoken softly but was so full of
power it stopped her in her tracks. This business was not

done yet. She could not embrace him publicly over the body of her dying husband, however vital her need.

She stood still beside them, looking down at her husband, who remained on his knees, clutching his wound fiercely as if he believed he could staunch the blood, heal the wound. His eyes were strangely unfocused.

"Did I draw blood, Leo?" he asked softly. "Tell me I did."

Leo glanced at his torn sleeve. The skin beneath was unmarked. As Leo looked at his arm, Michael, with one last effort, grabbed up his fallen sword and lunged at his enemy. Cordelia kicked the blade from him with a reflex action so fast her foot was a mere blur. Michael fell sideways onto the sword, his blood clotting the sand beneath him as his own blade sliced through his shirt into the flesh beneath.

Leo looked down at his fallen enemy, searing contempt in his eyes. "Die in dishonor, Prince," he said, and it sounded like a curse. Michael's gaze flickered away as he flinched from the dreadful derision. He could feel the poisoned blade cold against his skin, blood seeping from the cut, and his eyes closed.

And then the deadly triangle was shattered as people came running. Surgeons, officials, guardsmen surrounded the dying man, who now lay still on the ground.

Leo stepped aside, his expression cold, his eyes hard as brown stones. Cordelia stepped toward him. He stopped her with upraised hand and she fell back.

Leo walked across the sandy arena to the royal awning. He bowed before the king. His voice rang out across the square.

"Justice is done, monseigneur. I beg leave to remove myself from your court."

"Leave is granted, Viscount Kierston." The king rose and left the square with his family. Toinette looked over her shoulder to where Cordelia still stood, a forlorn figure, beside her husband's body.

Cordelia had heard Leo's words and they fell into her numbed mind like drops of frozen blood. He had formally

asked for leave to depart Versailles. Protocol demanded that
a guest of the king's could not leave the court without his
permission. But was he leaving her? He seemed a stranger to
her now. After what she had seen, after what had been said
between them, she no longer knew what to expect of him.

He came toward her, his face suddenly younger, his eyes
bright as if all shadows had been swept from their corners.
He looked as he had when she'd first seen him. When she'd
thrown the roses at him and he'd laughed up at her window.
An eternity had passed since then—an eternity of terror and
passion and confusion. An eternity in which she'd grown so
far from the child she'd been as to find that person now
unrecognizable as herself.

But now she waited for him to speak the words that
would bring an end to that eternity and an end to her own
happiness, or mark the beginning of her life.

Leo took her wrist—the one encircled by the serpent
bracelet. He unclasped the bracelet and held it in the palm of
his hand, looking down at it as if lay sparkling in the rays of
the new-risen sun. The diamond-encrusted slipper glittered;
the silver rose shimmered; the emerald swan glowed deepest
green. Precious stones that for him now held only the
memories of death and dishonor. It was not a jewel that his
wife would wear. Not a jewel that would accompany them
into their future.

"You will not wear this again," he said. He knelt beside
Michael's body and opened his still-warm hand. He placed
the bracelet in his palm and closed the dead fingers over it.
"Let him take the symbol of his own dishonor to his grave."

He stood up and took Cordelia's cold hands in his own
warm ones and smiled down at her. The smile he had first
given her.

"Come with me now, Cordelia."

She looked up into the golden eyes alight with the merry
hazel glints that warmed her to the marrow of her bones.

"You do love me, then?"

"O ye of little faith," he said. Cupping her face, he kissed her before the entire town of Versailles and the lingering, fascinated court, and Cordelia knew that with this public affirmation, he had laid the past to rest and embraced a future that had no ties to dark vengeance and the spun-sugar court of Versailles.

Epilogue

The Fisherman's Rest, Calais

WHERE WERE THEY? Christian gazed around the dim barn attached to the inn, peering into the shadowy corners. A stray ray of sun from the open door behind him was thick with dust motes from the hayloft above and the straw-littered floor.

"Girls!" he called softly. There was no one around to hear the oddity of the tutor addressing his little boy charges in such a way. "Amelia! Sylvie! Where are you? Your supper's ready."

He stood still, listening. A rat scuttled in the straw bales stacked at the far end of the barn.

Amelia pressed a finger to her lips, not that her sister needed the warning. They burrowed deeper into the fragrant hay in the loft, stuffing their fists into their mouths to keep the giggles in. They heard Christian's feet stomping impatiently below, his voice calling them again in the same insistent, frustrated whisper. Then Sylvie sneezed as a wisp of hay tickled her nose.

Christian glanced up at the loft, then with a sigh climbed the ladder. He stopped at the head and examined the low-ceilinged area. They hadn't ventured too far. The two lumps in the hay were a mere foot from where he was standing on the ladder. He stretched out a hand and grabbed. Amelia appeared from the hay, a bright-eyed, red-cheeked bundle of laughing mischief.

Christian slung her over his shoulder and reached for the second lump. Sylvie emerged in like manner, snuffling, her eyes shining.

"You wouldn't have known if I hadn't sneezed," she said gleefully, unprotesting as he bundled her down the ladder ahead of him, following with Amelia.

"I don't know why you *did* that." Amelia declared from her upside-down position.

"I didn't do it on purpose, silly!"

Christian set Amelia on her feet and tried to look stern, but it was not an expression that came naturally. "Madame Boucher has your supper ready," he scolded. "It's most impolite to keep her waiting, not to mention running me ragged looking all over for you." He surveyed them with something akin to despair. They had lost their caps, and wisps of hay stuck out from their hair, now tumbling untidily around their dirt-streaked faces.

Their hair was the bane of his life. Cordelia had shown him how to plait it tightly, so that the braids could be hidden under the caps that formed an essential part of their disguise, but his long, sensitive musician's fingers became all thumbs when it came to dealing with the fine, silky golden strands.

"Where are your caps?"

Amelia's hand flew to her head. "It's gone," she declared unnecessarily.

"So's mine," her sister affirmed with a nod.

"*Where* have they gone?" Christian asked.

"We must have lost 'em in the hay," Amelia ventured.

Christian glanced back at the ladder. He'd have to go and look, since the children couldn't appear in the inn's parlor without them. But what was he to do with the twins while he went up to the loft? If he turned his back on them, they'd be off again.

He felt absurdly like the hapless ferryman in the old riddle who had to ferry a carrot, a rabbit, and a wolf across the river but could only take one at a time in the boat.

"Amelia, you go and look," he said, pointing at Sylvie. He had given up even trying to guess which was which. Apart from anything else, he was convinced they switched themselves on him from time to time. Now he used their names indiscriminately except in public when he called them both

Nicolas. It seemed to serve perfectly well and the girls didn't appear to mind in the least.

Sylvie scampered up the ladder while he stood at the bottom holding on to her twin's hand. "Found 'em!" came the triumphant cry. In her excitement the child missed the top step and tumbled down headfirst into his waiting arms, still jubilantly clutching the two worsted caps.

"Stand still." He wrestled with untidy plaits until he could manage to cram the caps on their small heads. In their nankeen britches and worsted jackets, with their grubby faces, sparkling eyes, and grimy hands, they were an utterly convincing pair of little boys.

He shepherded them out of the barn into the stableyard just as a pair of riders rode through the gates ahead of a carriage and four.

"It's Monsieur Leo—"

"And Cordelia!" shrieked Sylvie, joining in her twin's ecstatic squeal.

Christian heaved a deep sigh of relief, his shoulders sagging as the great weight of responsibility was lifted from him.

Cordelia swung off her horse a minute after Leo, who had bent to receive the two small bodies as they'd rocketed into his arms. He was as astonished as he was delighted at this uninhibited greeting. The stiffly formal, repressed behavior of the overgoverned little girls had been transformed with their costumes.

They turned swiftly from Leo to Cordelia, babbling about the excitements of their journey, the fascinating people they'd met, the boats in the harbor across the road from the inn.

"My goodness me, what a pair of chatterboxes!" Mathilde declared, stepping down carefully from the carriage on the arm of an attentive groom.

"It's Mathilde!" the girls shrieked in unison. "Are we all going to England?"

"No," Christian said a little too quickly, a touch too fervently.

"You poor love," Cordelia said with instant comprehension. "You look worn to a frazzle. Have they been bad?"

Christian laughed as he returned her warm embrace. The children were regarding him with anxious solemnity. "No, of course not. But I'm not cut out for child minding, I'm afraid. It's much more complicated than I thought it would be."

"He can't do our hair properly," Amelia stated.

"But he tells *very* good bedtime stories," her sister put in judiciously.

"Much better than Madame de Nevry. She just reads the Bible."

"Yes, all about Job. And it's *so* sad. However good he is, bad things keep happening. Do you think that's fair?" Elvira's eyes, twinned, swung as one pair toward Leo.

"Probably not," he said with a smile. "Christian, I will forever stand in your debt."

"Nonsense," the younger man said, flushing slightly. His eyes met Leo's over Cordelia's dark head, and to their anxious question Leo nodded decisively. *It was over.*

"I must go back to Paris," Christian said.

"You won't come to England with us?" Cordelia shielded her eyes from the last bright rays of the setting sun as she looked up at him. "Ah, but no. There's Clothilde waiting for you. And your patron. Of course you must go back."

"Is our father coming to England?"

There was a moment's silence at Amelia's question, then Leo knelt down beside them, taking their hands. "Your father has had an accident," he said quietly.

"Is he dead?" The blunt question was Sylvie's.

"Like our mother?"

"Yes." Leo drew them into his arms and for a minute they stayed pressed to his chest, each sucking a finger as they absorbed this.

Then Sylvie said, "But you and Cordelia are coming?"

"Yes. We're all going to be a family now." Cordelia joined Leo on her knees on the cobbles, smiling into the two serious little faces. "You two, Leo, me, and Mathilde."

"Not Madame de Nevry?"

"No. She's gone back to Paris."

There was another moment of silence, then the children leaped as one out of Leo's arms, joined hands, and began to whirl around in a circle on the cobbles.

Cordelia stood up, regarding them with amusement. "I don't mean to cast aspersions on your sister, Leo, but do you really think those two are Michael's children?"

Leo, beside her, seemed to give the question due consideration as he watched the blur of the dancing children. "Highly unlikely," he pronounced finally.

"Well, all this excitement will lead to tears before bedtime," Mathilde declared, bustling over to the swirling girls. "Come along, now. You'll be needing your supper."

"Oh, it's been ready and waiting for them in the parlor for ages," Christian said, suddenly remembering. "Madame Boucher will be wondering what's happened to them."

"We'll go and set her mind at rest." Mathilde gathered the children in front of her and shooed them toward the inn door.

Christian, Leo, and Cordelia stood in the rosy glow of the setting sun, half smiling. "You will come and visit us?" Cordelia said, taking Christian's hand.

"Often." He squeezed her hand tightly. "And we'll write."

"Yes, of course. And you'll marry Clothilde?"

"Yes," he said definitely, and they both smiled.

"Be happy." Cordelia reached up to kiss him.

"And I know that you will be."

"Yes." She turned to Leo, her eyes radiant. "How could I be anything else now? I can't believe how lucky I am. I'm sure I don't deserve it."

"After what you've endured . . ." Christian began with sudden fierceness.

"It's over." She silenced him with a finger on his lips.

Leo came up behind her, slipping his arms over her shoulders, holding her against him. "Farewell, Christian. And remember that I owe you one very big favor . . . whenever you choose to claim it." He held out his hand and Christian shook it fervently. Then, with an almost embarrassed smile, Christian returned to the inn.

"It is really over," Cordelia whispered half to herself, wrapping her arms around Leo's encircling ones.

"My love, it's just beginning." He kissed her ear and she shivered deliciously, turning in his embrace, reaching her arms around his neck, her mouth seeking his.

Mathilde stood at the parlor window, the children's chatter at the supper table a faint buzz behind her, as she looked down on the stableyard with quiet satisfaction. Cordelia would not waste her life on a futile love as her mother had done. It was as it should be.

ABOUT THE AUTHOR

Jane Feather is the nationally bestselling, award-winning author of *Vanity, Vice, Violet*, and many more historical romances. She was born in Cairo, Egypt, and grew up in the New Forest, in the south of England. She began her writing career after she and her family moved to Washington, D.C., in 1981. She now has over two million books in print.

Coming from Bantam Books in Summer 1997

The Silver Rose

The next breathtaking romance
by the nationally bestselling

Jane Feather

Now, the second book in her new "Charm Bracelet Trilogy"
brings to life a tale of two noble families,
the legacy of an adulterous passion,
and the feud that threatens to spill more blood . . .
or bind two hearts together against all odds.

At the head of the stone staircase, Ariel paused. The Grand Hall below was crowded with guests, some eating a late breakfast at the long tables set before the fires, others already drinking deep as servants circulated with wine and ale. The castle housed at least two hundred wedding guests and the young bachelors, much to their amusement, were accommodated in the dormitories in the old barracks.

Ariel knew very few of these people. Only those of her brothers' inner circle came in general as guests to Ravenspeare Castle. Those she knew well. Her intimacy with Oliver Becket made her presence acceptable at their gatherings, except on the nights when the men went after female prey and she was banned from the Hall.

Reluctant to go down into the Hall and run the gauntlet of the guests, she turned aside, the dogs at her heels, and took a narrow stair set into the massive stone walls. It was a service staircase that emerged in the kitchens, where to the uneducated eye chaos reigned. Scullery maids, pot boys, sweating liveried footmen rushed through the series of connecting rooms, the great vaulted stone ceilings blackened by the smoke from the massive ranges, where suckling pigs, whole sheep and barons of beef roasted on spits turned at each end by red-faced pot boys.

Ariel weaved her way through the throng, who were all too frantic to pay any attention to her, the cause of all the uproar, until Romulus, whose head rose above the table top, found a succulent cooling pork pie too much of an attraction to resist. His great jaws opened, his tongue slithered across the scrubbed pine boards, and the pie was scooped whole into his mouth.

"You bleedin' varmint!" bellowed a woman, wrapped in several layers of flour-streaked apron. Romulus belted for the door, the pie still in his mouth, the woman, flailing her rolling pin, chasing after him.

"Oh, I'm so sorry, Gertrude." Ariel ran outside into the kitchen yard. The cook stood panting, her breath rising in the cold air. Romulus was nowhere to be seen, and Remus had taken off after him. "He's not really a thief."

"All dogs is thieves, m'lady," Gertrude stated. "It's in their nature, if you don't thrash it out of 'em. Their lordships knows that."

"Yes," Ariel said. Her brothers had very simple methods when it came to training animals. "It won't happen again, I promise."

The cook regarded her doubtfully, then her face creased into a smile. "Well, never mind. What's a pork pie now an' again? An' 'tis a weddin' day after all." She turned and bustled back to the kitchen.

A wedding day if it had a bridegroom, Ariel reflected, going toward the stables. It was surely inconceivable that the Earl of Hawkesmoor should fail to appear for his wedding. Such an insult would call for another round of bloody vengeance.

But perhaps that was his intention. He had forced his enemies to agree to a loathsome connection and now he would stand aside and laugh at their public humiliation. Curiously, she didn't feel in the least personally insulted. It was probably less mortifying to be jilted at the altar than compelled to be her brothers' bait.

Her groom was sitting on an upturned rain barrel cleaning tack as she entered the stableyard. "Saddle the roan, Edgar. I'm going to fly the merlin."

"Right y'are, m'lady." Edgar rose to his feet. "I'll be comin' along."

Ariel nodded. When her brothers were in residence it was wise to obey Ranulf's rules. She went into the mews, alongside the stable block. It was dark, the air heavy with the blood of small birds, the acrid smell of bird droppings. The hawks shifted on their perches, eyes bright in the darkness.

She went to the third perch and gently touched the

merlin's plumage. He turned his sharp, unkind eye upon her, his cruel beak close to her finger. "You are a nasty one," she said, scratching his neck, refusing to move her finger.

"You flyin' Wizard this mornin', m'lady." The falconer emerged from the darkness, moving as swiftly and silently as his birds. He held the hood and jesses.

"Just along the river." She picked up the thick falconer's gauntlet from a shelf along the wall and drew it over her right hand and arm as the falconer slipped hood and jesses over the hawk and released him from his perch.

Ariel took him on her gloved wrist and secured the jesses. "I'll be no more than an hour." She went out into the yard, where Edgar stood beside a roan mare and his own cob. The wolf hounds, looking very pleased with themselves, sat beside the horses, tongues lolling.

"I ought to lock you in the stables for the rest of the day," she admonished them, but without much conviction. It was too long after the offense for punishment to be effective. Edgar helped her into the saddle; the hawk sat on her wrist, his hooded head to one side, his plumage slightly ruffled with the wind.

They trotted through the castle gates and over the drawbridge. The air was cold but clear, the sun bright in a cloudless sky, the road winding its way across the fens toward the distant spires of Cambridge.

Ariel shaded her eyes against the sun as she looked down the road. She could see only a trundling wagon. No sign of a belated bridegroom. She nudged her horse into a canter down to the riverbank, where she drew rein, unhooded the merlin and held him up on her wrist to spy the land. A rook cawed from a copse a hundred yards away. A swift swooped low over the river, feeding on the wing. The hawk quivered. Ariel loosed the jesses, drew back her arm and with an expert movement tossed the merlin into the air.

·   ·   ·

The Earl of Hawkesmoor drew rein, looked up at the sun and judged it to be close to eleven. The bulk of Ravenspeare Castle stood out against the skyline, no more than half an hour's ride. Behind it rose the tall spire of Ely Cathedral.

"You're in no hurry, Simon," observed one of his companions. Ten men formed the cadre, ranged behind the Earl of Hawkesmoor.

"I intend my arrival to be timed with precision, Jack," Simon told him. "I've little relish for accepting Ravenspeare hospitality before I must." This had lain behind his reluctance to join the wedding festivities before the moment when he would stand at the altar with Ariel Ravenspeare. Once married, he would remain for the extent of the wedding festivities. It would be seen as simple courtesy, but it would serve a deeper personal purpose. While he was a guest at Ravenspeare Castle, he would have access to the communities that lived under Ravenspeare rule. Somewhere he would find the information he sought. Maybe even the woman he sought.

But first things first. He nudged his horse forward along the causeway ridged with frost-hard mud. He had no mental picture of the girl who would be his bride in a hour from now. He had asked for no description and none had been volunteeered. If she was wall-eyed, crook-backed, club-footed, doltish, it didn't matter. He would marry her and he would remain faithful. Because at some point the bloody line of vengeance must be broken. He would, God willing, breed a child or two on her body, and he would have done what had to be done. He had seen too many unnecessary deaths since he'd grown to manhood on the battlefield. Too many families wiped out. Too many young men destroyed. If he was to marry in the ordinary way and have children, his heirs would be touched by the feud however he tried to prevent it. They would hear of it on every tongue, from servants to relatives, and inevitably they would carry its burden into the next generation. Unless he put a stop to it.

He glanced up at the pale blue sky to watch a soaring

hawk. A plover rose from the reeds along the riverbank, then, as if alerted to the danger hovering above, swooped frantically, darting from side to side to avoid the killer now moving almost leisurely on its tail. Simon shaded his eyes and squinted upward.

"It's a merlin," Jack said. "No ordinary field hawk that. Look at its flight."

It was the most beautiful killing machine. It seemed to tease the desperate plover, hovering over it with its magnificent wingspan, before dipping lazily toward the little bird. The plover flew upward in response, but couldn't maintain its height. It flew down, heading for the copse along the riverbank. The merlin plummeted with the force and accuracy of a lead bullet, its curved beak caught in a weak ray of sun. The plover was snatched from the air in the vicious curling talons, and the men on the road breathed again.

"Someone's flying it along the river." Jack pointed with his whip to where two figures sat their horses.

On impulse, Simon urged his horse into a canter, directing him off the causeway. The cadre followed him, cantering down to the riverside.

Ariel was watching Wizard. He was newly trained and had still been known to take off with his catch. So far this morning, he'd returned to her wrist, but she could sense that he was becoming impatient at handing over his well-earned prey. So intent was she on willing the merlin to come back from what had to be the morning's last flight that she became aware of the horsemen only when they were almost upon her, the soft ground muffling their horses' hooves.

Her initial reaction was one of angry frustration. Couldn't whoever they were sense that she needed all her concentration for the hawk. But it seemed that they did sense it. They drew rein atop a small knoll, far enough away not to distract the merlin.

Wizard remained in the air, wheeling and hovering with his prey. Once Ariel thought he was going to head for the copse, where he could tear the plover apart in peace. The group of horsemen were absolutely still on the knoll. Then the merlin arced and flew with leisurely flaps of his wings toward the gauntleted wrist held up to receive him.

He settled on his perch, fluffed his feathers, and docilely yielded his prey to Ariel's fingers. She dropped it into the game bag at her saddle and fastened his jesses.

"Bravo." One of the horseman separated himself from the group and rode down to her. The hounds pricked up their ears, but the horseman gave them barely a glance. "There was a moment there when I thought he might renege."

Ariel's first thought was that she had never seen anyone as ugly as this giant of a man astride a huge piebald of ungainly lines but undeniable power. He was hatless, his dark hair cropped close to his head. None of his features seemed designed to go with any other. The nose was a jagged spur, accentuated by the livid scar slashing his cheek. His jaw was prominent, his mouth slightly skewed in a smile that revealed crooked, but strong-looking teeth. Thick dark brows met above deep set, wide apart blue eyes.

She took in the dark riding clothes, the short hair of a Puritan. Then abruptly she turned away, gestured to Edgar, snapped her fingers at the dogs, and took off at a canter along the riverbank, the hawk securely on her wrist.

Simon frowned. An unusual, not to mention ill-mannered, creature. But a striking sight in that crimson riding habit. "Come, we've dallied over long." He gathered the reins and returned to the road, the cadre falling in behind him.

They heard the blast of a horn from the castle's watch-tower as they reached the causeway. "Someone's on the watch for us," Simon observed with an ironic smile. "Maybe they were afraid we weren't coming."

Twenty minutes later, they clattered over the drawbridge and rode into Ravenspeare Castle.

The iron-studied doors to the Great Hall stood open and as the bridegroom and his party entered the inner court, the

Earl of Ravenspeare, flanked by his brothers, emerged from the castle's interior. They were all three dressed in the blue and silver colors of the Ravenspeare arms, wearing lavishly curled, gray-powdered, full-bottomed wigs. The family likeness was startling in the charcoal gray eyes, the angular features, the slightly sneering lips.

Simon's attention however was taken by the figure standing in the middle of the court beside a roan mare. The girl from the riverbank. Judging by her mount's labored breathing, she must have ridden her hard to arrive before them. It had obviously not been hard for her to guess his identity. At her heels stood the two massive wolf hounds, on her gauntleted wrist sat the hooded merlin. Ariel Ravenspeare. No crook-backed, wall-eyed, dolt this one.

She had removed her hat and held it under her arm. Hair the color of liquid honey tumbled unrestrained to her shoulders, framing an oval face. From beneath long curling sable lashes, clear, almond-shaped gray eyes met the Earl of Hawkesmoor's startled scrutiny with an unnerving intensity. Her nose was small, her mouth full, her chin slightly pointed. She bore little physical resemblance to her brothers, and yet there was something about her that he saw now was intrinsically Ravenspeare. Something about the arrogance of her stance, the tilt of her chin.

She was beautifully formed, he noticed almost absently. From the sloping shoulders, to the nip of waist, to the curve of hip. He had a sudden reluctance to dismount, to reveal his own clumsy lameness to this girl, so perfect in her youth and freshness.

The three brothers came toward him. "We bid you welcome, Hawkesmoor." Ranulf spoke with studied formality, but he was angry, his charcoal eyes dark, a muscle twitching in his pale countenance, his mouth so compressed as to be barely visible.

Simon dismounted, extended his hand. All three brothers shook it, but with noticeable hesitation. Simon glanced to where the crimson-clad girl still stood beside her horse, with her dogs and her hawk. She hadn't moved a muscle. Simon reached up to his saddle, sliding the silver-mounted cane from the loops that held it. He wondered when Ranulf would call her forward.

"You are very welcome to Ravenspeare, my lords," Ranulf declared, his harsh voice ringing out through the quiet. He moved forward to greet the party who had dismounted with Simon. He had expected a party of lords and ladies, friends and relatives of the Hawkesmoor. Instead the man had come with a troop of fighting men. Ranulf knew them all for what they were, all lords who had fought on the battlefields of Europe beside the Duke of Marlborough. They were armed only with the usual gentlemen's swords, but it was as clear as daylight to Ranulf that the Earl of Hawkesmoor was accompanied by a protective cadre. Or was it an offensive cadre.

But this was only part of his anger. The main was directed at his sister, who, instead of awaiting her bridegroom in her wedding gown surrounded by her attendants was standing with insolent insouciance with her dogs and a damn hawk on her wrist, for all the world as if she expected to be married on horseback in the middle of a hunt.

"The lady?" Simon inquired, his eyes still on the girl.

"My sister," Ranulf said harshly. "Your bride, Hawkesmoor, although you'd not be blamed for doubting it. Come here, Ariel!" The command was issued in a tone more suited to summoning a dog.

Simon's eyes flicked contempt, then before Ariel could respond to Ranulf's order, Hawkesmoor walked toward her, trying not to lean too heavily on his cane, trying to hide the slight drag of his wounded leg. She remained where she was, watching him, her gaze unreadable.

"Madam." He bowed as he reached her. "I believe you had the advantage of me at the river."

When he smiled, he was not quite so ugly, Ariel thought. His eyes had a faraway look to them as if he'd spent many years gazing into the horizon, but they had a glint of humor, too. She wondered whether his lameness was permanent, or merely the result of a recent wound. The scar on his face would never leave him, though. It might fade, but he would bear it to his grave. Not that his physical appearance was relevant to anything, she reminded herself sharply. If her brothers had their way, he would never be her husband in anything but name. He was an accursed Hawkesmoor and he would not know the body of a Ravenspeare. She had no interest in him at all. He must be a cipher, a man of no more substance than a ghost who passed for a brief period through her life.

"I knew of no other Puritan likely to be on the road to Ravenspeare," she commented with a cold curtsy, continuing with distant irony, "I am pleased to make your acquaintance, Lord Hawkesmoor. If you'll excuse me, I'll prepare myself for the altar." Then she was gone, through the archway that led to the stable yard and the falconer's mews, the dogs at her heels.

Thoughtfully, Simon turned back to his hosts and his own watchful friends. "Forgive me, but the Lady Ariel seems less than enthusiastic for this marriage."

Ranulf hissed through his teeth. Ariel was compelling him to make excuses to a damn Hawkesmoor. "My sister is headstrong, Hawkesmoor. But she is not unwilling, I assure you."

"Ariel is somewhat unconventional, Lord Hawkesmoor." It was Roland who spoke up now, his voice smoothly diplomatic, an insincere smile curving his thin mouth. "Her interests lie mostly with her horses, and, as you saw, she's a sportswoman. Her life on the fens has been somewhat isolated, she's not accustomed to society. But I assure you that you'll not find her any trouble. She'll settle onto your own estates easily enough, and won't pester you for visits to court or the like."

He was talking of his sister as if she were some highly bred animal who, handled correctly, would accept a change of habitat without undue difficulty. Simon could think of no response so he merely inclined his head and followed his hosts into the castle. From the little he'd seen of Lady Ariel, he hadn't formed the impression of a malleable personality.

"I daresay you'll wish to change your clothes." Ranulf snapped his fingers at a footman. "Show Lord Hawkesmoor and his party to their apartments." He glanced at his guest. "It wants but fifteen minutes to noon."

"Five minutes is all I'll need," Simon said with a pleasant smile, following the servant, leaving Ranulf looking astounded. He couldn't imagine how a man could ready himself with fresh linen, new garments, formal wig, all in the space of five minutes.

The bells in the chapel began to ring as the clock struck noon. The two hundred wedding guests crossed the courtyard to the stone chapel. The strangeness of this wedding was lost on none of them. The groom had been true to his promise and in five minutes had returned to the Great Hall in a suit of dark cloth, unadorned except for the lace edging to his cravat. His appearance was in startling contrast to the lavish ceremonial finery of the Ravenspeare brothers and their guests, the men in their rich silks and velvets, the women like so many bright plumaged exotic birds. His cropped head was almost shocking against the mass of luxuriant gray-powdered wigs as he took his place at the altar, his own friends, as soberly clad, standing in a semicircle to one side. Nothing could disguise the bearing of soldiers, and however hard they tried to keep their hands from their swordhilts, the tension of the effort was almost palpable in the dark, stone chapel.

Ariel listened to the pealing bells as a flock of maids dressed her for her wedding. She was feeling empty. As if the well of emotion and feeling that normally centered her had dried up. She was going through the motions of this charade as if she were a marionette and her brothers were pulling the strings. A Hawkesmoor had debauched her mother, caused her mother's death. Ariel had known this from early childhood, just as she had been fed the family hatred drip by drip until it ran in her veins. And in a matter of minutes she was to be wed to the son of the man who had caused her mother's death. The son of a dishonorable and dishonored family.

Wed but not wed. Wife but not wife. A woman was not a wife until she was bedded by her husband.

"Do sit still, m'lady. I can't do your hair if you wriggle so."

"I'm sorry, Mary." She sat still as the elderly maid fastened the pearl-studded velvet bands around her head. Her hair fell loose beneath them, teased into curls by hot irons in the hands of a rosy-cheeked girl, whose sucked-in lips and squinting eyes bespoke her concentration.

"The bells have stopped, m'lady."

Ariel stood up. She closed her eyes for a second, then opened them. She examined her reflection steadily in the glass, and decided that she liked what she saw even if it was a total mockery.

"Come, m'lady." Marie hustled her to the door. "His lordship will be waiting for you in the hall."

Ariel grimaced. "You'd best keep the dogs in here, otherwise they'll follow me to the altar."

The hounds' indignant barking followed her down the stairs to where Ranulf stood, black-browed and hard-eyed, waiting for her.

"I don't know what you think you're playing at, sister. But if you think to sabotage me, then you'd better think again. You make one false step, and I swear you'll rue it to your dying day."

"I'm here, aren't I?" Ariel said. "Dressed for the sacrifice. Virginal, pure, sweetly innocent. Aren't I, Ranulf?"

"You are insolent!" he said furiously, taking her arm in an iron grip.

He marched with her across the court and into the

chapel. His fingers bruised her arm, biting deep into the flesh. As the organ played and people gazed admiringly at the beautiful bride, his fingers bit deeper as if he were afraid she would suddenly pull herself free and run from him.

Simon Hawkesmoor watched the progress of his bride and her brother toward him. He noticed the position of Ranulf's hand on the girl's arm, read the strengh of his grip in the almost vicious determination in his eyes. The girl herself was white-faced, her lips taut. It was clear to Simon that she was not approaching the altar of her own free will. But then in essence neither was he, he reflected with a grim twist of his mouth, turning resolutely to face the altar. A greater good than personal preference was to be served by this union. The girl would come around eventually. She was young, it would be for him to use his greater maturity and experience to bring her to an acceptance of her new life.

Ranuld didn't release his sister's arm until she was kneeling at the altar rail beside Lord Hawkesmoor, and he remained standing slightly to one side of her, instead of stepping back into the body of the church.

Ariel's hands were clasped on the rail and she stared down at the serpent bracelet on her wrist, concentrating all her thoughts on its intricate pattern, on the delicate charms. The noon sun lit up the rose window above the altar and when she twisted her wrist slightly, the ruby in the heart of the rose sprang into blood red flame. Fascinated, she moved her wrist so that the emerald swan was caught in the swimming colored rays. It was quite beautiful.

The glint of silver, the glow of emerald, caught Simon's eye as he stared steadfastly at the intoning priest. He turned his head to the flickering jeweled light on his bride's wrist, resting on the rail beside his own hands. There was something oddly familiar about the bracelet she wore. He frowned, trying to retrieve the memory, but it remained elusive, leaving him only with a vague sense of disquiet.

Ariel was unaware that she was holding herself rigidly away from the powerful frame beside her, aware of the priest's voice reciting the service only on some distant plane that seemed to have nothing to do with her.

Lord Hawkesmoor's firm voice broke into her trance, startling her. He was making responses with a resonant conviction. Her mouth dried. The priest asked her if she took Lord Hawkesmoor to be her lawfully wedded husband.

Ariel's eyes fixed on the earl's hands resting on the altar rail. They were huge, with bony knuckles, pared nails, callused fingers. She shuddered at the thought of those hands on her body, touching her in the ways of love. The priest spoke again, nervously repeating his question. There was a rustle and shifting in the body of the chapel behind her, but Ariel didn't hear it. She was thinking that if she married this man she was signing his death warrant.

Ranulf moved forward. He put his hand on the back of her neck. It could have been interpreted as a gesture of reassurance, but Ariel felt the pressure, forcing her to lower her head in an assumption of acquiescence. There was nothing she could do. Not at this time. She was bait in the trap. And then it occurred to her that if she wished to, if she wished to save the Hawkesmoor from her brothers' vengeance, she could work to keep the trap from springing. But why would a Ravenspeare save a Hawkesmoor? And if she did so, she was condemning herself to a loathsome marriage. Her eyes fixed again on the bracelet. Ranulf's bribe for her cooperation. To keep her eyes averted, her mouth shut.

She murmured her responses and only when it was over did Ranulf remove his hand.

Simon helped her to her feet with a hand under her elbow. Her bare skin was cold as ice and he felt her shudder at his touch. *Dear God, what had he done?* She loathed him, was repulsed by him. He could see it in her eyes as she glanced up at him before swiftly averting her gaze.

Ranulf had joined his brothers in the front pew. He was smiling as he watched his sister walk back down the aisle with her husband. He could manage Ariel's rebellions. She was no fool; she knew which side her bread was buttered.

Outside in the cold sunshine, Ariel removed her hand from the Hawkesmoor's arm.

"It's customary for a groom to kiss the bride," Simon said gently, taking her small hands in his own, turning her toward him. She didn't look at him, but stood still, as if resigned to her fate, and he shrank from the image of his own self. He dropped her hands, said almost helplessly, "You have nothing to fear, Ariel."

At that, she looked up at him, her eyes as clear as a dawn sky, still filled with that piercing intensity. She said with pointed simplicity, "No. *I* have nothing to fear, my lord."

THE DIAMOND SLIPPER Sweepstakes

OFFICIAL ENTRY RULES

1. <u>No purchase is necessary</u>. Enter the sweepstakes by completing THE DIAMOND SLIPPER Sweepstakes entry form on the previous page, the coupon found on THE DIAMOND SLIPPER point-of-sale riser, OR by clearly printing your name, address, daytime phone number, and the answer to the question "Where will Cordelia's arranged marriage take her?" on a 3" x 5" card and mailing the entry form, coupon, or card to:

**THE DIAMOND SLIPPER Sweepstakes,
BANTAM BOOKS, DEPT. CW,
1540 BROADWAY, NEW YORK, NY 10036.**

2. One (1) Grand Prize: An elegant custom-made 10-carat gold diamond slipper charm encrusted with diamond chips totaling 1-carat. Approximate retail value: $2,700.00.

3. Ten (10) First Prizes: seven paperback books written by Jane Feather. Approximate retail value: $41 (U.S.); $55 (Canada).

4. All entrants must be 18 or older. Entries limited to one per person. Entries must be postmarked and received by Bantam no later than MARCH 3, 1997. The correct answer to the question is found on the back cover of THE DIAMOND SLIPPER and winners will be chosen in a random drawing by the Bantam Marketing Department from all completed entries containing the correct answer. The winners will be notified by phone on or about MARCH 17, 1997. Bantam's decision is final. The winners have thirty days from the date of notice in which to accept their awards or an alternate winner will be chosen. Odds of winning depend upon the number of entries received. No prize substitution or transfer allowed. Bantam is not responsible for lost, misdirected, or incomplete entries.

5 The Grand Prize winner will be required to sign an affidavit of eligibility and promotional release supplied by Bantam. Entering the sweepstakes constitutes permission for use of the winners' names, likenesses, and biographical data for publicity and promotional purposes. with no additional compensation.

6. Employees of Bantam Books, Bantam Doubleday Dell Publishing Group, Inc., their subsidiaries and affiliates, and their immediate family members are not eligible to enter the sweepstakes. This sweepstakes is open to residents of the U.S. and Canada, excluding the Province of Quebec. A Canadian winner would be required to correctly answer an arithmetical skill testing question in order to receive the prize. Void where prohibited or restricted by law. All federal, state, and local regulations apply. Taxes, if any, are the winner's sole responsibility.

7. For the names of the prize winners, available after APRIL 17, 1997, send a stamped, self-addressed envelope entirely separate from your entry to THE DIAMOND SLIPPER Sweepstakes Winners, BANTAM BOOKS, 1540 BROADWAY, DEPT. DS, NEW YORK, NY 10036.

Put some sparkle into your life with
THE DIAMOND SLIPPER
Sweepstakes!

Enter to win the Grand Prize:

A beautiful, custom-made gold slipper charm encrusted with diamond chips totaling 1-carat—ideal for attaching to either a necklace or bracelet.

10 First Prizes:

Ten First-Prize winners will receive the Jane Feather library from Bantam Books, consisting of her seven previous unforgettable gems: *Vice, Vanity, Violet, Valentine, Velvet, Vixen,* and *Virtue.*

ARTIST'S
RENDERING
actual size 1"

To enter: Just answer the question below, completely fill out this form (please print), and mail it to **THE DIAMOND SLIPPER Sweepstakes, BANTAM BOOKS, DEPT. CW, 1540 BROADWAY, NEW YORK, NY 10036.**

Enter Today—Entries must be received NO LATER THAN March 3, 1997!

Where will Cordelia's arranged marriage take her?_____

_____

(For the answer, see the back cover of THE DIAMOND SLIPPER)

_____

NAME

_____

ADDRESS

_____

CITY   STATE   ZIP

_____

DAYTIME PHONE

Bantam